DEADWOOD

KARLEY BRENNA

Deadwood

Paperback ISBN: 979-8-9888184-6-5

Cover illustration and interior art by Brittany Price www.bripriceartistry.com

Map illustration by Rena Violet @violet.book.design

Edited by Bobbi Maclaren

Proofreading by Emily in the Archives @emilyinthearchives

For grandma Chris.
I hope you're flying with the dragons high above.

IMPORTANT NOTE

Deadwood is a dark fantasy romance. There are elements within this story that may be unsettling to some readers. Your mental health always comes first. This book deals with heavy topics and may contain triggering situations such as physical abuse from a parental figure, isolation, mental abuse from a parent, brief discussion of suicidal ideation as well as suicidal thoughts, gun use, violence, blood, insinuation of rape/SA (it does not happen), and manipulation (not between MCs).

Please also keep in mind that Deadwood does end on a cliffhanger, as it is book one of a three book series. Like most fantasies, there is foreshadowing, as well as things left unanswered, and that is for a reason.

All that to say, I hope you enjoy. This book and its characters mean so much to me, and I hope you find the same within these pages.

TERMS AND KINGDOMS

Exitium Lunae: the "celebration" of the moon rupturing, and the dragons descending upon the continent of Serpentine.

Amosite Kingdom: King and Queen Tenere. First wife died, now remarried. Garnet color. Capital is Silicate. Provides magic. Dark magic mines are closed.

Feldspar Kingdom: King and Queen Pleum. Ivory color. Capital is Crystalline. Provides drinking water and timber.

Torbernite Kingdom: King and Queen Bular. Emerald green color. Capital is Anthracite. Provides tools, weapons, metals, coal, oil.

Sulphur Kingdom: King and Queen Alline. Yellow color. Capital is Payzin. Provides food: meat, fruits, vegetables, etc.

Deadwood: ???

Obscurum Mines
Opes Mines
Amosite
Silicate
Mines
Devil's Peak
Payzin
Sulphur
S E R P E

SUNWARD MOUNTAINS
INES
IRIS VERE
DEADWOOD
ALKALI
MINES
BRIMSTONE MOUNTAINS
THE HOLLOWS
FELDSPAR
ANTHRACITE
TORBERNITE
UNDERGROUND MINES
NTINE

PART ONE

CHAPTER 1

"We are under strict instruction to only allow you water tonight, Lady Auria," the servant said in mock apology. He wore a garnet suit, every inch of skin covered by some sort of material, save for his mouth and nose. Even his eyes were covered by a mask for tonight's party. The only sign he was a servant and not a guest was the metal tray of wine glasses he balanced on a gloved hand.

"Just another way to be controlled," I muttered as I gave up, moving on from him. I'd already tried to sway three other servers for a glass, and all of them had denied me. If tonight's masquerade ball was to get everyone together from the other three kingdoms, surely I should be allowed a drink. Their refusal only gave me the sinking suspicion my father was up to something.

My hands hung lazily at my sides, disappearing into the fluffed skirts of my garnet ball gown as I scanned the massive room. More people than I'd ever seen in the castle before danced and milled about, talking, laughing, and sending judgmental—and appreciative—looks at one another.

I ignored it all, focused on one task only: to get a gods-damned drink in me.

My eyes scanned the warm-lit room from behind my mask, the lace scratching at my cheeks as I turned. Giant garnet drapes hung from the walls, held back by a gold rope to reveal the deep night where the second, and only, moon shone bright on display. Two silver rings spanned the entirety of the sky, courtesy of the first moon exploding a little over a century ago. At night, they cast pearl-like lines across the land, and in the day, the sun reflected off them, vibrant and nearly blinding.

Around the grand room, Amosite's red colors were accented everywhere, between the tablecloths and napkins to the trays of food and bouquets of flowers. The dozen or so chandeliers lit up the room in a yellow glow, causing the beige walls with their intricate swirls of garnet and reflective polished floors to capture the same warm tone. My father had gone all out tonight, between decorations and sprucing up the hardly-used space, but I didn't pay any mind as to why as my gaze landed on an abandoned glass of wine where it sat lonely on one of the round tables meant for guests.

I weaved through people in grandiose suits and gowns, thankful none of them stopped me as I made haste across the room. As I approached the table, I felt eyes on my back, ones that burned, and a shiver crept up my spine, knowing who it was without having to look. I'd deal with that later. Nothing, not even my stepmother's scrutiny, could stop me from indulging in a glass.

Stepping between two dark oak chairs, I plucked the gold goblet up and held it to my stomach as I searched for a spot along the wall that wouldn't have too many prying eyes. With my stepmother likely very aware of what I was doing, I needed to get away from her judgmental gaze. The punishments were inevitable at this rate, so I might as well enjoy my drink in peace.

Aside from tables and groups of people, the walls were bare, not a hiding spot in sight. But as my eyes drifted, I paused on the drapes. It was a tad ridiculous, but with no other options, I aimed that way. The velvet curtains were large enough to offer me cover, at least until I finished the wine. My tongue was already salivating with the thought of the sweet berry flavor exploding over my taste buds as I shoved through the crowd. People parted while continuing their conversations, skirts and elbows brushing past me as I went.

As soon as I made it to the wall and out of the throng, I slipped partially behind the tied-back fabric, its material thick and offering more warmth than the room did on its own, almost like the heat was trapped behind the curtain, seeking its own private space away from the bustling of bodies.

Not wasting a moment longer, I brought the goblet to my lips. The sweet taste of berries coated my tongue as I took not one, but four sips. The aftertaste was tart, but instantly, my chest was warming. I didn't normally rely on alcohol—not that I could, even if I wanted to—but tonight, I needed it. With all the people and the unknown of why my father really threw this masquerade ball, my mind needed something to stop whirling. I wasn't much for parties, but even I could admit the bluster of colorful clothing attendees wore lit the place up in a way nothing else could. It was a welcome reprieve from the constant sea of red in Amosite, so I was making do. And if that contained alcohol, then so be it.

"Thirsty?" a deep, smooth voice asked, cutting through the sounds of chatter and elegant music around me. I jumped, thankful for the gulps of wine I'd taken so the liquid didn't slosh over the rim.

I gripped the edge of the curtain, holding it as if I was

keeping myself modest behind the fabric. I held the wine just out of sight, only my head peeking out as my heart nearly burst from my chest at being caught.

I tilted my chin up to look the man in the eye. His proximity and height was slightly daunting. Even behind the mask he donned, he was striking. From his dark pants to the leather jacket over his black shirt, he should have stuck out like a sore thumb, but rather, he somehow blended in, as if that was his goal, even with his more casual attire. It was almost refreshing to see amongst the sea of extravagant beauty in this room. While they wore gorgeous clothing, the man before me held it all in his physical appearance alone. His nearly-black hair was mussed and wavy, the curve of his tan jaw looking as if it was chiseled from granite itself, and his eyes... They struck through the mask like the North Star, the smokey blue devastating all they set their sights on.

"I don't know what you're talking about," I snapped.

He arched a brow, his gaze falling to the curtain as if he could see right through it. "I believe I just witnessed an unforgettable woman snatching my wine and hiding away to drink it behind a"—his chin tilted as he looked up at the curtain, and *gods,* his neck was just as beautiful as the rest of him—"curtain." He focused on me again, the attention nearly taking me out at the knees. "There's no hiding that you're guilty."

"*Guilty*?" I shrieked, dropping the curtain. It slipped past me, settling back against the wall behind me and revealing exactly what he was accusing me of.

This time, he raised both brows, and crossed his arms along with it.

To hell with hiding. I lifted the golden cup and took a long sip. I could practically feel his eyes sending zaps along my skin everywhere they roamed. My throat, my hair, my mask, my pale hand around the cup. He could take the wine from me at any moment, but he didn't, almost like he enjoyed this. Like it was *entertaining* to him.

He leaned a shoulder against the wall, a slight tilt to the corner of his mouth as I pulled the goblet from my lips. "Is that doing the job?"

I nearly choked. "What job?"

"Of hiding whatever you're feeling," he replied easily.

I gripped the cup in both hands to give them something to hold on to. "I'm not hiding anything."

His eyes darted to the curtain before settling back on me. Right. I was quite literally hiding to begin with.

"As much as wine can," I admitted. I sounded flustered, and it was almost embarrassing. If he was trying to flirt with me, I had no idea how to flirt back. I didn't talk to boys, let alone men that looked like...that. In my twenty-six years of life, I'd never been allowed.

He uncrossed his arms and plucked the goblet from my fingers, but he didn't bring it to his lips. Rather, he leaned closer. "Stolen wine, at that."

My nose scrunched as I grabbed for it. "This is not stolen."

He held it just out of reach. "No? Was it not at my seat?"

My eyes nearly bulged from my head, but I reeled in my reaction. "*Your* seat?"

He nodded, bringing the goblet to his lips and taking a pull. His neck moved with his swallow, and I forced my eyes away. I'd just poached his beverage, and now I was ogling over him. But the fact that he'd drunk the wine after I already had... I pressed my lips together as he lowered the cup.

His tongue darted out over his lower lip, savoring the last drops, all while he eyed me.

My cheeks heated, which wasn't ideal, because if I was caught standing here flushed in front of a man, nothing good would come of it. I needed to shut this down. Fast. "If you're expecting me to apologize, you're going to be disappointed."

"No apology necessary," he replied, tilting the cup to look inside. "I would only advise that you be careful of who you steal from next."

I opened my mouth to retort, but suddenly, a hand was on my arm, pulling my focus from him before I could speak.

"There you are!" Taylin exclaimed, turning me to face her. My best, and only, friend was wearing a garnet dress much like mine, but less flamboyant. Her blonde hair was draped over her shoulder in a braid, small red and white flowers tucked into the strands. Those, and the blush painted high along her cheekbones, accentuated her natural splattering of freckles along the bridge of her sun-kissed nose. "I've been looking everywhere for you. This guy—"

I glanced back to excuse myself from the man, but paused when I realized he was already gone. At least I no longer had to get out of my conversation with him. I turned back to Taylin as she continued.

"—he didn't tell me where he's from or anything, but he's almost too nice. I don't really believe all the things he's been going on about, but he's cute."

I couldn't help my laugh. "Are you saying you're pushing past his stories just because he's cute?"

"Well, I wouldn't say they're just *stories*. He's claiming he sees all kinds of things outside the chasm, but I don't know. People make shit up, you know?"

I eyed another lone goblet sitting on a table not far from us, the wine teasing me. "Now that's something I could drink to." My father made things up all the time. From his own rules to more tasks for me to fulfill for him, but never anything that included the duties of a princess. Being the king's daughter didn't mean I was prophesied to be a queen one day—I wasn't technically even considered a princess. My only title was being his offspring, and that's where the royalty in me ended. Every other kingdom passed the monarchy down to their firstborn child, but not King Tenere. I wasn't sure what his plan was for who would lead Amosite after he died, though I assumed it would be someone he thought more worthy of the title than myself. Growing up, he'd always told me it was simply because I wasn't fit to rule. I was only to do my duty, obey, and expect nothing more.

"Who was that man you were talking to?" Taylin asked, dark blue eyes searching the room for him from behind her mask.

"I'm not sure," I admitted.

She hummed before turning her focus back to me. "Are you enjoying yourself?"

I tried to crack a smile. "Should I be?"

She let out a small sigh, knowing exactly why I'd be skeptical. My father was a calculated man, and tonight was likely no different. I wouldn't let myself think otherwise. "Your father had quite the turnout," she noted, her skepticism matching mine as her brows raised slightly at the crowd around us.

"I'm only glad he allowed you to be here tonight. Everyone else, I truly couldn't care less about." Taylin and I were only allowed to see each other for a short period of time on select days, and when my father had notified me of the ball three days ago, he'd told me she was only allowed to come if I was on my best behavior. It'd been like this since we were young, shortly after my mother passed away. Taylin's mother was one of the best bakers in the city, Silicate, and my mother had her hand deliver her pastries to the castle twice a week. Then, when she passed, my father cut ties, but I'd grown a friendship with Taylin over the years, so naturally, he used that against me.

Do your tasks and behave or you lose your privilege of seeing her, is what he'd said the first day I told him I was too tired to continue my list. Duplicating magic, of any variety, from one vial to another was draining, but he never showed an ounce of mercy. Considering I was the only human with this ability, he put a lot of pressure on my shoulders to produce more and work harder.

Taylin was my only reprieve from this castle and the things that went on inside of it—the only person who made this life worth living—so I listened. But if I ever stepped out of line, I got my next visit with her taken away.

"Aren't you curious as to why?" she asked, adjusting her grip on something. My gaze landed on the glass in her hand, not gold like the one on the table, but it held the same colored wine through the clear crystal. I'd been too distracted to even realize she held it. I shouldn't have let that man speak—or flirt—with me, regardless of how entertaining he was for the short period. I was a fool to think I wasn't being watched, and I could only imagine speaking to him would be added to tomorrow's list of consequences.

With a deep breath, I said, "If I spent my entire life wondering why my father did the things he does, I'd never have a moment to think of anything else." I gave her a side glance. "And that's coming from a girl who never leaves the castle."

She reached up to itch her cheek under the edge of her mask. "As if you have much else to do while being forced to waste your life away in this dreary castle?"

My eyelids fluttered as I forced a swallow. Taylin didn't know I spent every waking day in the cellar filling vials. The castle had a cellar on the lowest level, one of each kind of magic lining the cluttered walls. The room was a small storage area crammed full of the things I needed to work.

I'd drain myself under my father's instruction to fill those vials so he could provide and put on a show as the richest king in all of Serpentine. To impress kings and queens from other kingdoms, as if his mines were producing at a faster rate than the rest of them. But he'd never let on that it was me creating all of it.

On the bright side, my magic ensured the mines were shut down and miners no longer had to suffer underground, digging up magic to provide for the kingdom. I could do all of it in their place, and knowing those people could be home with their families instead of wasting away surrounded by endless miles of rock helped spur me on on the days I felt like giving up. I'd never seen the mines, but I'd heard stories of the beauty of the different colors of glowing magic running through the rock like veins. Though beautiful, they were equally as dangerous, between the poor air quality and risk of collapsing.

I shoved the thoughts of my father and his expectations away. To hell with being modest tonight; I already went against his rule of no alcohol. What was the harm in more? I stepped around Taylin and crossed to the table along the wall, plucking the goblet up. I turned to find she'd followed, already holding her glass in the air. I mimicked her stance. "Let's have one good moment where it's not dictated by my father, shall we?"

Her eyes softened. The thing about Taylin was that, while she hated my father for the way he kept me locked up, she understood there was little to be done about it. Rather than fighting it, she adjusted.

Our cups clinked together before we both downed the sweet wine. While she finished hers, I noticed the glance of a blonde man from a few groups over. He must've been the one she'd abandoned to find me, if his longing stare was anything to guess, and I instantly felt bad. Taylin lived in Silicate, so events like this weren't an everyday occurrence for her. I wanted her to enjoy herself, and that included flirting with strangers.

"Go have fun, Tay. I'll see you tomorrow," I said, holding the now-empty cup in front of my stomach.

She followed where my eyes had been before turning back to me, something like guilt shining in her gaze. "Are you sure?"

I nodded, shooing her away with the flick of my hand. "Yes, I'm sure. Go back to that man." I stole another look his way. "He's practically fawning over you."

"Alright. I'll go," she conceded. "Tomorrow," she added with a pointed look.

I only hoped that was certain.

With a nod, she was off. I watched her retreating back as a server passed me with a tray of warm, buttery pastries. The sweet scent enveloped me, and I was nearly about to follow him for a bite when a guard stepped in my way. His brunet hair was slicked back and a typical sword was slung on his hip. While all the guests wore masks tonight, the guards did not. "My lady."

I pursed my lips, waiting for him to continue.

"King Tenere has requested your presence," he stated.

"Of course he has," I muttered as the familiar pit of dread hit me in the stomach like a rock.

I had no doubt that in a matter of moments, I was to be either escorted out or shown the true reason for tonight's party.

It didn't matter that I didn't care to find out which it was.

I never had a choice.

CHAPTER 2

Letting the guard lead the way, I followed him over to where my father stood beside the stage at the front of the room. As soon as I was delivered, the guard bowed and took his leave.

"You requested me?" I questioned, stopping directly in front of my father. His salt and pepper hair didn't have a single strand out of place, his face freshly shaven. The crinkles around his hazel eyes seemed deeper tonight, like he was stressed about something. Then again, my father was always tense.

"I did," he answered bluntly, his words clipped as he faced the stage and fixed his deep red suit jacket with stiff, pale fingers. "Remember, Auria," he started, his words low but still firm. "Behave, or your privileges are taken away."

I bit the inside of my cheek to keep myself in line. Of course he wasn't going to tell me why he'd requested me. But before I could ponder further, he began stepping up onto the stage, and I had no choice but to follow.

I stopped beside him in the center. One of his hands was clasped around the goblet he held, the other holding the mask he'd now taken off. I, on the other hand, had nothing to hold on to, and found my fingers itching with nerves. I clasped them in front of me, keeping myself still as I noticed my stepmother, Heidi, stepping up on the opposite side of the stage. Her brown eyes were dark, laced with malice as she kept them trained on me while she sidled up next to my father. Her blonde hair was piled atop her head, showing off her long neck and deep garnet dress. I forced my gaze forward, not wanting to feel her judgment up here. I could deal with her chastisement over sneaking a glass of wine later.

"Thank you all for coming tonight." My father's voice boomed over the chattering crowd in an attempt to quiet them. Instantly, they ceased their conversations and dancing, the music cutting off to give the king their full attention. "If I can steal a moment of your time. I promise to let you all get back to drinking and dancing in just a moment." He paused. "My family and I greatly appreciate you all joining us tonight," he continued, not sparing a glance my way.

I pressed my lips together, pasting on an obedient act. I didn't want to be up here. I'd prefer to find another forgotten glass of wine and down it like the last. My eyes moved on their own accord, searching the room for Taylin. But instead of finding her, my gaze landed on the man whose goblet I'd borrowed. I noticed he now held a new cup in his grasp, but rather than the playful posture he held before, he was stiff as a board, his mouth a tight line.

"While it wasn't on the invitation, we do have something to celebrate, if that makes you all feel better about getting through such a long evening." Chuckles floated through the crowd. Meanwhile, I stood by, impatient and slightly irritated that yet again, I was left in the dark.

My father held his goblet in the air, his other hand ghosting over my back. "Please, if everyone would raise your glass to congratulate my beautiful daughter, Auria Tenere, on her engagement to Lander Bular."

I nearly stumbled, my heart stalling in my chest right along with the air in my lungs.

Engagement?

Glasses rose in the air as cheers and claps sounded, but I barely heard a thing as everything became muffled. I stood frozen, the glint off my father's garnet mask in his hand blurring in my vision. My ears began ringing like they wanted to repeat the last few seconds and hear what he said again to be sure it was right.

Every eye in the room was on me, causing my cheeks to heat with...not embarrassment of the attention, but humiliation. He'd set me up. Gave my hand to a stranger and announced it in a room full of royals.

I was beginning to like this mask, aside from its rough material that beat down on my skin and made my cheeks feel like an inferno, for it hid some of me from the immense number of people in this room all finding out about my supposed engagement at the same fucking time I did.

For gods' sake.

I didn't even bother to smile, despite knowing I'd hear about that later, but did he expect me to be happy? Though, I shouldn't even question that. *Of course* he did.

My father made the decisions, and we were all meant to bow down and go along with them. *Especially* me.

I didn't even know what Lander looked like. Shouldn't he be up here with me if we were to supposedly be married? This was as much his announcement as it apparently was mine.

A hand at my back pulled me from my thoughts as my father led me off stage. The chatter in the room picked back up, people smiling as the music began again. Rather than an elegant tune, it was a fast-paced one. As if this was something to celebrate.

"King Tenere," King Bular greeted, stopping us at the bottom of the stairs. His greying hair matched the shade of his short beard, showing off his age. His finely pressed suit was an array of his kingdom's colors—muted greens mixed with deep emerald stitching—sitting flawlessly atop his sunburnt skin.

I noted Heidi stopping on the opposite side of my father.

"King Bular," my father gritted back. "Still no sign of your son?"

"No," Tonson admitted, not bothering to turn to the crowd, like he knew his son wouldn't have shown up since last time he had checked. "He has a horrible habit of tardiness."

"Tardiness or plain disobedience?" my father questioned.

Tonson's lips flattened for a split second before he changed the subject, but I didn't hear a word either of them uttered, as all I could focus on was my spinning thoughts of needing to get out of here. I wasn't staying until this ball was over—not tonight.

My father had done a lot of things to me in my life, but an engagement without consulting me beforehand was outrageous. *Married*? To a Bular? I'd hardly spoken to the king and queen, let alone their sons. My father never let me around the other monarchs' children, as he was overly protective. So protective that even he rarely left the castle himself, for fear of leaving me alone. At least, that's what I assumed. How could my father go from strictly forbidding I speak to any man, to suddenly marrying me off to one? And from the sounds of it, he didn't like Lander's behavior to begin with.

"Lady Auria, forgive me," Tonson said, pulling my focus back to the present. He was angled toward me, hands clasped together. "Congratulations on your engagement to my son."

Gods, this sounded so wrong. This whole evening was

wrong. But I dipped my chin anyway. "Thank you, King Bular, but if you'll excuse me, I really need to take care of some personal matters."

Pretending that I had to relieve myself probably wasn't the brightest excuse, given the glare my father sent me. I didn't care to see what Heidi's reaction was to my abrupt dismissal. I didn't give a fuck about any of this. I needed air.

I didn't stick around to hear Tonson's response as I slipped away, not bothering to look for Taylin. There was no question she was just as shocked as I was. We told each other everything, so if she knew, I'd know. It was a surprise to the both of us.

The guests had gone right back to mingling, as if the announcement hadn't even happened, and I was thankful their penetrating stares were no longer trained on my face.

I set my sights on the nearest exit. The balcony door. There weren't many places I could go from the terrace, but it'd get me out of this stifling room and give me the opportunity to tear this godsforsaken mask off my face.

If only I could unlace this suffocating corset, too.

My escape plan started to lose its promise of reprieve all too soon as people attempted to speak to me on my way out. I ignored every congratulations, despite hands grazing my arms and fingers bushing my skin in an attempt to stop me. I didn't want their attention. I didn't even want to be *engaged*. There had to be some kind of ploy behind all of this, but there was no use in trying to find a way out of it. What's done was done, and I'd have to live with that.

With Lander being from Torbernite, I had to guess that this was to bring some sort of twisted peace between our kingdoms. Trade had been rocky the past few years, and I'd often overheard my father's meetings about how things weren't looking good.

Yet he can turn around and throw a fucking party.

As soon as I was through the door, the cool night air offered a welcome bite to my heated skin. Letting it shut behind me, I crossed to the edge of the deck while simultaneously ripping the mask off. I looked over the amber glow from the city with it clutched in my hand.

The castle wasn't far from Silicate, the distance allowing the common eye a beautiful view of the bustling city. The light spilling from hundreds of lanterns, the stone buildings, the cobbled streets, it was supposed to be beautiful, a palace of sorts. But to me, it was just that—a collection of man-made structures set upon a once-beautiful landscape. Taylin had told me stories of the city, of the shops and markets and diverse citizens. I wanted to adore it, to find the same hope many did in a place such as Silicate. But my life would never take me there. It simply wasn't meant to be, and I'd come to accept the fact long ago.

Though, if I could give in to my dreams for just one moment, they wouldn't place me here in this castle. I was provided safety and a home, but that was as far as my thankfulness went for this place.

"Not celebrating with the rest?" a deep, husky voice spoke up from behind me.

Catching a gasp in my restricted chest, I whirled around.

I hadn't even seen the man standing there when I came out here, being far too distracted with my irritation. But as my eyes adjusted to the light, I realized with too much certainty that it was the same man whose wine I'd stolen.

Thank gods it was only him. I didn't have the energy to deal with anyone else tonight.

His back was to the building as he leaned against it, legs crossed at the ankles with arms folded over his broad chest. His mask was still tied around his head, making it difficult to figure out exactly who he was, even with the dim silver light cast from the rings in the sky. For some reason, despite feeling so exposed moments ago, the thought of wanting my own mask back on my face didn't seem appealing to me.

"Celebrating can wait," I snipped, trying to calm my racing heart. I wasn't particularly happy about the news sprung on me this evening, but I especially didn't need to be told what I *should* be doing. Nor did I need judgment for it. No one was privy to the fact that I was not aware of this engagement, aside from Taylin, and if I had to guess, my father would want me to keep that a secret, too. To keep up the act in front of this stranger, I couldn't let on to that.

I had a feeling a lot of acting on behalf of this engagement was to come.

"Already done enough of it?" he asked, and I hated how he stood there like there wasn't a party going on behind him. Like we were just two strangers talking, and my world hadn't been upended right before my eyes moments ago. Like him standing out here, with his dark, messy hair and bulging muscles under the jacket he wore was simply casual. Despite that, he had a bite to his tone, as if he'd conjured up his own idea of me in a matter of seconds and disliked me for it, whether it be the truth or not. That, and it was so different than how he'd spoken to me inside. What changed?

"Hardly." I tried to keep the irritation out of my tone, but seemingly failed.

The man quirked a brow. "Are you not happy with your betrothed, *Princess*?"

My eyes narrowed at his use of the nickname and the way he said the word like it was venom on his tongue. Was that what changed his attitude toward me? Seeing me beside the king? "I'm no princess."

He smirked at my neglect to answer his question. I was

already annoyed, and his childish little nickname got under my skin all too easily. "Are you not the daughter of a king?"

"That means nothing."

Malice lit his eyes, along with a hint of humor, as if he thought my response was funny. "Oh, it means *everything.*"

Ignoring his jab, I turned back to the scenery, setting my hands on the cold railing as I worked to take in one full fucking breath. If I could, I'd fire my maid for tying this damn corset so tight. Not only was my life dictated by this entire fucking kingdom, but now my breathing was, too.

"Trouble, Princess?" he asked, but the way he said it made it seem like he *wished* I was having some sort of problem, only so he could let me suffer from it.

My eyes squeezed shut as my chest was somehow strangled even tighter. *How was it possible this godsforsaken garment could be any more restricting?* "No."

Seconds later, he was beside me, but I ignored him as he faced me. I wouldn't let him continue to play with my head. Gods, how could he have been so flirtatious inside, then completely flip around and be so blatantly rude? Was everyone out to ruin my night?

"Your cheeks are red," he stated.

"And the stars are bright," I bit back.

"You look like you need some help. Can't do much on your own, I assume," he said blandly.

"As if I'd let a stranger touch my bodice."

He crooked a brow. "I meant grabbing you some water, but if it's your corset that's bothering you, I can be of use as well. Although, touching a Tenere is the last thing I want to get my hands dirty with tonight."

I paid his comment no mind, reaching up to tie the mask back around my head. I loosed a breath when my finger caught in my braid, but finally resecured the mask. Hiding sounded much more appealing now. Adjusting it over my eyes, I faced him, forcing in another deep inhale.

"My *betrothed* can do that for me." Even the word tasted bad on my tongue.

He gave a slow nod as a small smirk pulled at his mouth. "You sure about that?"

"What makes you think I wouldn't be?"

He jerked his head in the direction of the door. "Didn't seem like you were very pleased with the announcement, is all, Princess."

I tried my best to seem confident as I asked, "Why wouldn't I be?"

Behind the mask, his blue eyes were hooded by narrowed eyelids. "I don't like liars."

"It's a good thing I'm not marrying you, then, isn't it?" I spit back as forcefully as I could with still no breath in my lungs. If only he knew just how manipulative my father was with his half-truths, then this man wouldn't think so poorly of me.

He chuckled. Fucking *chuckled*. "The prince has his hands full with this one."

My jaw nearly dropped, but I held it in place. "I didn't ask you to like me." I tried to regain my composure with the statement, needing to back off from this, but realized it was just confirming that I'd lied about being happy with the engagement. "You're the one who's on *my* terrace anyhow."

Gods, I needed to shut up.

He took a step forward until we were practically chest to chest. Suddenly, I was thankful for the tightness of the corset, because if it weren't for the dress, my breasts would've brushed his body with every inhale I struggled to take.

He leaned into my space, but I refused to back away. I wouldn't give him the satisfaction.

"Don't waste your breath, Princess. Everyone else may fall for the act, but not me." His tone dripped with malevolence.

Despite my body telling me to cower, I refused. I tipped my chin higher, inching closer. "You were much nicer in the ballroom. Perhaps you need a bit more alcohol in your system to lighten up that scowl of yours."

He cocked his head. "If a certain thief hadn't stolen mine, I could have made your wishes come true."

My jaw dropped, unable to help itself this time. "A thief?"

His eyes darted down to my parted lips, then back up to my eyes, pinning me with twin sapphires. "A princess who steals. Would you look at that?" He hummed. "Not very well-behaved, are you?"

I hesitated, and I fucking hated that I did, because hesitation showed weakness, and I was *not* weak. He sounded exactly like my fucking father, and I wouldn't let yet another man make me feel this way. Turning on my heel, I strode for the doors, trying my best not to show that he had riled me.

"Enjoy your engagement party," the man called after me, causing my blood to boil. He shouldn't have this godsdamned effect on me, getting under my skin so easily. I was falling into whatever trap he had laid by letting him frustrate me further, just like he presumably wanted.

I hesitated with the door cracked, my hand gripped on the brass handle. "You, too," I replied with the sweetest tone I could muster, and with a glance back, I caught his lips pursing together, giving the slightest indication that he, indeed, would not be enjoying it.

Maybe parties weren't his thing either.

I left the man standing there, heading back inside to the last place I wanted to be tonight.

CHAPTER 3

The musty air in the room instantly sucked the cold from my skin, causing my palms to clam up. After a poor attempt to wipe them on my dress, I spotted Taylin searching the room, presumably trying to find me.

Shoving through the crowd of warm bodies and drunken dancing, I reached her, wrapping a hand around her wrist. Pulling her over to the wall, right below a massive painting of the hills that housed our barren mines, I dropped her arm.

"Did you know?" Taylin asked immediately.

I shook my head, giving myself a moment to catch my breath. "I had no idea. I don't even know who Lander is." Which only infuriated me more. My father used me like a pawn in his game of chess, and I had no choice but to play along.

"He's not here," Taylin said, confusion and frustration on my behalf marring her face. "I searched the entire crowd trying to find you after your father's speech, and not once did I see him."

"I know. His father admitted he wasn't here." I turned my

attention to the crowd. Women's dresses swayed and men laughed as everyone but me was clearly enjoying their evening.

Well, maybe me and the man outside.

There was only one reason someone would step out of a party.

I subtly shook my head, clearing my thoughts of the man. He wasn't important right now. Turning back to Taylin, I asked, "You know what he looks like?" I knew his last name, but I'd never met a Lander. I would've remembered if I was introduced to my future husband. He should've at least made a lasting impression. Well, I hoped.

"I know you're kind of a homebody, Auria, but no one would miss him. He's handsome. Blond hair, a dashing smile, beautifully tan skin, bright hazel eyes. He's been waltzing about Silicate for a few days now. That is, when he's not holed up in one of the gambling dens."

I tried not to roll my eyes at her explanation of him. I didn't want to hear about how beautiful he might look. Charming or not, it wouldn't lighten my reality.

My father rarely let me outside to see Taylin, and he sure as hell didn't let me go frolic around in the city, meeting boys of all ages and sizes, and that was for one reason. I was needed here. He always told me it was for my own safety. That if I was let out and didn't know how to handle myself, I could get hurt.

But I'd found that pain wasn't just a possibility from outside of these walls.

It came from inside, too.

"I don't care about his looks." Not that I should give a damn about that anyway. Regardless of if he was some egg of a man, it wouldn't have stopped my father from setting me up with him for his own political gain.

He told me long ago to give up hopes of ever finding love. His words: it's impossible to find it true anymore—might as well not waste my time and dream of it to begin with. Which was why I guessed he'd moved on so quickly after my mother's death. She died when I was just barely four years old, so I only had small memories of her, but even with that, she never truly seemed happy. Anytime I tried to ask about her in the years since, I was shut down by my father, so I eventually stopped bothering. All I knew of her death was that she was extremely ill before she passed.

I was never told the reason in the end.

"I suppose it makes sense he's not here. People say he's more of a gambler than a respectable prince," Taylin added.

"A gambler?" Why in the hell would my father set me up with a gambler?

Taylin nodded. "He's probably off blowing coin or magic, letting loose since he's away from home. A lot of people in Silicate get lost in stuff like that. Can be quite dangerous, I've heard."

Amosite was the richest kingdom in all of Serpentine, despite the mines having been shut down long ago. My magic was the reason we stayed afloat. The entire kingdom counted on me, which was why I couldn't wrap my head around him marrying me off to another kingdom. Marrying wasn't some kind of small agreement that didn't change lives. My father would never risk losing me, so why?

"What a coward," I sneered under my breath.

"Took the words right from my mouth," Taylin agreed. "I wonder if he knows?"

"I meant my father." I found him across the room in his garnet suit, talking with a few other men. "I'd like to believe Lander and I are blind in this together."

She quirked a brow. "Already saying you two are together, are we?"

I rolled my eyes, bile rising in my throat at the thought of the word. "At least I'm not alone in this."

Her face softened slightly. "Auria, you've never been alone."

I shook my head. She didn't get it. I loved Taylin as if she was my sister, but she didn't know what it felt like to be locked in this castle day in and day out, only allowed to leave the walls if I were in the garden with her. Even then, I barely got an hour with my best friend before I was forced back inside.

"Maybe it won't be so bad," she said, trying to lessen the load.

There was no bright side to this. I was being forced into a marriage with a man I didn't know, under circumstances I wasn't—and would likely never—be aware of.

Not only had my father been using me since I was young for his monetary gain and power display, but he was now using me as a political pawn as well.

"Maybe," I replied, but only because I was too tired to go on about it further.

It was no secret to Taylin that I didn't want this. I didn't have to say the words out loud.

"Come. Let's dance," she said, grabbing my hand.

Rather than spend the rest of the night stressing over the inevitable, I followed her to the middle of the floor. The rest could wait until tomorrow.

Every worry, every second thought, every doubt.

None of it needed to taint tonight.

I'd enjoy my time with my best friend and fight my battles in the morning.

After all, no war was won in a night.

CHAPTER 4

I put on a simple red dress that fell to my ankles as I got ready to see Taylin. I'd woken up only minutes ago, but with the questions and theories that had popped up in my head overnight, I'd barely rested, too confused about last night. It nearly felt like some crazy dream.

I opened the dark oak door but stopped short as I came face to face with a guard. He wore Amosite's typical garnet and silver armor, save for his helmet. He had dark blond hair and a scar through his bottom lip. With his uniform, he should've looked at least a bit intimidating, but I'd grown so accustomed to only having guards and servants in my presence that I wasn't bothered.

He glanced at the straps of my dress before quickly averting his gaze. "Your presence is requested in the throne room."

"I'm meant to meet with Taylin." I knew it was pointless to argue. He'd drag me to the king himself if he had to. Even with that thought, I still didn't fear him like I should. There were other monsters that worried me more.

The guard gave an almost sympathetic look. I never knew their names, as we were never to exchange such pleasantries.

The look was gone as fast as it had appeared.

"Sorry, Lady Auria. Orders are orders."

My chest rose with a heavy breath as he stepped aside to let me pass.

I'd much rather stay in my room at this point, but that was also a battle I would not win.

Passing the threshold, I closed the door behind me with a soft snick.

We began our walk down the hall, the guard beside me with his hands dangling loosely by his side. He knew I wouldn't try anything that would require him to wield his sword—I was the daughter of a king, after all. Even if I did, he wouldn't hurt me. My father had given strict orders that no one put their hands on me, regardless of the circumstances. I wondered how well he thought that might go if I had a husband.

Even Taylin wasn't supposed to touch me, but with a guard looking the other way, we'd always hug our farewells. It was too isolating to go so long without another human's touch.

"Were you at the dance last night?" I asked, my eyes trained ahead.

He was silent a moment, and I almost thought he might not reply, but then he said, "Yes."

"Did you enjoy yourself?"

His fingers twitched, signaling he was slightly uncomfortable.

Good. He knew what my next question would be.

"Yes."

"Did my father tell you what would be announced?"

It wouldn't shock me if he had told everyone but me, but I wanted to know.

The guard cleared his throat as we rounded a corner. Our

footsteps echoed on the stone floor, the red and brown rugs doing little to muffle the sounds of our shoes. My father made almost everything in this kingdom red, but I never shared the same adoration for the color. It only reminded me of blood.

"Yes," he finally replied.

I nodded once, slowly, as we descended the stairs down to the main floor. How could my father inform some random guard and not me, when I was the one being directly affected by this? But it wasn't a question for the man beside me, given I had already made him disconcerted. It was one only my father could answer, though I was sure he'd make up some excuse to try to justify all of it, and I'd have no choice but to accept his explanation and never bring it up again.

A moment later, we approached my father's throne room.

The guard opened the giant door for me, gesturing a hand forward for me to pass.

"Thank you," I said before stepping past him.

He closed the door behind me, most likely standing guard outside in the hall.

With one look around the room as I came to a stop in the center before the deep red and dark oak thrones, I was certain my father was not in here.

Instead, I found my stepmother sitting on her throne before me, one arm draped over the side casually, though the rest of her posture was rigid. Her dress was only the slightest bit more casual today, dark red lace draped over cherry fabric.

I didn't bow just to spite her.

"Did you know?" I asked, skipping right to the point.

To hell with pleasantries.

Regardless of the way I behaved in front of her, she'd still bring a flame to my skin. She'd punish me, day after day, and anyone who knew about it would turn a blind eye.

My father loved her, and he needed me.

There were no solutions in his eyes.

"Lovely night last night, don't you agree?" Heidi said, her voice grating on every nerve in my body.

"Did you know?" I repeated, my voice harder this time, each word enunciated carefully.

She snapped her finger, and in an instant, a guard was behind me, pulling my arms behind my back and hitting the soft spot at the back of my knees so I'd fall to the ground. My knees stung as they made impact with the hard floor.

I didn't bother straining against him, despite the discomfort that bloomed in my wrists at his grasp.

"That's no way to greet your queen," she said, as if she wasn't also my stepmother.

I'd really prefer she was neither.

I bowed my head slightly, enraged at the position I was in. How fucking helpless I was in every meaning of the word.

"Your father does everything for a reason. For the best interest of all of us. Are you insinuating you do not trust him?"

I raised my head to look her in the eye. "He's playing with my life."

"Because he loves you."

I swallowed, my posture stiffening slightly as the stone ground bit into my knees.

She was right. He loved me, and I had to remember that he did all of this so we could have a good life. So that everyone in this kingdom could.

The doors opened behind me, and I didn't have to look to know my father walked through them, the sound of his boots telling me all I needed to know. I'd gotten good at listening to the rhythm of people's steps through my bedroom door.

"Let her go," my father instructed, barely paying me any mind as he walked past.

The guard dropped my hands, and my shoulders slumped

forward as the strain in them eased. Getting to my feet, I rubbed at my wrists as my father took his seat next to his wife.

"Did your maid tell you about the dinner?" my father asked, looking bored as ever as he slumped back in the throne. His salt and pepper hair was neatly styled, much like his garnet suit.

"No," I gritted out. I didn't mention he could've told me himself.

He folded his hands together, his elbows perched on the sides of the chair. "Tomorrow night, you'll be attending dinner with the Bulars. Katie will bring your dress to your room beforehand. And I expect no stunts like you pulled last night." He recited the words like it was a message he was reading off a parchment.

My brows pulled together. If anyone pulled any stunts last night, it was him.

"Stunts?"

His eyes turned to slits. "You disrespected me at my own party. You must show your appreciation and gratitude in front of my guests. One wrong move, and I look weak. Is that what you want?"

I averted my gaze, hating his perlustration of me right now. He meant how I hadn't smiled on stage, and then excused myself immediately after the announcement. "No."

He seemed satisfied with my response as his cutting glare lost some of its edge. "You must understand, I am leading an entire kingdom. So much rides on my shoulders, and if all I ask is that you cooperate, then you will do so. Is that clear?"

"Crystal." Yet it wasn't the only thing he was asking of me. I was to duplicate magic, obey his orders, be a good daughter, hide myself and my magic, and now marry a man I'd never met before. Was I even allowed to be truthful with Lander? Could he know about my ability?

"Now, you know what chores are on your list. I've added a few more, as there are some requests from friends that I'd like to fulfill."

He meant me. That *I'd* need to fulfill.

I kept silent as he continued. "As always, the paper is posted in the cellar. You're excused."

I didn't hesitate as I turned on my heel and headed for the giant doors. It was a part of my daily routine to go down there and duplicate what I was ordered to. He always had a list of specific vials for me to work on, but even with the daily load, I was already left drained. With more on my list, I hoped I could get it done in time to turn in early and sleep the effects of it off before this supposed dinner tomorrow.

The guard that brought me here fell into step beside me as I made my way through the castle to the cellar. Every so often, the guard assigned to me would switch due to my father's paranoia of one of them catching on to what I could do. If one of them figured out why I was going to the cellars every day, they could spread false accusations, or even worse, true ones.

Aside from me and my father, no one was privy to what was locked in the confines of the cellar, which irked my stepmother. She wasn't allowed in, and that only added to the list of reasons she despised me. Being kept out of specific rooms in the castle left me frustrated, too. But with the way she treated me, I felt no mercy on her behalf. She might be a queen, but my father held the authority around here.

He'd chosen my stepmother for none other than the fact that her beauty would carry down into their children, but then he came to find she could not get pregnant at all. Still, with that knowledge, he had no plans for me to ever take the throne.

Keeping my power a secret was easier some days than others, but on a day like today, the urge to spill it all was strong. It was my spite talking, the aggravation from being blindsided at the party making me want to forget all the reasons I couldn't reveal the truth.

Unfortunately, though, if anyone did find out, my father would simply kill them.

Nothing had stopped him from doing it before.

Not even to someone I thought I could share a future with.

CHAPTER 5

The next day, the deep red fabric of the dress stared back at me where it was laid out on my bed. I'd been standing there for minutes, dread sitting in my stomach like an anchor at sea at the thought of having to put it on and attend this dinner.

I had no interest in meeting Lander or sitting through this torturous evening, but if I didn't go willingly, a guard would come fetch me, and knowing from past experience, it wouldn't be pleasant.

Accepting my fate, I let my ivory slip fall to the ground, opting for a clean one, as I'd been wearing the other throughout the day. I'd taken a short nap in it after my time in the cellar this morning, and if Heidi found out I'd been wearing something from this morning to such an important dinner, she'd only use it as an excuse to chastise me.

After I'd situated myself into the dress, I peaked out the door, holding the corset to my chest.

"Katie," I whispered.

My guard turned my way but quickly averted his eyes once

he saw the state of my dress. The floor suddenly became very intriguing to him.

Katie unfolded her hands where she stood across the hall, her faded red and white dress hanging limp on her petite form. She stepped forward, following me back into my room, and closed the door behind her.

I turned to face the mirror, giving my maid access to my back so she could tie the strings.

"Please, not as tight as the night of the dance," I instructed.

In the reflection, she gave a quick nod as her fingers worked. Her light brown hair was tied back in a ponytail as it always was, shorter hairs of gray springing out around her round face.

I changed alone in my room to avoid any eyes on the bruises, burns, or cuts that littered my body under my clothing. Typically, I could sneak a bit of a healing vial in the cellar when I was down there working, but if I didn't have the time, I didn't want anyone, even my maid, seeing my body and the things my stepmother had done to it.

There was little I could do alone when it came to the strings on my corset, though. If Katie ever glanced a wound, she never spoke of it.

As she tied the corset together, my mind wandered back to the night of the masquerade ball, when I'd assumed the stranger outside was offering to loosen the binds of my dress.

Heat crawled up my neck at the memory.

I'd been so quick to assume he'd wanted to undress me, which not only had to have shocked him—and annoyed him further—but my forwardness also surprised me. Given the events of the night, my mind was a blur of emotions, and he'd said just the right things to set me off.

His mockery of calling me Princess was what grated my nerves the most. I was no such thing. A princess was treated like royalty, pampered and expected to marry and have children and sit on a throne one day. I was none of that, least of all cosseted as one typically was. But after the announcement of my engagement, I wondered if that somehow made me more of one than I was before.

Even so, I didn't think I'd ever see myself as a princess, whether the title was appointed to me or not.

Not with the way my father used me like a tool for his own benefit rather than love me like the daughter I was to him. How he possibly knew of the way my stepmother treated me and made no moves to change the behavior would never be forgotten by me.

So long as I could work, the treatment was presumably acceptable in his eyes.

"All done," Katie said, stepping back.

I took a full breath to test the limits of the bodice, satisfied that I was able to at least breathe.

"Thank you, Katie." Despite my hatred for how tight she could tie a corset, I appreciated her. Aside from Taylin, she was one person I could talk to a bit more personally than the guards. As a child, she'd told me stories of the dragons that hid around our world, how when the moon exploded, they'd come to Serpentine and rid the land of fae. She never agreed with my father choosing to keep me uneducated on such topics, so she told me what she could in secret—though I was sure there was plenty more to learn. I was sure my father tried to keep me clueless purposefully. If I knew nothing of the world outside these walls, he hoped I'd have no desire to venture past them.

Katie wasn't around me as often as the guards, only coming to clean my room or help me dress, which meant she never had the chance to catch on to any of my magic. Because of that, she didn't have to be rotated like the guards did, so we knew a bit more about each other than the basic pleasantries.

"Of course, Lady Auria."

I pressed my lips together at the formality.

"I've told you countless times before you can call me Auria." I didn't like the way the titles felt. They were too formal. Katie and I were well past the stage of being proper with one another.

Her wrinkled cheek moved as she gnawed on it, like she was debating telling me something.

My forehead creased in concern. "What is it?"

"Have you met Lander?" she asked hesitantly.

"No. But how bad could he possibly be?" I wasn't sure how well she might know him, or the things she could have overheard, but I hoped that whatever it might be that he wasn't a horrid person.

"You haven't heard the stories?"

I frowned. "Who would be telling me these stories other than you or Taylin?"

Her shoulders sagged a bit in the reflection. "Just be careful who you trust out there."

I turned to face her, adjusting my skirts. "You think my future husband would lie to me?"

Maybe she knew his family better than I thought she did.

"People can be deceiving, Auria, and with your isolation, you may not know what to believe."

As much as I hated it, she was right. I was naive to the world and what went on outside the chasm that surrounded Amosite. The only way out of this kingdom was the one old bridge that had stood for decades. Inside the border, I only knew of some of the things that happened in Silicate, due to Taylin's stories. Everything else, I was clueless.

I faced the mirror again, at a loss for words. My eyes roamed over my reflection. I truly hated the color red.

"I'll keep that in mind, Katie. Thank you. I need a minute alone before I go down," I told her.

She dipped her chin, then slipped out the door, closing it behind her.

Moving away from the mirror to my window, I gazed out at the glowing city in the distance. The sky was beautiful as the dome of amber faded into the silver light from the rings, and while the world looked so silent in this moment, I knew it was anything but.

My hand instinctively reached up to loop a finger around my hair, and I thought about how it must be to wander the city streets and look up to see that sky looming above, rather than seeing it all from the outside, as if Silicate was kept in a glass bubble, and I might never enter.

I wished I could say I had hope that this marriage would allow me the ability to visit the city, to have a speck of freedom, but I'd lost my faith in much all too long ago.

A knuckle rapped on my door, and a small sigh slipped from my lips.

The size of this castle truly didn't matter when all the walls felt like a prison, caging me in from the world surrounding it.

Maybe Lander wouldn't be so bad. He could show me the various landscapes other than the grass and woods I could glean from my window, the city streets and how they cracked. The colorful flower beds outside shop windows and citizens that didn't only wear tight dresses and don swords on their hips.

Maybe he *could* be my key to getting out.

But something told me that wasn't my father's intentions with the arrangement, that it was rather a way to keep me hidden further.

How far could I go before I disappeared altogether?

My guard stayed posted by the door as I entered the dining room. Instead of searching the group of people for who might be Lander, my eyes landed on the full glasses of wine sitting on the table. I beelined for one of them, not caring whose place it sat at. They could get another glass. I just needed something to replace the buzz of my nerves.

Halfway to the table, I was stopped by a large figure stepping in front of me. My flats practically screeched on the stone floor as I halted and took a step back to steady myself.

"Excuse me," I said, narrowing my eyes up at the man. "Can I help you?" He should know not to get in the way of a woman trying to fetch herself a drink.

"I'd simply like to get to know my brother's fiancé," he answered. "Where's the harm in that?"

My brows shot up before I quickly cooled my expression. "I didn't know you two were siblings."

He smiled, the look anything but settling. "Ah, yes. But, in case you hadn't noticed, I'm the far more handsome one." He added a wink for emphasis.

"Cocky, too," I remarked. I didn't mention that I hadn't seen Lander in the flesh yet. The man before me, however, looked nothing like his parents—his hair shades darker and his eyes nearly more pitch black than the sky at night. Taylin had said Lander was blonde, but I supposed if I looked hard enough, I could have found some similarities in what she'd described. But I was too focused on craving some sort of buzz to care.

He chuckled, extending a hand out to me. I laid mine in his, allowing him to press his lips to the back of my hand. "It's a pleasure, Lady Auria. I'm Paxon Bular."

I arched a brow at the use of my name and pulled my hand from his grip after he lowered it, taking a mental note of the calculated look in his deep brown eyes rimmed by dark lashes. "Well, Paxon, I'm rather thirsty, so if you'd please excuse me."

He stepped to the side, gesturing toward the elegant setup. A thin, red tablecloth spanned the center, and shimmering gold trays were spread about. "Pick your poison."

Moving past him, I reached the table, grabbing a glass and downing half the contents. Alcohol might not make this dinner go by any faster, but a girl could dream.

"Auria," my father called, interrupting my sip.

I lowered the glass as I met his scrutinizing gaze across the table. He wore a pressed red suit with gold stitching tooled along every seam, and his graying hair was slicked back.

"Come."

Reluctantly, I set the glass down where I'd found it and rounded the long, wooden table.

"This is Lander Bular," my father introduced, gesturing to the man at his side. I hadn't cared to look at the stranger—my *fiancé*—on my way over. "Lander, this is my daughter, Auria Tenere. Your fiancée."

Our eyes met, and as I expected, no sparks flew. No heavy beating of my heart or a flutter in my stomach, like the old romance novels I used to sneak talked about. He was just a man, a stranger, a prince, one in which I had no physical attraction to right off the bat, despite his good looks. His hair was as blond as his mother's, his hazel eyes nearly sparkling in the light from the chandeliers. Beauty ran in their family, but I wasn't pulled by it.

"My fiancée," Lander said, testing the word on his tongue.

Maybe he was as happy about the news as I was.

"It's very nice to meet you," Lander added as I politely held a hand out to him. He took it gently, placing a quick peck to my skin before dropping it. His hair was mussed slightly at the top, strands of it sticking up in odd directions, like he hadn't cared to fix it before attending.

My father left us to speak, quickly getting lost in conversation with King Bular a few feet to the side. Neither seemed very interested in us meeting, which only proved my suspicions that this was simply a political move, not one set up out of love for their children.

"It's nice to finally put a face to the name," I stated hesitantly, not sure what else to talk about. I wasn't good at...this.

He forced a sympathetic smile. "My apologies. I was caught up in something the other night and couldn't attend the ball. I'm sure it was lovely."

"Caught up gambling again, brother?" Paxon interrupted, sneaking up on the two of us.

I took a small step to the side, putting space between Paxon and myself. Our shoulders did *not* need to be touching.

Lander's eyes narrowed on his brother. "And what were you doing that night?"

Paxon glared right back. I had no idea what was going on, but a brotherly dispute wasn't something I wanted to get caught up in.

"I don't mind," I said hurriedly.

Both their gazes landed on me, and I struggled to swallow. Attention was clearly not something I craved.

"If you like to gamble," I clarified. "And I didn't mind that you weren't there." But I should have, given we were now engaged. Minding if your fiancé was out enjoying himself rather than attending the ball where your betrothal was announced seemed like something I should feel.

Then again, I truly had no idea how to react to any of this.

"You two will get along just fine, then," Paxon said as he patted Lander's shoulder a bit too hard. They both wore dark green suits, yet Paxon's was more finely pressed. Lander's, on the other hand, was wrinkled, the top button undone.

Before either of us could say another word, Paxon walked off, joining his father.

"Did you know?" I asked, moving my attention back to Lander.

He was a few inches taller than me, his stubble-coated chin tilted down as he regarded my question. "About the engagement?"

I nodded.

"Somewhat."

I waited for him to continue, shoving down the frustration that threatened to creep up at the knowledge of him knowing more of this than myself. I'd never felt so clueless before, and that said a lot, given that my entire life was me being kept in the dark.

"Tensions have been high with trade between the other kingdoms, so it was no secret my parents were debating making an arrangement to keep the peace. I just didn't expect it would involve you."

I cocked a brow. What was that supposed to mean?

"Not that I'm upset it's you," he quickly clarified. "You're very pretty, Lady Auria. Your eyes alone feel like I'm staring into an icy forest, but just from our conversation, I can tell you're a warm person."

Was warm supposed to be some sort of compliment? Clearly Lander was not well-versed in speaking to women.

"I'm under the impression you were unaware?" he asked, his words hesitant as he realized he was talking out his ass.

I wished I was holding a glass so I could fidget with something other than my godsdamned dress. "I had no clue any of this would be happening." Gods, I wanted to say more, but I wasn't sure how much I was allowed to discuss with him.

He looked a bit taken aback, like that was somehow a shock to him. I supposed he thought the king's daughter would know of such basic information.

"Please take your seats," my father announced, interrupting our conversation.

I gave Lander a small smile before parting ways, heading to my designated spot at the table. I was to always sit on the side my father took.

To my satisfaction, my stepmother was seated where I'd drunk most of the wine from the glass.

In the spot next to her, at the head of the table, my father cleared his throat, gaining everyone's attention. "Thank you for joining us tonight to celebrate Auria and Lander's engagement a bit more privately. As I'm sure you two are"—he looked to King and Queen Bular on the other side of Lander and Paxon—"we are so pleased with their engagement, in the hopes it restores peace between the kingdoms."

I stared at my plate, not bothering to look his way as he spoke. This was the first time he'd ever mentioned anything of the sort in front of me, and while I'd had a sinking suspicion since the announcement, his words only solidified that I was being used as his pawn.

If this marriage was to bring peace the same way my magic brought him wealth, then what was I but a body to be moved around for convenience?

"In order for this to work," my father began again, "Lander and Auria will need to make their engagement known more widely than solely at the party I threw. Royals may be able to spread the news, but townspeople will surely have their doubts, and without them, we may not get the best in trade, as they are the biggest producers."

My head shot up, a small bit of hope blooming in my chest. Was he going to allow me outside of these walls? Outside of the chasm?

My father's gaze moved between Lander and me beside each other. "First, a stroll through the city, flaunting how deeply in love you two are. Then, with the protection of two dozen guards, you will travel to the three other kingdoms. You are not to stop in the other towns between visits. Is that understood?"

I blinked a few times, as if the action could help me process what he was saying any clearer. Did I hear his words right? Surely, I couldn't have.

"Other kingdoms?" I asked for clarification.

His eyes pinned me in place, clearly not appreciating my interruption. He wanted me to agree, not ask questions. "Yes. You will visit Sulphur first, then Lander's home in Torbernite, head to Feldspar, and then you will be back home, in Amosite."

My entire body was frozen in place, even my heart quieting its beat to take in this news. I was going to visit the other three kingdoms. That was...incomprehensible.

He was just going to let me walk out these doors, without him, cross the bridge over the chasm, and be free, even if only for a short time?

"Get that little gleam out of your eyes, Auria. There will be guards, and you are expected back within three weeks. If either of you do not arrive on the day you are expected to return, there will be consequences. Is that clear?"

I nodded, trying my best not to look too eager while Lander seemed entirely bored, not giving any indication how he might feel about this.

"All of the guards have been given detailed instructions with a planned route. There will be no straying from those directions. No exploring any cities. This is not a vacation. It is a show of power, of unification, that we will not crumble under their threats of breaking off trade. Understood?"

Though my father's voice boomed with authority, I couldn't care less what he was saying.

I was getting out.

Even if only for a few weeks, I would still be able to see something other than these drab walls.

That was enough.

"Yes, Your Majesty," I said, attempting to hide my excitement from my tone.

Across from me, Paxon eyed me curiously, not once taking his attention off of me. Lander had already begun eating beside me, seemingly in a hurry to be done.

"Along with the guards, Paxon will be accompanying the two of you on this journey," King Bular added after taking a sip of his wine.

My eyes moved from him back to Paxon, who now had the corner of his mouth tilted in a smirk.

"Plenty of time to get to know each other," he said, his expression twisted like a cat watching a mouse.

"Lovely," I mumbled before taking a large gulp of my wine. Not only was I supposed to become comfortable with Lander, I was now expected to be polite with his brother, too.

"May I be excused?" Lander asked, as if he hadn't been listening at all.

With a glance at his plate, I found it was empty, save for the leftover bones of the pigeon.

"Yes," Queen Bular answered, flicking her hand in a shooing manner.

I silently wished it was that easy for me to get out of things.

Lander's hand covered mine on the table for a split second before he stood, leaving his chair at least two feet from the table. He didn't bother to fix it before he left the dining room.

I got the feeling this fiancé of mine would not be saving me from any dreaded conversations and long dinners anytime soon.

But I could deal with that knowledge, knowing I would be

able to leave soon. I'd be tasting the air of other kingdoms in no time.

Excitement swirled with the slightest buzz of wine flowing through me as we ate. All the while, Paxon kept his eyes on me, only ever looking away for a brief conversation with my father.

As soon as my stepmother noticed how low her glass was, she frowned, calling for a servant to refill the cup immediately.

It should've filled me with some sort of joy to see her irritated, but all I could think of was the endless possibilities of what I might experience in just a matter of days.

The buzz of that knowledge alone was enough to make me forget all the pain I'd endured here, even if just for the evening.

CHAPTER 6

Two days after the dinner, I woke up particularly early in the hopes that Taylin would be in the gardens waiting for me considering I hadn't been able to see her since the ball. As I stepped outside the doors, I found her sitting on the stone bench we always met at. She stood as soon as she saw me.

My new guard who'd replaced my previous one yesterday was now a tall, lean redhead that seemed somewhat new to the job. He stayed posted by the doors, keeping a bored eye on our surroundings as I took a seat on the bench.

"Where have you been?" Taylin asked, worry evident in her voice as she lowered herself to the stone once more. Her pin-straight blonde hair flowed over her shoulders, the sun reflecting off the gold strands. The freckles on her nose were evidence of her time spent in the sun, the little spattering of dots a complement to her deep blue eyes. Her ivory dress hugged her figure beautifully. Though townspeople were encouraged to wear Amosite's colors, they were afforded some freedom to choose their attire. Aside from my jealousy of that, I always wished I had Taylin's curves and nearly flawless hair. Mine was wavy on a good day, but frizzy most.

I shook my head, easing her surely racing thoughts. "I had extra duties and couldn't make it down." She knew about my stepmother's punishments, and that sometimes, I'd be in too much pain for our visits. "I'm leaving."

Taylin's eyes widened to the point I thought they might burst from her head and fall to the grass at our feet.

"For three weeks," I explained. "With Lander."

Somehow, her eyes grew even wider.

I explained the reason my father was sending us away, and how Lander's brother would be accompanying us. I didn't forget to mention that Lander didn't seem too involved in this marriage either, which made it a bit easier for me to accept.

"So he doesn't want to marry you?" she asked once I was finished.

"I'm not sure. He seems okay with the engagement, but not so enamored with the political side of it that it's bothering him. I want to say that we have the same feelings about all of this, but that would be exaggerating, as I haven't had much time to talk with him."

She rolled her lips together like she was thinking on something. "And his brother, Paxon, he's really going with?"

I nodded.

"Do you think he might be up to something?" Taylin wondered out loud.

I tilted my head in question. "What makes you say that?"

She sat forward on the bench. "Why would Paxon take such an interest in his brother's fiancée? I mean, from what you told me, he seemed kind of creepy at the dinner. And accompanying your group on this journey? It's no business to him. This is for the two of you, not him."

"If we're being technical, it's mostly for the kingdom." I

understood why she might be skeptical, but that was how political moves seemed to happen in these places. It was never only between the two individuals involved, but their entire parties, and their families, too. "It affects him in some way. He's a part of their family, you know."

She sat back on the bench, her eyes full of concern. "Are you scared?"

I shrugged. "Somehow, not really. I'm excited to see what it looks like out there." My gaze moved in the direction of the city, though I couldn't see it past the foliage in the garden.

Taylin had never been outside the chasm, but she knew what all of Amosite looked like. She'd tell me stories about Silicate, the garbage in the streets, the people bustling about. It didn't always sound pleasant, but it didn't have to be. It sounded *real.* Sometimes I caught myself thinking of what it'd be like to be down there, a part of it all, to overhear gossip, take part in conversations with strangers just for the hell of it, and smell freshly prepared food. That was never to be my destiny, but now I'd get a glimpse at it.

The door to the castle opened and another guard slipped out, mumbling something to my appointed guard. After a few exchanges, the guard went back inside, and the redhead started for me.

"I suppose our visit is being cut short," I said, disappointment evident in my tone.

"I'll see you tomorrow?"

"I'll do my best." I'd miss Taylin for the days I was gone, but I'd see her as soon as I returned.

"My Lady," the guard started.

I stood, waving him off, then pulled Taylin in for a quick hug. Out of the corner of my eye, the guard tensed, but he made no attempt to split us apart.

"Love you, Tay," I said quietly.

"Love you lots, Auria. This will be good for you," she replied with a smile as I let her go.

Leaving Taylin in the gardens, I followed my guard back inside the castle. The doors closed behind us, taking the sunlight with them. The long hallway was dim as we walked toward the stairs that led down to the cellar.

The silence enunciated our footsteps on the stone as we descended the stairs. Once we reached the large, wooden door, the guard gave me a short nod before I twisted the handle and slipped inside.

I let loose a sigh when I glimpsed the list on the parchment stuck to the wall. After a quick read-through of the specific magics I was meant to duplicate, I eyed the vials, finding the first one on my list—healing magic.

He wanted me to fill half a dozen crates with the healing vials alone, then continue on to fire magic for the lanterns and hearths, and lastly, strength vials. I could only assume he needed an abundance of those for the guards that would be on the trip with us. He never listed what they were to be used for, but I always tried to guess, sort of like a game to make light of the work. If it was water vials I was to fill, I assumed the wells weren't producing as much as he liked; if it was fertile magic, I guessed he'd be sending them to Sulphur to encourage faster, healthier crop growth.

Today, though, it was simply the three types—healing, fire, and strength—but in great quantities.

I'd be tired, but it wouldn't be the worst I'd endured.

Using a ribbon on the shelf, I tied my hair back and got to work.

A BEAD of sweat dripped down my brow as a dim pink light glowed from my palms around the vials in each hand. To duplicate magic, I had to hold the existing magic, let it flow through me like blood in my veins from one hand to the other, and as a result, it would fill the empty glass.

I assumed what drained me was the magic passing through my body. Some magics were more extreme than others in the toll they took on my body, but healing salves, in comparison, were the easiest for me to deal with, as some part of it healed me as it flowed.

Almost like the healing magic cared for my body, not wishing to steal my energy as it heeded to my power.

I'd already fulfilled the fire and strength crates, along with half the healing ones, each labeled so I wouldn't get the numbers wrong. I'd purposefully left the other half of the healing vials for last, hoping they'd refill at least some of my energy so I didn't walk out of here completely drained.

The door to the cellar opened, and I jumped, the vial in my hand dropping to the ground with a crash. Tiny pieces of glass littered the floor, glowing magic oozing out onto the stone. I quickly willed the light to disappear from my palms. With the shards mixed into the green substance, the magic was useless. I silently cursed myself, hating that I'd wasted a perfectly good resource due to my clumsiness.

Remembering the door opening behind me and that I wasn't alone, I spun around to find my father entering the stuffy room.

His focus drifted to the mess at my feet. "You need to be more careful."

"Why are you down here?" I asked, slight panic lacing my words, despite now knowing it was only him. No one was allowed in here aside from me and my father, and even then, he rarely entered, so the sound of the door hinge creaking had sent alarm bells blaring through my mind.

He gave me a blank stare, but I didn't miss the judgment in my mess up hidden there. "It is my castle. I may go wherever I please."

"But you never come down here."

He closed the door behind him, taking a step further into the room as he surveyed the crates.

"You surprised me," I said, the silence all too loud, knowing he was disappointed in me breaking a vial.

"Clean it up," he instructed, not glancing my way.

I hurriedly grabbed two rags and a dustpan from the shelf. "I'm sorry."

He ignored my apology as I cleaned the glass and flickering liquid off the ground. It still held some of its shimmer, but it was dying out. Magic needed to be handled with care, and it knew more than any that it wouldn't be of use in this state, littered with shards of glass. My heart pulled at the knowledge it was letting itself wilt away, knowing its purpose was no more.

I stood, dumping the contents in the barrel by the door. I refrained from looking in to see the salve flickering out in the bottom. It'd lose its color, turning a murky gray as the life faded from it.

"Is it done?" he asked, his hands folded behind his back as he watched me move.

I set the pan on the shelf and the dirty rags in a cloth bag, making a mental note to bring it to the laundry when I got the chance. I gestured to the ground where there was now no trace of the mess. "It's clean, is it not?"

"The crates, Auria." He sounded irritated, and I inwardly cringed.

I shouldn't make his job harder than it already was.

I lowered my head the slightest. "I just need to fill one last vial, and the list will be finished." If I hadn't dropped the one, my father would have walked in with perfect timing.

He gave a curt nod, then turned for the door. "I'll send guards to bring the crates up. Leave them outside with the lids on."

Then he was gone, the door shutting behind him. I was once again alone.

With a sigh, I grabbed another full vial, along with an empty one, and repeated the process I'd been doing for hours. The familiar tingle flowed up my arm the moment my power lit my palms with that pinkish light. It traveled through my body, the burn paired with a cool aftertaste as it moved. In seconds, the empty vial was filled with the glowing green liquid, the color shining bright through the thin glass. It swirled around, almost happy to be there.

Once the duplication was complete, I let my power dissipate, the light leaving my skin, then set the original vial back on the shelf. I carefully placed the new vial in the crate, set the lid on top, then brushed my hands on my dress.

Satisfied with the now-filled crates, I turned for the door, opening it to find my guard where I'd left him.

"Done," I told him.

He nodded, moving a few feet up the stairs so that I could move the crates out of the room. Their lids covered the contents so the guards could move them without knowing what all was inside. It was the process my father made sure I followed down to the most minute detail to make sure they couldn't see inside the cellar, and that all the boxes going in and out were covered. They were not to know what was in them, only that my job was done once the correct amount of boxes were moved out of the cellar for them to bring wherever my father instructed.

After all the boxes were in the small area below the stairs, I slowly climbed the steps to meet my guard. The additional guards my father sent to retrieve the boxes headed our way. As they passed, one of them said to the redhead, "Care to help?"

My guard eyed the one who spoke, then glanced back at me in question. He was assigned to stay with me, but I was eager to be alone.

"I'm sure I can find my way to my room. You can help them," I said.

He contemplated staying with me, the indecision spiraling in his eyes. He then gave a tight nod, watching me a second longer to be sure I was okay with it and this wasn't a test. I offered a smile, which seemed to be enough as he turned to join the group of them, disappearing down the stairs.

I knew this castle like the back of my hand, so it wasn't like I could get lost. And with the heavy security around the perimeter of these walls, nothing would happen to me in the few minutes I was away from my guard. Plus, even if I wanted to get lost in the castle, I was too tired from overusing my power to try.

A warm bath and my bed were the only two things I could think of right now as I forced my heavy eyelids to remain open.

After heading down one of the halls, I rounded a corner, only to have my face immediately met with a hard wall. I staggered back, my palm coming up to my forehead as a hand wrapped around my upper arm to steady me. So it wasn't a wall I'd hit, then.

"Sorry," I mumbled, rubbing my head before looking at who it was I'd run into.

Even without the mask, recognition hit me in the gut like a punch. The man from the balcony stood before me, wearing the same leather jacket.

"Not very aware of your surroundings, are you?" he questioned, dropping my arm. His voice was smoother than honey, though a slight rasp hid deep within, and it tugged at me.

"The halls are typically empty," I defended, doing my best to put a bite behind my words, despite the exhaustion pulling at me. I wasn't in the mood to deal with this on the way to my room. I was tired, and he was a thorn in my slipper.

"Balconies, too? Or is it your guards that always check those for you?"

I lowered my hand to my side, narrowing my eyes at him. "I'm perfectly capable of being aware on my own."

He raised his eyebrows with a nod, not an ounce of him believing the words coming out of my mouth. Though, with the fatigue tugging at me, I feared he might be right in that I couldn't do it on my own. As if he could see it in my expression, that spot between his brows creased the slightest bit as he studied me.

I didn't have the energy for this.

"If you'll excuse me," I said, moving to walk around him. He stayed in place a moment before continuing the next few feet to turn into the meeting room.

Glancing around to be sure no one was in the hall, I pivoted, heading back to the door he disappeared into. Pressing an ear to the wood, I listened as muffled voices filtered through. Who did he think he was to waltz into that room like he was important enough to be a part of whatever discussion my father was having?

"Bowen." My father's voice carried through the door. He sounded surprised, which was strange, as he typically knew everything. "We were not expecting you."

Somehow, the name fit the stranger.

"It's rude not to invite all of us, isn't it?" Bowen asked, cockiness evident in his tone. The rasp had left, his words flowing together almost flawlessly.

I silently mouthed his name, testing the feel of it on my lips.

"Yes, of course. My invitation must have gotten lost on the wind," my father supplied.

"Those stubborn messenger hawks, always losing their parchments," another voice added, somewhere farther into the room. I couldn't make out who it was.

"Yes," Bowen drawled, boredom clinging to the word. "Those hawks. Maybe it was the same one I found downed in the desert. Though, that one was very clearly on its way to Feldspar, if the letter was any indication. Without its injury, I reckon I would've never known this meeting was taking place."

I could practically hear my father attempt to swallow his nerves.

A smile crept up on my face at the knowledge that this Bowen guy made him uncomfortable.

What about him made him so uneasy? Why did he not want him here?

Did my father know Bowen was in attendance at the masquerade ball the other night?

The fact that my father wasn't pleased with his appearance intrigued me when it shouldn't.

"What are you doing?" a deep, feminine voice asked, clearer than the ones in the room.

I spun to find Heidi flanked by three guards standing mere feet from me. "I'm heading to my room." It wasn't *entirely* a lie.

"And made a quick stop to press your ear to a door you have no business being near?" she questioned. I didn't miss the satisfaction shining bright on her face at catching me.

"I—" But I had no excuse, no explanation.

"Guards," she snapped, then immediately turned, heading in the opposite direction in which she came. One followed on her heels while the other two grabbed my arms.

"Wait, no. Please. I wasn't listening," I begged, but their hold was firm, their fingers digging in hard enough to bruise, as they forced me to trail Heidi. I was well aware of what was to come, my back already flinching with the phantom pain.

With my spent energy, it was useless to struggle against their grips. After a series of turns and a set of stairs that led below ground, we approached the room I knew too well. If there was one place I could erase from my mind, it'd be this one.

As the guard opened the double doors for my stepmother, the trapped screams echoed through my mind as memories all too real took hold. They were ingrained in me, etched into my brain. For being the protected daughter of King Tenere, pain was an all too familiar friend of mine thanks to this chamber.

"In the chair," Heidi instructed, waving a casual hand over her shoulder as she grabbed a vial of fire magic off the small wooden table in the corner. There were no windows in here, and the doors sealed seamlessly, keeping any sounds contained within the walls.

There was no use in begging anymore. It'd only drive the pleasure she got from doing this. Queen Tenere was a bored woman, and I was her toy. She had no ties to me other than marrying my father, and even so, he would never banish her for how she treated me. Anyone who knew kept her secret, turning a blind eye, and if I spoke a word of it, she'd surely burn off my tongue. By all means, she was protected in harming me, but in the end, I thanked the gods that it was me who endured her affliction and not some other innocent person.

Heidi never went as far as to render me useless with my wounds. My father needed me, and while she wasn't privy as to why, she was well aware that he'd lose his mind if something serious happened to me. While King Tenere was the shiny prize she somehow won in marriage, I was the golden egg he'd protect with his life, even if he didn't always treat me well in return. The power I held was too great a loss for him to risk, and it was no secret that elicited rage-inducing jealousy in her.

The guards shoved me into the chair, the top of the back slamming into my shoulder blades. They'd bruise, but it'd be nothing compared to what was to come. I welcomed the bite, as it only prepared my body to numb itself. To shut down from feeling, as it had become so well-versed in doing. From a young age, she'd been doing this, and eventually, my mind learned to find peace in a setting that offered none.

The back of the rickety chair was left purposefully open, no slats of wood or fancy intricate design. It provided perfect access to my back, and I always wondered if she designed it specifically for this. For me.

The sentiment was bittersweet.

Like usual, my wrists were tied to the armrests with leather straps that bit into my skin.

"When will you learn?" Heidi asked, uncorking the vial. The amber liquid bubbled at the top, begging for use. Purpose. That I might have been the one to fill that vial was... unfortunate.

I provided no response. My retorts were what she wanted, and I wouldn't give her the fuel.

"Quiet today, are we? Keeping those ears open?" She tsked as the guards tied my ankles to the legs of the chair. She reached a hand up to brush my hair behind my ear. "Perhaps today I won't go for the back."

She wouldn't follow through. She only said it to elicit fear, to get a reaction. She couldn't risk people seeing an injury on me without raising questions. While my father and the guards turned a blind eye, others might not.

After tying the knots tight, the two guards stepped to the side, joining the third by the door. It was a large room, despite being underground.

"Eavesdropping is a crime punishable by death," she went on, stepping behind the chair and out of my sight. My hands flexed under the bindings, but I didn't fight against them.

"It's too bad I can't die," I said through gritted teeth. My already-singed skin tingled in anticipation of the burn. The last ones had barely had time to heal, doing so on their own, as I hadn't been able to sneak a healing vial lately without getting behind in my work.

She laughed, then my head was yanked back by my hair. My back arched uncomfortably as the clammy air hit my exposed neck. "Don't be so sure of that, little wench. Anything is possible."

My breathing picked up, and I hated the show it put on for the guards. My body was in acceptance of its fate, but my mind was not. Thoughts swirled around frantically like fish caught in a net, desperate for a way out. Every time, I wished the magic wouldn't hurt me. Hoped and pleaded that it would grant me mercy. But one of the downsides of the magic that filled these vials—it gave its holder too much power.

"He'd leave you if you killed me," I seethed. Her title as Queen of Amosite was more important to her than anything else. Her ego reeked of it.

"He'd get over it." She let go of my hair, and I swung my head forward, wishing I could curl in on myself. Wishing all of this could just...go away.

The sound of fabric ripping filled the room seconds before a line of flames licked down my back like a river of agony. My teeth almost broke against the strain as it burned a path down my skin. The all too familiar smell of burnt skin wafted around me, and I wanted to vomit. I did all I could to hold back the bile. To calm the rolling of my stomach as pain erupted on every nerve ending.

I could beat this.

I could be strong.

CHAPTER 7

After Heidi was satisfied with the stream of burns following the length of my spine, two of the guards escorted me to my room. I'd been given a robe to cover up with for the walk, given my dress was destroyed and my back was too sore to put tight clothing on.

Tears sprung to my eyes each time the fabric ghosted over the burned flesh. I'd decided to hell with attempting to find a vial to heal the wounds first. I wanted a bath, to sink in on myself, and maybe, if I was lucky, I'd get lost under the water and fail to resurface.

The piney scent of the arnica oil I'd mixed in with the bath water lingered on my skin as I toweled off, squeezing droplets of water from the ends of my hair. I'd had to fight falling asleep in the tub, the cool water so blissful against the exhaustion and pain that threatened to pull me under. There was only so much a body could take in one day, and I feared I'd reached my limit. I almost couldn't help myself from allowing my eyes to shut, which was a clear sign to get out.

For the duration of my bath, I'd hunched forward rather than sit back in order to save myself the excruciating pain of the porcelain on my wounds. Not before long, my grumbling stomach stirred my half-awaken state in the water, further spurring me to unplug the drain. I hadn't eaten much today aside from the muffin I'd snagged on my way to see Taylin, and my stomach was finally protesting.

As it was now late and everyone was presumably turned in for the night, I threw a silk cardigan over my nightdress, careful not to wrap it tightly around my front so it wouldn't brush the wounds too hard, before heading out of my room toward the kitchen. I could snag a bite to eat and use a healing vial from the drawer they kept stocked with medical supplies in case a cook cut themself while prepping meals. They never noticed when I'd borrowed some in the past, as I was always sure to refill the vial exactly to where it was before I used any.

My hair was still damp, the ends cold as they dripped every so often, but the chill was welcomed against the burns.

I padded down the stairs before making my way down the hallway, then rounded a corner, coming upon the kitchen. It was dark, aside from the single candle lit in the center of the wood island. I didn't want to light any lanterns, lest a guard see I was in here and insist on escorting me back to my room. Nor did I particularly want to be around a fire vial at the moment. I had nothing against the magic itself—it wasn't its fault, but instead its user—but my mind still steered away from the idea of using it for a while after each punishment.

Opening the pantry door in the corner of the kitchen, I rifled through the few baked goods that were left in a basket from earlier in the day. Eyeing the flavors, my belly ached for something more than another muffin. Grabbing one of the blueberry ones, I scooted the basket back on the shelf and turned out of the pantry with a hand on the door.

My heart nearly leapt out of my chest at the sight of a person standing in the opposite corner, cloaked in complete darkness.

The muffin dropped from my hand, rolling across the floor as my back banged into the wall behind me.

"Fuck," I shrieked, but not toward the stranger in the room, but rather the unbearable pain that shocked through me, racing down my spine like a knife being dragged through my heart. My hand plastered to my chest, like that alone might keep the organ inside my body.

Bowen stood there, clouded in black as he watched me, as if he was simply a shadow in the room. "Quite the mouth on you, Princess."

I took as much of a steadying breath as I could, though it did little to slow my heart's frantic pace.

At least it knew to stay on edge around him.

"What are you still doing in my home?" I asked, clearly breathless from the scare and trying my best to keep the strain out of my voice.

"Staying a bit," he answered casually, crossing an ankle over the other as he leaned against the counter behind him. Even in the dim candlelight, I noticed his eyes fall to my bruised wrists. Quickly, I dropped my hold on my chest to hide them behind my back, careful to avoid the wounds.

"Please, do enlighten me on why," I said, trying to distract him. I truly didn't care about his reason for staying in the castle, I only needed to get the healing vial from the drawer he was currently blocking.

He tried to hide his smirk, like it was funny to him that I was bothered by his presence. "I have some meetings to attend before I return home."

"You mean like the one you forced yourself into earlier?"

The only thing that gave away his surprise that I knew he

wasn't meant to be there was the pause in his response. "Eavesdropping, are we, Princess?"

I scoffed. What was everyone's problem with that?

My eyes narrowed slightly. "Where *is* your home, anyway?" It was foolish of me to ask, but I'd never met him before, and I was overly curious for no good reason.

This time, he failed to hide the lift of his mouth. "Wouldn't you like to know?"

My jaw nearly dropped at his slight insinuation—that I was being nosy for something other than innocent reasons.

Moving on.

"Why doesn't my father like you?"

"Shouldn't that be a question to ask your father?" His tone seemed bored, like he'd rather be doing anything else than standing here chatting with me.

He wasn't the only one.

I only wanted a snack and to heal my burns. Then I'd be back in my room feeling an immense amount better and finally get the rest I craved.

"I'm asking you."

Bowen shoved off the counter, grabbing an apple from the bowl on the island before tossing it in the air once, his eyes admiring the shine on the red fruit as he turned it over in his fingers. "So many questions for a stranger." He hummed. "I'd think you were trying to distract me from something. Perhaps why you're really in here?"

My lips rolled together as I adjusted the cardigan over my shoulder, making sure it wouldn't slip down my arm. I shouldn't have thought I could get away with diverting his attention.

"I'm only here for a snack," I said innocently.

His thumb rubbed aimlessly over the fruit. "Little late for a snack, isn't it?"

I eyed the apple. "Not for you, it seems."

He spun the drupe in his fingers. "Go on, then. Grab what you're here for."

He was challenging me, all too curious as to why I was really in the kitchen while everyone else slept. Even my guard had turned in for the night, the only ones awake posted outside the castle walls.

Swallowing my nerves, I crossed the kitchen to him with as much confidence as I could muster, hiding my hands in the sleeves of my cardigan to ensure he didn't see the bruises. I stood directly in front of him, with mere inches separating his chest from mine. His head cocked ever so slightly, studying me.

His breath was a ghost across my cheek as he stared down at me. This was a bad, bad idea. If anyone were to walk in and word got back to my father, he'd never let me be without a guard again. Worse, I feared what he might do to Bowen.

"You're in my way," I stated, breaking the tense silence hanging thick in the air between us.

He took one small step to the left, keeping his eyes trained ahead. I stepped forward and reached for the handle, pulling open the drawer. Quickly, in the hopes he wouldn't see what I grabbed, I pocketed a healing vial and closed it again.

When he didn't speak up, I turned around, heading for the exit.

"Now, why would a princess need a healing vial in the middle of the night?" Bowen asked, stopping me in my tracks.

I inhaled deeply, clutching the sleeve of my cardigan. "It's a good thing I'm not a princess or I'd be wondering the same thing."

Before he could question me further, I hurried out of the kitchen and toward my room.

On my way, I mentally kicked myself for asking where he lived.

I had a godsdamned fiancé now. I shouldn't be asking random men those types of things.

Frustration forced away the exhaustion I'd felt moments before, making me forget all about my grumbling stomach and the muffin I left on the floor. Typically, I handled healing myself right then and there, but now I'd left with the vial, which meant I had to find a time to bring it back so no one would notice it was gone.

Once I was back in my room, I popped the cork off the vial and slipped my cardigan off one shoulder. Doing my best to reach behind me without straining the wound, I angled the glass upside down at the top of my back, letting it dribble down the sensitive, scorched skin. The thick liquid might not hit every inch on the way down, but it'd work its magic on the parts that it did. It'd be enough to at least make the pain ebb.

I braced my hands against the end of my bed and sucked in a breath through my teeth as a cooling sensation followed the trail of magic. The contrast against the burns sent shivers skating over my arms. I gave it a moment to settle in, knowing my skin would scar regardless of healing the wounds because of how much time had passed since they were inflicted.

Before slipping the rest of the way out of my cardigan, I called for my magic, the pinkish hue instantly glowing bright in my palms. With a few drops still in the glass, I duplicated it until the vial was once again full. Corking it, I placed it in the drawer in my bedside table.

As I settled into my bed, lying on my stomach, I decided that if I stayed in here until we left for our journey to the other kingdoms, I wouldn't have a chance to run into Bowen again and risk him questioning me further. In a perfect world, I might be able to, but I'd come to find long ago that my life was anything but perfect. I'd be forced to leave my room eventually.

However long his *meetings* were taking place here, I could avoid him.

Besides, staying hidden was my specialty.

CHAPTER 8

Another dreadful dinner.

It was a record how many my father was able to squeeze into the span of a week. I was aware we had other royal parties visiting, but I didn't think it called for a formal dinner with everyone in attendance nearly every night.

To go along with my feelings on this dinner, I put as minimal effort into getting ready as I could, leaving my hair down and not caring if my dress was wrinkled. I was tired from another day of filling crates full of vials for my father. He was gifting them to the other kings and queens as a show of his wealth—and I supposed his gratitude for their visit.

I never saw where the crates went after the guards brought them up, and truthfully, I didn't care to. My job was to duplicate the magic, not follow its every move, which was my excuse to slip away this morning and return the healing vial to the kitchens. I'd told the redhead I'd grab a snack while I waited for him to help them with the crates, and while I technically had stolen a few berries, I'd wanted to be alone in there for an entirely different reason. Surely, the guard wouldn't have asked why I had the vial in the first place, but I didn't want to raise any unnecessary questions.

Now, as soon as I stepped foot in the dining hall, my father's voice boomed across the massive room, grating on my eardrums. "A moment, Auria."

Eyes snapped between the two of us but quickly averted as I walked to my father's side. His deep red suit was buttoned all the way to his neck, not a single thread frayed or out of place on it.

"Yes?"

"What is wrong with this picture?" he asked, surveying the painting on the wall in front of him.

I craned my neck back to take in the entire scene. Men and women were gathered around a table, smiles lit up on each of their faces as they raised glasses full of deep red wine. Each guest was dressed to the nines with regal gowns and ironed suits.

"Nothing...?" I replied, not sure what he thought I might find in the painting. It was the same one that had hung here since before I was born, and he hadn't mentioned anything wrong with it before now.

"Look at their hair." His words were low and clipped.

My eyes roamed over the women in the photo before realization hit me as to what he was trying to say. I took a step back, my hands coming together in front of me. "My hair."

He nodded, not giving me his full attention as his eyes stayed trained on the painting. "Fix it."

"Yes, Your Majesty," I answered quietly before turning around and hurrying back through the doors with my gaze downcast.

My steps were quick, each footfall light on the gray floors as I headed down the hall. I saw the boots a moment too late and landed face-first into a chest.

How many times would this happen to me this week?

I was so used to the castle being empty with no one in the halls, save for the few guards, that I wasn't being cautious of where I was walking.

My hands shot up to push off the man I'd run into, but I briefly hesitated when our gazes caught.

"Second time this week," Bowen so helpfully pointed out as I stepped back.

I ran both hands down the front of my dress. "Yes, well, as I said before, the halls are usually empty."

"Auria," my father's voice boomed from behind me, echoing through the hall.

I flinched, quickly averting my eyes back to my feet, but not before noticing Bowen's brows inch together in skepticism. He didn't move his gaze from me, and I knew that pissed my father off more than he already was, seeing me speaking to him.

"My apologies," I whispered before moving to walk around him.

I wasn't sure if Bowen continued walking once I was out of his way, too afraid of the repercussions to look back and check.

Humiliation ran its way up my spine, only solidifying the fact that I didn't want to sit through another dinner or paste a smile on my face in front of kings that looked at me like I was more a courtesan than a Tenere.

All the magic I'd been using the past week caught up to me, the emotions I typically kept carefully tucked away threatening to overflow and show themselves.

I inhaled deeply through my nose, then out my mouth as I did when I needed to hide how I felt. It did little to ease my mind, but it worked wonders on the rock lodged in my throat.

I made it to my room and worked my hair into two flawless braids, then looped them to create a makeshift bun at the back of my head. The shorter pieces in the front frayed out, but if I used water, they'd only get frizzier, so I did my best to twirl the strands around my finger to shape them, tugging a few times.

I gave myself a quick once-over in the mirror, running my hands down my bodice. The whites around my green eyes were slightly bloodshot from the strain of my magic the past few days. It was a normal reaction, but nonetheless, I hoped no one at the dinner took notice.

If they did, it'd be easy to excuse it as sleep deprivation, so long as they didn't look too far into why I might be losing sleep.

Knowing there was nothing I could do besides pinch some pink into my cheeks, I headed back down to the dining room to find everyone was already seated and eating. The food smelled lovely—an array of pigeon, imported chicken, and pork chops laid out on the table among various greens and a few potato dishes. It was a waste of food, given that my father's guests never ate it all. They didn't need all these options, especially if trade between the other kingdoms was getting to be as bad as it seemed to be. We depended on the others for specific goods. While Amosite produced various types of magic, we weren't strong in other areas like farming, lumber, or weaponry. So if Sulphur was cutting our food supply, it'd be wise for us to conserve our stock of it. At least, I'd think so.

I took a seat on the side closest to my father and set my napkin on my lap. Though the food smelled delicious, my stomach was currently sour, giving me no desire to eat. My eyes scanned the room. Aside from Sulphur's leaders, everyone was in attendance—monarchs from Torbernite, Feldspar and Amosite. And, somewhat to my surprise, Lander was even here, too.

"The food is magnificent," King Pleum from Feldspar spoke up. He and his wife both wore Feldspar's color—ivory. They both had long, rich brunet hair, and while King Pleum's was tied in a neat knot at the base of his skull, Queen Pleum's cascaded down her back in luscious waves, showcasing her sharp features and natural beauty from the plumpness of her lips to the crisp edge of her cheekbones.

"My chefs are the best in all of Serpentine," my father bragged. "I pay the spice harvesters a hefty price to get this sort of seasoning. Bland food doesn't sit well in the stomach, as you know."

Queen Pleum grinned, though it didn't seem very sincere, like all this talk of how much was wasted either brought her some sick delight or made her literally nauseous. I assumed the latter.

"Speaking of payment," King Pleum started, "let's hope Sulphur brings back their end of our trade agreement with this marriage being boasted about in front of them. Their attitude toward our treaty due to your wealth does not make me feel good about our ability to get meat and crop for much longer."

My father waved him off, wiping his mouth on the corner of his crimson napkin. "No need to worry, Desmond. Once Auria and Lander visit Sulphur, they will see how well we are all getting along and uphold their end of the deal. Things will be well again in no time."

King Pleum nodded with a closed-lip grin, like my father's words failed to settle an ounce of his concern. All the while, Bowen remained eerily silent from where he was seated at the other end of the table, observing the conversation rather than taking part in it.

So that truly was the problem, then? Other kingdoms were breaking their agreements because they didn't like how wealthy my father was?

"It is rather unfortunate that we were not able to speak with King Alline further. He had to leave shortly after the ball to return with Patreesa. As we all know, she's expecting their child soon. But rest assured, all will be as it was before soon enough," my father assured him.

I looked around the table, finding eyes trained on me—ones that'd barely left my face since I arrived.

Paxon's.

After a silent dinner while everyone ate, King Pleum finally spoke up again. "It is quite impressive, King Tenere, how much you are producing. How many workers do you have down in those mines, if I may ask?"

My palms grew clammy. Did he know about the cellar, about my magic? I couldn't bear to look up, but out of the corner of my eye, I noticed Bowen's attention pique at the subject. I might have missed it if I wasn't so hyper aware of the way he'd been relaxed in his chair the entire dinner.

The mines were closed, but others didn't know that. It was a cover-up for the use of my powers.

I didn't dare meet Paxon's gaze again to save myself from seeing his damn smirk he'd worn during our last meal. I had no doubt he likely held the same expression tonight, given he'd flashed it my way when I joined them.

"Quite a few," my father said, excusing the question with his vague response. "They're all very hard workers, doing what is necessary for their kingdom."

Servants filed into the room, grabbing empty plates and used cutlery to take them back to the kitchen to be washed. They disappeared as fast as they came, leaving the table clear of everything aside from our glasses of fizzing berry wine. I hadn't taken a single sip of mine, though I ached to. Alcohol would do wonders for me right now, but the last thing I needed tonight was to slip up in front of these monarchs.

With the meal now over, people stood, King Pleum and his wife coming over to talk to King Bular while my father came around the table to find me. I abandoned my chair as well, making sure to push it back in.

"Did you enjoy your meal?" my father asked, though he sounded more annoyed than curious. The question nearly took me off guard.

"It was delicious." I'd barely touched the plate.

"You may be excused so the men can talk," he ordered.

Ah, so that's why he'd pretended to care.

I assumed the queens would soon go to the tea room to have a drink, but I wouldn't be invited.

I nodded, lowering my chin. "Yes, Your Majesty."

I was about to turn to head for the doors when Bowen came up beside me and my father, his hands held casually behind his back. "A wonderful meal, King Tenere."

My father's jaw twitched as he pasted on a very clearly forced closed-lip smile. "Yes. Like I said, I owe it all to my chefs."

Bowen looked down at me, and I quickly averted my eyes to the chair as if it was the most interesting piece of furniture in the room. "I wanted to personally congratulate Auria on her engagement. I haven't had the chance yet."

I couldn't help that my focus spun back to him. He'd already congratulated me. Although not in the most pleasant way, he still had.

"Thank you," I said quietly.

"She's very happy with the arrangement," my father added, as if Bowen would care if I truly was or not.

"Is she." It came out more like a statement than a question as he studied my response. "You'll miss your daughter, though, won't you?" His attention turned back to my father. "When she's off with him?"

My father's teeth ground together, the action evident in the way his jaw flexed. "She will not be living with him."

A crease formed between my brows as my eyes shot to my father.

How could I not live with my *husband*? Though I'd been curious what my father's plan was for that all along, I hadn't had the chance to ask him. He likely wouldn't have given me an answer, even if I had.

Bowen must have had the same thought. "Interesting marriage, then."

My father was quite a few inches shorter than Bowen, yet he tried his best to look as built and lethal as him. "It is what she wanted," my father defended, sounding too bold for his statement not being even slightly true.

I wasn't sure how he could lie so easily about words I hadn't spoken or arrangements I hadn't agreed to right in front of me, as if his words simply spoke it into existence and I had no feelings of my own.

"And Auria," Bowen started, his ice-filled eyes directed at me again, "how do you feel about this marriage?"

If my father wasn't irate before, he sure was now.

I didn't have a say in any of it, and Bowen was giving me the opportunity to speak up.

But I couldn't. Not in front of my father.

I knew what would happen if I did.

I pasted on a small smile, my cheeks straining at the effort. "I'm excited for my trip."

At least that much was true.

Bowen's eyes never left mine, and I feared he could see it all written in my own.

"Well, I must excuse my daughter. She has a big day ahead of her tomorrow, prepping for the journey."

Bowen's brow cocked ever so slightly, like he was challenging me to go against my father blatantly telling me to leave.

"Yes, right. Thank you for being so kind," I told Bowen. If he was disappointed in me obeying, he didn't show it. "I must be heading to bed now. Enjoy your evening."

Without looking at my father, I headed for the door, feeling the burn of Bowen's eyes on my back as I exited the room.

There was something going on between the two of them that I didn't want to be in the middle of. Bowen was baiting my father, and I didn't like that he was bringing me into the mix. The last thing I needed right now was my father thinking I was encouraging Bowen's behavior or was even on his side.

With my father's reaction to Bowen's appearance in the meeting room the other day, their dislike for each other was clear. I wasn't sure where it stemmed from, and I shouldn't be curious. It was none of my business.

But being locked behind these castle walls my entire life, boredom was an all too close friend of mine, and this new tension piqued my interest.

With my departure in a few days, I was sure I'd get no information out of subtle snooping and light eavesdropping, so for now, I'd let it go. Bowen would be gone by the time I was back anyway.

Might as well forget about the issue altogether.

CHAPTER 9

I startled as I woke to a dress hanging in the open window of my room. The breeze ruffled the fabric, making my tired mind believe it was a person at first glance rather than a gown. Once I realized it was only a piece of clothing, I groaned and covered my face with the sheets. Through the thin fabric, the sound of the door to my room opening caused me to peek an eye out.

"Oh, good. You're awake," Katie said, floating across the room in her usual drab attire.

"Unfortunately," I muttered, but then she grabbed the sheets and yanked them back. "Hey!"

She ignored my protests, moving to the hanging dress. The brisk morning chill wafting through the window ate at my bare legs.

"What could possibly be so important that I have to wear that?" The dress was pure silk, silver lace covering the top half of the garnet outfit.

"You're going to the city, Auria."

I froze in my movements to get out of bed. "I'm going where?"

"Silicate. You've heard of it."

"Of course I have," I said, exasperated. Was this actually happening?

"Oh, Auria," my maid began, a look of understanding on her face as she regarded me. "Do not be scared."

"I'm not scared, I'm...in shock."

That had to be an acceptable reaction for someone who had never been to the city that was only a thirty-minute ride away on horseback. Would I get to ride a horse? Talk to the people who live in the city? Visit Taylin where she grew up?

"But excited, right?"

"Yes," I answered, finally getting up from the bed. The cold stone seeped through the rug beside my bed, biting into my exposed toes.

"You'll enjoy your time there, I'm sure. I don't visit often, but try not to judge it at first appearance. Not everyone is as well-off as your father. Not every place looks like"—her eyes roamed the room—"this." Her hand ran down the side of the dress, as if her mind was somewhere else as she spoke.

I didn't expect the town to be lavish and sparkling. Just seeing different scenery than the same stone walls and long hallways would be enough for me.

"The guards will keep you safe, as I'm sure Lander will as well," she continued, holding the dress out to me.

I froze at the word. "Safe?" Was it dangerous there?

She eyed me hesitantly, like she was debating how much to tell. "You need to be careful outside the chasm, Auria. There could be things—" She stopped herself.

"What things?" I pressed.

She shook her head, pushing the dress closer to me. "I've said too much."

I slowly took it from her, the soft fabric running through my fingers as her warning rang through my head.

"You're the king's daughter, Auria. People may not treat you the same as you are treated here." But the way she said it, it seemed it wasn't only the people she was trying to warn me about. "Just stay close to them, okay?"

I'd never seen such concern in her eyes, let alone hear it in her voice. Katie was more a mother figure to me than Heidi had ever been, regardless of her title as my maid.

"I will," I assured her, dropping it. She said I'd be kept safe, and I didn't doubt that. I couldn't hold too much fear in this, knowing I was finally getting what I wanted—to leave. "Will I visit the cellars before we depart?"

She shook her head, rearranging various items on my vanity. "You are excused today."

The shock of knowing I was going to the city was nothing compared to her response.

"I-I'm excused?"

Never in my life had I been given a day off from my time in the cellar. Not even when I was running a fever or down with a stomach bug.

"Yes, Auria." Hope shone in her eyes as she twisted to face me, like she was just as excited as I was. "You are excused."

The slight tilt of her lips told me she knew exactly what this meant. I was finally getting what I dreamed of for so long.

My smile mimicked hers, though we both tried to hide them, despite being in the privacy of my room. I felt almost foolish being this excited when it was only a day.

But a day held so much potential. So many possibilities. And soon, I'd be on a three-week trip. Three weeks without duplicating magic, without draining my energy for my father's benefit.

I wondered what my body and mind would feel like after a day away from using my magic, and how weeks might feel.

Katie dipped her chin. "Right. Well, get dressed, my lady. There are only so many hours in the day."

I gave her a nod before she exited my room so I could have privacy to get ready.

I'd never stripped so fast in my life.

I DIDN'T GET to travel by horse like I'd hoped. Even if I only got to see the scenery through the tiny window of the carriage I was currently stuffed in, I was enamored enough with the view of the forest we passed through that it didn't matter.

I'd take what I could get.

The cart rocked side to side as it maneuvered over rocks and divots in the dirt path, jostling Lander and I where we were seated across from each other.

"Are all rides this bumpy?" I asked. I wouldn't lie and pretend I wasn't the slightest bit perturbed, and the uneven ground did little to ease those nerves.

"Have you never ridden in a carriage before?" Lander questioned, cocking his head slightly as he studied me.

I reckoned he didn't know my situation very well, then.

I shook my head. "This is my first time."

His eyes trailed to my slippers. "You'll need better footwear for our journey."

"Won't I be in a carriage like this one?" I assumed I wouldn't be allowed to ride a horse then either—as much as I was dying to.

A crease formed between his brows. "You'll still need to walk, Lady Auria. The carriage won't simply drop you inside the doors of wherever we'll be staying."

I shifted my posture, folding my hands tightly in my lap as I moved my gaze from Lander to the window. "I don't expect that. I just thought I'd be under orders to stay inside as much as possible." Did he really think I was that presumptuous to have an entire horse-drawn cart go inside the doors of a home? He was demented if so. But the one thing I had come to like about Lander so far was that he didn't seem to judge others—at least me—given his guilty pleasures in gambling were far from perfect. It seemed he'd come to accept that people wouldn't particularly like how he spent his free time, and rather than let that bother him, he chose to not care what others thought at all.

Regardless, he was right. I'd have to let Katie know that I'd need new shoes before we departed.

I turned back to face him. "Have you traveled to the other kingdoms before?"

He leaned back on the bench. "I have. And if you're wondering, you're not particularly missing out."

My brows furrowed in confusion at his response.

"Not much to do in kingdoms full of oppressed people," he went on.

Puzzlement hit me harder than before. "Why do you say that?"

He studied me a moment, almost like he was gauging if I was serious or not. "Common folk don't have much to be happy about with trade being the way that it is right now."

"Is it that bad?"

He shrugged. "In some parts. Some are better off than others, but that doesn't make anyone particularly happy. Leaders are doing what they can, but with tensions high, uproar seems to be more common than not recently."

I nodded, my mind at a loss on how to reply as his words did little to ease the nerves building in my stomach. "I haven't,"

I told him, though he didn't ask. "Been to other kingdoms, I mean. I'm excited to see what's out there, though."

He let out the smallest snort. "There isn't much. Besides, we won't have time to explore, per your father's orders. He's sending us on the quickest route for a reason."

I folded my hands together on my lap, straightening my shoulders. "Then I guess I'll do my best to take in what I can as we travel."

His brows rose as he slowly nodded.

"What's that look for?" I asked.

He placed his elbows on his knees as he leaned forward. "Are you not aware of how dangerous it is outside the kingdoms?"

"I thought you said there isn't much out there," I snarked. He was only trying to scare me.

"There are precautions taken inside Amosite's borders to keep the people safe. The same goes for the other kingdoms, though they don't have the same benefits of the chasm. The laws that protect you in here"—he pointed to the carriage floor—"will not be in place out there." His finger aimed toward the window. "So I suggest you put your life before your sightseeing, Lady Auria."

I inhaled deeply through my nose in an attempt to keep my composure. He wasn't going to ruin my excitement of crossing that bridge by adding fuel to my reservations. If I died out there, so be it. At least I wouldn't have lived without seeing some of the world.

"If this trip is so risky, why is my father sending us? Surely the kings and queens seeing the engagement announcement was enough to convince them."

Lander's eyes narrowed on me, though more so in confusion than annoyance. "It's not just royalty that's angry with your father."

Of course it wasn't. "Who else?"

"The people," he answered like it was obvious. "What he's done has essentially severed the peace between common folk and their royal leaders."

I opened my mouth to ask what my father could have done, but before I could get a word out, the approaching city caught my eye through the window. I turned to peer out, excited to see it up close for the first time, but instead of feeling awe, more confusion coursed through me. Silicate didn't look nearly as beautiful at this distance as it did when I saw it from the castle.

Every building was a different shade of mottled gray, the uneven stone streets reflecting the same trite palette. As we entered the city limits, the driver steering the carriage to where I assumed was downtown. There, the street turned to pure dirt, deep divots worn into the path from years of use.

As we ventured deeper, the social status of certain city folk was clear, as some wore nicer clothes than others, but nothing among the multitude of people compared to the finery Lander and I wore. Most of the townspeople wore fabrics lacking any color, aside from varying shades of white and brown, causing them to almost blend in with the buildings around them. Upon closer look, I realized most of the brown clothing was faded from its original red color, either the sun or age depleting the pigment.

Every few blocks, an establishment would reach three or four stories high, but most of the residences didn't expand beyond the first floor. They were piled upon each other, not a gap to be found in between the houses.

Once we entered the main square, the carriage jerked to a stop. I braced a hand on the wall to keep from sliding forward onto Lander. The sound of boots hitting the dirt filtered through the carriage, and a moment later, the door was thrown open.

I looked to Lander, not sure if that meant I was supposed to get out.

He gestured to the door. “My lady.”

Using the wall to balance myself, I pushed off the seat, bending slightly at the waist so I wouldn’t hit my head on the ceiling. My excitement nearly made me rush, but I forced myself to slow. I set my hand in the waiting palm of the attendant outside the carriage and stepped down the two wooden steps, taking in our surroundings as my slippers hit the ground. I was barely aware of it as my hand slid back to my side, my mind trying to wrap around what I was seeing.

Lander exited as well, stopping beside me as the guard closed the door behind us, then stood post next to the wheel.

One glance around the square at the feet of the civilians told me enough. What looked to be compost sat in small piles littered about. Children had dirt-stained cheeks, mothers greasy hair, and men’s hands were caked with oil and littered with untended cuts.

But all the healing vials I produced... The water magic. Was none of it being sent here? Were they not able to bathe?

“Is it what you were expecting?” Lander asked as he meagerly attempted to straighten his button-down.

I swallowed, not sure how to respond. I never would have expected this was the reality of Silicate from my view at the castle. Taylin had told me stories of the city, but I guess I didn’t think it was this bad.

“Not quite,” I admitted quietly.

“Don’t hate that castle on the hill so much now, do you?” he asked, working on the top button of his shirt.

If anything, the sight before me made me hate my home more. Seeing Amosite’s people living in such conditions, with dogs wandering the streets, piles of manure stacked high behind buildings, and trash littered about. No one seemed bothered, as if this was normal to them. It almost made me... angry.

My father was sitting up in his castle, hoarding resources and hosting lavish parties, all while his people lived like this.

Did he purposefully hide this from me thinking that if I knew, I'd demand he do something about it?

I could help these people. I could replenish more magic if they needed it. Why would he keep it from me, knowing I could do more?

But worst of all, why was he okay with these conditions?

I didn't give Lander a response, for if I told him the truth, he might take the information back to my father. Or worse, word could get back to my stepmother that I was ungrateful.

"Care for a stroll?" he asked, holding his hand out to me in offering.

Right. That was what we were meant to do. Show our presence, and look happy doing it.

I nodded, adjusting my skirt before placing my palm in his. We began walking side by side through the dusty street, the feeling of his skin on mine for so long foreign to me. The rocks hidden in the dirt threatened to pierce through the bottom of my slippers, quickly proving Lander right. I'd most definitely need better shoes for the journey.

Three Amosite guards trailed behind me, while two others stuck closer to Lander, their hands at the ready to grab their swords if they needed to act fast. I could feel the magic flowing through their weapons like my very own heart beating in my chest. Blacksmiths crafted daggers and swords with the ability to hold vials of magic in the pommel. Once a vial was placed in the compartment, its power would flow through the steel. If they inserted poison, it would infect whoever was cut by the blade. If they chose fire, the weapon would light with flames as soon as it was unsheathed.

I'd sometimes steal a quick peek at the guards training on the fields behind the castle, but I'd never seen them use magic during lessons. I could only feel magic being used from a certain distance, depending on the strength and type of power, but when it was amplified through steel, it was easier to detect.

We passed mostly empty carts of various fruits and vegetables, but what was left on display was either dirty or near rotten. Though what remained didn't look appetizing in the slightest, people still milled about, making trades to purchase the foods so they'd at least have something in their stomachs. All the while, townspeople sent wary glances our way, rightfully confused as to why we were here.

Nausea rolled through me just thinking of how these families were living. How they must feel to live in fear of starving or wilting away from improper conditions. I hated that they had to endure such things. This wasn't *right*.

As we continued on our way, Lander never strayed from my side. He stayed close, as did the guards. Being the king's daughter, I was sure they were afraid someone might try to harm me, but for some reason, I didn't carry the same fear I had felt a sliver of in the carriage.

The people had a right to hate me.

I caught a few glares as we made our way through the main square. Who we were went without question. Word of our engagement had probably already traveled, but now they had proof. It didn't help that our means of transportation was so unnecessarily flashy that one glance and even a fool would know it held someone of royalty.

My focus snagged on a dark-haired man walking past us in a hurry, some kind of black ink traveling up his exposed arms in swirls and shapes I'd never seen before. I wasn't aware people had the ability to stain their skin in such a way.

Beside me, Lander tensed a bit, dropping my hand as his

eyes narrowed on the man passing an alley. Suddenly, the stranger switched direction, turning right back around as two city guards came out from a shop. They wore a different sort of armor than that of the castle's guards, more silver weaved throughout with only accents of garnet.

The man's clear attempt to avoid their attention failed as the guards drew their swords.

"Stop!" one of them shouted at the man.

Lander put a hand on my arm, halting me where we stood.

The man had to be barely twenty feet from us now.

He immediately took off in a run, the city guards following suit as one of their swords lit with flame.

My three guards quickly surrounded me while Lander's did the same, ushering the two of us toward the nearest building to keep us out of the way. The one with a bald head and dark red beard grabbed my upper arm, yanking me against the wall. I let out a small gasp as his fingers dug into my skin, but my attention was too trained on the man with ink running down his arms to do anything about it.

"I said stop!" the guard shouted again as he sheathed his sword and yanked a firearm from his hip. It had a curved wooden handle with gold accents, the worn tip long and narrow.

My eyes widened at the sight of it.

Why would the guards in the city need to carry firearms? I'd only ever heard stories of them being used in battle, their magic bullets much more effective than close combat with a blade.

As if in slow motion, the guard's thumb pulled back the hammer, his finger adding pressure to the trigger, and it fired.

An ear-piercing boom echoed off the stone buildings, the sound traveling down every nearby street.

I didn't think to cover my ears, and as a result, ringing filled my head as my eyes trailed to the man now lying in a heap on the street, his blood seeping into the dirt like water breaking through an unstable dam.

"Get her out of here," Lander instructed as the guard holding my arm yanked me closer to him. "Now!"

My body felt numb as I was rushed back to the carriage, my mind spinning with questions as the ringing subsided.

Why did they shoot him? What did he do to make himself a target?

Why did he have ink running down his arms?

Did the shapes mean anything?

In a flash, I was being shoved inside the carriage. My skirt caught under my foot as I stumbled inside, and I braced my hands on the bench to keep myself from face-planting.

Lander stepped in behind me, helping me into my seat with a steadying hand on my waist.

I plopped onto the cushioned bench, yanking my skirt away from my feet. I hated all this damn fabric.

"Are you okay?" Lander asked as he took his spot across from me at the same moment a guard slammed the door shut.

"What just happened?" I hadn't realized how out of breath I was until I spoke.

His eyes searched my face. "They were trying to arrest a citizen."

The carriage jerked forward as a whip sounded, but this time, I didn't have time to catch myself. Lander set his hands on my shoulders to steady me, and I scooted back on the bench.

"Why? What did he do?"

A crease formed on Lander's forehead. "You saw his tattoos."

I shoved my hair away from my face, suddenly feeling hot. "Yes, and? That doesn't tell me why they needed to shoot him."

I didn't say what we both knew came after the shot. That he was dead.

Lander was silent a moment, studying me like he couldn't figure out if I was being honest or just snippy. "The ink means he stole."

"Stole what?"

"Magic."

I shook my head, more questions arising than before. "You're telling me someone etched black swirls into his arms and hands because he stole *magic*?" It didn't make any sense.

"Are you testing me?" he asked, his tone accusatory.

"What?" How would I be testing *him*? None of this was logical.

He dropped the question, finally taking me at my word that I had no clue what the fuck was going on. "Magic stains people when they steal it with ill intent. It's not a...pleasant process. But it's basically just a blaring sign saying they're criminals."

I blinked rapidly, trying to process what he was telling me. I truly thought I knew everything there was to know about magic, given that I worked with it every day. "So because he took magic against the law, it *inked* him?"

Lander nodded, though the rocking of the carriage made it hard to notice.

"And he deserved to die for that?" I asked.

His features softened a bit before he said, "It's your father's law that thieves are to be killed, Lady Auria. Magic inks for its own reasons, but he uses it as a way to rid the land of criminals. Other kingdoms follow the same rules. Your father is just a bit more...strict about it."

My mind whirled as I tried to process his words, the unstable movements of the coach churning a sea of nausea in my gut.

It all hit me—how much I truly didn't know. Being stuck in

that castle might seem like a luxury to those on the outside, but it was my own personal prison. I knew nothing of the real world, and yet, I was expected to travel throughout the entire continent in just a few days.

Maybe Lander and Katie were right—Serpentine was dangerous. Not only for me physically, but mentally as well. Once I got a taste of the world outside of my father's walls, I feared I wouldn't want to go back. I wouldn't want to be locked away again, forced to do the same draining tasks every day until I died. I wanted to know these things I'd learned today. To know...more.

I couldn't even begin to imagine what else I was blind to when I'd already found out so much in the small amount of time we were in Silicate.

There had to be a way to convince my father to let me have a sliver of freedom outside of the castle after my return from our journey through Serpentine.

I just had to figure out what that was.

CHAPTER 10

I awoke before dawn the next day by the demands of my father. He'd sent a guard to escort me to the throne room because apparently, I had some making up to do on my chores since I was gone yesterday.

As if he wasn't the one who sent me to Silicate.

"Every crate," he drawled from where he was seated on his throne, inspecting his nails as if a speck of dirt could be found on his perfectly clean hands.

I was already exhausted just a few hours in. Not only was I woken up long before the sun had risen, but I'd had a hard time falling asleep to begin with, images of that man being shot flashing through my mind every time I managed to close my eyes.

I didn't believe thievery was a big enough reason for someone to be killed, but what did I know?

"I need a minute, Father," I said from where I was sitting on the floor beside one of the many crates spread about the room.

"The longer you take, the longer you prevent me from getting to my job."

It wasn't *my* idea to do this in the throne room. Since I hadn't fulfilled my typical load of vials yesterday, I was now tasked with filling every empty crate in this room. If I had to guess, there were a little over two dozen neatly set out in rows. I'd filled at least seven so far, which was already more than I typically did, but I still had a long way to go.

Sometimes, I really loathed that he'd closed the mines in return for me providing Amosite's magic supply, but one look at Silicate yesterday told me the work I'd been doing wasn't enough. But if he was so hellbent on me getting through this load with no breaks, I could at least distract him to take a moment to rest.

"Why don't you let me leave the castle?" I asked, leaning an elbow on the crate next to me for support. Even my spine was tired of holding my body upright.

"I do. I allow you to see that girl." He spoke as if that was a luxury.

I scoffed, which earned me a glare and the thinning of his lips.

"Aside from my short visits in the garden with Taylin," I clarified.

He waved me off. "It is too dangerous. Look what happened yesterday. That could easily happen again." His eyes narrowed. "People are unpredictable, Auria, but you wouldn't know that. How could you?" His tone was accusing, as if *I* was the reason I was so left in the dark. "Now stand up and get back to work. I have no time for an unnecessary chat."

I bit back what I really wanted to say and reluctantly pushed myself up to stand. I wanted so badly to defend myself, to tell him I would've been more prepared if it wasn't for him, but I didn't. Instead, I shook out the heavy feeling that had settled into my arms. It felt like I'd been lifting fifty-pound weights with only the tips of my fingers for hours.

"What if I had guards with me?" I continued, bending to grab the vial of fire magic from the crate, along with an empty vial off the table beside me.

I could practically hear my father's teeth grinding to dust. "And what if I were to lose you? Who would fill all these vials to provide for the people?"

The silence that followed his question echoed louder than the words he spoke. Was that all I was to him?

I had no answer, so I focused on my power, letting it course through me as it duplicated what flowed from one vial to the next. Fire magic sometimes left a tingle in my arms, my skin and bones feeling slightly hot with the substance as it traveled.

My eyelids drooped as I filled vial after vial, the glass glowing a vibrant amber hue. I'd just gotten done filling half the current crate when the door to the throne room opened. My father instantly jumped from his chair, hazel eyes blazing bright with rage.

"No one is allowed in," my father's voice boomed. "Guards!"

Quiet panic filled me as I quickly bent to set the two vials in the crate, but as I straightened, my head spun from the sudden movement.

"They must not have received the memo," a male's voice stated, sounding bored. "They're snoring just outside the doors."

I set a palm to my head as it pounded, my hand on the table beside me to keep me from swaying.

"No need to wake them," the man said. He sounded familiar, but I couldn't pinpoint who it was in my current state. "I only came to say my goodbyes."

Pinching my eyes shut, I waited until the dizziness subsided before letting go of the table. I turned to see my father's nostrils flared, a clear sign of his anger, as he stared the man down from up on the dais. Then my gaze moved to find Bowen standing in the doorway, looking directly at me.

The prickle of my magic through my veins was nothing compared to what his eyes on me felt like. His curious gaze heated my core and sent shivers over my skin all at the same time. He was...entrancing. Nearly making me forget we were standing among other company.

"I was under the impression you left yesterday," my father said, snapping me back into the now. But even so, my focus stayed glued to Bowen. His hair was as messy as every other time I'd seen him, as if he ran a hand through it one too many times quite often.

Bowen's hard gaze trailed down my body, catching on the crates behind me, before moving to my father. With his inspecting eyes now off me, I sucked in a breath. It was almost as if a weight had been lifted off my body, but still, I felt a ghost of the pressure.

Bowen folded his hands behind his back. "I decided to stay another night."

My father tried his best to cover up his irritation as he stiffly returned to sitting on his throne. "Well, you must be on your way, then. Better to make the journey in the morning, and it's nearly past that." He was being oddly polite, but I could tell in the way his words were clipped that he was hiding how he truly felt, fighting the urge to kick Bowen out. Aside from the clear vexation in his tone, that same waver from before trickled in, proving he was, even in the tiniest amount, intimidated by Bowen. But why?

Bowen silently eyed my father, then moved his gaze back to me. "I was busy looking for something, but I've found it."

"Glad to hear it was not truly lost, then. Now, if you'll excuse us, we have other things to attend to," my father said, doing his best to politely urge Bowen to leave.

More like *I* had work to complete.

If Bowen had any idea of what was going on when he walked in, he didn't show it.

"What are the crates for?" Bowen asked, surveying the space.

My father's cheeks instantly reddened when Bowen very clearly didn't take the hint.

"My daughter is double-checking inventory."

My palms grew clammy when he failed to sound convincing.

"Of seven crates full of fire magic," Bowen said blandly. "And a multitude of empty ones?"

My father's jaw pulsed. His composure would soon crack, though Bowen surely saw through it already. "She is assuring the stock is all accounted for before her trip."

Bowen arched a brow in question. "You don't have workers to do that for you?"

I wanted to ask, *Yes, Father, why am* I *the one counting inventory?* But I thought better of it, knowing the consequences of speaking out of turn.

"I do not trust them. Now, if you will excuse us—"

"You may be right in that traveling so late in the day might not be wise. Perhaps I'll stay another night," Bowen interrupted.

If I wasn't so tired, I'd be amused by Bowen toying with my father like this. He was bold, that much was certain.

My father's lips rolled together, likely thinking on how to respond to that. "I will have to insist you leave today."

Bowen meandered toward the crates—toward *me*—with his hands still lazily clutched behind his back. "Is that an order, King Tenere?"

"My daughter is leaving on her journey with her betrothed tomorrow. We will need the castle clear, as I am sure the grounds will be quite hectic leading up to their departure."

It was the poorest excuse I'd ever heard.

If I was questioning it before, I wasn't any longer. Bowen and my father clearly didn't get along. But what game was Bowen playing here? My father wasn't the bear he wanted to poke.

Bowen stopped directly in front of me, and I dared not move for fear that if I did, I'd get another dizzy spell. My father would have Bowen's head if he put a hand on me in his presence, even if it was to save me from falling.

His intense gaze searched my face, lingering on the bags under my eyes. It was no secret that I was exhausted. On a good day, using my ability drained me, but with little sleep and more work, my magic was taking every bit of life from me today.

He unfolded his hands, only to reach past me to grab an empty vial off the table.

"You are to leave this instant," my father said hurriedly, hands fisting at his sides. I could practically feel the fumes blowing out of his ears from the rage he tried to keep tightly contained.

Even so, Bowen took his time. He held the vial up to inspect it, twisting it in his fingers. By the look in his eyes, it was clear he knew as much as I did that I wasn't simply counting inventory like my father claimed.

What if my secret got out?

Would he tell people? Or possibly blackmail us with it?

Would my father kill him for knowing?

The beat of my heart picked up its already pounding pace, crashing against the cage of my chest. My father had easily ordered someone to be killed for simply getting close to me before. What was stopping him now if he already disliked the man in front of me?

As Bowen set the empty vial back on the table without so much as a sound, two guards filed into the room, hands at the pommels sticking off their belts.

"I suppose it's time to get going," Bowen said, more so to my father, but he was looking straight at me.

He gave me one last once-over before turning on his heel and striding out of the room. As soon as he left, I inhaled a deep breath in an attempt to slow my racing pulse.

"Where were you?" my father demanded, not trying to hide his aggravation any longer.

"Our deepest apologies, Your Majesty. We didn't mean to doze off. I don't know what came over us," one of the guards answered, followed by a rough chorus of coughs from the both of them.

"No excuses!" my father boomed. "One slip-up, and everything could be ruined. Is that what you want?"

The guards shook their heads in unison, keeping their eyes downcast.

He'd have them killed, I was sure of it. Not only for falling asleep while on watch, but for seeing what was in this room.

My entire life, my magic had been a secret. Now there was the possibility that Bowen knew. The way he'd looked at that empty vial, how he saw the crates full of glowing amber—he *knew*.

Would he send someone to harm me? Or would my father give orders to have him killed before he could step foot outside this kingdom?

"Auria," my father snapped. I flinched, my eyes shooting to him. The guards were gone, the door now closed. I hadn't noticed them leave the room. "Finish your job."

I bent, grabbing the vial I held minutes before and palming the empty one Bowen had held in my opposite hand.

Only a little less than two dozen crates to go, and I'd be that much closer to leaving this castle.

That much closer to knowing what a sliver of freedom might feel like.

CHAPTER 11

The chest holding the clothes my father had picked out for me was removed from my room an hour ago. Already, I had another packed and waiting by the door. Katie didn't have a choice but to follow my father's orders in packing only the most elegant of dresses, but I couldn't imagine spending the entirety of this trip in suffocating outfits. The tight girdles atop bulky piles of skirts would be unendurable during our journey. If the dresses in the first traveling case were anything like the one I was forced to wear the night of the masquerade ball, I was making the right decision in bringing spare clothing.

"This one as well, my lady?" a servant I'd never seen before asked, gesturing to the case.

I gave a curt nod, doing my best to keep my chin held high, despite my reservations about leaving. I was beyond eager to cross the bridge leading out of Amosite, but unsure of what to expect once we did.

"Very well," he said, hefting the chest in his arms and exiting the room.

Aside from what I'd packed, my wardrobe was still overflowing. All the garments in the other case were newly sewed, and it made me feel all the more guilty for wearing them. The people in Silicate needed them far more than I did.

"Auria," Katie said from behind me. I tore my attention from the window, where I'd been etching the view I saw day in and day out into my memory, as if it wasn't already stuck there like a preserved painting. "Are you ready to leave?"

I took one last glance at the city in the distance, knowing my answer before she even asked the question. "Yes."

"Your father would like to say his goodbyes."

I turned, facing her. I inhaled as deep as my corset would allow, having half the mind to ask her to loosen the strings before my departure, but knowing it would be no use. My father had given strict orders that I must look my best on our way out of the city. My lungs would be aching for air until we stopped for the night and I was finally able to change, though I wasn't sure they were ever truly filled in this dreary castle. Some people starved for food or water, but I was peckish for a whole different reason.

I wondered what a change of scenery might do for me.

Katie leaned close as we walked side by side down the hall, two guards trailing behind us out of earshot. "Taylin is waiting in the gardens if you would like to say your farewell. It's on the way to the throne room, after all," she muttered.

My heart seemed to skip a beat, the realization that I'd miss her more than ever while I was gone hitting me in the gut. "I would like that. Thank you, Katie."

She gave the barest nod. "Of course."

After heading down the stairs, my slippers padding lightly on the steps, we emerged through the large doors leading into the garden. The servants hadn't had time to make me proper shoes for the trip, so I'd have to deal with the ones I had. I was almost certain I wouldn't be doing much walking anyway. If I knew my father at all, he'd have ordered them to keep me in the carriage and on a tight leash at all times.

"Auria." Taylin stood from the bench, immediately throwing her arms around me with not a single worry that someone might see and pull us apart. Even if someone saw her as a threat, I'd forfeit my life before she was ever put in danger.

I bit my bottom lip to keep myself composed as I hugged her back. Leaving Amosite was bittersweet, but I refused to cry. I'd be getting away from the place that was more a prison than a home, but I'd be far from the only friend I had ever had.

"It won't be long," I told her.

"I'll be sitting on this bench in three weeks' time, waiting for you."

All those stories I'd heard of true love, but they never said that love didn't just come in the form of a significant other. It came in the form of friendship, too. Taylin was living proof of that.

"I'll try to bring you something," I said, pulling back.

She let me go, a smile on her face as she waved me off. "Don't bother. You enjoy your time. From what I've heard, the rest of Serpentine is a beautiful place. Take it all in, and don't you for a second waste time thinking about me. This trip is for you. In the end, I'll be happiest seeing you walk back through those doors"—she glanced at them towering behind me, a sadness in her eyes—"gift or not."

"You're too good to me, Tay."

"And you, to me."

We'd recited those words many times before, and I was sure we'd say them a hundred more.

"I'll tell you all about it when I get back," I promised.

"And about Lander, I'm sure," she added, with a dance of her eyes.

I shook my head, unable to hide my grin. "If there's anything to tell."

"You never know," she teased.

We would definitely not be doing what she was indicating.

"Maybe this vacation from you will be a good thing," I joked.

Her mouth gaped, and I laughed. I'd miss this.

She sobered her expression. "Be safe, Auria. Don't trust anyone out there. You're a special person, and anyone could be looking to take advantage of that."

"I will. Don't worry about me. We'll have two dozen guards, and Lander and his brother will be there, too."

She frowned. "He's handsome, but that doesn't mean you should immediately put your life in his hands."

"Believe me when I say my confidence in others does not come easy. I'll be unassailable out there."

"As if that doesn't sound as confident as ever," she said with a roll of her eyes.

I smiled, then pulled my friend in for one last hug. "I'll see you soon."

She nodded in response before letting me go. I reluctantly headed back into the castle, dreading my visit with my father before I departed.

Katie faced me before we entered the throne room, folding her hands together in front of her. "I will see you in three weeks, Lady Auria."

I rolled my eyes at the formality. "I'm sure you'll enjoy every moment of my absence," I said, attempting to make light of the situation.

She inhaled through her nose, doing her best to keep herself together. It was improper for her to laugh with me in the eyes of my father. "One might say it will feel like a bird's first flight, the rest of the flock waiting back at the nest for their return."

"It'll be a smooth flight, I'm sure." Though I couldn't tell if I was reassuring her or myself. There was something exciting about the unknown, yet it remained formidable.

"Safe travels, Lady Auria." With a dip of her chin, she was heading down the hall, leaving me to face the doors before me.

How many houses could have been built rather than wasting such resources on all these grand doors?

The guard standing post stepped forward, opening them for me. I entered the room, leaving him in the hall.

"Auria," my father greeted. *How welcoming.* "Being tardy to your own trip is not the best impression."

Heidi glared at me from her throne beside him, her eyes promising chastisement had my father not been present. Surely, I'd receive her infliction upon my return.

"My apologies," I said quietly. "Packing took longer than I thought, as you'd expect, given I've never been away for so long." *Or at all*, I wanted to add, but thought better of it with my stepmother seated only ten feet away. I'd rather not add to her already growing list of reasons to punish me when I returned.

"As you are aware, you will be traveling for three weeks. After you have visited Sulphur, Torbernite, and Feldspar, your traveling party has direct orders to return to Amosite immediately. The wedding ceremony is set for one week after your return." My brows shot up at that, but he continued. "There is no room for debate, and if you are not back when you are expected, there will be consequences. Is that clear?"

I fought the urge to turn my eyes to the ground, instead keeping them trained on my father. Even in the small bit of freedom I was being given, I was still to be controlled, but did I expect anything else? It was the way my father talked of objurgating me if we were unpunctual, as if it'd be my fault. He rarely, if ever, was the one to dole out threats to me, so what was different with this? The risk of losing me for good? If instilling fear was his assurance that I would return, I worried it might only do the opposite.

I didn't miss the hint of a smirk on Heidi's face.

"Yes, Your Majesty. We will return in three weeks, and not a day later."

Not so much as a blink indicated he heard me. "I will see you then."

So much like the words I told Taylin moments ago, yet with a completely different emotion behind them. No pleasantries or hugs, just a formal farewell. I should have expected that from my father, yet somehow, I thought this goodbye might go differently.

I turned to leave, but my stepmother's voice stopped me in my tracks. "I'd suggest following the rules laid out by your guards and being on your utmost behavior." Her eyes narrowed, her voice lowering on what she said next. "Word travels."

Her threat was loud and clear.

"Yes, Your Majesty."

And then I left, heading for the carriage that would take me away from the only place I'd ever known.

A place I wasn't sure could be called a home.

CHAPTER 12

"Sulphur's the farthest kingdom from us right now," Lander stated from where he sat across from me in the carriage. He had offered to accompany me for the first leg of our trip, while Paxon had opted to travel on his personal horse outside, along with his brother's being led just ahead of the coach. "But we're heading there first due to the ease of travel along the land bordering the chasm. We can get there in prompt time on this route."

I shifted on the seat, glancing at the small, curtained window. My dress was too tight, and the carriage was stuffy, a sort of musty smell invading me ever since I entered. We hadn't crossed the bridge yet, having only left a short time ago, and I honestly wasn't sure how far it was from the castle. Regardless of the uncomfortable space, excitement thrummed through me.

Before this moment, I never thought leaving Amosite would be possible for me. Sure, my father had talked about the trip and made plans for it, but like all else I longed for, I assumed it'd be taken away at the last minute. Something so desired put within arm's reach, only to be snatched away before even the tips of my fingers could graze it.

But such wasn't the case for this.

"Sulphur has livestock?" I asked, remembering some of what Katie had informed me of last night. She'd given me a quick rundown of details she thought I might need to know before my visits to the other kingdoms. She never brought up her near-warning again, though.

"And crops," Lander added. "From cows to chickens, and corn to berries. We eat it, they grow it."

"Is my father's arrangement with them the problem?" I was trying to glean as much information about the trade issue as I could, given my father preferred to keep me ignorant on political matters. A woman with knowledge was powerful, so he did the one thing he could to prevent that—he kept me naive. And it worked. I didn't know enough to go against his word.

I might as well take advantage of the opportunity to learn more from Lander while I could.

Lander folded his hands between his knees, swaying side to side as the carriage ran over dips in the path. "Such hard questions before we've even crossed the bridge."

I shrugged. "A lady doesn't waste her time."

"She does not, indeed." He was quiet in thought. The wheels creaking over the dirt and horses' hooves stomping the ground were the only sounds in the enclosed space. "Not solely with them, I'm afraid."

The knowledge frustrated me as his daughter because I couldn't do anything in regards to easing that tension, but if I was to show myself as a figure of power on their land, I needed to be educated on the matters at hand. I supposed the days of traveling could make up for the holes in my conversance.

"Who else?"

He eyed me before glancing at the small, curtained window. "Is this a topic we should be discussing?"

My fingers wanted to fist in my skirts, but I held them at bay. I had to show composure. "Is it one we shouldn't?"

"It's the beginning of our marriage, Lady Auria," Lander started.

"Please, just Auria."

"Auria," he corrected. "I wouldn't like to know firsthand what your father's wrath might look like, should he discover I've told you things he would rather you not know."

"His mistake for marrying me off, then."

He pressed his lips into a thin line, the corners turned down. "You don't want this."

"You do?" I questioned.

"To be honest, Auria, no. I don't wish to be married. You're a lovely woman—"

"Save it, please. There's no need for flattery."

"You are. And you should know that. I know being locked away in that castle, you likely haven't heard it often, so hear it from me because you deserve at least that. While we both clearly don't want to be betrothed, neither of us have a choice in the matter. At least we can endure it together."

I blinked. "Are you asking to be my friend?"

"If nothing else," he said.

Any man Taylin had ever told me about had turned out to be a pig, and here Lander was, my fiancé, offering *friendship* in light of our marriage.

"A friend, then," I decided. It couldn't be the worst proposal.

His lips lifted the slightest as he gave a dip of his chin.

Possibly, what I'd been forced into wouldn't be as bad as I once thought.

It surely started on a bad note, but being able to see some of Serpentine? It was a dream.

I might be seated in front of a good-looking man, but he wasn't what I pictured when I closed my eyes at night.

It was trees and mountains and snow and desert. My imagination ran wild with what I thought the world might hold, and what I wished to one day see with my own eyes. And this engagement? It was the key to the locked door that I'd been searching for for so long.

It opened me up to a sense of freedom I never thought I'd have, and here it was, merely a breath away.

"We'll be celebrating Exitium Lunae in Torbernite," Lander added, changing the subject and pulling me back from my thoughts.

I tilted my head. "Exit-what?"

A small chuckle passed his lips. "Gods help me." Regaining his composure, he went on, "It's the celebration of when the moon exploded a century and a half ago. Have you really never been to a Lunae Festival?"

I shook my head. "Given I didn't even know the holiday existed, no. I've never celebrated anything of the sort."

Sorrow flashed in his eyes before he quickly masked it. "Well, you'll make up for all you've missed at this year's celebration."

I folded my hands together in my lap, a smile pulling at my mouth. "I suppose I will."

Yeah. This new freedom was feeling pretty good, if I had to admit.

~

I'D BEEN ALONE in the carriage for what had to be hours now. The only bright side was that I'd slowly become immune to the damp smell. With the shift of the sun through the curtained window, I could tell it was nearly dusk. Lander had exited at our last stop, shortly after we crossed the bridge, opting for his horse in light of the endless bumps. I, on the other hand, had no option.

"It's not safe," my guard had said. "What if we were to be ambushed?"

And that was the end of that. I truly had no idea what to do if we were attacked, as I hadn't had an ounce of training in hand-to-hand combat my entire life. My safety was in the hands of the guards, and presumably Lander. Did he know how to protect himself? How to wield a sword or throw a punch?

The carriage rolled to a stop as someone shouted something outside, which was followed by the sound of footsteps. I dared a peek out the curtain, seeing that guards were dismounting their horses, others unpacking loads off mules.

On the horizon, where the sky was turning a vibrant pink as it melted into the mountains beyond, a bird flew directly in front of the sun, its dark silhouette against the bright colors the perfect painting.

The door to the carriage flew open, pulling my attention from the view. Immediately, the warm air invaded the cab, swirling with the once-stagnant stale scent.

"Time for supper and rest," a male voice said as I turned.

My eyes widened at the sight of him. "Your Highness?"

A smirk bloomed on Paxon's mouth. "Not expecting me, my lady?"

I sobered my expression as best I could, though my brows remained furrowed. "I knew you were with the group, I just wasn't aware you were the door-opening type."

He held out a hand, and I hesitated a moment before placing my palm in his. "I like to leave some things a surprise."

I stepped down from the carriage, my hand resting in his as I got my bearings on solid ground, taking in my first true look of our surroundings. The grass was a vibrant green, stretching so far that it disappeared into the mountains altogether. Wind rustled the blades, causing them to flow in sync. Even the air smelled different, almost more fresh, as it flowed through and around the breathtaking landscape. The smell of new leaves and the aromatic scent of pollen on vibrant flowers nearly pulled a smile to my face. It was more jaw-dropping than I could have imagined.

I was actually outside of Amosite.

"It's beautiful, isn't it?" Paxon asked from beside me.

I finally pulled my hand from his, gazing out at the rolling hills that butted up to towering mountains with magnificent peaks. A constant gray haze always sat stagnant over Amosite, dampening the beauty it had the potential to hold. But out here, the sun seemed to touch everything, even as it began to slowly fade behind the mountains in the distance. The sky was pink, yet it shone just as bright as it had midday, rays of light reflecting off the rings spanning the entire length of the sky. They looked somehow larger out here than inside the border of the chasm. More birds chirped in the sky as a small group flew over, and a lone frog croaked somewhere in the distance.

"Beautiful doesn't even begin to describe this." My eyes caught on Lander laughing near a cart with some of Torbernite's guards. King Bular had insisted a few come along, which meant we had more than enough protection, with over two dozen men at the ready. They donned rich shades of green on their armor, whereas Amosite's wore their typical garnet.

I turned to find a couple of the guards setting up a large tent, pounding stakes into the ground and tying string to the ends to keep it restrained.

"That one is all yours," Paxon informed me, his voice rather close to my ear.

I inhaled as deep as my corset would allow, fighting the urge to inch away. "And where will you and your brother be?"

I glanced to the side, seeing his hands tucked in the pockets of his jacket as he leaned into me. "On the other side of camp. Or would you rather we be close?"

For him, the other side was not nearly far enough. I'd been wary when I'd met the two of them, but with our short interactions, Lander had come to grow on me. I couldn't see myself falling for him romantically, but with our friendship, I could tolerate him.

Paxon, on the other hand, almost made uncertainty crawl up my spine like a spider whenever he was near. While he was Lander's brother, I didn't need to be *his* friend, too. I only needed to tolerate Lander. I could do without Paxon's presence altogether.

"The setup is fine," I replied.

"Three's a crowd," he surmised, stepping back.

"Are you leaving us once we get to Torbernite?" I asked, turning to face him while putting some space between us.

That permanent smirk still pulled at the corner of his mouth. "So quick to get rid of me? I'm hurt, Lady Auria."

"It is not you I am to show a presence with," I pointed out.

He dipped his chin, glancing at his shoes. "You're correct. But my brother, you see, he needs my support." His eyes met mine again. "I'm sure you understand."

"I don't." As far as I'd seen, Lander could uphold himself just fine on his own.

He sucked his tongue, the sound rather irritating. "As you are aware, my brother enjoys his leisure time."

"This isn't leisure." Surely, he wouldn't be off gambling when we were to deliver the ridiculous speeches prepared for us.

Paxon smiled, though it was gone as soon as it appeared. "To you, no. You have an image to uphold. But it's no secret that Lander is...feckless."

My brows furrowed. "Are you saying you're his coach in his appearance with me?"

He let out a breathy chuckle. "If that's what you would like to call it."

"I'm sure he can handle himself."

"If you'd rather he be off spending his time gambling magic and drinking every jug of ale in sight, then by all means. But me being here is not a bad thing, Lady Auria. Don't let yourself think otherwise."

His words didn't reassure me in the least. My stomach felt sour from hours of traveling in the cramped carriage, and while I wished for nothing more than to stare at the sun as it fell below mountain peaks, exhaustion was quickly taking hold.

"I'm rather tired," I said, excusing myself.

His smirk was gone now, the glint in his eye showing dubitation to my dismissal. "Right. I'll have a guard retrieve you when supper is ready."

"Thank you."

He dipped his chin in response, and I headed for my tent. Thankfully, the guards had made quick work and it was ready to go.

The garnet material flapped in the breeze as two men stood post outside. One of them reached for the flap of the door, holding it open as I approached. Before I ducked to dip inside, I glanced back to find Paxon still watching me. His chin was lowered, his hands still slung casually in his pockets. One emerged with a slow wave, and I offered no response back as I continued on my way into the tent.

In the corner, heaps of blankets sat folded atop the makeshift bed they'd laid out for me. A lantern sat lit beside it, a vial of amber magic in the bottom to keep the flame alight.

Crouching in front of it, I set two fingers on the thin glass. With barely a thought, the tips of my fingers glowed pink as the liquid rose, hitting the cork at the top. Immediately, the tightness in my stomach eased, a wave of tension leaving my muscles.

While I wasn't afraid of the dark, being in a new environment with people I'd never been alone with before didn't make me feel all too eager to let the light go out sometime in the night. Once I returned from dinner, I'd do the same, giving the lantern as much magic to fuel it as I could.

With the risk of bandits attacking our camp, I felt much more comfortable keeping the tent dimly lit. Should anyone get past the two guards stationed outside, I'd at least look death in the eyes before I went out, rather than face it in an endless pitch black void, only to be in it for an infinite amount of time after life seeped out of me.

With that thought in mind, I reached behind myself, working at the laces to finally loosen my bodice. But rather than undress completely, I remained in the clothes I'd traveled in, figuring going out for my meal in night clothes wouldn't be entirely appropriate.

Because even in death, my father would prefer me presentable.

CHAPTER 13

The light from the roaring flame flickered amongst the group's faces as we sat around the campfire, eating our supper. It cast shadows in the distance, the peculiar shapes looking all too similar to people watching us as the fire snapped and popped over burning wood. The smoke wafted away from me, leaving the crisp, earthy scent to wrap around me like a caress.

"We're alone out here with the light from the fire. No need to worry," Lander said from where he sat on the dirt ground beside me. He'd already finished his bowl of porridge, listening as others talked. I'd half expected him to excuse himself as soon as he was done, but he'd stayed, keeping me company.

Paxon sat across the circle, every so often observing the two of us in between bites. He'd ignored the guards as they attempted to strike up conversation with him, and I had to believe it was because he was eavesdropping on everyone.

"Because of the light?" I asked, setting my bowl in the dirt in front of me.

Lander nodded, shifting his leg under him. "Have you heard those scary bedtime stories?"

I gnawed on my lip. "Sort of. But they're not real, are they?"

He looked out at the dark expanse past our camp, as if the thought of what might be out there haunted him. "Some are. Different environments hold different predators."

"Are you saying we're their prey?"

He turned to me, the orange ambience lighting up his hazel eyes, as if they themselves were the fire. "We're always the prey."

"Ignore my brother," Paxon spoke up from his spot across from us, drawing our attention to him. "He's too into those old stories of things that go bump in the night. You needn't worry about what's out there."

"So long as the fire keeps burning," Lander said, and the rest of the circle quieted.

Paxon's jaw pulsed, as if he was holding back some retort. "That's what we have the guards for."

"I'm only educating her," Lander defended, sensing his brother's growing irritation. I wasn't familiar with sibling relationships, given I was an only child, but if Lander and Paxon were anything to go off of, I was glad for my situation. The bickering seemed nonstop between them.

Paxon's hand flexed before he set it on his bent knee. "You're to be her husband, not her teacher."

Lander's teeth ground together beside me, the sound apparent.

"I heard they aren't actually getting married to rebuild peace," one of the guards said.

Everyone's attention jumped to him. He wore a green short-sleeved shirt with gray pants, having taken off his armor once we arrived. His light brown hair was greasy, sticking up in odd angles, evidence of our journey already taking a toll on our hygiene.

I sat forward, curious for him to go on. I knew as much about this marriage as the rest of them, so I'd take any information I could get—rumor or not.

Paxon's narrowed eyes landed on the guard, but the man seemed oblivious.

"What's the union for, then?" another guard asked, this one from Amosite. He took the question right from my mouth.

"Some s—" the first guard started, but was quickly cut off by Paxon's hard tone.

"Is it your job to gossip?"

The guard rolled his eyes, as if Paxon was being dramatic. Truthfully, he was. "We're just talking, Your Highness."

"Chitchat is done for the night." Paxon stood, straightening the cuffs of his jacket. "Finish your meals and return to your posts. As my brother so helpfully brought up, we're the prey out here, lest you forget."

The guard let out a sigh, a look of annoyance crossing his face. He didn't say a word as Paxon retreated to his tent, leaving the rest of us to finish our bowls of bland food in silence.

As one of the other guards made a round to collect the empty bowls, Lander offered me a hand to help me stand. I took it, getting to my feet.

Lander shot me a sympathetic half-smile. "Ignore my brother. He tends to be a bit dramatic about things."

"You don't have to make excuses on his behalf. I think we're all bound to get a little stir-crazy with the long days."

He ran a hand through his mussed hair. "You're probably right."

I turned to head for my tent, Lander accompanying me on the short walk. "Do you think that guard knows something we don't?" I asked.

Lander shrugged. "Maybe. They all gossip, though. Someone probably made up a rumor to stir up some drama, and now people are believing it. I wouldn't worry too much about it." We stopped outside my tent, facing each other. "I wanted to ask, though. Are you enjoying seeing some of Serpentine so far?"

A genuine smile crept up on my face. "Enjoying it would be an understatement." My eyes scanned the darkness surrounding the camp. "It's so much more than I ever could have imagined. Wildflowers and colorful trees I would never have thought existed just...do. I can feel the sun and see the soft grass and smell the fresh soil." I inhaled for emphasis, taking in the warm scent of the smoke from the fire and the earthy undertones that followed it as I looked at Lander again. "I never want to leave it."

He offered a closed-lip smile in return, the corners looking sad. "I wish you never had to. Maybe your father will change his tune once we return unscathed."

"Maybe," I said, the thought of never seeing such beauty again threatening to bring me down. "But for now, I'll enjoy it while I can."

"That's the spirit." He inched away. "Sleep well, Auria. We have a long few days ahead of us. You're going to need it."

I reached for the flap of my tent, pulling it back. "You, too, Lander."

Then I disappeared inside, making sure to refill the vial of fire magic that kept the lantern lit in the hopes it'd keep the monsters at bay.

For the physical ones, it'd work. But the ones that lived inside my head?

If only such was possible.

~

The next morning, I emerged from my tent to find the camp had already been packed up, the only things left to be stowed away on the mules were a few packs of clothing. The coals from the fire that had burned out overnight still released small gray tendrils, the pungent scent of smoke lingering in the air.

"Did I sleep in?" I asked Lander as he passed me, hurrying to match his pace as he continued walking.

"No."

I waited for him to continue, offering any explanation as to why we were hurrying to leave, when he did a double take, noticing me staring at him. He stopped, grabbing my arm to halt me with him. But before he could speak, the presence at our side sent pins and needles down my arm.

"You didn't happen to see anyone sneaking off last night, did you, Lady Auria?" Paxon asked.

I looked at him while Lander kept his focus trained on me. "No? Why would I have? I was asleep."

Paxon nodded slowly, as if he didn't believe me. Meanwhile, guards entered my tent to begin packing it up. "If you hear anything, you'll tell us." It wasn't a question.

"Of course I will," I replied, not sure what I was even agreeing to.

Once Paxon walked away, I turned back to Lander. "What is he talking about?"

Lander rolled his lips together, like he was debating what to tell me. "That guard who doubted the reasons behind our marriage deserted sometime during the night."

My eyes widened. "Deserted?"

He nodded, but he had the same look his brother did moments before.

"You don't believe that, do you?" I asked.

His gaze hardened on me as he thought. "There's an explanation for everything, and my brother always seems to be the first one to provide it."

Realization at what he was trying to say hit me. "You don't trust him?"

"I grew up with him, Auria. But as we both know, family is family."

I knew all too well what he was getting at.

"Don't ask questions. Don't raise suspicions. And if you hear anything..." He trailed off, searching the busy area for his brother.

"I'll come to you," I said.

He gave a nod of approval before continuing on his way to continue packing up the camp.

I didn't know who to trust or what to believe, but I wanted to think Lander wouldn't be messing with my head. Either way, keeping to myself was probably in my best interest for the duration of our trip.

CHAPTER 14

The next five days went as smoothly as they could. No other guards deserted, and no one spoke of the one we'd lost after Paxon made it clear we wouldn't be looking for him.

Each day, we'd depart at dawn and travel until the sun began to set before we finally arrived on the outskirts of Sulphur. I hadn't complained once during the long stretches in the carriage, no matter how hot it grew. I was too transfixed by the view as the mountains turned into rolling hills, which then became fields and fields of crops and livestock as we got closer to King and Queen Alline's territory. I didn't think I could ever tire of the scenery surrounding me.

We'd traveled along the chasm most of the time, but far enough away to where I couldn't quite see the depths of it. It was better that way, though. Out of everything, I didn't want to see the gorge that kept me separate from the rest of the world.

On our way into Sulphur, much like the rest of the trip thus far, my gaze had been trained out the tiny window. Before the land had turned to tall grass pastures and fields of assorted crops, it'd been miles and miles of meadows sprouting various colors of wildflowers. In the distance, Lander had pointed out Devil's Peak, one of the only active volcanoes on our continent. It hadn't had a major eruption in over a century, but lava was always slowly seeping from it, puddling at the base. It was a dangerous crater surrounded by beauty and peace.

Lander wasn't kidding when he said every protein, every fruit and vegetable, came from Sulphur. Even without him telling me, I would've been able to guess it. There wasn't a single parcel without something being raised or grown. Even the homes in the town had small gardens in their yards.

The people lining the dirt roads as we traveled past last night wore all kinds of colors and attire. On our cross-through to reach the kingdom, I saw workers extracting colors from all kinds of flowers and fruits, dyeing clothes in buckets and hanging them on lines to dry. It was serene—how they all worked in harmony with children running amuck. There were no arguments, no raised voices or weapons being drawn at each other. But even so, the tension in their shoulders was obvious, accompanying their narrowed eyes as we passed.

It was so opposite of everything I'd seen in Silicate, yet so similar. The streets didn't smell nearly as rancid; instead the aroma from the flowers wrapped around me, mixing with the hint of salt in the air. But despite the inviting atmosphere, I could see the stress on each citizen. Maybe Lander was right, and the tensions with trade really were having an effect on every single citizen, whether their leaders treated them better than King Tenere or not. Even the castle looked more welcoming than my father's, more like a home than a fortress.

"The ocean borders one side of Sulphur, much like it does Amosite," Lander said from beside me. We were now standing in the foyer of the home I'd stayed in last night.

King Alline had been kind enough to let our group sleep in some of the empty houses near the castle after we'd arrived too late to visit with the king and queen. They didn't have as large of an estate as Amosite, so there were no spare rooms for us to occupy. I'd been in my own cottage with three guards posted outside while Lander and Paxon slept in a separate one just next door. The guards who weren't on shift got one house to themselves. After days in a tent, we were all thankful to have at least one full night's rest in a real bed.

But somehow, even with the unpleasantries I'd learned came with travel, I'd never felt happier.

"I smell the salt in the air," I replied, almost hating the small talk Lander and I forced at times.

I'd chosen to wear a looser dress today. The tight-fitting gowns I typically wore didn't seem to fit in with the citizens of Sulphur. Much like the land and its people, I wanted to feel free, and that meant no restricting corset. No dreary colors either. Red was not in my vocabulary—at least for today.

"Not as humid, though. And a much cleaner aroma than Amosite," Lander acknowledged, nudging my shoulder with his own. He clearly wasn't missing the damp, seaweed smelling air in my kingdom. Truthfully, I wasn't either.

"You're not wrong," I said with a hint of a smile before taking a deep breath, mentally preparing myself for what the day held. I wasn't used to any of this, but I was trying.

He stepped forward and opened the door, holding it wide for me to pass through. The morning air warmed my skin instantly as I moved past him.

"My lady," a guard said, stepping in front of us before we descended the steps. The sword at his hip clanked against the garnet armor on his leg.

Lander and I both paused.

"I have to ask that you go back inside," he went on.

"Is there a threat?" I asked. With the mention of it, Lander inched closer to my side.

"No, my lady." He cleared his throat as he averted his gaze, eyes darting to my clothing before looking at me. "But King Tenere has given us strict orders that you are to only wear his colors and the wardrobe he had picked for you."

His colors. As if I didn't spend every day of my aching life in Amosite. As if I hadn't grown up there.

A bit of the tension left my body at the reassurance there was no real danger. I should've known, though, that even outside the chasm, my father would still find a way to control the smallest of things.

I glanced at Lander, but he had his gaze downcast on his glossed shoes.

I turned my attention back to the guard. "Surely, for a day, my father would excuse it."

"I cannot make that decision for him, my lady," the guard said, something like uneasiness coating his words.

I looked down at my simple white dress, realizing there would be no getting around this. If the worst that came to me on this trip was being forced to wear Amosite's colors every day, then I considered myself lucky.

"I can wait here. Changing will not take long at all," Lander assured me.

I swallowed, already feeling the binds of a corset caging my torso in. But how would it look if my first impression outside of Amosite and in another kingdom was arguing with a guard over something as minute as clothing? It wasn't worth my—or my father's—reputation.

"Thank you," I muttered, not sparing the guard another glance before turning around. Lander kept his word, standing outside as I changed, and when I reappeared wearing the desired red dress, the sleeves itchy and the neckline suffocating, he offered a sympathetic smile.

I didn't return it.

"King and Queen Alline will be meeting us in the town square," the guard said, trailing beside Lander and I as we walked.

"Is that where we're to do this speech?" I asked.

"It is, my lady. We can get everything done today and be gone by morning."

"I wasn't aware we were leaving so quick," I said.

"King Tenere has us on a tight schedule. If we hit poor weather, we may have to stop, and with days of travel in between each kingdom, we're hoping to get ahead of anything that could hinder us arriving back in Amosite on time."

It seemed my father's guards were just as fearful of him as everyone else. Although their jobs were on the line, I worried it wouldn't be them who got the worst of what was to come if we weren't back in a few weeks.

Though I was the one forced to change my attire, Lander looked much worse for wear. His hair was astray, his lapel crinkled, and the cuffs of his sleeves were unbuttoned.

"Are you okay?" I muttered to him as we walked.

"Why wouldn't I be?" he asked.

"You don't look very..." I wasn't sure what to say. We weren't close enough for me to say he looked unkempt.

"It's my style. No need to be worried."

I snorted. "Style?"

From my peripheral, I saw the corner of his mouth tick up as he fought a smile. We had to act as if people were watching constantly. Our images were our families' images.

"Just as you have a style of being rebellious," he said.

I shook my head, snuffling my laugh. "I'd hardly call wearing a white dress rebellious."

"Is white your favorite color?" he asked.

I nearly tripped on my skirts.

He looked at me before facing forward again. "Was that the wrong thing to ask?"

I gave a shake of my head. "Sorry, no. It's not that. I've just never thought of it that way."

"That you abhor garnet so much that you'd rather wear no color at all?"

"White is a color."

"A rather bland one," he muttered, a light lilt to his voice.

My mouth popped open. "If it was my favorite, you've just insulted it."

He dramatically set a palm over his heart. "My sincerest apologies, Lady Auria. I most certainly didn't mean to insult your favorite color."

I rolled my eyes and smiled, not caring to hide it this time. "I'm sure."

We approached the town square where people were gathered, a wooden dais sitting in the center of the crowd. Fabrics of every color popped among the people, oranges and purples, pinks and blues, and once again, I found myself envying them. It wasn't just the clothes—it was their freedom to express themselves. I longed for that, in any way I could get it. The comforting scent of cinnamon and sugar wafted through the air, likely from a nearby bakery. I could nearly taste the sweet pastry. It made me think of Taylin and all the baked goods we used to steal bites of, whether from her mother or her smuggling one for me during our visit.

I tamped down the nostalgia. She wouldn't want me to spend my time missing home. She'd rather I enjoy this small bit of freedom I was offered, so that's what I'd do.

Through the crowd, I couldn't find King and Queen Alline. I guessed Lander wasn't able to spot them either by the tight set of his mouth.

"The speech, my lady," a guard said, coming up beside me to hand me a rolled parchment.

I took the paper, unfolding it and glancing at the words. I'd read them at least a hundred times in the carriage, but no matter how many times I recited it, the words didn't feel like something I'd say. I supposed that was the point of my father's advisor writing it and not me.

"Thank you."

I shoved aside my feelings for the letter and pasted on a smile. Lander and I were to be married, and we had to look strong in our union if this was to work. Whatever *this* was.

Lander held out a hand to assist me up the step onto the low wooden platform. As we stood in front of the crowd, a bead of sweat rolled down my temple. It wasn't hot by any means with the breeze rolling through, but my body was warm with the coverage this dress provided, my chest pressing against the binds of my bodice with every breath.

On the opposite side of the dais, King and Queen Alline stepped up, finally presenting themselves. When our gazes met, they both gave a dip of their chin, their bronze crowns perched atop his white hair and her black as night locks glistening in the midday sun. Their clothing was various shades of yellow—their kingdom's color. Queen Alline's vibrant sunshine dress had short sleeves, showing off the deep brown skin of her arms. Beside her, her husband's suit was a darker shade than her gown, the top two buttons undone to show a sliver of his brown chest. They were nearly identical in height, both tall and lean. Both equally as beautiful.

King Alline's lips were pressed into a tight line, judgment clear as day in the way he watched us, while the queen set a hand on her round belly and nodded at me, signaling me to start.

I looked out at the people standing before us. With the

makeshift stage raised only a few inches off the ground and my short height combined, I could see only the first few rows of people standing shoulder to shoulder. The rest disappeared behind them, though the crowd wasn't massive, indicating most of the town hadn't bothered to show up. For some reason, the knowledge that not everyone had come made me more nervous, feeling as if this was all a joke to them. Likely, it was, but I had no choice but to follow orders.

I held the parchment in front of me, scanning the words. "People of Sulphur. We are here to put your worries to rest," I started.

"Bullshit," a bulky man with brown skin said from the front of the crowd.

"All Amosite is good for is thievery!" a woman shouted, her thick accent clinging to every word.

"Filthy thieves!" a young child with blonde hair bellowed.

My eyes darted between each irate citizen before turning to the king and queen. They stood there with nothing more than pitiful looks on their faces.

I looked back down at the paper, my stomach tightening. "Amosite and Torbernite have come to a union," I continued.

Before I could get another word out, something hit me in the hip. I took a step back to steady myself, glancing down to find a bright red stain on the garnet fabric.

The shouts grew louder as people began chucking various fruits and vegetables our way. It wasn't long before the guards were in front of me, shielding me from the worst of it as they ushered Lander and me off the stage.

"My lady, are you injured?" a guard asked hurriedly as the others formed a half circle behind the two of us, blocking the barrage of foods.

I wasn't sure if I was injured.

Was the red simply residue from a tomato?

The hit hadn't hurt, but pain was such a familiar feeling to me that perhaps my mind didn't register it at the same time as my body.

"My lady," he said again, but I barely heard him, his voice nearly blending in with the shouts around us.

There were so many noises. So many angry people. So many colors and stones and buildings.

Our footsteps hurried down the path to an awaiting carriage. Was their hatred aimed at me? Or my father? What could he have done to cause these people to be so angry?

"Auria," Lander said, interrupting the echo in my mind. His hand was on my shoulder, his gaze narrowed on me. He must've seen my eyes working to focus themselves. "They need to know if you're hurt."

With a glance at my dress, I knew now that I wasn't. Yet though I wasn't physically injured, my emotions were a mess. To have food thrown at us... It was beyond embarrassing. But most of all, shameful. I didn't want these people to hate us—to hate *me*.

I shook my head, words still unable to form on my tongue as nausea built.

"She's okay," Lander relayed to the guard.

He was standing beside us as the others had their backs to us now, watching to make sure none of the mayhem followed.

"You need to get in the carriage, my lady," the guard said as he opened the door.

I stepped up, my hands fisted in my food-stained skirt. I situated myself on the bench as Lander sat across from me. The guard closed the door, and in seconds, we were moving.

"Won't they follow us to where we're staying?" I asked, finally able to think clearly enough for logic to seep back in.

"I presume we'll depart Sulphur tonight," Lander replied.

I swallowed, the jostling of the carriage leaving a sour taste in my mouth. "But the guards need rest."

Lander peeked out the curtain. "They're trained for far worse than some flying rotten food and no sleep, Auria."

My eyes fell to the stain of red and the seeds splattered throughout. Would it truly be so tragic had it been my blood and not the juice of a fruit?

I ran a finger through the pulp. "If they're not well off, why would they waste all this food only to humiliate us?"

"I don't believe it's food they have a shortage of here," Lander said.

I wiped the juice off my finger, looking at him. He was barely stained with the remains of a blueberry or two on his shirt. "Is that why they called Amosite thieves?"

His forehead creased. "You truly don't know?"

"No. And that's what frustrates me the most out of all of this. My father sent me out here with no knowledge on any of what's going on, and I'm expected to act like I know everything. How am I to serve as a face of peace between Amosite and these kingdoms if I don't even know what goes on behind closed doors?"

Sympathy filled his expression, his eyes softening. "Some doors shouldn't be opened, Auria."

But Lander was wrong. I wasn't scared of what I would find —only frustrated they were locked in the first place. Like apples plucked from a tree, my father chose only the sweetest information to tell me, and left the bad for his ears only.

That wasn't how I would be able to stand up for the kingdom I grew up in. Being fed the good only led to an influx of the bad later on.

And if being given a taste of freedom taught me anything, it was that the bad would eventually come out.

I only had to find a way to get it.

CHAPTER 15

Four days later, we made it to Torbernite, Lander's home. Due to our arrival being so late into the night, Lander had shown me to a guest suite in his parents' castle and suggested we take a tour of the kingdom in the morning. Traveling had exhausted me, and my body ached, so I'd quickly agreed and sunk into bed.

I'd awoken early the next morning, eager to explore. Sulphur as a whole had been much smaller than Amosite; the size, homes, and capital itself reflected their seemingly simpler way of life. But already, I could tell Torbernite would be more like Amosite in its grandness. There was nothing *simple* here.

I slid into my slippers as I emerged from the warmth of my bed before crossing the room to shove open the window. The morning chill met my skin, my hair blowing back from my shoulders. I inhaled the salty scent of the sea that carried on the air wafting into the room. Torbernite was directly southeast from Amosite, sitting across the continent on the opposite shore. From the back of the castle, the view of the ocean was spectacular. The water stretched for miles, not another land mass in sight, despite other continents being out there, only reachable by ship.

Though the view from this room was beautiful, I ached to see more. Hurriedly, I dressed in a long sleeve garnet dress with a deeper red thread wound throughout the bodice in intricate detail. It stood out amongst the green accents in the room, just like I was sure it'd do the same out there among the emerald attire of Torbernite's people.

Lander had briefly given me more insight into Exitium Lunae, explaining how the town decorated the meadows that butted up to the sandy beaches, right by the forest bordering Feldspar. Apparently, every kingdom was invited to celebrate the one hundred and fiftieth anniversary of the moon's explosion. Some got together in their respective territories while others traveled elsewhere to partake in festivities on this particular day every year to commemorate when the moon burst into millions of pieces. With the explosion came the silver rings that highlighted the land in the day and illuminated the world at night.

Tomorrow, I'd make up for the lost years and celebrate Exitium Lunae like the rest of the continent.

I opened the door to the bedroom to find one of Amosite's guards stationed beside my door, as well as Paxon standing across the hall with his hands held behind his back, almost as if he was waiting for me. His hair was perfectly styled, slicked back flat against his head. He'd clearly cleaned off all evidence of our travel, taking advantage of being home.

"Sleep well?" he asked, stepping toward the threshold.

"As well as one can away from their home." But the truth was, I'd slept better than I ever had before. Perhaps it was the change of scenery from my pretty prison. "Is Lander awake?"

He dipped his chin in a nod. "He's waiting on us, actually."

"Oh?"

He swung a hand in the direction of the hall as he tilted his head to the right. "Come with me."

Crossing the threshold, I shut the door behind me. The guard moved to step forward, but Paxon held up a palm, halting him.

"The lady is perfectly safe with me," Paxon assured him.

"But the king—" the guard started.

"Would agree," he interrupted. "If she's to marry my brother, King Tenere has clearly entrusted us with her safety. There are no threats here, I can assure you of that." But the slight smirk pasted on Paxon's lips did little to back his statement.

With a hard swallow, the guard dipped his chin. "Yes, Your Highness."

As Paxon and I walked side by side through the hall and down a set of stairs, I said so only he could hear, "The guard was so quick to see me off."

He kept his gaze forward. "He's well aware we have guards stationed throughout the castle. There is nothing to worry about, Lady Auria. It is merely his job to stay by your side, and today, that will not be needed."

I didn't say anything more as we continued on. I merely wished I had as much authority to demand my guards leave me alone for even a few minutes.

The foyer we passed through was decorated with their signature emerald green colors. A grand statue showcasing a massive crystal stood tall in the center of the space, a large rug underneath it. It was noticeably carved from stone, and I wondered if healing magic ran through the rock, causing it to glow that familiar green. I'd never seen magic in its raw form, only after it was placed in vials, but I had to guess this was what it'd look like before being extracted from its natural state.

Rather than exiting through the large front doors, we walked down a long hallway to a side door that opened up to a wide expanse of a perfectly-cut field. The smell of grass baking in the sun was a welcome embrace to my senses as I found Lander standing in the center of some sort of game with a wooden mallet slung over his shoulder, another supporting his weight as he leaned on it. His jacket was unbuttoned, the cuffs wrinkled, and his hair blew in the slightly chilled breeze. In the trees surrounding the grassy area came the chirps of birds and the rustling of leaves.

Lander squinted his eyes against the sun as he smiled at me. "Care for a game?"

I approached him, shading my eyes with my hand. "I'm not sure how to play."

Paxon picked up the mallet lying in the lawn. "We'll teach you."

Lander handed me one of the ones he held as Paxon began explaining the rules of the game. Once I'd figured out the basics of what the goal was, we fell into an easy routine, yet I could tell Lander was bored. He took his time whenever it was his turn to make a shot, often checking out of whatever topic Paxon was going on about.

"So, Auria," Paxon began after tapping the ball through one of the hoops. "Have you been enjoying your time outside of Amosite so far?"

Lander took his turn, adjusting his hands on the stick as he slumped his shoulders.

"It's been more than I expected," I replied. The incident in Sulphur had taken me by surprise, though I should have guessed not everyone would be particularly happy seeing King Tenere's daughter.

"So my brother has let on. Torbernite has been much calmer than your time in Sulphur, though, no?" he asked.

"It has. So far, at least," I answered, plopping the end of the wooden stick in the plush grass.

"And you're looking forward to the Lunae Festival?" Paxon questioned.

"Do you ever stop asking questions?" Lander piped in after hitting the ball.

Paxon slowly moved his gaze to him. In the bright sun, his deep brown eyes seemed to darken. Perhaps they reflected his mood. "Problem, brother?"

Lander propped both hands on top of his mallet, leaning into it. "The entire game, all you've done is yap your mouth."

"Just helping you get to know your fiancée," Paxon replied innocently.

Lander's fingers flexed. "I know Auria just fine."

Paxon looked to me. "Is that true?"

"I-I suppose. We've had quite a bit of time to talk during the days of travel." Lander and I didn't know each other much past surface level, but we were content with that. This was only a friendship, after all. His brother wasn't aware of that, though.

"What's her favorite food, then?" Paxon asked, peppering yet another question.

Lander dropped the mallet in the lawn. "I've no time for this."

Paxon tilted his head at him. "Better things to do than spend time with your soon-to-be wife?"

"We have different hobbies," Lander bit out.

My grip on the mallet tightened. "You—" I shook my head, stopping myself before I could say something I might regret. "We don't have to defend ourselves. Our relationship is none of your business."

Amusement flitted into Paxon's eyes. "No? My brother is marrying an absolute stranger, a daughter to a corrupt king, and it's not my business to be sure he is well aware of the woman he is betrothed to?"

"That's enough," Lander barked.

My eyes narrowed on Paxon. If that's how he wanted to play, fine. I'd play.

"That king supplies your kingdom with magics of all kinds, so I'd watch what you say."

Paxon leveled his gaze on me. "And Torbernite provides yours with weapons." He took two steps closer, swinging the mallet in his grip casually. "How weak a kingdom is without a means to protect itself."

Tension rang through the air between us, so thick not even a bird could flit its wings in it. It nearly sucked the air from my lungs and shoved me back a few steps, but I held firm. He was trying to intimidate me, to make me bow down and tell him everything he was digging to find out. I wouldn't be fooled by the superficial questions, only to be taken off guard by something that could ruin me later.

In the span of a breath, Lander was standing in front of me, shoving Paxon away. "Enough with the bullshit. Auria and I are leaving."

Paxon picked a piece of lint off his jacket where Lander's hand had made contact, then slung the mallet over his shoulder, sending me a wicked grin. "Enjoy the town. Lander may disappear after you pass the gambling hall, so be sure to stay safe on your own. People can be quite unpredictable the day before Exitium Lunae."

The warning held true in his tone, but I ignored it as Lander and I turned our backs on him and walked, leaving our mallets in the grass. Two of the guards that had been standing post quickly caught up to us, flanking us as we went.

Paxon had played his cards well, but he hadn't won the game.

I wasn't scared of him and the threats he doled out, and for that, he should fear *me*. I didn't have nearly as much to live for, and pain was all too good of a friend of mine. He could say whatever he wanted. Dole out whatever empty threats he found pleasure in.

He wasn't the only monster in my life.

~

We hadn't been in the city long before I began to feel queasy. One of the guards brought me back to the castle, leaving Lander behind to presumably indulge in his hobbies while he had the spare time. His family might fault him for his addictions, but I envied him for having the luxury of being able to form them. He had the ability to leave as he pleased, to partake in whatever activities he liked, while I, on the other hand, wouldn't know what to do with myself if presented with the opportunity to do as I chose.

As soon as I returned to the room and was alone, I used my power to refill the fire vial in the lantern. Right as I did, the sourness in my stomach eased. My brows pulled together, taking notice of the pattern I'd been feeling during the trip. At some point each day, I'd grow nauseous, but I'd been assuming it was due to the long hours in the carriage. Each night, when we'd settle down and I'd refill my lantern vial away from any prying eyes, the rolling of my gut would ease.

Was I having...withdrawals?

I stared at the vial glowing a bright amber in the compartment of the lantern, then moved my gaze to the tips of my fingers. That had to be what was going on.

Was I truly so accustomed to using my power day in and day out that even one day away from it was whittling away at my body?

If that was the case, I'd have to find a vial to use my magic on in private each day until we returned, which wouldn't be difficult in the grand scheme of things, but making sure no one witnessed what I was doing might become tricky. Thankfully, since we had been in Torbernite, my guards had been a little more lenient on watching my every move, so I hoped it'd stay that way until we returned to Amosite.

Accepting that was the case, I laid down, falling into a deep sleep shortly after. I must've rested all through the afternoon and well into the night, because when I opened my eyes, it was the next morning.

Feeling like I'd woken from the dead, I climbed out of bed and bathed before dressing for the day and heading downstairs. The Bulars were holding a grand breakfast in the dining room to begin the celebration of Exitium Lunae, and I was thankful for it as I was starving since I'd skipped lunch and dinner yesterday. With the festival, I was sure there'd be plenty of food to indulge in, and my stomach was already anticipating the delicacies.

The doors to the dining area were wide open as I entered. My guard stayed posted by the threshold, leaving me to my own devices. I assumed none of them told me their names, despite our traveling together, due to my father's instruction. I didn't mind very much, given that as soon as we arrived back in Amosite, I likely wouldn't see them again.

"Lady Auria, I'm so glad you joined us," Queen Bular said from where she sat at the end of the table. Her blonde hair was placed atop her head in an intricate style, pins and clips holding the multitude of curls in a seamless display. Her eyes were lined with brown eyeliner, her blush heavy.

The dining area wasn't quite as long as my father's, the room feeling much more intimate, but I guessed it was due to the nature of the holiday that we were eating at a smaller table. Today, as Lander had informed me on our way into the kingdom, was a day to celebrate equality. To honor each other.

"Of course. Thank you for inviting me. I'd never miss a delicious breakfast," I replied, taking a seat next to Lander. Paxon sat across from him, and their father was seated at the opposite end of the table. The warm smells of various foods coming from the kitchen made my stomach growl.

"Just lunch and dinner," Paxon remarked with a wink in my direction.

My fingers fumbled over the cloth napkin as I unfolded it. "I—"

"It's no problem to skip a few meals," Queen Bular said before I had a chance to come up with some excuse and apologize. "You have all been on quite the journey, and rest is important to take care of yourselves. I'm sure sleeping on the road is not the most comfortable."

I gave a small nod, flattening the napkin on my lap. "That's quite the understatement."

Three servants wearing finely pressed light green suits appeared from a small door that led to what I assumed was the kitchen. Their attire wasn't as grand as the royals, but even so, they seemed better off than Amosite's. They carried covered plates of food and sat a platter in front of each of us. I thanked the one who placed a silver tray in front of me, earning me a peculiar look from the queen.

"Lander tells us this is your first year celebrating Exitium Lunae?" King Bular sent a glance my way as he sliced into his fried egg.

"That's correct," I replied, grabbing my fork.

"Does Amosite not partake in the celebration?" he asked before taking a bite.

"I'm not sure." Without knowing the holiday even existed

before last week, I wasn't sure if Silicate ever threw their own festival to celebrate.

Paxon stared at me from where he sat, not touching his plate. "Why is that?"

My thumb ran along the intricate etching on the handle of the fork as I tried to think of a suitable answer. It was one thing to never have celebrated Exitium Lunae, but to admit I knew nothing about it was almost embarrassing. What king's daughter was so uneducated that she'd be clueless about a holiday celebrated all across Serpentine? Me. And depending on how I answered, it could lead to questions I couldn't respond to altogether, which would look all the more suspicious.

"Now, Paxon, leave the poor girl alone," Queen Bular piped in.

Poor girl? Was that how they saw me?

Paxon gave a closed-lip smile. "My apologies." He finally grabbed his cutlery and sliced through an egg with the side of his fork, the yolk leaking out onto the plate. "It's only interesting that you know nothing of your kingdom's traditions around such a widely celebrated holiday."

His mother didn't scold him this time. She simply glanced at me, half expecting me to explain.

I set the fork down, smoothing a crinkle out on the napkin in my lap. "You're right. It is interesting. But I'm eager to take part in Torbernite's festivities today."

King Bular pasted on a glowing smile. "We do hope you'll enjoy."

I returned the expression with ease. "As do I."

We ate the rest of the meal in silence until the servants returned to gather our plates and clear the table.

Queen Bular sat forward slightly in her chair. "I'm not sure how much Lander has told you about Exitium Lunae, but every year, citizens come together to celebrate the equality in the people of Serpentine by wearing our finest masks and dancing together under the ring-lit sky. As I'm sure you weren't expecting the festivities during your journey, I had something made specially for you."

As if on cue, a servant filed into the room holding a small box. He set it on the place mat before me, gave a curt bow, and left. I eyed it, not sure if I should open it in front of them or not.

"Go on." Queen Bular gestured to the green box. "Don't be shy. Open it."

With all eyes on me, I gently slid the lid off the box. A garnet mask sat on an emerald plush cushion. Where it flared up to a point at the tips on either side, it faded from deep red to pitch black with delicate black lace laying over the entirety of the piece. Tiny silver gemstones framed the upper half of the eyes, giving an almost wing-like look. It was far more precious than any mask I'd worn in Amosite, and it felt too great a gift to accept.

"I can't—" I started.

"You can," Queen Bular interrupted. "Consider it an engagement gift. With the amount of dances your father will likely throw before and after your wedding, I'm sure it will come in great use."

After one more look at the mask, I placed the lid back on. "It's truly beautiful. Thank you."

The servant reappeared, taking the box back from me.

"It will be brought to your room for when you get ready tonight." The king and queen both stood, and she crossed to him, hands clasped in front of her as she turned to me. "Enjoy your stay in Torbernite, Lady Auria. We are so ecstatic to be hosting you."

With that, the two of them left. Paxon stood shortly after

they disappeared, facing Lander. "I expect you to be at your best tonight."

Lander sat back in his chair, draping an arm over the back of mine. "Of course," he drawled, the response sounding anything but sincere.

Paxon looked at me. "Keep his nose out of the barrel until the festivities begin, will you?"

"That's hardly my job," I responded.

He straightened his jacket. "Prepare yourself for a lifetime of it. Lander never matured past the age of twelve."

"Better that than a stuck-up prick," Lander murmured before sipping from a glass of water.

"Watch it, brother. The guards only protect from the outside, not from within." Paxon turned on his heel without another word, leaving the two of us alone.

Lander stood, looking down at me. "I'll see you tonight?"

"Wouldn't miss it."

Then he left, leaving me alone in the dining hall.

I stared out at the empty table and chairs, taking in the stark silence of the room. The dynamic between the Bular brothers was anything but pleasant, and yet, I found myself enjoying their company much more than I thought I would.

Perhaps I preferred a little bit of chaos, and chaos preferred me.

CHAPTER 16

I spent the day exploring Torbernite, admiring all the decorations that were thrown up in honor of Exitium Lunae. The gardens, beach, and meadows were all set up in preparation for the celebration. Blue and silver tablecloths were draped over tables, cushioned chairs set out around fire pits. There were multiple locations set up with assortments of appetizers, giant banners, and colorful drinks, all of which I wanted to see and taste, but my temporary maid had informed me that the Bulars requested my presence in the meadow tonight.

After returning to the room to get ready, my hands gripped my large skirt as I descended the stairs. I'd weaved the tie on the mask into my hair, keeping the strands around my face held back. The rest flowed down my back in loose waves.

The dress was heavy, the bodice thankfully not too tight, courtesy of my maid heeding my request to give me room to breathe. Already, Torbernite was growing on me, and I was somewhat sad to be leaving here so soon. Lander and I had given our speech halfway through the day to the townspeople, standing in the street in the city, and while they didn't seem too pleased with my piece, they adored Lander. I had expected that, but thankfully, it had gone much better than Sulphur. No food was thrown, and I survived the day.

The sun had since set, the rings turning their typical purple hue before transitioning to silver. People milled about as I exited the castle, some wearing extravagant attire, and others more casual clothes. The Lunae Festival was all about equality, and wearing whatever felt comfortable was a big part of that. Tonight, people weren't judged for their clothes or their actions. They were celebrated for their freedom of expression.

Perhaps that was why my father never spoke of or attended the festival.

Lander's mother had given me the dress I was wearing, having it specifically made to match the mask she'd gifted me. Though it was still Amosite's typical garnet colors, the detailing through the dress was intricately beautiful, making it feel like my own rather than something I was forced to wear. The full skirt was a deep maroon with bits of sheer black fabric spread throughout the folds while the bodice carried the same black lace as the mask. It stretched above the top of the corset, looking slightly risqué against my skin. Given the nature of the holiday, I'd chosen to ignore that bit. For the first time, I felt pretty in my kingdom's colors.

I crossed the gardens, maneuvering around a few large groups of people drinking and laughing. Before attempting to find Lander in the crowd, I grabbed a glass of berry wine from a nearby table, downing it to shove aside my nerves. I savored the rich flavor as I inhaled the scent of smoke from the bonfire and the distant smell of roasting pork. I'd been to many balls before, but never anything like this. I couldn't help the nerves being tossed around in my stomach like a boat on rocky water.

"Enjoying yourself?" Paxon asked, striding up beside me.

I coughed after gulping down the last drop of the sweet wine. Clearing my throat, I set the glass back on the table. "I've only been here a couple minutes, but so far, I am."

He wore a dark green three-piece suit, every inch of it perfectly tailored for him. "This is what you get to look forward to in marrying a Bular."

"A once-a-year holiday celebration?"

He turned, and I followed his gaze to find Lander swaying around the bonfire, a handle of bourbon in his grip.

"Lander's habits are not of my concern," I said, understanding what he was trying to say.

Paxon faced me with a raised brow. "No?"

I shook my head. "He's enjoying his life."

"He's ruined it."

"He doesn't look ruined to me."

Paxon sighed, reaching past me to grab a drink. "The people think he's a joke. A spectacle to laugh at when he overindulges in alcohol or wastes vials of magic by gambling them all away."

"He bets magic?" I'd never heard of such a thing. I was aware that people with an abundance of vials were considered rich, but I never would've thought they'd be used in a game of luck.

Paxon slowly sipped from his glass before replying, "It's a dangerous addiction. But perhaps the citizens of our kingdom will overlook it once they fall in love with you."

"I highly doubt that will come anytime soon." Being the daughter of a greedy, selfish king wasn't a good look, as I'd come to find.

"Perhaps magic could persuade them," he said, watching me carefully.

What he was insinuating would never happen. People kept secrets for a reason, and mine couldn't be revealed.

"Perhaps," was all I said before heading into the throng.

The nearby flames from the bonfire warmed my bare arms and shoulders while the wine heated my cheeks. A small band played off to the side, and many danced with their partners to the beat. In a flash, I was pulled into the embrace of a man, and I blinked to find Lander grinning down at me. He smelled of booze, but he looked happy, smiling from ear to ear. He swung me around until the song was over, then another upbeat tune began, and he passed me to another dancer. Everyone traded partners every few steps or so, and I threw my head back with a laugh, letting the music and wine flow through me as it fueled the joyous race of my heart.

Halfway through the song, I twirled into the arms of another man, his hands gripping my arms stronger than the rest, but the buzz nearly made me blind to it. The stranger didn't spin me like the others. In fact, he kept me quite close to his stiff chest.

"Enjoying the last night of your life?" he asked, his voice low and close to my ear.

My feet stumbled slightly as we continued moving while it took me a moment to process what he'd said. "I'm sorry?" I tried to pull back to get a better look at him, but he held me in place. To anyone else, it'd look as if we were simply dancing.

His fingers dug harder into my shoulder. "Oblivious thing, aren't you?"

My heart skipped. *Play dumb. Act naïve.*

"I'm not sure what you mean." I mustered as much confidence behind my words as I could.

The hand pressed to my lower back slid around to my waist and gripped, the tips of his fingers brushing the underside of my breast through my corset.

"I have to ask you to let me go." I tried to keep the fear from my voice, but it shook anyway. Were there people here to kill me?

"I don't take orders from weak little bitches like you."

My eyes darted around until they landed on Lander, who was inebriated as ever, laughing with a tall, dark-haired woman. He didn't so much as glance this way, infatuated with whoever the girl was. Paxon was nowhere in sight, but for some reason, I felt a bit of relief at that. Knowing him, he'd watch and see how I handled the situation. Everyone else was so caught up in their conversations and dancing that no one noticed what was happening before them.

But I was *not* weak.

Putting all my force behind it, I brought my knee up to meet with his groin, the act hidden in the mess of my skirt. He let out a grunt, the impact enough for him to loosen his hold on me. I shoved his shoulders away, leaving him keeled over with his hands cupped between his legs.

My dress suddenly felt suffocating, and despite the cool night air, I needed somewhere I could breathe, away from the stifling bodies moving every which way. I bundled my skirts in my fists and hurried away from the crowd, weaving through people lost between dancing and drinking.

Maybe the festival was a bad idea. The citizens of the other kingdoms weren't particularly happy with my father's hold on trade and his hoard of supplies he refused to share, and with that, I should've known tonight might be a dangerous event to partake in. My guards had been here, but they were now distracted, as I'd suspected they would be. I'd have thought that to be a relief, but it clearly wasn't. Threats loomed, even on the night where equality was supposed to be celebrated.

The festival butted up to the edge of the forest, and as I entered the tree line, an opening in the distance revealed itself. My dress snagged on various twigs and rocks, but I carried on in the hopes of the man not seeing where I'd disappeared to. He was drunk, allowing himself to act unruly simply because of the holiday.

My body was confused whether to enjoy its buzz from the dancing or to let fear seep in with the thought that the man might come looking for me. I had to hope my knee had done enough damage to keep him away.

Emerging from the trees as the sound of the party faded behind the foliage, a small pond sparkled under the rings above. The crisp scent of dew on the blades of grass was a welcome reprieve from the multitude of invading smells at the celebration.

Lightning bugs danced in the air above the water, stars glittering across the surface. I looked up to find one shoot across the sky, and while it might've been foolish, I whispered a wish to the stars. Perhaps they'd hear it and give me mercy just this once.

Tell me the world is not truly all this bad.

Crossing to the pond, I perched myself on my knees and trailed a finger through the still water, watching as it rippled. The water was like glass, showcasing the world above, and in the reflection, I stared at my mask. It was breathtaking, there was no doubt in that, but it wasn't me. It was a perception, hiding who I truly was behind distracting beauty. I was wearing Amosite's colors as if I was proud, and yet, all I felt was shame. Shame to have a father so greedy, and to live in a kingdom so rich, yet so poor.

Among the faint croaking of frogs and chirping of crickets, a twig snapped, but before I could turn, my head was thrust down, water instantly surrounding my face and flowing up my nose.

"Keep her under!" a man shouted, his voice contorted by

the water around my ears. Another pair of hands grabbed my shoulders, forcing me farther into the water.

I thrashed against the hold of the two people, trying not to scream, as it would only spend what oxygen was left in my lungs. I tried to blindly reach behind me to find a weapon, a body, anything, but found nothing of the sort. My hands plunged into the water, trying to push off of the sandy shore, but it only kicked up debris, the dirt stinging my eyes. I squeezed them shut, but the sting was nothing compared to the rest. I was drowning, my lungs burning with the natural urge to breathe. If I let the water in, that would be the end.

"Bring her up," the man who had spoken before commanded.

Hands pulled at me, and then my head was above water, and I was sucking in air. My face and hair were drenched.

"Please." I gulped, my lungs raw from the sudden intake of oxygen. I coughed hard, my throat feeling like it was torn to shreds. "Please. I'll do anything. Please don't kill me."

The man behind me chuckled. "We've got a beggar, boys."

The one to my right said, "I like it when they beg."

A hand gripped my chin hard, forcing me to face the guy to my left. He had a shaved head with black ink swirled over every inch of skin, aside from his face. "She'd look even prettier begging for me to fill her tight cunt."

My chest heaved as nausea rolled through me, but I was too starved for air to think about vomiting. Instead, I spit at him, the glob landing right on his cheek. "Fuck you," I seethed in between pants. I might not have the upper hand here, but that didn't mean I had lost all my fire.

His hand released my chin and flew back, a crack splitting through the air as he slapped me. Rough fingers gripped my chin again as pain stung my skin, my mask barely taking the brunt of the hit. "You want to spit on something, bitch? I'll give you something to soak." His free hand moved to his pants.

I thrashed my body, but the other man wrapped his arms around my shoulders, keeping me in place. I tossed my head back, and a crunch sounded right before he yelled out in pain. His arms fell from around me, and I instantly twisted, landing flat on my stomach in the grass. The bald man grabbed my arm, but with the water slicking my skin, I slid free and scrambled to my hands and knees.

The one who had spoken commands grabbed my hair, and I screamed out in pain as he lifted me off my hands, my knees barely touching the ground now. I reached up, scratching at his arms, but he held firm.

"Lucky for you, we like a little fight." As he spun me, I recognized that the bald man with the now bloodied nose was the one who'd danced with me.

"You fucking coward!" I spit. "Bringing your friends because you couldn't fight a girl on your own!"

The short-haired man holding me up chuckled. "She's feisty."

I tried to pry his hand off my hair, but he kept his hold firm. "Let me go," I bit out.

"I'm having far too much fun to do that," he said, like holding a woman against her will was *amusing* to him.

"You heard the girl. Let her go," a deep voice said from behind us, interrupting the chaos like a wish whispered on the wind.

He spun, keeping me in his grip as he faced whoever spoke. "We're not sharing."

I blinked rapidly, trying to clear the water and sand from my eyes to focus on whoever it was that was speaking. I recognized the voice, but I couldn't pinpoint from where.

The man stepped out from the shadows of the tree line,

dagger in hand as he picked at his nail with the tip of it. My heart picked up its pace as I instantly recognized him.

"Doesn't look like she wants to be shared," Bowen said, not bothering to look up from his dagger.

"She's having a grand ol' time. Aren't you, honey?" the short-haired man asked, jostling me a bit. "Just a bit of foreplay."

I breathed furiously through my nose, not giving him a response.

Bowen looked up from his dagger, his eyes immediately landing on me, like he, too, was waiting for a response. "See, I have a hard time believing that," he finally said. "It looks to me like she was putting up quite the fight."

"She just wanted to play, is all," the bald man said from behind me.

Bowen cocked his head slightly. "Are you having fun, Princess?"

Short-haired man tightened his grip on my hair in warning, so rather than shaking my head, I tried my best to plead with my eyes. Bowen wasn't buying their story, but I wouldn't survive if he walked away.

Bowen flipped his dagger a few times, his eyes following it as he tossed it into the air. "One chance, boys. Let the girl go."

"We ain't scared of you," short-haired man said.

"That's unfortunate." Bowen didn't hesitate as he gripped the handle of his dagger and threw it directly at us. The man holding my hair yelled out as he dropped his hold on me. My palms hit the grass as I coughed from the impact, the short-haired man falling to his knees in front of me. My stomach twisted at the sight of the dagger protruding from his wrist, and I frantically crawled away as the bald man darted toward Bowen.

In the blink of an eye, Bowen produced another dagger,

taking aim and landing it directly in the side of the man's neck. He fell to the ground, not moving as blood spurted into the grass like a fountain. The one with the broken nose tried to stand, slipping in the wet sand, but he barely made it a foot before another one of Bowen's daggers lodged itself into his shoulder. He screamed out in pain as Bowen landed another in his hand where he'd reached to grab the knife.

I crawled backwards, fear threatening to lock my muscles and shut me down, as Bowen approached the group. My shoulders hit the trunk of a tree, halting my retreat. The pungent scent of iron hit me like a fist to the chest.

Blood.

My blood?

"You see, boys"—he grabbed his dagger from the one man's neck, wiping it on his jacket—"if a woman doesn't say yes"—he straightened, admiring the blade to be sure it was clean—"it means no."

He turned on the short-haired man with the blade still sticking out of his wrist and approached him where he sat holding his arm. Bowen brought the tip of the dagger to his jaw, forcing the man's chin up, then shoved it through his skin. Blood poured from the man's mouth as Bowen removed the blade, wiping it on his shoulder pad. The man fell back in the grass, and as Bowen stood, he didn't bother turning around as he threw his dagger at the man by the shore. It landed right in his heart, and he fell face-first into the sand.

I hardly saw as Bowen approached me. As my eyes moved from the bodies to him, my feet scrambled in the dirt, but my back was already scraping against the bark of the tree. There was nowhere for me to go.

"I won't hurt you," he said, slowing his steps.

"You expect me to trust you?" The words barely got out through my rushed breathing.

"I did just kill three men for you," he pointed out.

My fingers dug into the dirt as I pressed my back harder against the tree. "Please. Just— don't come near me."

He held his hands in the air, palms out. "Okay."

We stared at each other for a moment. A slight crease formed between his brows as his gaze scanned my face before he asked, "Are you hurt?"

"N-no." But it hardly sounded convincing, even to my own ears.

His eyes fell to my dress, and I looked down to find the front of it had torn. Instinctively, my arms wrapped around my torso in a poor attempt to cover myself. I hadn't realized how hard I was shaking, how cold my skin now was.

He shrugged out of his jacket, and I instantly stiffened at the ink swirling along his muscled arms. The blue hue from the glowing flowers by the pond illuminated the way the tattoos wound up his arms like rivers on a map. With his bulging veins, his sculpted muscles were silent proof of the strength he'd just showcased by killing three men without so much as breaking a sweat.

"What are you doing?" I asked.

"Giving you my jacket."

"Why?"

He took a step toward me, jacket in hand. "You're wet, cold, and exposed. Unless you would rather not have it?"

"People will wonder why I'm wearing it," I said, which was such a vacuous excuse.

"You can tell them whatever story you'd like, Princess, but covering up would best suit you tonight." He crouched a few feet from me, holding the jacket out toward me, his blood-stained dagger in his other hand.

I stared at the jacket in his grip, my mind warring with itself over the fact that he was, in fact, a criminal, and yet, he'd saved me. Why was he in my father's castle if he was a criminal? "They wanted to kill me."

Bowen studied me as he inhaled. "They did."

"Why?"

His Adam's apple moved as he swallowed. "There could be many reasons."

Our eyes met. "Are you like them?"

He hesitated, thinking on his answer. "No."

"Then why do people fear you? Why does my father not like you?"

He stood, stepping closer, then kneeled again to wrap his jacket around my shoulders. For some reason, I let him. I realized my question wasn't the brightest, as he'd clearly just buried multiple daggers in three men and was covered in ink, proving he was a thief, but my mind wasn't working coherently at the moment and his voice kept me in the present rather than the spiraling of my mind.

"People fear things for an abundance of reasons," he replied.

I brushed a wet strand of hair off my cheek. The mask stuck to my face uncomfortably, and with the tangle of my hair, it'd be a pain to get the knot undone. "What are your reasons?"

His eyes met mine again, and somehow, I found a sliver of escape in them. What beauty was found in the sky, when he held it all right there?

"We all have our secrets, Princess. Some are just kept for better reasons."

"Is there ever a good reason to have them?" With the removal of his jacket, he clearly wasn't afraid of me seeing the tattoos littering his skin. But what else could he be hiding?

His shoulders slumped the barest amount as his eyes softened. "I like to believe so."

"You're not wearing a mask," I acknowledged, changing the

subject. I needed to keep talking or I feared the panic would set in.

"I'm not."

"Do you not celebrate Exitium Lunae?"

His body instantly went rigid again before he straightened, turning to grab his dagger from the man's body on the shore. "No."

"Why not? I thought everyone did." I kept peppering him with questions for fear he'd leave. If he did, I'd be alone again. Vulnerable.

He shoved the body onto its side with ease, extracting his dagger from the man's chest. With a thump, the man was face-first in the sand once again as Bowen moved to run his dagger through the water. "Holidays aren't my thing."

"But killing is?"

He wiped the blade on his thigh, sheathed it in his belt, and stood. "If you believe the deaths of these men were all in good fun, I think you should replay the events of what happened before they took their last breaths."

A shiver skated down my spine at the all too fresh memory.

"You should get back to the castle," he said, not looking at me.

I pushed to a stand, his jacket still draped around my shoulders. I pulled it tighter around me, my wet hair and dress catching the cool night air like a web. I should heed his direction and turn in for the night, but curiosity kept me rooted in place. "Why are you out here if you're not celebrating?"

With the silver rings casting an ominous glow over his dark pants and black shirt, he looked almost like a painting, with rough edges and wind-strewn hair. He was so unkempt compared to the men I was used to, so much more dangerous, and it seemed to draw me to him like a magnet. The shadows only succeeded in emphasizing his tan forearms and sharp jawline, and I fought to keep my eyes from straying to them.

I shook my head, finding myself having taken three steps toward him. The adrenaline was messing with me.

"Keeping you alive, apparently," he muttered.

"Aside from that."

He subtly shook his head, his jaw ticking, and began walking toward the tree line.

"Wait," I called after him before I could stop myself.

He paused, not turning back around.

"What do I say if someone asks what happened?" I suspected Bowen wasn't welcomed here, and for that, I needed to know if he wanted his presence known. Being out in the forest during Exitium Lunae gave me the impression he was here on another agenda.

"It's your story to tell, whether you'd like to or not. It can be our secret or the world can know. Your choice." With that, he continued on his way, disappearing into the tree line.

Maybe it'd be the last time I saw him, but I'd thought the same back in Amosite, and here he'd been, showing up when I was on the verge of being killed. Given his sneaking around, I figured he wasn't from Torbernite, which made me curious as to why he was here in the first place.

Perhaps this secret was best kept close, for his sake and mine.

CHAPTER 17

The morning after Exitium Lunae, we left for Feldspar as the sun rose, despite the hungover state of our group.

Somehow, I'd snuck up to my room after the incident in the woods without being seen. Most of the guards had been too caught up in celebrating to the point they hadn't noticed me wearing a man's jacket as I quietly found the back entrance of the castle. It had been mostly empty inside the home, save for a few servants wandering about as they refilled trays outside, so it'd been relatively easy to get back to my room. I'd peeled out of my torn dress, leaving Bowen's jacket on the bed as I bathed the sand and dirt off, somehow managing to untangle my hair from the ribbons of the mask. I'd then changed into my night-gown and tossed the clothes in the trash, along with the mask. They were all ruined anyway, and it'd be easier to have a servant dispose of them than explain why the clothes were so battered, and why I had a man's jacket.

I still wondered why he'd been so easily willing to give me his coat.

From the moment I'd met Bowen on the night of my

engagement announcement, he'd been harsh with his words, careful with his phrasing like everything he said and did was calculated. But last night, he'd killed three men simply for threatening me. Well, it was a bit past a threat, but the sentiment remained. He didn't have to put himself at risk for me, and yet, he did. For a stranger. For someone he'd made clear he wanted nothing to do with. For someone he'd mocked before. He could have walked away, but he didn't.

And not a soul could know of it.

We'd traveled through the Hollows most of the day, the cover from the thick forest of black pine trees a relief from the beating sun. It reflected off the rings, scorching us with heat as we moved. I was thankful we were heading into Feldspar, known for its fresh water rivers and towering trees, as shade, snow, and a swim in one of their hot springs sounded lovely after the long day of travel.

Feldspar and Torbernite were quite close to one another, not nearly as far apart as the other kingdoms—though their biomes were complete opposites, with Torbernite being warm and sunny and Feldspar being overcast and snowy—so we reached Alkali, their city, shortly after nightfall.

After a full night's rest to recover from travel and lingering hangovers, we had awoken to freezing temperatures. The salty ocean breeze rolled through the snow-covered pines that battled for height against the massive castle. The building itself had been impressive, with its dark tan architecture against ivory accents weaved throughout the intricacies of each carefully sculpted piece of art. The palace was a painting in and of itself as it stood grand amongst the thick trees.

I'd never have thought such a place to exist. Amosite had forests containing a variety of smaller trees not far from the castle, but those didn't hold a candle to Feldspar's. The timber were beasts of their own, swaying with the wind that rolled in from the ocean miles away, sending loads of snow to the ground as piles fell from their branches.

After having tea with Queen Pleum, Lander and I had gone into downtown Crystalline to present our speech to the citizens. King and Queen Pleum had been much more warm than our brief interaction with Sulphur's monarchs, but the people had treated me the same. Rather than food being thrown at us, though, they chucked balls of snow, soaking my dress through.

As Feldspar and Torbernite were close, Lander and Paxon had been welcomed with open arms. During my time to speak, though, they'd made crude comments, shouting over my words. From what I wore to the way I looked, they had picked on all of it.

But the comments that stuck with me the most were when they'd said Lander deserved better than a fragile woman.

The word had repeated itself in my brain all night. *Fragile.* And as much as it hurt me to hear, maybe they were right. I wasn't prepared for any of this. All the slander, the glares, the judgment. My father knowingly threw me to the wolves with no means of preparing myself.

Through it all, Lander had apologized profusely. It wasn't his fault—the two of us knew that. This was my father's doing, and I was simply paying the price. He thought he could stick me in front of crowds of irate people, and I would give some simple speech and they would trust me. But what trust would they have in a kingdom that ruined their trade agreements by withholding resources we had an abundance of?

Our world relied on magic for so many things that when my father cut their supplies to such a meager amount, they suffered. They had no choice but to make do, none of these kingdoms having someone like me to replenish their resources.

I'd filled half-empty vials when no one was watching, my magic flowing through my body eagerly when I did, but what little I was able to do was hardly enough. There were hundreds of thousands of people in each kingdom we visited, and one or two vials wouldn't fix their problems.

But it was a start.

With our unwelcome presence in the city, we had left Feldspar the next morning, hoping to get an early start on the journey over the Brimstone Mountains. I'd been on edge since our departure, memories of the attack in Torbernite plaguing me like the flu.

"It's not your fault, Auria," Lander said across from me in the carriage.

"I know." He'd told me at least a hundred times.

"Then why are you moping?"

I looked up from my lap to find his eyes on me. "I'm not moping."

"Two and a half weeks with you, and you think I can't tell the shift in your mood?"

How did he expect me to feel? I'd been so excited to leave Amosite, even for just a few weeks, and with each day that passed, that spirit was being pulled out of me. I didn't take any of this for granted, and yet, I wondered if I hadn't left the kingdom at all, would I feel better? After all, I couldn't be hurt by things I didn't know.

I folded my hands together on my lap, attempting to straighten my posture, despite the wheels of the carriage shifting on each bump in the snow we passed over. I was thankful the strength vial I'd refilled this morning was enough to keep the queasiness from setting in so far. The Brimstone Mountains, as Lander had informed me, were treacherous to pass no matter the time of year. The weather conditions were so severe that many didn't take the risk, but the guards had wanted to return to Amosite as early as we could, so they hadn't chosen the longer route that went around the base of the mountain. "As if yours hasn't shifted, too."

Outside the carriage, the howling wind was deafening, and I was thankful for the thin barrier between us and the elements.

"For all different reasons," he said.

I raised a brow. "Is that so?"

He crossed his arms, leaning back against the cushion. "Marriage is a leash."

This time, both my brows shot up. "You think I'll force you to give up what you love?"

"Why would a wife be okay with her husband gambling?"

I fought the smile threatening to bloom. "If you haven't yet realized, Lander, we are not a common husband and wife duo."

The stiffness of his arms loosened slightly. "You won't force me to stop?"

I shook my head. "You can do whatever you'd like. If the roles were reversed, I'd hope the same."

"But your father already controls you," he surmised, pulling the unsaid words from my mouth.

"Yes," I said softly. I wouldn't allow my father to ruin this trip, even from miles away. Though the people of the kingdoms we visited were all too eager to judge me for his actions, I refused to let it get to me. Not here. Not when this was my one chance to be away from Amosite, and I only had days left. "Do you know when we're stopping next?"

"I'd assume not until sundown. The weather isn't kind out there," he said with a glance out the window. We'd pulled the curtain back, giving us some light in the dim carriage, though the thick snowfall blocked almost all of the sunlight.

To get from Feldspar back to Amosite, it'd take at least two days to get over the Brimstone Mountain range with the deep snow covering the ground, slowing us down tremendously.

Once we made it down, it'd take a day to reach the bridge over the chasm. That'd leave us with one day to spare, but still, the guards were worried about time.

Lander had opted to travel in the carriage today. He'd insisted it wasn't because of the weather conditions, but I knew better. Two and a half weeks with him taught me some things, too. I'd done my best to avoid Paxon for the duration of our trip, but with every stop, he was there, assisting me down from the carriage. He'd been mostly polite since our game of croquet in Torbernite, ever the gentleman, but regardless, I was still skeptical of him.

"If you need to relieve yourself..." Lander started.

My nose scrunched. "Please. If I did, you'd be the last I'd tell."

He grinned. "Who would be the first?"

I returned the smile, rolling my eyes, but the look quickly disappeared when the carriage jerked to a stop. Lander set a hand on the wall to keep himself steady as my hands gripped the cushions on either side of me.

"I guess we're stopping sooner than sundown," Lander muttered.

Shouts rang out from behind the carriage, and then the clang of metal on metal filled my ears. Realization hit that the sound was coming from swords.

Lander stood as best he could, having to remain ducking so he wouldn't hit the ceiling, and looked out the window. "We're under attack," he said hurriedly, confirming my fear.

I looked at him, eyes wide, but before I could ask him what we should do, the carriage door flung open. It hit the outside of the coach with a bang.

Hands reached in and grabbed Lander by the coat, yanking him out. A gasp escaped my lips as my legs came up on the bench, shoving myself backwards to press my back to the wall of the carriage. My eyes remained on the opening of the door. Snow blew in on the howling wind, but no one appeared. Chaos ensued outside as I tried to calm my breathing, but it was no use. I wasn't trained to fight, and I was now alone.

The smell of blood on the icy air invaded the space as a body entered the doorway, two hands grabbing the frame to heft themself up into the carriage. I screamed, kicking out, but fingers wrapped around my ankles.

"Auria! It's me!" the man said in a hushed whisper.

I stopped my thrashing, squinting my eyes to focus on him.

"Paxon," I breathed.

"I'm going to get you out," he whispered, letting go of my ankles to hold a hand out to me.

I took it, getting to my feet. "Where's Lander?"

Paxon peeked his head out the door, looking both ways. The snow made it hard to see much of anything. "Currently fighting for his life."

With his hand still in mine, Paxon pulled me out of the carriage. My slippers landed in the snow, the ice instantly licking at my feet. I'd freeze out here.

"Paxon," I said hesitantly, looking warily at the snow.

He glanced back at me. "I know. It won't be for long. We'll find horses, and we'll—"

A person clad in all white hit him in the side of the head with the pommel of his sword, and he went down, dropping my hand. A scream escaped me as snow sprayed in the air where Paxon landed. The man narrowed his gaze on me from behind the mask he wore that covered the entirety of his face, leaving only his eyes to be seen, but even then, so much snow was on him that even those almost disappeared.

I stepped back. His mask lifted slightly as I assumed he grinned maliciously, and then I turned at the same time he bolted. With my slick slippers unable to get a grip in the snow, my ankle twisted. I fell as pain shot up my leg, my bare hands burying in the snow in an attempt to catch myself. I hadn't had time to grab my gloves from the carriage, and I quickly wished I would have.

Doing my best to ignore the pain in my ankle, I shoved up with my arms to attempt to get on my back, but the man was faster. He grabbed my hair, yanking my head up. My back protested at the odd angle, my spine straining.

"Little bitch isn't so protected now, is she?" he mumbled through the mask.

All around me, guards were fighting off bandits. They were clad in white, presumably to disguise themselves in the snow. I couldn't tell who was winning, but with the amount of blood staining the ground, I hoped it was us.

His fingers tightened in my hair, but the burn was nothing compared to my screaming ankle. "How does it feel not having someone to save you now?" he seethed.

His words stopped my whimper from escaping at the pain flickering through me. Was he friends with the men who had attacked me the night of Exitium Lunae? Had this group been following us?

With the dagger in his other hand, he pulled my head back farther and yanked open the fur cloak I wore. Buttons flew in all directions, disappearing into the deep snow. He let out a groan—the tops of my breasts were on full display within the confines of my corset.

Slowly, he drew the tip of the dagger down my right breast, trailing it over to the other. I couldn't hold in my fear any longer. My eyes welled with the burn of every emotion in my body coming to the surface.

"Scared?" he murmured, caressing my chest with the blade.

I pressed my lips together so tightly, I thought blood might seep from where my teeth bit into them.

"You should be," he continued. "I might just have to play a bit before I kill you. The price of your head will be high, but I think I want to have some fun first. It'd be a shame to put this little body to waste." He brought the tip of the dagger up my neck to my cheek, then attempted to wiggle it into my mouth. "Open."

Every single one of these men were vulgar.

With fear enveloping every nerve in my body, I had no choice but to obey, if only to spare myself a few more minutes of my life.

I parted my mouth, and he trailed the blade across my bottom lip.

"These will look good wrapped around my dagger, won't they?"

The tip of the blade touched my tongue as a tear rolled down my cheek, and then the earth shook.

The man wobbled, the knife leaving my mouth. "What the f—" But before he could finish, his weight left my body, and my chest fell to the ground. In moments, his screams went silent.

I didn't spare a single second as I flipped onto my back, using my hands to prop me up as my ankle shot pins and needles up my leg.

My eyes narrowed in an attempt to see through the flurry of snow coming down in thick sheets of white. Shouts erupted around me, but I couldn't make out what any of them were saying as adrenaline made blood rush in my ears and pound viciously in my veins. Smoke invaded my nose, and a glance to my right revealed the carriage tipped on its side, flames enveloping it.

I managed to get on my hands and knees, crawling toward where I thought Paxon might be. He'd clearly passed out when he was hit over the head, so shouting his name would do no good other than draw attention to myself.

My entire field of vision was filled with white, and then my hand hit something hard and cold—so cold that it stood out amongst the snow coating my skin. I looked up, and the sight immediately stopped me in my tracks. I scrambled backwards, my ankle protesting at the use of it. I muffled my yelp with my hand once I stopped, staring up at the statue.

But it wasn't a statue.

It was one of Amosite's guards.

Frozen completely solid in ice.

An ear-piercing roar filled the air, and my eyes darted around frantically. I had no idea what could make a noise such as that, and I didn't want to find out. I needed to get to Paxon or Lander or a guard. *Somebody*.

Before I could continue crawling, a thick, white whip lashed out and shattered the frozen guard, his body flying into pieces along with the ice.

My eyes widened, and all too quickly, I realized that what looked like a whip wasn't that at all. It was a tail.

And the being attached to it was now standing directly in front of me, towering over my body with razor sharp teeth bared, a growl rumbling low in its throat.

A dragon.

All the air in my lungs was sucked from me as fear froze me in place.

Its white scales blended easily with the snow as it took a single step toward me, standing so close now that not a single snowflake fluttered between the two of us.

Its crystal blue eyes narrowed in on me, and my body shook—from fear or shock, I couldn't tell.

A scream pierced through the air, pulling my attention from the dragon. I looked just in time to see a bandit coming straight for me with a sword raised high above his head.

Fear lodged in my throat, concealing the scream that threatened to escape, and I scrambled backwards once more. My ankle was useless, and I was going to die. I couldn't move fast enough. Especially not at the speed these attackers were capable of. Were any of my people even still alive?

Accepting that there was no way out of this, I squeezed my eyes shut. Maybe death would be peaceful, less full of the hate that littered Serpentine. Maybe I'd finally get my freedom in the after.

I sucked in a breath, and then the battle-cry of the bandit went silent. Nothing touched me, but maybe death was merciful that way. It didn't let you feel the pain before you departed, giving you that final moment of bliss so the last thing you felt wasn't despair.

Open your eyes, burned one, a rough, feminine voice said, the words echoing in my head, likely from the adrenaline.

With the release of the breath I held, my eyes opened. I looked at my would-be attacker, directly in front of me, with the tip of his sword merely a foot from my face. Yet he had never gotten to strike before he was frozen to the core.

My gaze moved to the towering white dragon. It was no longer growling, its teeth hidden now.

Look at your attacker, not me, that same voice said, making my mind spin.

My eyes widened as my heart picked up its pace, realization settling in. The dragon was *talking* to me?

Do not be afraid of me, girl. It is them you should fear.

My chest heaved with my breaths coming in short pants now. The corset, the adrenaline, the dragon standing in front of me—it was all taking over every thought in my mind, weighing down on me like boulders from a landslide.

Somehow, the beast wasn't talking with its mouth, though. It seemed to have the ability to speak in my mind.

It is rude to stare.

Was it...female?

"Auria!" a voice shouted from somewhere in the distance.

Paxon.

He was awake.

I opened my mouth to shout back to him, but before I could get a word out, the dragon swung her head around in a snake-like movement, looking for something.

My stomach dropped as I realized she was looking for him.

"No!" I yelled up to her. "No! Don't hurt him!"

The greater evil always wins, she growled.

"He's not like the others!" I shouted, trying to stand, but my ankle refused.

I twisted until I was on my hands and knees, my body nearly frozen from the cold, but I couldn't let her turn him into an ice statue, or eat him, or whatever it was she planned to do to him, too.

"Please! Please don't hurt him! They're on my side!"

The dragon's nostrils flared as she faced me again, white eyelids blinking slowly before she subtly shook her head, almost like she'd been caught in a haze. A low rumble sounded from her throat. *Be careful who you hold close, burned one. Loyalty does not always guarantee integrity.*

Tears welled in my eyes with the slight horror of her looking down on me. She was massive. Taller than any tree I'd seen before, bigger than any of the houses I'd seen on our journey, and she was standing directly in front of me, her head lowered to get a better look.

It seemed almost as if the hardness of her gaze softened the slightest before she blinked it away. Her wings flared out seconds before she took off into the sky, disappearing from sight as her white scales blended into the flurry of snowflakes.

"Auria!" Paxon shouted again, pulling me back to the wreckage around me.

I tried to calm my breathing, but it was no use. She was in the sky somewhere above, able to strike at any moment. She could kill me. Kill them. Kill *all* of us.

But she'd had the opportunity to, and she hadn't. She'd even *protected* me. If she hadn't been there, I'd be dead right now.

"Auria, fucking hell, there you are," Paxon said, relief clear in his tone.

My focus moved from the white sky to him, where he crouched beside me, taking his coat off to drape over my shoulders.

"Are you okay?" he asked, helping me sit back. I hadn't realized I was still on all fours.

As I sat, my ankle twinged in pain, and I hissed in a breath. "I think I twisted my ankle."

He looked down at it, but my attention remained focused on our surroundings. At any moment, a bandit could attack or the dragon could swoop back down and freeze us all where we sat. If there even was anyone else to freeze other than me and Paxon.

The snow began to lighten up, revealing the aftermath of what had ensued only moments ago. Chunks of ice sat perched in the snow, pieces of the bandits'—and some of our guards'—bodies sticking out at odd angles. Their blood was frozen, none seeping out from the thick layer of ice. Whatever was sprayed on the snow had happened before they underwent the wrath of the dragon. She'd frozen them all in place, using just her tail to shatter the ice formations when she so pleased.

"Want the good or bad news first?" Paxon asked, surveying my injury.

"The good. Please," I replied, still reeling from what had happened.

"The cold is keeping the swelling at somewhat of a minimum," he said.

"Okay. And the bad?"

"You won't be able to walk on it."

I bent my leg at the knee, eyeing my ankle. It was already a deep shade of purple, clearly not well enough to be of use.

"I figured as much," I muttered.

If Paxon saw the formations of ice around us, he didn't mention it. He had more knowledge out here than I did, so perhaps he already knew what they were and didn't care. If he knew they'd come from a dragon, how could he be so calm about it, as if she wasn't about to freeze him where he stood? Had he even seen her?

"Paxon! Auria!" a voice called out, and I immediately recognized it.

"That's Lander," I said quickly, frantically looking around to see if I could spot where he was. My teeth chattered in the cold, shivers wracking my body as the adrenaline wore off. My wet dress and thin slippers were no use against the freezing temperatures, and sitting in the snow was doing me no favors.

"I know," Paxon acknowledged, glancing over his shoulder a moment before turning back to me. The furrow in his brow told me he was conflicted. "The bandits are all dead. Can you wait here?"

I nodded, though I wasn't certain how he could be so sure. What if they were only hiding, waiting to strike when our guard was down?

He stood, walking in the direction of the carriage that was still smoldering. The entire cart was destroyed, burned to a crisp.

"My lady," a voice croaked out, barely audible from somewhere behind me.

Looking over my shoulder, one of Torbernite's guards lay

trapped under the neck of a deceased horse. From what I could see, the man was bleeding from his thigh. I glanced back in the direction where Paxon had disappeared, not seeing him or Lander anywhere in sight. He had asked me not to move, but the guard wasn't far. If I could get him unpinned, he could put pressure on his wound to stop the bleeding.

Digging my hands into the snow to brace myself, I crawled toward the guard, doing my best to avoid putting any sort of pressure on my ankle.

"Can you shove it off?" I asked after rounding the body of the horse.

He shook his head, and upon closer inspection of his wound, I could see an arrow sticking clean through his leg. "It's too heavy, my lady. If you get help, they may be able to."

The horse's neck was completely draped over the bottom half of his leg, keeping it pinned in the snow.

"I don't know how many are left," I admitted softly, setting a hand on the horse's jaw. The animal didn't deserve this. None of us did.

The guard winced as he tried to move his leg, only successful in creating more pain with the arrow stuck inside him. "Prince Paxon—he might be able to. He was just with you."

I glanced in the direction Paxon had walked off and still saw no sign of him. The snow hadn't completely stopped falling, clouding some of the distance he'd gone, so I couldn't tell how far he was.

"I can try," I said, determination ringing in my tone.

"Lady Auria. With all due respect, this is a thousand-pound animal and you are injured."

I ignored him, angling myself beside him to get the best advantage to push the horse's head. I braced two hands between its eyes while the guard braced a hand on its neck, his other behind him in the snow to keep himself propped up. With the position he was in, he wouldn't be able to stay upright if he wasn't supporting himself.

I gritted my teeth against the anticipation of the pain in my ankle and pushed as hard as I could, squeezing my eyes shut. My knees dug into the snow, the muscles in my arms straining with the effort, but I put every ounce of my strength into it. I wouldn't let another guard die. They were out here because of me, and we were most likely ambushed because of me. I wouldn't let him die because of me, too.

I began sliding forward and opened my eyes to find the neck of the horse sliding off the guard's leg, its head gliding into the snow at his feet.

"Well, I'll be damned," Paxon said from a few feet away.

My gaze shot up to him now standing there with Lander by his side.

"Your fiancée is quite strong," Paxon added.

"Auria, are you alright?" Lander asked, quickly kneeling beside me.

I sat back, careful not to use my leg much. "Just a twisted ankle. You, on the other hand, look nearly untouched."

"Couple of them got a few good punches in, but I'm still breathing, thankfully," Lander said.

Paxon snorted. "A miracle, honestly."

Lander ignored him, holding out his hand. "May I?"

I nodded, and he positioned himself under my shoulder. I wrapped an arm around his torso and leaned most of my weight on him as he helped me stand.

"Can you walk?" he asked, looking down at my feet. They were buried in the snow, the bottom of my dress scrunching on the surface.

I attempted to set my foot down, adding a small bit of

weight to it, and instantly regretted it. My eyes squeezed shut as I held back my wince. "Not really, no."

Paxon moved to talk to the guard that was assisting the one I'd just freed from the horse, leaving Lander to help me on his own.

"It might be more than just a strain, then. It's a long walk to the nearest town, and we have no carriage. I can carry you, but—"

"I can do it." I was weak in so many ways, but I wouldn't let a hurt ankle slow us down.

"Are you sure?" he asked, clearly concerned.

I gave a determined nod. "I am. I can do it."

CHAPTER 18

The descent down the mountain was anything but graceful. With Lander's arm to help support me, we did our best not to tumble in the snow down the precipitous terrain. We chose the way down that seemed the quickest, yet unfortunately, was the steepest. Each groan from the guards echoed in my ears, the smell of blood sticking to the insides of my nostrils as if it'd never leave.

If we fell, there would be no stopping as we careened down the side of the mountain. The guards assisted one another, grabbing onto arms if one nearly slipped or supporting the men with the worst injuries. Out of the twenty-three that accompanied us at the time of the ambush, only four remained, not including Paxon, Lander, and myself. That left us with a total of seven people. All of our belongings had been burned, the horses shot with arrows, leaving us only with our bodies and the clothes on our backs.

Once we finally reached the bottom, I could see the desert terrain close ahead through the haze of fog and sprinkle of snow. As I'd come to find on our journey, the landscape changed abruptly from one biome into the next. The immediate warmth of the desert would be a relief after the frozen tundra we were currently stuck in.

My ankle was throbbing, though the snow helped numb some of the pain. My feet were beyond frozen, having lost feeling in them ages ago. The only thing that propelled me forward was the promise of warmth and the hope of getting off my injury.

"Almost there, Auria," Lander muttered close to my ear. He was shivering all the same, his jacket ripped on one side and his shirt wet from the flakes of snow. I didn't have the energy to check behind us to see if all four of the guards remained following. Paxon was ahead of us, and by the look of his gait, he seemed barely affected by the elements. If he was hurt at all during the ambush, he didn't show it.

What had to be nearly an hour later, we finally reached the desert. As soon as we passed from the snow to the sand, my body began to thaw. The telltale smell of the warm sun baking over the ground did little to overpower the sickening scent of blood. The sand was somehow thicker than the snow, and trailing my useless foot through the terrain was no longer working. With each step, the sand put resistance on my ankle, pulling at the limb. With the injury thawing from the snow, I no longer had the frigid temperatures on my side. The throb became insistent, a pulse of pain ricocheting up my leg with each beat of my heart.

"Wait," I whispered. I could barely catch my breath or muster the strength to speak any louder.

"We have to keep going," Lander said, barely sparing me a glance.

At his words, my body gave up. The light pressure I'd been putting on my ankle was too much, and my knee buckled. Lander's grip slipped from my shoulders, and I landed in the sand with a thud, my hands out in front of me to prevent my face from planting itself in the warm ground. My fingers dug into the coarse sand, the particles covering my nails.

Lander quickly crouched next to me as I worked to take in air. The adrenaline was still coursing through my body with the danger that had presented itself to us, and now we were exposed without the snow cover. There couldn't only be one group of bandits out here, and it was clearly no secret we were traveling. If their hatred for my father ran that deep, surely I was a bigger target than he'd initially thought I'd be.

Lander set a hand on my shoulder as Paxon turned and barked, "We won't make it there like this."

"I just need a minute," I choked out. A million needles prickled up my leg, and I wasn't even sure if the pain was centered in my ankle anymore.

Footsteps shuffled through the sand, and then two hands grabbed my arms, hefting me up. I winced, muffling my groan as I used my hurt foot to balance myself.

"We need to cross this desert before nightfall or we're all dead," Paxon said, his voice stern, leaving no room for argument.

"We can sleep in the desert, rest until morning, then get to whatever town you're taking us to tomorrow," I replied as Lander wrapped an arm around my waist. I leaned into him slightly, using him for support to take some of the weight off my ankle.

Paxon's mouth was set in a thin line, judgment shining in his gaze. I knew the look well. "We won't survive the night in the desert."

"Why not?"

"There are creatures that hunt out here. Beings that should only appear in nightmares. They'll smell all the blood from miles away and have a lovely midnight snack. Is that what you want?"

Monsters in the desert? Were they dragons or other creatures I had no knowledge of? My mind hazily went back to the night Lander said we were prey out here.

"No," I admitted. But I wasn't sure how he expected us to keep going at this pace. With the sun high in the sky, dusk had to be only hours away.

"Then let's get moving," he ordered, turning around to continue on his way.

It was so easy for him to keep pressing on with barely a scratch on his body. Even though Lander's injuries weren't visible to me, I could tell he was hurt. I glanced over my shoulder at the small group. The guards were much worse than the two of us, some still bleeding as they limped. One's arm dangled freely at his side, another holding a soaked piece of clothing to his ribs where a wound openly flowed. I had no idea how long it would take us to cross the desert, but we'd certainly lose a few more of them. The ones with bleeding wounds were pale, their armor doing nothing to hide the aftermath of the ambush. With all our belongings destroyed, the vials had been ruined, too, leaving us with not a drop of healing magic.

Lander and I began walking again, following behind Paxon. The guards were farther back, and I honestly believed that if we lost some or all, Paxon wouldn't hesitate to leave them. Over the course of our travels, I'd come to find that Paxon was not at all soft or able to lighten up like his brother. He was stern, always keeping us on course, where Lander wouldn't mind taking a few hours to sit in a gambling hall and enjoy a drink or two.

Hours later, the sun began to kiss the horizon. Though we were still in the desert, we could see the approaching town in the distance. If we kept our pace, we'd just barely make it before darkness crawled over the land.

All around us, cacti sprouted from the sand, tumbleweeds rolling by them with each surge of wind. Lander had told me to keep an eye out for rattling, as the sound would alert us to any snakes. We didn't have such animals in Amosite, so while I didn't know exactly what sound I was listening for, I kept silent just in case.

The cacti towered over the desert, three to four times the size of an average person. A particularly large one stood proud in the distance. Beside it, a smaller one sat, but with narrowed eyes, I quickly realized it wasn't a plant. It was a person.

"Lander. Look." I pointed in the direction, and he followed my finger. "Someone's out there."

He took a moment to find it, but once he did, his eyes widened, his body turning as stiff as the ice sculptures the dragon had created. "That's not a person, Auria."

"It has to be," I said, studying it further. But upon closer inspection, I could tell he was right. It was a shadowed figure floating at least a foot off the ground, watching us from afar. Its form blew with the breeze, tendrils of dark strands casting out to the side of it, but it didn't move.

"Will it attack us?" I asked, suddenly feeling the danger as if it was the very blood in my veins.

"Not until the sun is gone." He tore his gaze away from the creature, calling up to his brother. "Paxon."

Paxon looked back at him, then followed where Lander's finger was aimed toward the creature. The only indication that he saw it was the slight stiffening of his movements. "Pick up the pace," he ordered.

I glanced back at the guards. They were farther behind than I had hoped, but they would make it. We'd only lost one of them so far, the guard falling due to blood loss. Attempting to carry him the rest of the way would have put the rest of us at risk. We'd made the decision to leave him behind after Paxon confirmed his pulse had stopped.

Keeping a wary eye on the creature, we approached the run-down town. The being didn't make any moves toward us, staying in place as it hovered over the land rather than standing on the sand. I didn't want to find out what it could do if it got to one of us after the sun sank behind the distant mountains that surrounded us.

With another glance at the creature, my eyes caught on a cluster of tiny dots in the distance. I tried to focus in on them, and with a narrowed gaze, it seemed to be a herd of livestock. But the animals didn't look like the cows I'd seen in Sulphur. Instead, the brown mammals had slightly hunched backs and short legs, and I instantly recognized them from a book I'd read as a child.

They had to be bison, based on their shape. But they couldn't be, could they? Bison had been extinct for years. I shook my head, blinking a few times to help focus. My vision was slightly blurry due to dehydration and the exhaustion that threatened to claim me. I had to be seeing things.

Coming up on the edge of the town, the sand turned to dirt, leaving the desert behind. Ahead, Paxon waited by one of the wooden buildings for us. Going in together was smarter than going in alone.

"I'll do the talking," he muttered as Lander and I reached him.

We both gave a nod. I didn't think I'd be up for much chatting anyway.

We followed behind him as we entered the town, the guards only a few paces behind. The buildings lining the dirt street looked worn down, the wood stained with years of wear from the elements. Porches sat barely elevated above the ground, doors wide open with warm candlelight emanating from the insides. Even the air held a tinge of dirt, the distant smell of whiskey and cigar smoke laced with it. Just that alone made a sense of unease crawl up my spine, but even so, this was immensely better than the way the desert made me feel.

People bustled about, but they were dressed in clothes so unlike that of the kingdoms we'd previously visited. Everyone on the street before us was wearing something different, whether it be the colors or the way they layered their clothing. Some looked like they were a sort of guard, wearing black, dirt-stained outfits with boots that laced up their ankles and thick leather around their chests, which appeared to be some sort of armor. The others were dressed like everyday citizens with more worn, wrinkled fabric, neutral colors layered upon leather wrist pieces, boots, and the odd hat here or there, with a wide brim that went all the way around. Very few seemed concerned with their appearances, wearing cleaner clothing with their hair neatly styled. Though, despite the effort put into their appearances, it was still not as nice as I was used to.

A sun-bleached sea-green building stood tall on the right, catching my eye. A spiral staircase led up to the balcony where two women and a man were perched, leaning over the rails wearing clothes that left little to the imagination. They hollered down at the people walking the streets, some acknowledging them while others continued on their way.

We'd barely made it past one of the businesses when two men stepped out in front of us, stopping us in our tracks.

"State your business," one of them demanded.

"My men are hurt," Paxon said, his voice stiff with restraint. He clearly didn't appreciate being ordered around. If the men blocking our path knew who we were, they didn't indicate as much.

"That's none of our concern. Turn around and continue on your way," the other man ordered.

We wouldn't make it if we did, not if what Paxon said was true. The shadow-figure was out there, waiting for us to be vulnerable, without light to protect us. I wondered if it would wreak havoc on this town, but the people didn't seem too worried with the sun going down, so I assumed we'd be safe here. Safety was all we needed right now, at least for the night. I couldn't let him turn us away.

"Please," I begged, stepping out of Lander's grasp. I put some weight on my ankle, ignoring the pain that shot up my leg as I limped forward. "We only need to stay until we're well enough to travel."

One of the men turned his attention on me while the other kept his eyes trained on Paxon, watching him closely. "We're not a rest stop for royal folk like you."

I came up beside Paxon, standing a few feet to his right. The pain in my ankle was a constant throb, but with being so used to it now, I could bear to put some weight on it. "Where is your king? Surely he will allow us to stay, if only for one night."

The man snorted, shaking his head. "King or not, you're not welcome here."

My brows drew together. "I'm from Amosite, the daughter of King Tenere." I nearly cringed saying the words aloud. "You aren't a part of the other four kingdoms, so you must have your own leader here."

He glanced at his equal, amusement dancing in his eyes as he crossed his arms, a sardonic smile cresting his lips. "This is Deadwood, sweetheart. There is no king."

My mouth parted, but any words I'd been about to say were lost on my tongue. A town without a leader? Land without a king?

"Leave her alone, Billie," a smooth, deep voice said from somewhere beside me.

I barely recognized it, my mind pulled in a hundred different directions, but as I turned to face the man who had spoken, realization hit me.

Bowen stood with his arms and ankles crossed, leaning a shoulder against a wooden post supporting an overhang over one of the porches. He was dressed similarly to how he'd been at my father's castle, yet looked more so like the night of Exitium Lunae: lethally calm. Still, he exuded the same confidence as before, like danger appealed to him and he wasn't afraid to give in to those urges. His dark hair was messy, as it'd been every time I'd seen him, and the black shirt he wore hugged the inked muscles of his biceps, stretching across his chest. His leather pants were tucked sloppily into his black boots, and as my eyes traveled back up his body, I found his focus homed in on me.

He unfolded his arms, stepping off the porch to approach Billie and the other man.

"Want me to scare them away?" Billie muttered, dropping his smile.

Bowen shook his head, facing me. He didn't spare Paxon a glance. "What's the problem here?"

I swallowed and attempted to hold my chin higher. If he was going to look to me for an explanation, I couldn't cower.

But before I could answer, Paxon spoke up. "Bandits ambushed us."

Bowen lazily moved his gaze to Paxon. "I asked the lady."

Paxon's jaw clenched as he held his tongue. Bowen looked at me again, raising a brow as if to say, *Go on.*

"We were attacked," I answered.

His eyes trailed down the sullied dress that clung to my body. His perusing gaze paused when he reached my ankle peeking out from the torn fabric, the one I was currently trying to keep some weight off of.

"My people need rest before we can continue on our journey back to Amosite," I added hurriedly.

Bowen looked me in the eyes again before regarding the guards behind me for the first time. The silence gnawed at me, and I worried he'd turn us away.

"You can stay until your guards are ready to move, but once they're able to travel, you're gone." His penetrating gaze fell back on me. "Is that clear?"

I nodded. "Yes. Thank you. We won't overstay our welcome."

He didn't acknowledge what I said as he left us standing there. I watched his back move under his shirt as he went, disappearing into a building and leaving us with the two men.

"Follow me," Billie said, turning to head deeper into the town.

We did, the eyes of every passerby following us as we moved, and I wondered if this truly was the better choice than risking our lives in the desert overnight.

Only time would tell.

CHAPTER 19

We were brought to a spot on the edge of town and given tents to set up on our own. The spot seemed like it might have been an old section of housing or businesses, but had been torn down—in quite a messy manner, might I add. The old cobblestone foundations still stood, but the buildings had been decimated. Piles of boards littered the dirt, nails and old pieces of metal thrown in with the rest.

It'd taken us hours to set up the tents, given the state of our group. An elderly woman had stopped by with a few medical supplies after the tents were secured, not uttering a word when she dropped them off.

No one had checked in on us since, but I guessed that was a blessing. By the looks of the townspeople we'd glimpsed, I didn't want to get on their bad side and draw more attention to our group; though I was certain we'd already failed the latter. We'd walked into town, full of injuries—there was no way we had managed to be discreet with how battered we were.

"Do you need help with that?" Lander asked after having

just removed the remnants of an arrow from one of the guard's legs.

"Please," I replied from where I sat by the fire, stretching my leg toward him. The flames cracked and popped as they licked at the air, sending plumes of smoke all around. This time, I was thankful for it covering up the lingering scent of blood and sweat.

I'd been fumbling with the cloth for a while now, having a hard time wrapping it tight to hold my ankle in place. As long as I couldn't bend it, I hoped it would heal enough for me to make it back to Amosite. If they had healing vials in this town, they didn't offer them willingly, but there'd been a pain-reducing tea in the supply bag the woman had dropped off. I'd drunk a cup so far, and the warm, herb-flavored liquid had eased some of the swelling.

Lander crouched in front of me, unwrapping the cloth to start from scratch. Paxon had disappeared into one of the tents, likely already asleep and not worrying himself with the state of the guards.

I looked away, trying to distract myself. "Can I ask you something?"

He nodded as his blood-caked fingers worked the cloth around my swollen ankle. "Of course."

"Did you see what happened when the bandits ambushed us?"

He was silent a moment, focusing on the wrap. "We were...attacked?" His answer was left open-ended, like he couldn't figure out why I might be asking such an obvious question.

I chewed the inside of my cheek, debating if I should clarify. Maybe I'd only imagined the dragon. "Not that, necessarily. More like a beast kind of...stepped in."

He tied off the wrap, tucking the ends in to keep it in place, then sat back on his heels. The look on his face told me all I needed to know.

I shifted my leg to a more comfortable position. "You did."

His eyes fell. "Briefly. The snow was thick, and I was rather occupied fighting for my life."

"So I didn't imagine it," I whispered, more so to myself.

"No. You didn't."

I kept my voice hushed so only he could hear. "I thought dragons were in hiding?"

He looked conflicted on what to say. "Auria..."

I let out a breath. "I know."

"It's just...your father. He made it clear he didn't want you knowing of certain things."

"Is that why I've been forced to stay in the carriage?"

He nodded, the movement slow. "That's part of the reason for his orders, yes."

I didn't doubt that the other reason was for my safety. As we'd seen, a majority of the guards that had been trailing the carriage were killed. If I had been outside, that easily could have been me lying lifeless in the snow beside them—or worse, frozen in place and shattered by the tail of that dragon.

Lander stood. "No need to worry, though. We'll be ready to continue on our way back to Amosite soon, and you can leave the snow bandits and all of the death behind you."

He walked away, heading over to the jug of water by the fire, as if it was that easy. My stomach felt queasy, but I wasn't sure if it was due to the smell of blood all around us or the fact that my powers ached to be used. I decided to shove the feeling down until I could get into a tent and refill a fire vial we had been provided.

With my ankle now wrapped, I stood, testing my weight on it. It felt slightly better now that the cloth held it firm and the tea was setting in further, yet it still ached and sent tiny bursts of pain springing up my leg. Compared to how it felt on our trek here, it was bearable.

To get away from the groans of the guards and the scent of iron, I made sure everyone was preoccupied before sneaking away to the edge of town. Immediately, the cleaner, warm air filled my nose, the welcomed breeze blowing strands of hair away from my sweat-slicked forehead. The calmness was night and day compared to what we'd endured only hours ago. Ahead of me, the street was cast in an amber glow from the lanterns hanging on wooden posts outside businesses. Guards clad in all black stood watch outside some of the doors, daggers and swords strapped to their bodies.

More people than I expected walked down the street, confirming the shadowed creature in the desert likely couldn't hurt us here. The biome was different once we crossed into town, more dirt than desert, which must act like some sort of barrier for the desert and its monsters to not pass through.

I unknowingly took a step forward when Bowen appeared in the street, walking alongside another man. They were discussing something, their voices too low to hear from where I stood, but they ceased talking when the one I didn't recognize saw me. Bowen's gaze followed, landing directly on me.

I quickly turned my eyes to the ground, but they'd both already seen me watching. I should turn back, go to my tent, and fall asleep. I needed the rest, but even so, my mind wouldn't quiet. Whatever I decided to do, I couldn't stay out here. There had to be a reason my father didn't like Bowen, and I was unsure if I should hold the same feelings, regardless of him killing three men to protect me.

Just as I was about to turn back to camp, Bowen's voice wrapped around me. "How are your guards?"

I startled, looking up to find him much closer than where he had stood only seconds ago. The man he was with had since left, and I couldn't find him anywhere in the direct area. Bowen, on the other hand, didn't so much as glance at the camp behind me. His blue eyes were so light, I almost wondered if there was color to them at all.

"They're stable." Though I was sure he didn't truly care for the answer. His being nice all of a sudden made no sense.

"And you?" he asked.

My brows curved inward slightly at the question. Showing my weakness to him wouldn't be smart, so I lied. "I'm great."

A low hum sounded in the back of his throat as his gaze fell to the bottom of my tattered dress. "That why you're limping?"

"I'm not limping," I defended, but it was no use. I was very clearly catering to my injured foot, leaning most of my weight on my opposite side.

He didn't look like he believed it for even a moment.

"Did you wrap it?"

I swallowed. There was no use in trying to hide it anymore. "Yes."

He searched my face, most likely for the truth, then bent, lowering himself to a crouch in front of me until his head was level with my stomach.

My eyes widened down at him as I quickly took a step back, but my ankle sang in pain and I nearly fell backwards. In a blink, his hand shot out to grab my wrist, our connection the only thing keeping me upright.

As I steadied myself, he let me go and gestured to the bottom of my dress. "May I? Or are you too proper for a man to be in such close proximity?"

My eyes narrowed, too stubborn to let him think I'd much rather not have him below my skirt, before I said, "Have at it." He had done his best to push my buttons every chance he got, but I didn't want him to think I was weak or scared of him, that he might be winning in whatever battle this was between us.

His fingers wrapped around the hem of my skirt, slowly lifting it to expose my ankle. All I could do was stare down at him, nearly in awe. This man was *kneeling* in front of me.

"You know, the last time I offered my help, you politely declined." His hand reached forward, disappearing from view.

I snorted. I was far from polite that night at the masquerade ball when I'd thought he wanted to unlace my corset.

Pain bloomed in my ankle as he tried to move it, and I sucked in a breath. His brows furrowed as he studied the injury.

"So, if there's supposedly no king here and everyone seems to answer to you, what does that make you?" I asked, trying to distract myself from what he was doing.

"Just a male," he answered.

"That makes no sense," I said, but the end of the sentence was cut off as I hissed in another breath. Heat spread up my leg along with the pain this time. Even through the wrap, the prodding of his fingers hurt.

He let my skirt fall back into place. "Doesn't have to make sense, Princess."

Bowen stood, his body all too close to mine, and if it wasn't for the fear of causing any more strain on my ankle, I would've stepped back again.

"You'll live. It should take about a week to heal."

"A week?" I exclaimed, deciding he was too close to be appropriate and finally taking that step away. I fought the wince at the throb in my ankle. "We need to be back in Amosite in a few days."

"How did you expect to leave any sooner with the state your group is in?"

I glanced behind me at the camp where two of the guards that hadn't retired to tents were lying around the fire, one noticeably asleep, the other doing all they could to ignore the pain that still lingered.

If we don't get back...

My father had made it clear there would be consequences.

I turned back to Bowen to find him staring at me, waiting for an answer, and I wondered if I'd voiced my thoughts aloud.

"You don't have healing vials?" I asked.

He gave no response. "Nothing heals better than time."

I held back the sigh that wanted to escape. "I should get some rest."

I had no idea what we would do about the delay in our return. Sure, Paxon and Lander might be fine, but the guards and me? We'd pay the price.

Bowen dipped his chin, and I turned, limping back to camp.

We had to heal quickly because I worried that if we didn't, we'd be in way worse of a condition come our return.

CHAPTER 20

Overnight, the winds had picked up tremendously. The tent flapped loudly, and at times, I thought it might up and fly away. I silently wished it would, only to get all of us back to Amosite before our deadline.

I hadn't left the tent all morning, aside from relieving myself, but even on the short walk, the dirt in the air had stung my eyes. While I'd briefly been outside, I'd found that no one was milling about the town like they had been when we arrived. Whatever the wind was a warning of, the people knew to take shelter.

I was still in my destroyed dress, but I had no other options. All of our luggage had been burned in the ambush. My forehead felt warm, my hands clammy, making me all the more glad I didn't have to leave the tent anytime soon, giving the weather enough time to hopefully die down.

With the wool blanket wrapped tight around my shoulders, I watched from the corner as the knot on my tent string was pulled loose, and the flap was yanked back.

None other than Bowen entered, ducking inside, along with

a gust of warm air that carried hints of cinnamon and something earthy, like wind through the pines.

My eyes grew wide as I sucked in a breath and shot up. "What if I was indecent?" I said hurriedly, pulling the blanket tighter around me. With the state my dress was in, I wasn't far from it at this point. The rips had only gotten worse in my sleep.

Bowen ignored my question, pinning his gaze on me. "You all need to move inside."

"We're in our tents, are we not? This"—my eyes flicked around the small space—"is where you wanted us."

His jaw hardened as his brows lowered slightly. I tried to avoid shifting uncomfortably. Maybe that hadn't been the right thing to say.

"These storms only get worse before they get better. You and your guards won't want to be caught in the eye of it in these flimsy tents."

"My fiancé and his brother are here, too," I reminded him. He had been at the ball when it was announced, and even asked me about it in my father's castle. Bowen wasn't blind to my engagement.

"They can take shelter, too," he added, as if it might not have been an option for the two before I mentioned them.

"I don't want to be far from my guards," I added quickly. I didn't trust anyone in Deadwood.

He raised a brow the slightest bit. "What about your fiancé? Where would you like to be in terms of his presence?"

My lips pursed together. Lander and I were only friends, so I wasn't sure I wanted him in the same house as me for the duration of a week, let alone the same bed.

"Say the words, and I'll place him in a separate house," Bowen said, his voice deeper this time.

"We don't sleep in the same bed." Shame filled me with the

statement. The fact that I even had to tell Bowen that at all was embarrassing. He didn't need to know anything about me and Lander.

His eyes scanned my face, looking for something, though I wasn't sure what. "He'll go to a different house, then." With that, he turned, reaching for the flap.

"Wait."

He looked over his shoulder, waiting for me to continue.

"Are there more...dragons out there?" What if the storm somehow confused them, and they came here? Or worse, were they already around Deadwood?

Displeasure filled his features before he said, "They will not harm you."

Then left.

~

THE WIND STORM had picked up immensely in the past twenty minutes, making it impossible to break down the tents. I'd quickly refilled a fire vial before leaving my tent, not knowing when the next opportunity would come to use my power. We'd decided to leave the tents, as watching the injured guards attempt to break them down alongside Paxon, Lander, and myself was proof enough that it'd be no use fighting the flimsy fabric. Hodge, one of Deadwood's guards, had shown me to a small, two-story house. The guards were placed in a similar sized home to the right of mine, and on the other side was Lander and Paxon.

Though my room was upstairs, I stayed seated on the couch in the living area, listening to the wind howl outside. I'd never seen a storm this bad in Amosite, but with each biome came different weather conditions. Lander had mentioned that dust storms typically sprouted in the desert, and this seemed to be the beginning, before the worst of it arrived.

A knock sounded at the door, and I left the couch, walking over to open it. Warm wind blasted me where I stood, staring at the blonde-haired woman standing before me wearing a light coat with the hood up. She immediately pushed her way in once the door was cracked.

"That wind is terrible," she said as I started to close the door, but a hand shot out to stop it. A man, wearing similar clothing as the woman, slid in and shut it for me.

"Uh..." I started, unsure who these people were and why they were in here.

"Oh, my bad," the woman said with a smile, dropping a beige sack on the ground before removing her hood. Her long hair flowed down her back, and with the lanterns now illuminating her face, I noticed freckles spattering the bridge of her sun-kissed nose, making her teal eyes pop. "I'm Siara, and this is Flynt."

I glanced at the man, who stood a few inches taller than Siara. He was wearing black pants and an ivory long sleeve, the top of the v-neck exposing some of his tan chest, the hood pulled up halfway over his head. The ends of his shaggy hair—a few shades darker than Siara's—sprouted out from the fabric.

"Excuse her. She's a bit pushy," Flynt said, side-eying Siara.

"Am not," Siara defended, her eyes narrowing. "He's just shy."

Flynt crossed his arms, frowning at her. "I can't be *shy* as Bowen's right-hand man."

"Then maybe *you* should've introduced us," Siara snapped back, leaning toward him to add emphasis to her words.

I shook my head, thinking I might've heard him wrong. "Wait. Bowen's right-hand man?" Was Bowen more than he was letting on?

They both looked at me. Flynt made no move to clarify as Siara grabbed the bag and came forward, setting a hand on my arm. "Come. I have clothes for you. This dress is a disaster."

Flynt stayed downstairs as Siara guided me to my room, setting the sack on the bed. She opened it to reveal a pile of clothes, a pair of boots sitting on top. "You can wear whatever you'd like. They're all yours now." She pulled out the boots and plopped them on the ground, then each item of clothing, holding them out in front of her before laying them neatly on the bed. "There's pants, shirts, coats, some underwear—"

"I can't accept this," I said, interrupting her.

She paused her movements, giving me a curious look. "Why not?"

I searched for an answer, but realized I didn't have a good one. I truly did want to get out of this dress. It was caked in dirt, torn in various spots, and the corset was far past uncomfortable at this point. "I'm only here temporarily."

She set the shirt she'd been holding on the bed. "Would you rather be wearing that during your temporary stay?"

I looked down at my dress, inwardly cringing. It even smelled odd. "Not exactly." She quickly inhaled as she was about to speak, but I added, "But I don't need this many clothes. We're hoping to leave by the end of the week."

The corners of her mouth ticked up, and she dipped her chin. "Right. Well, feel free to wear whatever you'd like from the pile until then."

She headed for the door as I regarded the clothing on the bed. "Are there dresses?"

She paused, her hand on the knob. "There are some in the bag. You can sort through it, choose what you like."

I nodded. "Thank you for bringing these."

Her eyes softened. "Of course. I'll wait downstairs."

She closed the door behind her, and I moved for the bag,

reaching in to empty it. After laying out the few dresses that were in there, I stood back, admiring them. None had corsets, and the fabric was soft like silk, shining in the dim sunlight coming in from the overcast sky outside the window. I'd never been offered such simple dresses. They were mostly black, but some had beautifully simple details on the skirts or the tops, weaves of lace or various colored stitching decorating them. One was completely solid black, a bit shorter than the others, and I assumed it was for sleep.

I opted for the dress with the more simple skirt, weaves of dark gray flowing through the soft fabric, blending with the black. Looking in the mirror, I attempted to run a hand through my hair, but it wouldn't be fixable until I had a bath. I'd take care of that tonight. The water would feel good on my ankle, but already, it was feeling better with the wrap and tea I'd been drinking. I was still limping and moving slower than usual, but the pain wasn't as bad as before. Even better, if they had warm water, it would help immensely with the swelling.

Once I was changed, I headed back downstairs to find Flynt and Siara sitting at the table. Upon seeing me, they both stood.

"It looks like it was made for you," Siara said, admiring the dress.

It hugged my body in a way my usual dresses didn't, and I felt somewhat vulnerable.

"You look nice," Flynt added, barely sparing the gown a glance.

"Thanks." My cheeks felt warm, and I wanted to sit, but it felt wrong to do with them here.

"How are you feeling now that you're out of that sad excuse for a dress?" Siara asked, clasping her hands in front of her.

"Better." I offered a small smile.

"Tomorrow night, we're hosting a dinner in the main hall, if you'd like to join," she said.

"We?"

"Bowen, Raiden, Siara, me," Flynt clarified, drawing out the last word like I should know who these people were by now.

"Who's Raiden?" I asked.

"The commander," Flynt answered.

My brows pulled together. "Like the head of the guard?"

Siara nodded. "He's also our friend. Acts all big and tough, but he's a softy." She tipped her head to the side. "Sort of."

My eyes fell to the ground as I tried to process all of this. I'd gone from being isolated and dining alone, save for the nights my father bothered to invite me to eat with him and Heidi, to being surrounded by people at all times, especially for meals.

Siara elbowed Flynt's arm. "You scared her," she whispered, though I heard it loud and clear.

"You're the one coming in here like a bat out of hell," he muttered back.

I lifted my head. "I'm not scared. This is just...a lot."

They both pasted on a smile, as if they hadn't bickered at all.

"Will you come?" Siara asked, a small plea behind her words.

A dinner with a bunch of strangers in a town I'd never heard of before. Not only that, but Bowen would be there, too. What could possibly go wrong?

"The Bulars are invited as well," Siara added.

Just what I needed.

"It sounds lovely, but—"

"Please," Siara begged. "It'd be nice to have another girl there, other than myself. These men are insufferable sometimes," she added on a mutter.

Flynt shot her a look.

I inhaled, hoping it wouldn't be too bad. "Okay. I'll go."

Flynt grinned, but it was small compared to Siara's gleaming smile.

She came forward, grabbing both my hands. "I'll come get you before."

The front door opened, letting a burst of wind inside the house that rustled my hair, and Lander appeared. He still wore the clothing from our trip, the fabric torn and dirty.

"Auria," he said sternly. "A word?"

Siara dropped my hands, glancing at Flynt as he gave a small nod toward the door. She turned back to me with a slight furrow in her brow. "If you need anything, come find one of us."

I almost didn't want them to leave, despite the two being strangers. "Thank you. I appreciate the clothes."

"Of course." Then she and Flynt left, closing the door behind them, and leaving Lander and I alone in the foyer.

"An entirely separate house?" he practically snapped. He didn't sound happy.

"It's how it's been the entirety of the trip," I said, moving to sit in one of the chairs at the table. The weight off my ankle was a relief.

"This is the longest stay we'll have, Auria. Not to mention in a town like this."

My brows pulled together. What did he mean by that? "What difference does it make?"

His fingers stretched before he balled them into fists. "We're supposed to be engaged."

"Yes, and we're not yet married."

"But we will be."

"And you said it yourself, you'd rather be friends."

He inhaled deeply through his nose, visibly trying to control himself. "To the eyes of the people, we aren't *just* friends. We have to keep up appearances. We're the underdogs here. Do you know how irate Paxon is?"

"More than you?" I surmised.

He crossed his arms. "You should be glad it was me who came to you first and not him."

I unconsciously rubbed my arm as a chill worked its way over my body. "I don't see the problem. It's the same arrangement we've had."

"It's not me who has the problem with it." He took a seat beside me, his shoulders hunched.

"Could've fooled me," I mumbled before he continued.

"My brother is breathing down my neck, Auria. He thinks the image we portray here is important."

I tilted my head. "Compared to any other place we've visited?"

"Deadwood has no rules. They do whatever they want, whenever they want, and there are no consequences."

Deadwood was lawless? But that couldn't be possible, could it? Every kingdom, every town, was ruled by *someone*.

"Shouldn't that mean we can lay off the theatrics for a few days?" I asked. Not that we'd been showing our engagement off much to begin with. Aside from holding hands occasionally—only when it mattered—and looking like a perfect, happy couple in front of citizens that couldn't care less, we'd been behaving more as acquaintances than anything.

"It means we need to look united."

If what he said was true, then why had Bowen checked the binding on my foot like he cared? Why had Siara brought me clothes, and Flynt acted polite? Why give us supplies, or even refuge, if they had no obligation to? No leader to look good in front of?

"We are," I defended.

He arched a brow. "By you being in this house alone?"

"I asked for the guards to be placed next to me, and they are."

He released a sigh, subtly shaking his head. "Did you request they keep me and Paxon far from you, too?"

"No," I answered hurriedly. "No, Lander. That's just how it worked out. Besides, you two are right next door. If anything happens, someone will hear."

He scoffed, but I had no energy to fight.

"It's been a long couple of days, okay? I'm just... I'm tired." I ran a hand down my face for emphasis, my eyes heavy. With the lack of sleep and his high emotions, we'd only bicker back and forth about it, getting nowhere.

He ran a hand down his jaw. "Alright."

He stood to leave, placing a hand on his stomach like he was going to straighten his coat, but paused.

The act reminded me of what Siara had asked. "They've invited us to dinner."

His gaze froze on me. "Dinner," he repeated in a monotone voice.

I dipped my head in a nod. "With their..." What even were they to each other? Remembering what Siara had said of Raiden, I filled in, "Friends."

"That's what they were here to talk to you about? A *dinner*?"

I nodded again.

He shook his head, but not in answer, more so in thought. I was about to open my mouth to explain further—as if there was anything else to say—when he said, "I'll talk to Paxon."

He turned, walking away, but before he could slip out the open door, I spoke up. "I apologize if I caused any problems."

He offered me a closed-lip smile, the wind rustling his hair, then left, tugging the door shut behind him.

I hadn't seen him act like that for the entirety of this trip, and now all of a sudden, he wanted to pretend we were more than what we agreed. It made no sense. But then again, not much did lately.

CHAPTER 21

After Lander left, I couldn't settle. I was tired, but not in the way that sleep would relieve. I itched to explore outside, but a peek out the window told me the winds were still high, and I wasn't sure when they'd calm.

There wasn't any way I could predict how long it might be until the sun reappeared. Dark clouds covered the sky in a thick sheet, allowing no splotches of blue to peek through. It cast the land in an eerie gray, making everything seem unsettling, like danger lurked not only above, but on the streets, too.

I wasn't sure if I was allowed to wander through Deadwood, so I needed a reason if I were to leave this house. If a guard asked, I could use an excuse of enjoying the day, but the conditions outside were barely tolerable for that to be believable.

I paced the living area for a few minutes, testing my ankle for a walk and trying to think up a reason to leave the house. Ultimately, I decided to check on the guards. I hadn't spoken to them since we had moved out of the tents, so making sure they were okay wouldn't be out of the ordinary if any of the townspeople were curious as to why I wasn't in the house.

Wrapping the wool-lined coat Siara had lent me tightly around myself and tugging on the pair of boots she had provided as well, I headed out the door, making sure it clicked into place so the winds wouldn't blow it open. My knotted hair whipped in the wind, and I wished I'd thought to comb it out better before going out in this. I'd bathe once I returned. I wouldn't be able to sit still long enough in the bath to properly soak the dirt and grime of traveling off of me—I was too anxious.

The houses we were placed in were off to the side of the main street, on the edge of town. It seemed most of the citizens' houses were the same, lined up in rows that led to the businesses of Deadwood.

Though I'd planned to visit the guards, now that I was out here, I figured a short stroll wouldn't hurt. Well, aside from the pain in my ankle and the soreness in the soles of my feet. That, I could ignore. But being cooped up for not the first time in my life? I needed air.

If someone approached me and asked why I was out, I could tell them I got lost. How believable that might be, I wasn't sure, but the likeliness of someone asking seemed slim. Deadwood wasn't massive, as far as I'd seen.

Dirt kicked up in flurries as I walked, coating the bottom of my dress, while other bits flew into the air. It wasn't cold out, despite the powerful winds that whipped my hair around my neck and face as I walked out of the neighborhood and into the town.

Most of the old buildings looked the same, whether they were houses or stores, but a few on the main street stood out amongst the others. The one with the winding staircase on the exterior was a faded green, while another shop a few doors down was black. The paint on the buildings had chipped with the weather and sun, which was most likely why there were only a few painted.

Every other building stood uniform with their wooden planks turned various shades of brown from the sun bleaching the slats. Some had overhangs over small porches, others with signs dangling above their doors, but none were built of stone like in Amosite.

Last night, Lander had briefly told me there were other towns like Deadwood spread about Serpentine, but each was presumed to be under a monarchy. Deadwood, however, was not.

The town was truly lawless.

I shouldn't have been intrigued, but there was a sliver of me that couldn't help it. Bowen had been in Amosite. He'd stayed in the castle, had a history with my father, and yet, he came from here. A town without rules. Without a leader.

I wanted to know more.

The boots Siara had lent me felt a hundred times better on my sore feet than my slippers had, and the high laces helped support my aching ankle. By the time we'd crossed into Deadwood, my slippers were full of holes and soaked to the sole. I silently hoped Siara would let me keep the boots for the journey back to Amosite.

We weren't close to the chasm or to the bridge that led back to the kingdom. There was only one way to cross over, and I'd been told there were two reasons for that. One, to better control who could enter and exit the kingdom. And two, because the ledges were unstable almost the entire way around the chasm. Where the bridge sat was one of the few places rockslides hadn't occurred, and it'd stood strong for centuries.

"Auria," a voice spoke up from behind me.

I stopped in my tracks, turning to find Paxon approaching me.

"Out for a walk?" I asked. I really didn't want company, so I hoped he'd continue on his way.

"Looking for you, actually," he replied, stopping a few feet in front of me. He still wore his battered clothes, his shirt unbuttoned at the top, exposing a bit of his chest. Upon glancing at it, I noticed the button was gone altogether. Did someone bring them clothes, too, and he chose not to wear them? Or was I the only one?

"Oh?"

"Take a walk with me," he said, not a hint of a question in his tone.

Without waiting for my response, he turned, heading away from me. I glanced around, noting a few of the townspeople talking in the street or going in and out of businesses. A few guards clad in black leathers stood outside shops, and one in particular had his eye on me. He was talking to a man in similar attire, but it seemed he was hardly listening as his gaze was dead focused on where I stood.

With a deep inhale, I followed after Paxon. He passed a row of houses, then continued on into the desert.

I hurried to catch up to him, my limping and the wind battering against us slowing me down. "Where are we going?" I called to him.

"I wanted to talk to you about a few things," he said, his hands folded behind his back as he walked.

I finally made it to his side, nearly out of breath. "About?"

He was silent, staring straight ahead. I waited for him to answer, but he didn't. For ages, we walked in silence, and the wool coat I wore suddenly became all too hot. The wind only seemed to get worse as we went, the bottom of my dress kicking up around my calves.

We approached a hill, and as we reached the top, a split in the ground at the base revealed itself. The open mouth of nothingness stared up at me like a warning as it seemed to stretch on as far as the eye could see. I wasn't sure if it was attached to the chasm that separated Amosite from the rest of Serpentine, but it seemed similar enough that I would almost expect it to be.

"Paxon, there's not much farther we can go," I warned hesitantly as he descended.

"Come now, Auria," was all he said, not bothering to look back.

I ran my fingers together, my palms slightly damp. I wasn't sure if it was from the coat or the nerves that ran through my body. I should've demanded he talk to me in town, and now here I was, alone with a man who had to be nothing short of mad at me for not only speaking out of turn when we arrived in town, but also being the reason Lander was placed in a separate house from me.

I slowly followed him down the hill to the edge, approaching him from behind like a sheep might a sleeping lion. He stopped near the edge of the cliff.

"The ledges aren't safe," I stated. He hadn't grown up in Amosite, so I wasn't sure if he was at all knowledgeable on the state of such natural phenomenons.

"We'll be fine," he said, almost as if he was bored.

The fissure stood before us like a predator. Its black depths had to go on forever, and I was sure it had claimed many souls in the past. Though it was inanimate, it looked almost hungry. Ready to take its next victim at any moment. With the wind, sand brushed off the sides, falling in small wisps of clouds to be swallowed whole by the midnight mouth. At least the sky had stars and the rings to brighten itself in the dark. The split was an infinite black void.

"You don't love Lander," Paxon said matter-of-factly.

My eyes locked on the side of his face. "It was a forced engagement. Surely that much is obvious."

"What I mean is that it seems certain he won't grow on you," he clarified. "One does not request to be placed in an entirely different home than her fiancé if she wishes to make things work."

"I'm not sure what I want out of this yet." I didn't mention that Lander and I had agreed to be friends through all of this or that these had been the sleeping arrangements for the entirety of the trip. The only difference was that I'd had a hand in that this time. I wasn't sure if Lander had brought it up or if he'd kept quiet, with the fear that Paxon wouldn't be happy hearing about it. I also didn't mention the fact that he was likely correct—I would never love Lander. He seemed to be a great man, aside from his flaws, but already, he was like many other people I'd met.

Under the grips of my father.

"It seems you're not sure about a lot of things, Auria."

"I'm confused—"

He spun, a hand grabbing my arm, another my shoulder, and instantly, I was thrust forward and flying through the air. Before a scream could manage to pass my lips, my chest ricocheted off a rocky wall, my body dangling off the cliff solely by my arm held in a tight grip.

Paxon loomed above me, staring down at me with thick locks of hair blowing across his forehead.

My free hand tried to grab for purchase on the cliff, but each edge only cut into my hand. It was as if tiny teeth sprouted from the rock itself, hungry for blood and craving a soul. "Paxon, *please*. Please bring me up." I could barely speak through the short breaths rushing in and out of my lungs. "Whatever it is, we can talk about it."

"You've had a lot of decisions to make recently, haven't you?"

he asked, his tone flat, as if he wasn't dangling me over certain doom and holding my life in his hands.

"I'll love Lander. I can." I swallowed hard, glancing below me at the infinite black. My gaze flew back up to him. "I will. Please, just pull me up," I begged, my voice desperate and trembling. The wind howled, thunder cracking in the sky. The sound echoed down into the ground like a growl, the void threatening to swallow me whole.

"It's not a matter of love, Auria. Love is not what leads kingdoms."

I tried to find purchase on the ledge once more, but it was no use as he stood there, staring down at me like I was wasting his time.

Sand flew into my eyes, causing me to blink rapidly to attempt to clear it from my vision. I tried to reach up with my other hand to grab his arm in case his grip slipped, but my body was weak from the last few days, protesting the movement. It was no use.

"I can get you out of this marriage."

My blinking immediately ceased as I focused on him with stinging, watery eyes. "What?"

"If you agree to come with me back to Torbernite, I'll get you out of the engagement."

"W-why would you do that?" If I could, I'd shake my head, but I feared to move any further. If he lost his grip, I'd fall to my death.

"Not only kings can make plans, Auria."

Plans? What plans did Paxon think he had that needed to involve me? No one knew of my power, so surely it couldn't involve that. If he wanted to marry me, it wouldn't be any better than being with Lander. At least Lander and I were similar in some ways and were able to come to an agreement with all of this. If I knew Paxon at all, I was certain he wouldn't be as easygoing as Lander.

In a flash, Paxon hauled me back up to land, leaving me lying on the ground by his feet. I coughed, tears springing to my eyes as he wiped his palms on his pants like I'd dirtied them.

"You have until we are able to travel to give me your answer," he said, not sparing me a glance. "Don't make a choice you'll regret. The ground isn't the only thing that might accidentally claim you."

He left me in the sand with his threat ringing loud and clear in the raging storm.

There was no choice to be made. And if I thought there was, after the way he'd threatened my life just to present the ability to get out of my engagement, I was a fool.

I might have been locked in a castle for the entirety of my life, but I knew what potential death looked like when it bared its teeth at me.

Paxon Bular would make sure I chose him whether I wanted to or not, and I had a mere week to make my decision.

Die or follow him.

Only one seemed enticing.

PART TWO

CHAPTER 22

BOWEN

I was losing my godsdamned mind over this woman when I should be focusing on the fucking task at hand.

The storm was only getting worse, and with the amount of sand and dirt being kicked up, it was only a matter of time before magic joined the mix. Though a lot of magic had to be mined from deep inside the mountains, there were enough minuscule fragments on the surface that it could affect those who breathed it in when the weather got this out of control. Which meant the citizens of Deadwood needed to either get inside until it passed or cover up, and as of right now, Auria and her little group were part of Deadwood, whether I liked it or not.

"Are you going to give them bandanas?" Flynt asked where he stood with his back leaned up against the wall in my living room. As my advisor, he kept his hard exterior up when he wanted to, but like everything, there were cracks. His just opened a little too wide sometimes.

"He has to," Siara voiced. "I highly doubt Auria knows

anything about the weather outside of Amosite to cover her mouth and nose in the storm."

Flynt crossed his arms, scoffing. "Her dumbass fiancé might know."

"If you're using dumbass in the same sentence you're claiming he might be smart, you're kind of contradicting yourself," Siara pointed out. She had no true ties to me like Raiden or Flynt did, other than sticking around to constantly point out everything I was doing wrong. There weren't many ways to do things right when I was constantly babysitting a town full of careless criminals and stir-crazy fae. But she'd been there for me when I lost someone close to me, never leaving my side even when I tried to push everyone away, so I owed her. Fuck, I owed all of them in some shape or form.

If Auria and Lander both had half a brain, they'd leave before the storm got worse. There was no telling how long it would stick around, and with their limited knowledge of the real fucking world, I didn't need to be responsible for any of them.

Especially not when their fathers wouldn't hesitate to pin anything on me. I couldn't let them ruin what I'd worked so hard for.

"They need to leave," I muttered from where I sat in the chair with my elbows braced on my knees, my back hunched.

Siara gaped at me. "I'm sorry, but if you haven't noticed"—she threw a hand out, gesturing to the window—"there's a dust storm currently rolling through the town."

"Not to mention, their guards are injured," Flynt added.

Sometimes I wished these two would leave me the fuck alone, but unfortunately, I cared about them too much to outwardly tell them to fuck off.

The door to my house opened, a gust of air whipping in as Raiden appeared. With little effort against the wind, he shut the door tight behind him, the veins in his massive arms bulging under his light brown skin.

"She left with the guy's brother," Raiden announced, not bothering to brush off the dust caked onto his black jacket as he crossed the room.

Siara and Flynt kept their eyes locked on me, where I sat now pinching the bridge of my nose. A headache was sure to come when the three of them were around on anything other than business. They helped me run Deadwood, kept the chaos from becoming too much, but when they expected me to handle things that weren't mine to handle, I silently wished they'd chosen a different leader.

As if that was a choice.

Dropping my hand to dangle between my knees, I asked, "And what does that have to do with me?"

The two knew each other, and though everything about Paxon Bular rubbed me wrong, he had every right to be in communication with King Tenere's daughter. She was to marry his brother, after all.

"He returned without her," Raiden stated, as if that wasn't a vital piece of information. He did that on purpose, if the look on his face was any indication.

He stood a few feet from me now, and I could smell the storm like a perfume coating his leathers. Raiden wasn't a man of many words, so the fact he had come in here to tell me this at all meant he expected me to do something about it. The man had a steel heart that only proved to still be beating in times like this.

I straightened in the chair as Siara bounded for the window, presumably searching outside.

"How long ago did he leave with her?" I asked.

"About two hours," Raiden reported. "Saw her following him into the desert."

I silently cursed. If she was lost out there, the sandwalkers would snatch her up easily once night fell.

Though Auria was none of our business, my commander, my advisor, and my friend all felt it necessary to keep an eye on her for some fucking reason. From the second she'd set foot in Deadwood, they monitored her from afar. Many pretended to be blind to the fact that King Tenere kept his daughter locked in that castle day in and day out, never letting her step foot outside the walls, but we knew. With my brief stay in Amosite, I found the only time she was allowed outside the castle walls was to see a girl in the gardens, who I assumed was her only friend.

With the knowledge of Auria's past, Siara obviously felt remorse for her, and with the limited friendly female population in Deadwood, I was sure she thought she might make a friend out of her. But her and her group's presence in this town was temporary, and I didn't need my friends growing attached. I especially didn't need her father putting a target on us.

"Do you think he killed her?" Siara asked, her breath fogging up the window.

Raiden's jaw ticked, his instincts to find a threat and diminish it fighting to take charge.

"Being a king's sheltered son, he seemed far too casual to have just killed a woman, let alone King Tenere's daughter," Raiden said. I was sure he'd watched every movement Paxon made when he returned alone, too.

With King Tenere keeping Auria locked up the entirety of her life, it was no secret there had to be a better reason for that choice than to simply keep her safe from the world. Raiden, Flynt, and Siara didn't seem to have a clue as to why, but I had an idea.

"What should we do?" Flynt questioned.

"It's not up to us what he does with her," I answered, though it was clearly a lie. Questions bounded around my mind like a stampede of horses through the meadows. Where was she? And why hadn't she returned with him?

Siara's head whipped toward me, her long hair catching on her shoulder. "So you're fine with her being out in this storm, possibly hurt?"

I didn't mention that she was hurt to begin with.

My teeth ground together as I stared at her. "They were careless enough to go out in the storm in the first place. I warned them to stay sheltered, and they refused to listen. After that, it's not up to me what happens."

Flynt sighed, shaking his head as he eyed his boots.

"Got something on your mind, Flynt?" I asked. Disappointment rolled off the three of them like salt off the ocean breeze, and I nearly hated it. The problem was that I did care about what happened to Auria, I just didn't have the right to show it. She wasn't mine to protect, let alone worry about. I had people to look out for.

He confidently met my gaze from across the room. "Just curious why you don't give a shit."

Oh, if only they knew.

Raiden was back to being quiet as usual, watching as the tension escalated. He informed me of things I needed to know, and it typically ended with that. He was the leader of Deadwood's army, and he took his role seriously.

I slowly got to my feet, keeping my gaze pinned on Flynt. "I do not protect Amosite or Torbernite. I look out for Deadwood, and Deadwood only."

"Because you care," Siara said from where she'd returned to staring out the window.

"Because it's my job," I corrected. If I got distracted with what everyone else was doing in their grand castles, we'd never stay on the objective.

Flynt pushed off the wall. "You can do your job and still have a heart, Bowen."

I shook my head only to alleviate the ache settling into my jaw with how tightly it was clenched. He was wrong. I'd lost that organ a long time ago.

"There she is!" Siara whisper-shouted, pointing out the window.

Flynt gave me one last glance before coming up beside Siara, following her finger. I wanted to look, to make sure Auria was okay, but I kept myself grounded.

No distractions.

Even Raiden sidled up beside them, which just pushed the point home. I was being an ass.

"I'm going to talk to her," Siara said, pushing away from the window to grab her coat off the hook beside the door.

"Siara," I said gruffly.

She looked at me as she untucked her hair from the jacket and tugged her hood on. "What?"

I wanted to say more, possibly even offer to go with. But instead, I said, "Make sure they're all at dinner. We have things to discuss."

She reached for the door, barely giving a nod before wrenching it open and disappearing outside. I was left in the quiet room, the silence ringing loud as Flynt and Raiden both stared at me.

I had to do what was necessary, whether I agreed with it or not. It wasn't just for everyone's safety, but also mine. If for some reason a kingdom found me a threat, everything we'd worked so hard for would be ruined.

Distractions of any form had to be kept at bay.

We were too close.

CHAPTER 23

AURIA

"You're sure you're okay?" Siara asked as we approached the house I was staying in. Her blonde hair whipped around her face as she reached up to tuck it behind her ears, her hood having blown off when she joined me.

"Really, I'm fine." She hadn't mentioned Paxon on our way through town after she'd approached me. I'd been scared she was going to reprimand me for being out in the storm, but she'd only wanted to make sure I was okay. She hadn't asked where I had been or why I was alone. It was odd having her only curious about how I was doing and not pestering me over my whereabouts.

We paused before the door, and she turned to me. "I guess I believe you. You're still coming to dinner tonight, right?"

Shit. With everything that happened after Siara and Flynt had left earlier, I'd forgotten about her invite. I know I'd agreed, but now my mind was reeling with the ultimatum Paxon had given me—the ability to get out of this marriage, but the potential of putting myself in a worse situation.

"About that..."

"Please don't cancel," she begged. "I'm tired of sitting at a table full of boring men."

Didn't she know I was only here temporarily? That this was likely a one-time thing?

"I'm any better?"

She laughed. "Auria, please. I can already tell you're much better company than the men in this town, and I've only talked to you once."

My brows furrowed. "I guess that's why I'm confused."

She angled her head in question.

"My group stumbled in here unwarranted, and you're inviting us to a dinner? It doesn't make sense," I explained.

Her shoulders dropped. "I can see how that might be confusing. It's not really a dinner out of courtesy, more so to inform your group."

"Inform us of what?"

"Well, you're here for about a week, right? And you're not exactly..." She searched for the word, tossing her head back and forth. "Liked?"

I rubbed at my chest, where it ached from slamming into the cliff's wall. "Thanks?"

"What I'm trying to say is that Deadwood isn't like your heavily guarded castles. We have a few guards stationed around the town, but that's mainly to be sure no one's getting killed in the streets. The people, they mostly do whatever they like, and sometimes those aren't the best...activities."

Her use of the word *activities* sent a shiver down my spine. "I didn't assume we were safe here."

She tilted her head, studying me. "And yet you're out here walking alone."

My throat worked on a swallow. She was trying to get more out of me, and I refused to fall for it. Paxon would most likely kill me if I said anything about what had happened. I didn't know the lengths he'd go to protect himself or his brother, and I didn't want to find out.

"It won't happen again," I assured her.

She shook her head. "That's not what I'm saying, Auria. Just — please come to dinner. And cover your mouth and nose when you're outside while the storm is bad."

"Why?"

She walked backwards a few steps, facing me as she did. "I guess you'll just have to come to dinner to find out. I'll come get you in one hour." Before I could say anything else, she spun around and headed away from me, into the street.

I opened the door, the force of the wind causing it to swing in fast. Bracing my hands on the back of it, I managed to shove it shut after I was inside. Despite being in the house, the wind still howled through the walls. Already from when I'd left, the speeds had picked up.

Given I had an hour and no choice but to attend this dinner, I decided to take a bath and finally get the days' worth of grime, blood, and tangles out of my hair. I headed upstairs, still catering to my hurt ankle, and found the bathroom next to the main bedroom. I turned on the faucet to the tub, thankful they had running water like we did in Amosite—and, as I'd hoped, it was coming out hot. Going up and down those stairs with buckets would have been a pain. Many of the kingdoms seemed to have the same luxury, but there were certain parts of the cities that weren't as lucky, so I'd been told.

Once the tub was full, I undressed and left my clothes in a pile on the floor. My fingers carefully undid the wrap around my ankle, and after it was off, I tested the movement in the limb and instantly regretted it. It wasn't as bad as it first had been, but it still hurt to move much without the support from the wrap.

I set the fabric by the sink and lowered myself into the tub, nearly moaning as I did. The hot water instantly felt blissful on my aching muscles, so I gave myself a few minutes to enjoy the warmth before getting to work scrubbing myself from top to bottom with a bar of soap. It coated my skin in a beautiful floral scent, which was a wonderful change from the stench I had before.

As I sat back against the porcelain, I stared at the ceiling, wondering how we'd ended up here. Being stranded and losing nearly all of our guards was the last thing I'd expected to happen on this trip, and yet, here we were. I couldn't help but feel lucky that we had landed here, as bad as Deadwood might seem on the surface. Siara and Flynt had been welcoming so far, and I wondered how they had grown so close to Bowen. I'd admit I was curious to meet Raiden, partly to see the company Bowen kept aside from the other two.

As soon as I was done soaking in the last moments of warmth, I rinsed off best I could and got out, using a rag to wipe myself dry. After I put the black dress back on, I braided my hair, figuring it'd be easier to keep tame in the wind that way.

Then, I sat on the edge of the bed to rewrap my ankle and stayed there while I waited for Siara to come and get me.

THE HOUSE the dinner was held in was more like a massive, narrow room. The table stretched nearly the entire length of the space, the top made of fresh-cut wood, sealed with a glossy finish. Each knot and groove was left in its imperfect state, not filed down or filled like I'd normally seen them.

Siara had come to gather me not long after I'd finished my bath, and on our way over, she'd told me Flynt was fetching Lander and Paxon. Like Bowen, she hadn't questioned why

Lander was in separate quarters from me, and I was thankful for it.

As I was taught, I kept my feet flat on the ground, my elbows off the table, and took small bites so as not to make a mess. All the while we ate, Paxon kept his eyes on me from down the table. I'd avoided his intimidating gaze as much as I could, but anywhere I looked, I felt his stare, unease crawling over my arms with each passing second.

Bowen sat directly next to me at the head of the table, with Siara, Flynt, and Raiden—who I could finally put a face to—across from me. On my other side was Lander, with Paxon beside him. Whether I leaned forward or back, he somehow kept finding me.

It'd been a silent dinner, aside from some of the side chatter between Flynt and Siara. Raiden, Bowen's commander, had been silent the entire meal. He gave each of us equal attention, most likely watching our body language to tell if we were about to strike or not.

I'd avoided the meat on my plate all evening, only picking at the mashed potatoes and roasted asparagus. I hadn't seen any protein look the way it did, and I wasn't in the mood for food poisoning tonight. Who knew what they ate in this town?

"What's wrong, Princess? Never seen food before?" Bowen asked, interrupting my stare down of the food in front of me. Siara was peppering Lander with question after question now, drowning out Bowen's voice from the others.

"Is this bison?" I asked quietly. It sounded outlandish, voicing it aloud.

He studied me, likely trying to gauge if I was being serious.

My gaze moved back to the plate in front of me as shame filled me. "My apologies. That was a stupid—"

"It is," he interrupted.

My eyes shot to his. "That's impossible. They're extinct." He had to be playing some sort of joke on me. The innocent, naïve girl staying in his town would surely have a prank or two played on her. I should've been expecting it.

"Maybe in Amosite, but not here."

"You'll have to excuse her. She's a little unacquainted," Lander said beside me, inserting himself into our conversation.

Bowen gave Lander a flat look. "Is that so?"

Lander nodded while finishing his bite. "Kept locked in the castle and all that."

"I wouldn't say that makes her unacquainted," Bowen said blandly. I wanted to shrink in on myself. If I had to make bets on the two of them, Bowen would surely win. No offense to Lander, but Bowen had him beat by a long shot. Lander had barely any muscle on him, while Bowen was built like he trained for battle every day. Lander wouldn't stand a chance.

"It's okay—" I began, but neither paid me any mind as Lander's eyes narrowed on Bowen.

"Do tell. What does it make her, then?" Lander asked.

Bowen moved his gaze to me, the two of us locking eyes. In his, I found remorse... almost like he regretted something, but that had to be wrong. He had no right to feel pity for me. For all he knew, I lived a great life.

"I'm not one to put a label on a person," Bowen said, his voice quieter now as he didn't bother to look away as he spoke.

"I wouldn't be so quick to jump to her defense," Paxon said from down the table. I didn't need to glance his way to know he had distaste in his gaze. It was polar opposite from what I saw in Bowen.

Bowen regarded him, a bored look on his face. "Because you won't?"

My mouth parted slightly at the shock from his response. Across the table, Siara and Flynt watched with rapt attention while Raiden sat with his arms folded across his chest, a subtle shake to his head as he watched his leader. Though he was casual in the way he was seated, it was clear he was ready to jump in if needed.

"Because she's gotten men killed for less," Paxon said without hesitation.

My fork fell from my hand to the plate in a clatter, my eyes fixating on the ceramic in front of me as my mind threatened to be pulled back to that day. My father had told Paxon about my past? After he'd been so careful to keep me hidden away, along with my secrets, for so long? He not only controlled my present and my future, but held my past in his hands and did whatever he pleased with it.

I wished it was anger I felt, but instead, it was embarrassment.

Bowen gave no reaction, as I assumed Paxon expected him to ask for clarification. For some reason, Bowen didn't. He simply grabbed his napkin from his lap and set it atop the table.

A man came out from the kitchen and grabbed the plates, retreating back through the door with them. I'd barely had a few bites the entire meal, my appetite nonexistent tonight.

"We appreciate the hospitality your people have shown us, but we'll be leaving in the morning," Paxon stated, moving on from the topic when he didn't get the reaction he was clearly seeking.

Bowen leaned back in his chair, leaning an elbow on the armrest. "Oh?"

"Torbernite will be much safer for the newly engaged couple," Paxon explained.

"I didn't know you called the shots," Flynt spoke up.

Paxon lazily looked to Flynt, letting out an annoyed breath. "I'm here for the best interest of Lander and Auria."

"The best interest of Auria, yet you just insulted her," Siara muttered.

My gaze shot to hers. Was she *defending* me?

Paxon didn't bother acknowledging her. "I may have spoken out of line. Regardless, we will be leaving at first light."

He knew just as well as the rest of us that he'd said it for a reason. He didn't regret the words passing his lips one bit.

"Not a good idea," Flynt said. "The storm is only getting worse, and even if it breezes over down here, it'll stick to the mountain pass. I'm sure there's more than a dozen feet of snow up there at least, and it's only dumping more."

"I agree with him," Lander piped in. "It'll be too dangerous to try to get back over the Brimstones. Plus, the guards haven't had any time to recover yet."

Paxon eyed his brother with something akin to disgust for not agreeing with him. "I'd send a team back to get them when we arrive in Torbernite."

"You wouldn't take your own guards?" Siara asked, her tone incredulous.

"It's easier to travel in a smaller group," Paxon answered.

"I won't go," I spoke up. "I'm not leaving anyone behind. We can wait the storm out." That, and I didn't think we'd survive if we were ambushed again.

Paxon tried to keep his mask of calm in place as he stared at me, but I saw the crack in his façade. He didn't want me to have a say in the decision.

"I'm with Auria on this one," Lander agreed.

I glanced at Bowen to find him watching me, but once silence rang through the room, he finally spoke. "Now that that's over with. In regards to the storm, you'll all need to cover your nose and mouth if you go out in it. With the wind kicking up so much sand and dirt, there could be magic in the air, and you don't want that entering your body if you don't know what it is."

Paxon scoffed. "Surely it won't do much damage."

Bowen's lips lifted with the slightest amusement. "You may not get the kind of storms we do, but I can assure you that the magic will poison your lungs, and it's a long, painful recovery if it does." He sat back in his chair with the flick of a hand. "But by all means, Bular, feel free to go against my advice."

Paxon's teeth ground together, indicating he was pissed at the way Bowen was talking to him. I had to admit that I felt a bit of satisfaction at the way Bowen put him in his place with only his words. It served Paxon right for thinking he called the shots. He wasn't untouchable.

"Right." Paxon's lips pressed together, his nostrils flaring the slightest bit. "Well, if there is nothing else, we will return to our homes." Every word was stiff, forced through gritted teeth. He was at his end with the conversation, holding himself back from blowing his mask clean off.

Bowen gestured to the door. "Enjoy the weather."

Lander and Paxon stood, but while Paxon immediately headed for the exit, Lander looked down at me.

"I'll catch up," I said to him. I didn't want to hear their recounting of the evening and the nasty things they were sure to say on the walk back.

He nodded, giving Bowen a wary glance before following after his brother. On his way out, he grabbed a bandana from the small table by the door. I wasn't sure if Paxon had done the same.

I stood from my chair and the others did the same. I looked at all of them. "Thank you for dinner. It was lovely."

"Do you want some food sent to your home?" Siara asked. "You barely touched your plate."

"Siara," Flynt warned, sending her a look.

"She must still be hungry," Siara defended.

I gave her a small smile. "I'm okay. Thank you, though."

Siara nodded, then headed for the door with Flynt. Raiden had backed toward the wall so he was cast more so in shadow than the lantern light. I turned toward the door, wondering how painful it'd truly be to have magic in your lungs.

"Auria," Bowen said from behind me.

I twisted, careful of my ankle, despite it feeling slightly better, and found him standing by the corner of the table. We were maybe four feet apart, but it felt like mere inches.

"What happened before dinner?" he asked.

I swallowed the surprise at his question. I wasn't expecting him to ask about *that*.

"What do you mean?" Had he seen me? Had he been out near the fissure when Paxon dangled me from the ledge? "I bathed, and—"

His lips pursed into a thin line before he interrupted, "Not that. You disappeared with Paxon."

I blinked a few times, pasting on a smile. "Right. That. We only went for a walk. I hope that's okay?"

Bowen shook his head. He wasn't dumb, and yet here I was pretending he would take nonsense answers. "You came back alone."

"I tripped, so I was a bit slower on the way back," I said hurriedly.

As if on instinct, his gaze fell to the bottom of my dress, like he could see through the fabric and gauge how injured my ankle really was. His lips pressed together. He wasn't believing it for a second, but making the story believable wasn't my concern. It was the way he asked, like he truly wanted to know what had happened, that worried me more.

"You don't need to feel guilty, Auria," Bowen said, his eyes finding mine again.

"Guilty for what?"

"It's written all over your face."

It dawned on me he was no longer talking about the walk, but rather what Paxon had said during dinner.

My father, nor Paxon, had any right to bring up what had happened when I was younger. But rather than being angry, it mostly hurt me that my father would share my secrets so easily with someone else. A stranger, nonetheless.

It wasn't my fault the boy had been killed either. He'd been visiting the castle with his father, who'd come to show the king his newest perfume scent. He had snuck off, and I'd found him in the halls. We'd...clicked.

The act was innocent, yet my father made it out to be my fault. He'd been irate to find him in my room, watching as I filled a vial of ice magic. My father hadn't hesitated to kill him right there on my bed, shoving a sword right through his chest. The image of his lifeless body visited me some nights when I was weakest from the pull of my magic, and I wished sometimes I could erase it from my memory altogether.

He hadn't deserved to die.

"I won't pry into your life, Auria. But little piece of advice?" Bowen said, interrupting my thoughts. I was thankful for his voice in that moment, for it pulled me from a place I didn't want to be. Not when I was vulnerable in a room full of people I didn't know I could trust.

"What's that?"

"Don't live the one life you get with regrets."

Before I could reply, he walked past me. Raiden followed him out of the room, leaving me alone in the flickering lantern light.

His words couldn't be for me. Not when I didn't even get to *live* the life I had, no matter how that might be. What could I do with being stuck in a castle for the rest of my days? My father had already made it clear I wouldn't be living with Lander, which proved that even the one relationship I could've had was a farce, and I wouldn't even get to enjoy it if I wanted to.

I loved Taylin, and if she was the only friendship I got out of this life, I'd be grateful. But being out here, especially in Deadwood, gave me a sense of freedom I didn't want to give up. I should've known this would happen, and yet, I'd been naïve.

Maybe the life I was already living was the right one for me. I clearly couldn't make choices for myself or even so much as stand up for myself when it mattered. I was a puppet.

Grabbing a bandana from the basket on the table, I tied it behind my head and walked out into the night.

Tonight, I'd start making a change.

CHAPTER 24

BOWEN

Raiden stayed back by the door to the dining hall, giving me the space I needed. If I didn't get it, I'd likely rip the heads from every being in this town clean off.

Paxon's ego dripped off him like dew dropped off the stalactites in the mines, and I was already at my end with it. If Auria wasn't here, I'd have gladly urged him to leave, to attempt to cross the mountain pass in treacherous conditions. He'd wind up dead, either from exhaustion or freezing, but when the elements claimed a soul, it was simply population control. Let fate have its way with the man.

But if Paxon left, he'd force Lander and Auria along. He claimed he was keeping them safe, but he seemed to be doing quite the opposite. It was a surprise he hadn't gotten their entire group killed—hell, he nearly had. It didn't slip my observation of their arrival in town that every single one of them was bruised, bleeding, and injured. All aside from Paxon. His chin stayed high, right along with his ego, and he had no patience for the pain his group felt.

If I hadn't felt off about him before, I did now. He'd been content with leaving their guards behind, and that was a problem in itself. Would he have treated Auria the same had she been too injured to make it over the pass, leaving her in the snow to freeze to death?

The possibility of it made my veins surge.

Leaves crunched under my boots as I walked out of town, the wind blowing them into the air around me. The forest bordered the opposite side of Deadwood as the desert. I wasn't in the mood to fight off sandwalkers, so I'd opted to disappear into the woods, though the dark, no matter the biome, held danger as well. It was just easier to detect among the rustle of the forest floor.

Vibrant flowers and mushrooms sprouted up from the trunks of various trees, adding color and dimension to the two-toned forest. The rings in the sky glowed a bright silver, despite the cloud cover, but with the canopy of the leaves, only certain areas of the forest were illuminated in an almost crystal-like glimmer. In the few old paintings my ancestors were able to save generations ago, there were no rings. Instead, two giant moons sat perched in the sky. One of them still floated in our atmosphere, while the other had been obliterated into millions of pieces and disappeared forever. The two rings left in its wake shifted with the orbit of the planet, following the rise and fall of the sun.

But the universe wasn't the only thing that had changed when the moon exploded.

Bison were on the long list of beings thought to be extinct in some kingdoms. Before the trigger of the moon rupturing one hundred and fifty years ago, humans and fae lived peacefully among each other. They all worked in unison, keeping their civilizations afloat, but then dark magic was discovered in the mines. Shortly after it was harvested, humans found it could hurt the fae, weaken their powers, making them almost equal in strength with humans.

So naturally, they took advantage of it. Corrupt leaders ordered armies to use dark magic on fae, and in the fae's weakened state, humans committed mass murders and burned entire villages to the ground in their wake.

Every power had a price when used in abundance, though, and dark magic had triggered what no one thought was possible.

After days of humans targeting the fae, killing thousands of faekind, the moon had exploded, and beasts fell from the sky. Dragons had had no choice but to flee their home on the floating rock, coming to the next closest refuge. In the beginning, dragons had thought we were the enemy. That they had to kill us in order to have a life here, as the one they knew was destroyed. Humans had taken advantage of that, leaving the dragons to rid the land of the fae while they hid in what was now the kingdom of Amosite.

While the humans had kept themselves locked away and protected, an alliance was formed, and what they now thought was extinct wasn't truly after all.

Cresting the top of the small hill that breached the tips of the trees, I looked out over the land, admiring the silver gleam illuminating everything the light from the rings touched. A stronger gust of wind rustled the tops of the trees around me, then the earth vibrated under my feet.

"Hello, Vulcan," I greeted blandly, my voice slightly muffled by the bandana wrapped tightly around my head.

The dragon huffed a hot breath of air by my shoulder as he settled his wings, but I didn't bother looking back at him. His scales were midnight black, the tips of them shimmering a bright gold. The highlights flared brighter when he was pissed —or, in this case, irritated.

You stink of stress, Vulcan chastised rather loudly in my head. They had the option to speak aloud so everyone could hear them, but I assumed he kept this private so no one that might be lurking could listen.

I shook my head. Dragons were *so* polite.

"You need to stay away for a few days," I said. It was unwise to turn your back on a dragon, but Vulcan and I had been together since I was a kid. He had basically raised me, which meant attitude wasn't unheard of between us.

He let out a snort. *I do not need to hide from those humans.*

I wiped my shoulder before turning to look up at him. "They won't take kindly to dragons."

He cocked his massive head to the side. *Then they shall roast.*

"You can't kill them," I instructed, though my word did little against him. There was no controlling a dragon. They'd only feel more inclined to do the opposite.

His gaze moved in the direction of Deadwood, his onyx eyes thankfully not the glowing red they turned when he was mad. *I will spare the burned one. You need not worry.*

My brows pulled together, but before I could question him further, my gaze caught on something in the distance. With narrowed eyes, I realized it wasn't some*thing*, but rather some*one*.

Vulcan's head swerved in an almost snake-like manner to follow my line of sight. *Her.*

"What about her?"

She is trouble.

"Is that supposed to be your warning to stay away?" I'd have no problem doing that. She was leaving in a few days' time anyway, and after how I'd left her father's castle, I highly doubted I'd be visiting again.

It is my advice to stay wise.

"I'm not sure why you believe I'm ever not," I defended.

If a dragon could give someone the side eye, that's exactly what he tried to do as he looked down at me.

I focused in on Auria in the distance as I said, "I've been smart in every single decision I've made."

Befriending a dragon is where you first went wrong.

"Not like you ever gave me a choice," I muttered.

His head swung so that his nose was directly in front of me, his eyes narrowed.

I didn't take my focus off Auria, watching as she climbed up an old rockslide. Following where her current path might lead her, I spotted a cave in the side of the mountain and internally cursed.

Of course the princess was exploring. What else should I have expected her to do? Stay inside during a storm I'd just advised her was dangerous? Rest her injured ankle? No. *Of course* she had to go out in it alone and find an unstable cave, risking hurting herself further.

Vulcan followed my line of sight again, then dramatically sniffed the air. *I must be off to find my hiding spot.*

"Offended?" I teased.

He flared his wings wide, casting a shadow over me. *If you must know, it is due to your stench.*

He took off into the air, flying over the forest toward the mountains. Thankfully, he stayed far out of Auria's path. I wasn't sure what she'd do if she saw a dragon near Deadwood, given they couldn't get into Amosite. If she thought bison were extinct and was surprised by that, she'd be a hell of a lot more shocked when she saw these in close proximity to where she was currently staying.

I began walking down the hill, heading in the direction of the cave. She shouldn't be out in this storm, even if she was wearing a face covering. The caves were unpredictable, and exploring them alone was a disaster waiting to happen. Weather like this triggered other natural disasters like tsunamis or earthquakes, and with the chasm bordering the ocean, if a tidal wave flooded the ravine and entered the caves, she'd drown.

The caves were all connected by a system. Some said if you traveled long enough, they took you to the other side of Serpentine, but I'd never been curious enough to test out the theory. Getting lost underground was not my idea of fun.

As the wind battered against me, I couldn't get what Vulcan had called Auria out of my head. Why would he think she was burned? Dragons could smell pain in some instances, but her ankle wasn't scorched—it was sprained. Regardless, she had stayed hidden away in that castle her entire life. No harm could come to her, even if it wanted to. She was too precious a gem, and her father was well aware of that. It was a wonder he'd been able to keep her abilities hidden for so long, given I'd discovered their secret in just days of being in Amosite.

I hadn't been invited to the masquerade ball, but as Deadwood was directly affected by all trade deals and negotiations, I had a right to have been involved. Though anything the kingdoms typically discussed was boring, Deadwood relied on me to keep us afloat. I wouldn't let my people down, and that meant crashing King Tenere's daughter's surprise engagement party.

I made it to the old landslide and climbed the rocks with ease, the rough surfaces doing nothing to my callused hands. Auria had been much slower, and I guessed it was due to her ankle, which made me all the more curious as to why she felt the need to come out here. She was still clearly injured, and there were beasts in these woods that would tear her limb from limb if given the chance.

As I reached the top of the rocks, I stared into the black depths of the cave. Farther in, a small light flickered, causing a smirk to bloom on my mouth. She'd brought a lantern.

How cute.

But even a flame couldn't save her from what lurked in the dark.

CHAPTER 25

AURIA

Change probably didn't need to involve hiking into the woods after the sun had gone down, but I'd already made it to the cave I'd spotted on my walk, so there was no point in going back now.

The protection of the tunnel was a welcome relief from the almost-painful winds outside. I was thankful my hair was tied back in a braid, otherwise it would have been all over the place, and I'd have turned back not even twenty feet in. Hiking in a dress, though, was not the most ideal. I should have opted for the leather pants and shirt Siara had left for me, but it had felt inappropriate to wear to a dinner, no matter how informal it might have been.

It wasn't just my curiosity that led me into this cave, though. It was the urge to be alone. In Amosite, I had had no company aside from the guards who were always strangers, sometimes a chat with my maid, and a visit with Taylin if I was allowed. Other than them, I was typically by myself, with only my thoughts to keep me company. After so long of that, the social interaction that'd been required on this trip was exhausting, and I needed a moment away.

Did I need to do it at night by exploring a mysterious cave system? Probably not. But in being able to make my own decisions, I wanted to do something risky and not be told, *No, you can't do that. It's not safe.*

I wasn't a shard of glass, fragile in its imperfect state, yet I was treated like I might break at any moment. It wasn't for the fear of losing *me*, though. It was for the services I offered that might be lost. Which led me back to the confusion of my father forcing me into an engagement with Lander. Did he truly plan on us having a wedding or was this all simply for show? To bring the kingdoms back together so trade could be as it once was, but never with the intent for us to get past this stage?

Ahead of me, a drip sounded, echoing throughout the tunnel. I paused, waiting to hear if it continued, but it was only the one. To be sure it didn't actually come from behind me, I turned around, but as soon as I shone the lantern into the dark space, my heart leapt into my throat.

"Scared of the dark, Princess?"

I sucked in a breath, jumping back at least a foot as my hand came up to cover my heart. The shock was more than enough to cover the pins and needles that worked their way up my leg. "Holy gods."

"What are you up to?" Bowen asked, not moving from his spot.

"Living with no regrets," I spit at him, trying to calm the racing beat of my pulse.

He cocked a brow, and I turned back around, heading deeper into the cave. He quickly caught up, matching my stride. "Exploring caves during a storm was not my suggestion."

"No?" I acted oblivious, like maybe he truly had advised such a thing.

"I told you to have your freedom, Princess, but not to be foolish about it." His voice didn't hold the same stern edge the guards' did when they commanded me to do things. A small vibration rolled through the ground, and he gritted out, "We need to get out of the damn cave."

I ignored the sudden bite in his tone. "You can leave at any time if you're so scared. Plus, I don't think I need to listen to you." My eyes searched the textured walls around us.

He hummed, our steps echoing off the stone. He was matching my slower pace due to catering to my ankle. "You should."

My fingers around the handle of the lantern tightened. "Will you lock me away if I don't?"

In the faint glow of the flame, I could see the firm set of his mouth and the frown that pulled at the corners. "No."

"Will you punish me for not obeying?"

Another vibration beneath our feet had his hands flexing at his sides. "No."

"Are these orders to turn around?" With each question, we moved deeper and deeper into the tunnel. The glimmer of the rings in the sky no longer lit up a portion of the cave. It was truly pitch black, save for the fire.

"No."

"Then I don't see why I should turn back if it's not what I want to do." I was aware of what I was doing, how stubborn I was being, and yet, I pressed on.

"Because it's not safe to be in the caves during a storm of this severity," he stated.

"Why's that?"

He stepped over a stray rock in our path. "The storms can influence the shifting of the earth, and you don't want to get stuck down here. Believe me."

"Have you before?"

"No. But I know people who have."

I dipped my chin, keeping a close eye on the ground to be sure not to trip. "Ah, so they lived to tell the tale. We'll be okay."

"I never said they lived, Princess."

My steps barely faltered, but it was enough for him to reach a hand out to steady me, the ghost of his touch on my waist sending sparks through my limbs.

I opened my mouth to speak, but quickly shut it as a low rumble vibrated the ground, stronger than before, sending dust falling from the ceiling. All around us, chunks of rock began to rain down, barely missing us where we stood. Bowen grabbed my arm, and I had not a moment to breathe before he was pulling me to the ground and covering me with his body. My back hit the floor hard, knocking the air from my lugs, but his hand cradled my head, protecting it from the impact.

The sound of rocks crashing to the ground was the only thing filling my ears. Panic surged through me, and with each rock that hit Bowen, his stiff body flinched.

This was all my fault.

If we died—if he got injured—it was on me.

Maybe this was why I wasn't allowed freedom. Why I wasn't allowed to make my own decisions. Why I was kept locked away from everyone—so as not to bring them harm, too. I was reckless. Coming into this cave was injudicious.

"Auria." Bowen's voice filtered through my thoughts, and I realized my ears were ringing.

"Auria," he said again.

I blinked away the dust coating my eyes, my vision blurry as I tried to focus on him hovering above me.

His hands roamed my body, but I barely felt it through the adrenaline coursing through me. "Are you hurt?" His face was in mine again, his hands now placed on the ground on either side of my head.

My head lolled to the side to find rocks everywhere. Close. Too close.

"Hey," he murmured, setting a hand on my cheek and bringing my gaze back to him. "Eyes on me. Are you hurt?"

Had he always been this breathtaking? Or was it the panic that had closed my lungs?

"I think I'm okay," I croaked. My nose and throat felt dry, like they were coated in chalk. At some point, he'd lowered my bandana. Or it had fallen in the chaos. I didn't know. But he'd lowered his as well, and our noses were almost touching, our breaths mingling through the dust trying to settle.

"We need to be careful moving," he said, examining the destruction around us. "The rocks could still shift." His eyes landed on me again. "I'm going to get up now, okay?"

I nodded, and he shifted, pushing away from me. As soon as his body was off mine, I quickly missed his weight. Being vulnerable in an unstable cave wasn't comforting in the least.

He held a hand out, and I took it. As he pulled me up, a rock slid down the wall, dust following in its wake. My grip on him tightened as I realized the lantern had been crushed, and the magic from the vial that had been tucked in the holder seeped out onto the cave floor. It was the only source of light we now had, but it wouldn't last for long.

I reluctantly let his hand go as he surveyed the space. Rocks had fallen in a heap, covering the way we'd come, which meant our exit was blocked.

"Did you tell anyone where you were going?" I asked, my voice higher than normal.

He walked the few feet to the wall of rubble, searching for any weak points. "No."

"Great," I mumbled, though it wasn't his fault. It was mine.

I crouched by the fire magic, watching it flicker and shimmer along the stone. A part of me hurt for the waste it had become in the destruction I'd brought upon it. It had had a task, and I had been trusted to use it, and yet it would die here. Because of me.

"Auria," Bowen said, and I looked up to find him watching me. "We're going to be okay."

"A few feet back and we would've been crushed," I pointed out quietly, my voice breaking.

He crossed the distance, kneeling beside me to study the magic. "We're alive, and I'm going to make sure we stay that way."

The magic flowed in a stream, coming closer to my boot. My fingers ached with the urge to reach for it. To build it back up again and give it the life it so needed. "You can't be sure of that," I whispered.

"They'll figure out we're stuck eventually. Raiden or one of the others will come looking. They can never seem to leave me alone for long."

The ache built, running up my arm and pulsing at my muscles. "What if the light runs out before then?"

"It won't," he said confidently, standing.

"It will." With the amount left, it'd survive maybe an hour.

"You won't let it."

My gaze jumped to him. "What?"

"You keep it flowing, and I'll find us a way out."

"I'm not sure what you—"

He pinned me with his eyes, stopping me. "Let's pretend we both know each other's secrets right now."

My brows pulled together. What were *his* secrets?

"You know what I can do?" I asked as he went back to the wall and set his hands on it.

"Very aware," he grumbled.

"What is yours, then?"

From the open end of the cave, an echo sounded, much like

the same drip I'd heard before. Bowen's head turned in that direction.

"Water might mean there's a way out," he said, ignoring my question.

I'd make it a goal of mine to figure out what his answer was before I left for Amosite.

"Or another way to die," I snipped.

He crossed to me again. "Only one way to find out. Grab some of that." He gestured to the amber liquid.

"Just...grab it?"

He nodded. "In your palm. It won't hurt you unless you will it to."

I lowered my hand to it, but rather than it allowing me to scoop it up, it flowed to me like I was a magnet. As it pooled in my palm, it tickled my skin, then warmed as it settled. I'd never seen it react like this outside of the vials, so I wasn't sure exactly what I was expecting, but it wasn't this.

"It likes you," Bowen observed quietly.

I straightened, gently cupping the magic in my hand. It glowed through the cracks of my fingers, lighting our way. "I don't think *it* knows what it's doing."

He began walking deeper into the cave. "Oh, it does."

Again, the drip sounded, louder this time, which meant we were getting closer to whatever it was.

"Are you feeling okay?" he asked, not looking back at me as I followed.

"Are you?"

"What makes you think I'm not?"

"You're being nice."

We followed the tunnel, and the farther we got, the more persistent the drip became.

"I've been nothing but welcoming since you arrived in Deadwood," he defended.

"You barged into my tent without warning," I reminded him.

"If it makes you happy, Princess, I'll knock from now on."

Our boots echoed along with the drip, centuries of dust shuffling under our feet.

"Why do you have a right-hand man?" I asked, interrupting the silence.

"Not sure what you mean."

"Flynt. Siara said that's what he is to you." He was playing dumb, unless Siara and Flynt had lied?

He was quiet, and during his silence, I decided to pull at the magic with my body, seeing if it would duplicate in order to keep itself alive. To my surprise, it did. Amber liquid squeezed through the cracks in my fingers, and I pulled my power back a bit as it threatened to drip to the floor.

"He's an advisor of sorts," Bowen finally admitted.

"But you aren't a king."

"No," he agreed. "I'm not."

"Then why do you have an advisor?"

He looked back at me. "Why do you have a friend when your father keeps you locked away?"

He waited for a response, but I had none. What was he trying to say?

"Are you telling me you keep him close because you're lonely?" I asked as I stepped over a hole in the ground.

He stopped, and I almost slammed into his back. "Lonely isn't what I would call it."

"What would you call it, then?"

He turned, and I was far too close to his chest. "An entire town relies on me to keep them alive and fed. While you may not know what that's like, *Princess*, it is anything but an easy job." He hissed the nickname at me like an insult.

I lifted my chin. "I never said it seemed easy."

"Then don't chalk my desire for others' opinions on important matters up to me being lonely. I am far from that."

He faced forward again, continuing on his way.

I followed suit. "Right. The brothel." Lander had told me what the green building was, and I had to admit, it didn't shock me to know what they did in there. People had desires. There was nothing wrong with giving in to them.

He chuckled, the sound low as it bounced off the walls. "I don't need to find company there."

"Are you insulting them?"

"Far from it. Not many can handle the tasks of what those men and women do every day. If anything, I commend them."

I stopped in my tracks. "Really?"

He must've heard my footsteps cease, as he stopped and turned to face me once more. "Yes. Is that so shocking?"

"It is," I admitted. My father didn't allow prostitutes of any kind in Amosite, as far as I was aware. I'd eavesdropped on many meetings where he'd yelled about the disgust of it. Yet, it was no secret that his guards hired the few who worked under the table in the city. There were many secrets to be heard when you had nothing to do but listen.

"Well, it's true. Now may we keep moving?"

I went to take a step forward, but as soon as I did, a massive, ivory face appeared from the wall of black directly behind Bowen.

"Bowen!" I screamed, and he turned just in time to avoid the beast's teeth tearing his head from his body.

It had no scales like the dragon that had found me in the snow. Instead, it was all bone with hollow black holes where its eyes should have been. Its teeth were a mangey yellow, and its jaw snapped as Bowen dodged the attack.

It let out a roar as its head thrashed to the side, hitting the wall of the cave to knock more rocks from the ceiling. The sounds clashed together, reverberating through me. Bowen was on the other side of the cluster of rocks that fell, pressed up against the wall.

"Auria! Are you okay?" he shouted over the chaos.

"Fine!" I yelled back, but it was followed up by my breath getting caught in my lungs as the dragon pinned its hollow eye sockets on me. A rumble poured from its throat, echoing through the cave.

Bowen attempted to distract it, throwing a rock at its skull before unsheathing a dagger from his belt.

"What are you doing?" I shrieked.

"Getting its attention off you," he replied, keeping his eyes on the beast. "You want to eat someone? Eat me."

Its head swiveled in his direction, and though it was fully made up of bones, I could tell it was annoyed just in the way it moved. And probably hungry. *Very* hungry.

Its teeth snapped again, and out of nowhere, its tail whipped out, crashing into the rocks. They shattered into hundreds of pieces, flying every which way. I covered my face, pressing the front of my body up against the wall while trying to keep the fire magic tight in my grip. We were going to die, most certainly so if I let the light die out.

"*Darkness has no place for mercy*," the dragon growled, its voice deep and grainy.

I looked back at it, finding its head facing me again. From my peripheral, Bowen moved toward it as the dragon took a step. The force of its talons hitting the ground shook the cave floor.

"We don't want to harm you," I told it, my voice trembling. I'd never seen a dragon before that day on the mountain pass, and now here I was, face to face with one that bore no scales, no skin—only bones. It was a sight to behold, watching a skeleton of a dragon prowl toward me.

Maybe my father had hidden me away for good reason. The real world was no place for someone as weak as me.

"*You are in my home*," it rumbled, coming closer with each step.

"Auria, back up," Bowen warned from the other side of the rocks. He tried to make his way over them, but loose ones prevented him from getting very far.

I stood my ground, staring the dragon in its face. Its wings were tucked close to its body to avoid hitting the ceiling, cobwebs spread wide between its limbs. Was it stuck underground?

"We got lost, and our way out is blocked," I said, trying to keep my voice even.

Its head cocked to the side, but it continued its prowl. It filled the entirety of the cave, its body barely fitting in the tunnel. By the way the bones of its chest contracted before widening, it looked like it took a deep breath, and then Bowen was yelling, "Auria! Cover your mouth!"

A burst of green gas released from its mouth, and I ducked down, dropping the magic in my hand in order to cover my mouth and nose. Bowen lunged, making it over the rocks. He stuck his dagger directly in the center of its ribs, but it was no use. The dragon let out a roar, the gas cutting off and lingering in the air like a fog. It swiped its tail at Bowen, catching him in the leg, but he somehow stayed standing and ran for me.

The dragon snapped its teeth as Bowen sprinted by, and then he was scooping me up into his arms, running back the way we came. The beast thundered behind us, gaining momentum quickly. We turned corner after corner, but it only got closer with each passing second.

"Bowen," I started.

"I know, Princess. Don't look back," he panted as he sprinted faster, harder, speeding through the tunnels. Magic was stuck to my hands after I'd dropped the majority of it, but I was thankful, as it was our only source of light to see where we were going, my hands glowing as I held on to him.

Despite his command, I kept my eyes on the dragon, my heart racing in my chest. If I was to die, I wanted to look it in the face, not hide. I was weak, not a coward.

We were close to where the rocks had fallen, and we both knew what would come once we reached them. We couldn't fight it off, and the exit was blocked. It'd corner us.

Almost as if an invisible wall had sprouted up out of nowhere, the dragon slammed into it. Its bones clinked together as it impacted whatever was there, its body curling in on itself. It let out a frustrated roar, growling as it shook its head.

"Bowen. Look."

He glanced over his shoulder, stopping in his tracks. He kept me cradled close to his chest as he turned, looking at the dragon, where it stood trapped in the cave. It tried to ram its head into whatever it had run into, but it had no luck getting past whatever was there. It was surely stuck.

Bowen slowly lowered me to my feet, steadying me with a hand on my back as my arm slipped off his shoulder. After another try, the dragon roared in our direction, its head outstretched from its neck, jaw wide. If it hadn't been stopped, we'd be dead right now.

With a defeated huff, it pivoted its giant body around, swishing its tail back and forth as it disappeared into the darkness. With the sight of it, my eyes shot to Bowen's leg—the one that had been hit. "Your leg."

He glanced down at it, all that was left in its wake a small tear in his pants. His skin was untouched. "It's okay. It barely got me."

On the other side of us, a noise that sounded like a rock

being moved echoed through the cave, followed by the wind whistling into the tunnel. We both turned in the direction the sound had come from.

"Someone's moving the rocks," I said, seeing a thin strip of dim, orange light shining on the wall beside us.

I hurried toward where the light was coming from, Bowen close on my heels. My ankle screamed with every step, but I ignored it. We had to get out.

As we rounded the last corner, we found the top half of the wall had been taken down already, flickering lantern light illuminating the men at work removing rocks from the other side.

"Ah, Vulcan *was* telling the truth," Flynt announced over the sound of the wind as he hefted a rock off to the side. It landed with a crash, blistering into multiple pieces, and I flinched.

Bowen stepped to the side of me, his arm brushing mine. "I wouldn't let him know you thought he was lying if I was you."

Flynt snorted. "As if I'd ever do that."

"He's dumb enough that he would," Raiden piped in. I hadn't noticed him there until he moved the rock blocking his view from us. He was taller than Flynt by a few inches. His arms had to be bigger than my thigh, and he moved the rocks like they were little more than a piece of parchment.

From somewhere behind the two of them, a low thud sounded, and the ground shook again. I grabbed Bowen's arm, fearing the cave would collapse.

He looked down at me, concern in his gaze, until he realized why I was scared. He turned to face me completely, blocking me from Flynt and Raiden's view. His hands moved to my neck, and I realized he was readjusting my bandana before fixing it back over my mouth and nose.

"You don't have to be afraid anymore. And don't be fooled

by them," Bowen muttered to me. "They're using strength magic." He did the same to his own mask after he spoke.

"He's just trying to make up for the fact that he couldn't move a few pebbles," Flynt teased, clearly having heard Bowen speak. He and Raiden both had their masks in place, and it seemed the storm was only growing stronger, if that was even possible. It was foolish of me to come out in this, and now they were all dealing with the fallout.

Bowen stood by my side again, keeping us a safe distance back in case any rocks rolled.

"*They have been complaining about the task for over an hour,*" a deep, rough voice said, but it sounded far away. My body tensed with the knowledge that I now recognized it being a dragon that spoke.

Bowen's finger grazed my wrist, but he didn't look my way.

Flynt wiped sweat from his brow, turning toward where the voice came from. "Don't you have anything better to do, like find some poor sheep to eat?"

"*I'm hungry for a different flavor tonight,*" he said casually, as if he was insinuating that one of us was on his menu.

"He won't hurt you," Bowen murmured to me.

"*Don't be so sure,*" the dragon purred back.

"Why don't you go relax until the storm passes? The winds will only get stronger, making it harder to fly," Bowen said, having to raise his voice so the dragon could hear him over the howl.

Something like a chuckle echoed through the cave. "*A small breeze has never been a problem for me.*" Then the sound of wings beating flowed through the tunnel, and I assumed the dragon had taken Bowen's advice.

Bowen left me where I stood to help with the rocks, moving them one by one until we could step over the mound safely. All the while, I watched his back flex under his shirt, his arms straining with each boulder he moved after using the strength vial on himself. He was already strong on his own, but the magic only emphasized it.

Though it seemed as if he disliked me, he'd protected me tonight—covered me with his own body so that I wouldn't be injured by the earthquake, and distracted a dragon dozens of times his size from eating me alive. All of that combined, I wondered why he would do such things. As far as I could tell, making sure I was unharmed wasn't on the top of his to-do list, and yet, he'd shown up here himself, asking me to return to the town. In addition to all of that, he hadn't commanded it. He'd simply *recommended* it.

I had had a choice in the matter. And sure, I'd chosen wrong, but Bowen had given to me what no one ever had before.

A say in what I did.

And I couldn't help but wonder why.

CHAPTER 26

BOWEN

The entire walk back to Deadwood, Auria had insisted she was fine, but I wasn't risking it. Not only had rocks fallen all around us, one or two surely hitting her in the chaos, but the bones dragon had sprayed its toxic gas directly in front of her. She hadn't seemed affected in the cave, but it could still be dormant in her lungs, slowly poisoning her blood if she breathed enough in.

"So it just hit a wall you couldn't see?" Siara asked, reiterating what I'd told her, Flynt, and Raiden multiple times now. We were in the corner of the infirmary, far from any listening ears. I hadn't wanted to leave Auria alone while she was checked out by Doctor Quinn. The citizens of Deadwood listened to me, but I didn't trust they wouldn't try anything with her. She was the daughter of a loathed king, and the people in this town had a liking for vengeance.

I nodded, peeling my gaze away from where Auria sat perched on the edge of a table. Quinn had a finger on her wrist, checking her vitals. She'd already examined her eyes, along with her balance—which was presumably bad due to her already injured ankle—and I assumed her lungs were next. There were two rows of twelve tables each, only a few occupied with patients that had gotten into fights at the saloon or those that had gone out in the dust storm without a face covering and were now suffering the consequences.

"It was chasing us one second, and bashing its skull against some sort of invisible wall the next," I said. My hands were fisted, my palms burning with the memory of Auria in my arms. I hadn't meant to touch her so many times in that cave, but I'd had no choice.

Flynt bit the inside of his cheek in thought. "Do you think the earthquake had anything to do with it being unable to go further? It was a pretty strong one. We felt the aftershock of it down here."

I shook my head, adjusting my arms across my chest. "I don't think so."

"It had to have been there for a while, right? I've never seen a dragon like what you described," Siara said.

"I have," Raiden piped in. "In the mines." Before Raiden had taken residence in Deadwood and become my commander, he had been enslaved in the mines of a kingdom on another continent. He'd tried to kill a guard in order to escape, but had been caught and sentenced to be hung. I was lucky I had found him in his cell when I was over there for a meeting and was able to sneak him out. The way in which he held himself gave me all I needed to know that he wasn't a man who deserved to die for trying to escape cruel conditions. Ever since, we'd looked out for each other. "Dragons decay, but don't die unless by some other force."

It was no secret that dragons couldn't die of old age. They simply kept living until they were killed in battle, ate something poisonous, or some other unfortunate element took them out. Not many lived to see the day their scales wilted off their bones, though.

"You think it's been trapped down there for years, then?" Flynt asked.

I nodded. "To be in that state, decades, at least. If not well over a century."

Flynt's brows pulled together. "And there's no way to get it out?"

"I'm not too sure that it wants out," I said, moving my gaze back to Auria across the room. Quinn seemed to be done with her and was heading my way as Auria spiked up a conversation with the patient she'd been seated beside.

"Bowen," the doctor said, giving a small dip of her chin before stopping a few feet from me. She was tall, freckles dotting the entirety of her pale skin, with bright red hair that fell to her shoulders.

"Doctor Quinn," I greeted. "How is she?"

My friends' attention was focused raptly on her as they waited for her response. I wondered if they hoped for good news as much as I did. Siara grew attached to things—and people—rather quickly, which was what I didn't want. She was far too emotional at times, which would only hurt her more when Auria had to leave. Flynt, on the other hand, didn't want to see harm come to those who didn't deserve it, and Raiden was simply curious. He was never too concerned unless it came to one of the three of us. We were the closest thing he had to a family. So his interest in Auria's health was...suspicious.

Doctor Quinn laced her fingers together in front of her. "She's going to be fine. Her vitals are okay, but she does have a slight wheeze when she breathes, likely due to the gas. I don't believe she inhaled enough for it to affect her much worse than that. Some warm tea and staying indoors until the storm is over will be her best route to a quick recovery."

"Thank you." That was all good. She was going to be fine. Now I could stop worrying about the woman and return to my duties.

She pressed her lips together, eyeing the others before explaining. "She does have the slightest fever, but nothing major. From the adrenaline, possibly. I wouldn't be worried. And her ankle." She pinned her gaze on me. "I gave her a healing vial for the sprain."

I tried not to give a reaction, but I knew she expected me to explain why I hadn't done the same in the first place. Truth was, I didn't know why. I didn't want anyone to suffer, but if I'd given her a healing vial when she had arrived, I'd have had to provide them to her entire group. And the sooner they recovered, the sooner they'd be gone. I'd wanted that, and yet—

I gave a curt nod. "Thank you for taking a look at her."

She dipped her chin. "Of course. Wouldn't want to see her in pain longer than she needs to be, regardless of where she came from." With one last suspicious look at me, she moved back across the room to one of her patients—a brawny man I recognized from the gambling hall. He visited often, and fought even more.

I knew people expected me to treat Auria cruelly due to the past, but it wasn't that. If she had been healed and able to travel, they would have left first thing, taking her back to that castle to be locked away, not to see Serpentine ever again. Her injury was her key to freedom. I was just helping lead her to the lock so the door never shut.

A burst of wind whipped into the room as the door to the infirmary slammed open, then was shoved shut. One of Deadwood's guards rushed over, eyes wide as they landed on me.

"Bowen," Hanklie panted, attempting to catch his breath as he pulled his mask down. "The bridge." He swallowed roughly. "It collapsed."

Raiden went rigid beside me as Siara and Flynt leaned closer, like they might've heard him wrong.

"What do you mean it *collapsed*?" I asked, my voice taking on its authoritative tone flawlessly.

"The bridge to Amosite?" Siara clarified.

Flynt shot her a look. "What other bridge, Siara?"

She glared at him in response.

"Meritum told me. It fell when the earthquake rolled through," Hanklie explained. Meritum was Hanklie's desert dragon.

"The entirety of the bridge?" I asked. That couldn't be possible. The bridge had been standing for centuries, and one earthquake had managed to take it out?

Hanklie nodded. His eyes were red-rimmed from the debris in the air outside. "All of it, sir. Meritum was flying near the chasm when the earthquake hit. He watched it fall."

"Watched what fall?" Auria asked, coming up behind Hanklie.

"The bridge, my lady," Hanklie quickly answered, stepping to the side to give Auria some space to join us.

I inwardly cursed. That was her only way home.

Her eyes went wide, moving from Hanklie to me. "The bridge is gone?"

"Let's not jump to conclusions here," I said hesitantly. "I'll send Vulcan that way to check it out. I'm sure it's all a misunderstanding."

Hanklie shook his head. "All due respect, sir, but Meritum showed me."

"Showed you?" Auria repeated.

Hanklie nodded frantically, his hair sticking up every which way from the wind. "Flew me right near it. On the desert side, of course."

"You can ride dragons?" Auria exclaimed. She looked pale,

whether from the information or the chaos of the caves, I wasn't sure. But this wasn't helping her recovery.

"Hanklie," I cut in, giving no room for argument in my tone. "Thank you for reporting this to me, but I can take it from here."

He nodded. "Yes, sir. I'll be on patrol if you need any more information." He headed back out the way he had come, leaving Auria gawking at me.

Everything was crashing around her all at once. Today was too much, and I could see it in the bags under her eyes and the way she looked like she was trying her damndest to process everything.

"Bowen," Siara started, coming closer to me.

"Not now, Siara," I snapped, and she backed off.

Auria looked like she'd been struck by lightning, her mind practically spinning in her eyes.

"Would you like me to walk you home?" I asked, ignoring the others as Siara, Flynt, and Raiden started mumbling about what the bridge being down meant.

She blinked a few times, and in the flickering lantern light, her skin looked like it had a sheen to it. With a small fever, she shouldn't get worked up. It'd only make it worse. If she wanted to stay and discuss it, that'd be her choice, but I wanted to give her the option.

Auria gave a small nod in response, the green around her pupils looking brighter than before. Without thinking, I reached for her face covering and pulled it up over her nose, then did the same with mine.

I didn't have to say the words to the others for them to know we'd talk more about this later. Doing it in the infirmary wasn't the most ideal place, and while the bridge falling caused problems for all of us, it could wait.

I held the door open for Auria, letting her pass through. As soon as the wind hit her, the hairs that had come free from her braid whipped around her face. She was wearing a dress that left much more of her skin showing than I'd seen before, which had been a surprise at dinner. As King Tenere's daughter, I would have thought she'd prefer to stay as covered as possible. It seemed the princess was more daring than I'd originally thought.

We walked in silence. It was no use to try to speak over the howling storm. Dust kicked up everywhere, bits of magic caught in the mess whizzing past our ears like whistles on the wind. Magic took its form in many different ways. It flowed through rock like a stream or was hard like stone itself. Some of it gathered in big chunks or large rivulets, and others were so small, the common eye could hardly see it. Sometimes it hummed or had a melody much like a flute, or it was quiet, stagnant. It was like a living creature in that way—taking on different personalities. Even magic of the same type behaved differently, depending where it was found. Most of it varied based on the region it originated, like fire magic from the underground mines near Devil's Peak or healing magic from the Hollows. Most was found in mountains, caves, or underground, or where it would sometimes form near bodies of water. It found its home and where it wanted to grow, and it was respected. At least, it had been, until humans used it for the wrong reasons. There was no mistaking the inky black current of dark magic, the substance itself looking as if it was on a search to destroy, weaken.

We approached the house Auria was staying in, her dress moving wildly around her boots as she trudged up the steps. She opened the door, and I waited for her to disappear inside, but rather than closing it behind her, she faced me.

"Would you like to come in?" she asked, raising her voice over the storm.

I hesitated a moment, taken back by her offer, then nodded. I'd expected her to want to be as far away from me as possible, not to continue our time together. I stepped inside and made sure the door clicked shut before turning to find she'd barely moved away. Our chests were now mere inches from each other.

I couldn't see the bottom half of her face due to the mask, but her eyes spoke volumes. She was perplexed by what had happened, while I was confused for an entirely different reason.

Frustrated with the fact that I could get lost in her so easily, I stepped away, pulling my bandana down. "How is your ankle?"

She untied her own, holding it in front of her with both hands. "Better with the healing vial Doctor Quinn gave me."

"Good," I replied.

"You said the dragons wouldn't harm me," she started.

"They won't."

"But the one in the caves, it seemed like it wanted to."

I moved to the small living room off the foyer, taking a seat on the couch. Explaining this to her when she had not a clue about any of it was not how I had expected to spend my night, but I should've known she'd be curious.

Auria followed suit, taking a seat next to me.

"You've just found out your only way home is destroyed, and you're more concerned about the dragon in the cave," I stated. I wanted to give her answers but...I also wanted to distract her. See how far I could push her until that perfect mask snapped.

She gave no response. I had her figured out.

I moved my gaze to hers. "You don't truly care about returning home."

Her chest rose as she inhaled deeply. "Of course I do."

The corner of my mouth pulled up in a smirk, and I set a hand on the cushion behind her, leaning into her space. "You secretly have a little rebellious side, don't you, Princess?"

Her eyes bounced between mine, her lips parting slightly. "I'm only curious about the world."

My gaze fell to her neck, drifting down from her collarbone to the swell of her breasts. The dress left little to the imagination. It reminded me of how soft her skin had felt under my hands in the cave, how despite the danger we had been faced with, something inside me had awakened, perking its head up in attention while my heart rate skyrocketed with our touch.

"What else are you curious about?"

Her eyes narrowed the slightest bit, her breath quickening. "What are *you* curious about?" she snapped back.

Fuck, what was I doing? She was a Tenere, the precious, protected daughter of Amosite, and I was...me.

"Oh, Princess," I murmured, unknowingly shifting closer. "There are so many things I want to discover, but none of it has to do with the continent, and all of it has to do with you."

This. This was my distraction from her peppering of questions. The less she knew here, the better. Our plan had to be kept secret, and I didn't need her poking around.

I didn't admit that distracting her made me feel things I shouldn't ever dream of feeling for a woman like her. From our first interaction in Amosite to now, I couldn't help the intrigue that lit me like a match every time she was around... The same flame that touched both me *and* my magic.

Our lips were inches apart now. I could smell the lilac soap wafting off her skin, and my tongue betrayed me by craving a taste of its own.

In a flash, she stood, backing away from the couch and me. "I know what you're doing."

Casually, I leaned back with an arm over the armrest, letting my knees fall open as I looked up at her. "What's that?"

"You're distracting me, just like everyone else does when I want to know more." Her voice was thick with emotion, betrayal clinging to the end of her sentence, almost like she expected something else from me. A part of me hated myself for it. She deserved her freedom, the knowledge that everyone else was privy to, and here I was, hiding it from her just like the rest.

I sat forward, setting my elbows on my knees. "You're right."

She paused, taken back by my admittance. I got the feeling she wasn't told that very often in the castle.

"You're admitting to veering the conversation off course?"

I nodded. "Ask me one question, and I'll answer."

"Why did the dragon want to kill us?" she asked.

I was surprised she again brought the discussion back to that.

"Dragons that live longer than they should sometimes lose their mercy." There was no easy way to explain it.

A crease formed between her brows. "Longer than they should?"

"That's more than one question, Princess," I warned.

Her lips pressed into a thin line, determination clear in her gaze.

I sighed, giving in all too easily. "They don't die naturally," I answered. "They have to be killed in some way. That one we saw is called a bones dragon. He seems to be stuck down there, likely awaiting his death."

Auria's eyes fell to the ground as she mumbled, "Death would be its freedom."

I watched her. Her expression was blank, but her eyes screamed with...pain. So silent, so hidden, that I hadn't seen it before. But now, it flared bright, like it wanted someone to recognize it. Like it needed someone to relieve it.

Was she insinuating...?

"Princess." The word was a quiet caress.

She shook her head, blinking away unshed tears. "It's true."

"Death is not freedom, but only another sort of prison. You don't wish that."

More had to be going on inside that castle than what met the eye. I was certain of it now.

"The bridge collapsing is not the most tragic thing." Now *she* was the one deflecting.

I got to my feet, eliminating the space between us to set a finger under her chin, lifting her head so she'd look at me. I couldn't help that my thumb ghosted over her skin. "Such a change of heart since you arrived. What will your fiancé think of this new you?"

Her lips pressed together. I'd ticked her off just like I wanted. She needed her mind out of whatever dark place it'd traveled to, and I'd gladly be the one to get her out of it while I could.

Rather than go at it with me, she changed the subject once again. "What about the barrier the bones dragon couldn't cross?"

What a shame. I quite liked the flame that ignited in her eyes when she came alive.

I dropped my hand from her. "That, I don't have an answer to."

"So you don't know everything," she surmised.

I quirked a brow. "Careful, Princess."

Her eyes turned curious. "What is your secret?"

I cocked my head in question.

"In the caves, you said to pretend we knew each other's secrets. What is yours?"

"Next question."

Her bottom lip pouted out with a frown. The look was... torture. "That's not fair."

My shoulder lifted in the smallest shrug. "The world was not built on a balanced scale, I'm afraid."

She set her hands on her hips. "Fine. What does the collapsed bridge mean for my people?"

I began to take slow steps, circling where she stood in the center of the living room. "That you cannot cross."

Her arms unconsciously fell back to her sides. "Can't dragons get us across the chasm?"

A low chuckle came out of me. "Have you ever seen a dragon in Amosite?"

Her brows pinched together as she thought on that. "Well, no. But I assumed I hadn't seen one because I can't leave the castle."

I took note of her phrasing. Her sequestering in the castle was not voluntary, it seemed. "Dragons won't cross the chasm."

"Why not?"

I shrugged, continuing my prowl around her. It was something we hadn't been able to figure out for decades. "You ask any of them, and they won't do it."

"Perhaps the bones dragon would let us pass," she thought aloud.

I stopped behind her, eyeing the back of her head. "Are you searching for a way to die?"

"It'd be trading one prison for another, like you said. Maybe I truly cannot be free."

Sadness laced her tone, and it lit something inside of me I didn't want to feel. That I *couldn't* feel. Not when it came to Auria Tenere.

"Freedom will not find you if you choose to stay in that

mindset. If you're so content with trading one prison for another, why haven't you?"

"I guess I've had some semblance of hope." She shook her head, her gaze falling to the ground. "What a foolish thing."

My hands flexed at my sides. There was always hope. She just had to keep her faith.

My voice quieted the slightest bit. "It's quite brave, having hope. After all, when the horrors of the world are no match for the demons in our heads, the true battle is not the physical, but the mental. And you, Princess, are beating all odds."

A burst of air blew through her nose. "I'd hardly say I'm beating it."

"You're alive, aren't you?" I asked.

She nodded.

"I'd say you've already won, then."

She turned in place, tilting her head up to look me in the eyes. Hers were the color of the leaves in the forest as the bands in the night sky reflected silver light off the tree canopy. They were magnificent, and I feared I'd get lost in them if I stared too long, but something about Auria made me want to keep looking.

"We'll see about that when my father finds a way to Deadwood."

I dipped my chin. "Ah, yes. You mentioned there was a deadline. Surely King Tenere will understand your delay with the bridge being destroyed."

She let out a small laugh, but it was void of all emotion. "If there is one thing my father can't do, it's understand that something didn't go his way."

I folded my hands together behind my back. "He's about to be in for a treat, then, isn't he?"

The corners of her lips twitched, hinting at a smile, and my job here was done.

By the looks of it, Auria was conflicted between staying on her father's side and going after what she truly wanted. It was a choice she'd have to make, but without the entire truth, I feared she might choose wrong. But it wasn't my decision whether she could be privy to the plan at hand.

There were more forces at play here than just me and Auria, and despite my loathing of her father, I couldn't put her at risk.

She deserved more than to be caught in the crossfire, and I'd make sure she remained unharmed while in Deadwood. But once she was back in Amosite, I couldn't protect her.

She'd have to learn to do it herself.

CHAPTER 27

AURIA

The morning after the incident in the caves, my lungs were already feeling better. There'd been a slight burning in my chest, but Doctor Quinn had assured me it was just the wheeze that would clear up soon enough. My ankle no longer hurt to put pressure on, the healing vial having sped up the process immensely. I was grateful for that as I put all my weight on it to swing my other leg over the bench at the breakfast table in the dining hall.

I'd felt queasy before breakfast and dipped into one of the shops on my way, refilling an ice vial near one of the chests holding an array of meats. I was already starting to feel a bit less sick as the time between using my magic lengthened, and I hoped it was due to my body getting used to not using it as often.

Our guards had retrieved their breakfast before returning to their house, opting not to sit with us. I wondered if it was because they were humiliated over the attack or they simply didn't feel comfortable in Deadwood. Either way, they weren't doing much protecting.

Lander sent me a wink from where he stood in line behind Paxon, the two of them filling their plate with an abundance of baked goods, fresh eggs, and herb-roasted ham. I'd been taking to eating at the house, but decided if I was going to make the best of my last days on this trip, I might as well do my best to enjoy the company of others as much as I could.

Paxon had found somewhere to launder his only outfit, the previous dirt stains no longer visible on the dark green fabric. He stuck out like a sore thumb among the people of Deadwood, though I assumed that was his goal. His ego would never opt to blend in with the masses.

Paxon didn't spare me a glance as he seemed to be intently listening to the conversation just ahead of him, the set of his mouth strained. Lander reached to grab a pastry off the wood-carved platter to the side of Paxon, but then Paxon moved. All of a sudden, Paxon had the back of one of Deadwood's guards to the buffet table, his fist gripping the man's black shirt.

The commotion pulled everyone's attention to the two of them as Paxon got in the man's face, shaking him. "What the fuck did you just say?"

The guard seemed completely calm, and then I realized it was Hanklie, the same one who'd come into the infirmary the night before with the news of the bridge collapsing.

Two of the guards who'd been with Hanklie in line, a man and a woman, stepped forward like they were going to intervene, but Hanklie held up a hand, stopping them.

"I said your precious way home is gone, and you're stuck here," Hanklie answered with a wicked grin.

His cockiness was going to cost him, if the reddening of Paxon's face gave any indication. I couldn't let him make a scene by hurting one of Deadwood's own. What if we were kicked out? Forced to survive in the elements, now with no way back to Amosite? After Paxon's threat, I didn't want to temporarily stay in Torbernite. It'd only give him the upper hand.

I quickly stood from the bench, flinging my leg over before hurrying to the scene.

"You have five seconds to tell me what the fuck that means," Paxon seethed.

Hanklie let out a chuckle, despite the awkward position he was in. "I don't answer to you, filthy scum."

Then Paxon started counting, and I picked up the pace. I weaved between benches and chairs, people standing about with trays of food, all watching as Paxon ruined our chances of surviving out here and put a target on all our backs.

"Five," Paxon said, gripping Hanklie's shirt tighter, who only rolled his eyes in response. "Four."

"You royal shits are always so fucking dramatic," Hanklie spit, his slight accent hanging on thick to every word.

"Three."

I elbowed past two people, careful not to dump the plates in their hands.

"Two."

I had ten feet to go. Nine. Eight.

"One."

Paxon reared his arm back, and I jumped for him just in time to hook my hands around his elbow and hold it back. But he didn't bother to look at who grabbed him as he shoved me away, and I easily lost my grip. My foot slipped, and I stumbled to the left, right toward Lander. He dropped his plate to grab my arm, the ceramic landing on the floor in a crash, but in doing so, I slipped on the eggs and careened forward, landing right on my knees in the mess of berries, pastries, and other assortments of food.

I squeezed my eyes shut against the burst of pain in my knees, Lander's hand still gripped tight on my elbow. I partly braced myself for the sound of Paxon's fist landing true on Hanklie, but surprisingly, no such sound came. Instead, a familiar voice intervened.

"Hit one of us, and I'll throw you to the fucking wolves before you can so much as blink," Raiden threatened, his voice full of lethal intent, like he'd take great pleasure in doing what he promised.

I opened my eyes to find Raiden's hand dwarfing Paxon's fist, having stopped the hit inches before he landed it. Siara stood beside Raiden, eyes peeled, arms crossed, and a hip popped out. But as soon as her gaze met mine, she softened, dropping her arms to her sides.

Fuck, I didn't want their pity. I just didn't want to get kicked out of the one place we had found refuge for the time being. We'd gotten so lucky ending up here, and Paxon was ruining that. Was that his intention, so we had no choice but to go to Torbernite?

Siara moved past Paxon, making it a point to bump him with her elbow as she did. She bent to grab my other arm, she and Lander helping me off the messy ground.

"This backwoods hick said the godsdamned bridge collapsed," Paxon defended, like that gave him the right to punch a fucking guard.

Raiden shoved him back by his fist, causing Paxon to let go of Hanklie and stumble backwards two steps. Siara bent at the waist, doing her best to brush the food off my pants, as if two men weren't about to rip out each other's throats behind her.

"That's because it did," Raiden said. "And if you want to fight someone over the fear you feel in being stuck in our town" —he stepped toward Paxon, looking all the more intimidating —"you fight me." He leaned in, muscled arms flexing. "Little secret, I don't go easy on pathetic royals."

Satisfied with her work, Siara straightened, standing at my side as we both watched Paxon try to contain his anger.

"We were to cross that bridge in a matter of days," Paxon hissed.

"You think we dropped the bridge on purpose?" Raiden accused.

Paxon's hand flexed at his side, like maybe he'd gotten the bright idea to punch the fucking commander of Deadwood's army. "I don't know what this town full of outlaws is doing, but I'm not sticking around to find out."

Lander spoke up now, unable to take any more of this. I was getting to that point, too, if it weren't for the humiliation building in my core. "The guards still need time to heal, Paxon. We're not leaving."

Paxon spun on his brother, not sparing me so much as a glance. "You don't call the shots."

"And you do?" Siara quipped.

Paxon's nostrils flared as he pinned a glare on her, but rather than continue the argument, he turned and stormed out of the dining hall, leaving the mess and havoc he created behind.

Once he was out the doors, Raiden checked on Hanklie, ensuring he was okay before turning to me. It seemed everyone's eyes were on me, watching to make sure I wouldn't crumble. I'd been shoved, fell in food, and was now standing here looking more like a fool than someone who'd tried to protect one of their own.

Though I wasn't wearing a corset, the pants and shirt I had on suddenly started feeling all too tight, the walls suffocating as they boxed us in. I needed air. To be alone with no eyes on me. To change out of this godsdamned outfit, and stop reeking of breakfast and shame.

"I need a minute," I quickly muttered before spinning

around and finding a door at the back of the dining hall. I beelined for it, shoving through and into the warm air.

As the door closed, I pressed my back up against the building, setting a hand on my chest to find my heart was beating erratically. I took a deep breath, then another, counting to four in between. I let my eyelids drift shut as my head lolled back against the warm wooden slats, the rays of the sun seeping into my skin like an answered whisper through the wind that still howled.

Was this really the life I wanted to go back to in Amosite? Being talked over, having no power over anything, treated like I didn't even exist?

Lander at least wasn't being irrational about being stuck in Deadwood, much unlike his brother. It was a small positive out of an ocean of negatives.

"I didn't think food fights were your scene, Princess, but you continue to surprise me," Bowen said, startling me from my moment of calm.

My head snapped up, finding him standing a few feet from me wearing leathers, a belt full of daggers wrapped around his hips. "Bowen," I breathed, adjusting my stance.

"Everything okay?" he asked, the spot in the center of his forehead creasing.

I gulped, nodding as I pulled a hand through my hair. "Yeah. Of course. Why wouldn't it be?"

He stepped forward, and my gaze caught on a folded piece of parchment in his hand. "Well, you're standing out here looking like you've seen a sandwalker, you're covered in food, and"—his eyes fell to my pants—"you're bleeding."

My focus shot down to my legs at his observation, thinking he was playing a trick on me. Through the mess of food, I couldn't tell what he was referring to. "It's just berries."

He shoved the parchment in the back pocket of his pants

before he walked closer, only stopping once he was directly in front of me. Then, this man dropped to his knee before me, *again*, and wrapped delicate fingers around my thigh. I braced my hands on the building behind me, staring down as he prodded my skin through my pants.

A breath hissed between my teeth as he hit a sore spot.

"Right there," he murmured, dropping a hand to retrieve a dagger from his waist.

My eyes widened. "What are you doing?"

"Checking your wound," he stated, bringing the blade to my pants.

I tried to pull my leg back, but he held it firm with his other hand. The way he kept me rooted before him sent tingles flowing up my spine.

"You're not going to dig in it, are you?"

He paused with the tip of the blade pressed against the fabric, as if he had so much control over the steel that he knew it wouldn't pierce unless he wished it to. His eyes met mine. "No, Auria. Not unless I have to."

Before I could protest once more, he sliced through the material. I waited for the bite of pain to follow, but none came. He studied me carefully. "You think I'd hurt you?"

"I don't know what to think," I replied honestly. He was hot and cold with me, day and night. One minute, he was behaving as if he was irritated with my existence, and the next, he was protecting me from falling rocks and an angry, decayed dragon.

He raised a shoulder before moving his attention back to my leg. "Your opinion of me hasn't changed."

"Should it have?" I asked.

With a small portion of my leg now exposed, he sheathed the dagger, pulling out a healing vial next. "You can think whatever you'd like, whether it's wrong or right."

I let out a snort as he uncapped the vial.

"Something funny, Princess?"

"You act so kind, yet you seem so..." I trailed off, trying to think of the right word.

"Charming?"

"Pernicious," I filled in.

He frowned, dribbling a small portion of the magic over my minor cut that very easily would have healed on its own.

"You think I'm evil," he stated.

"I don't know what to think," I repeated.

He looked up at me again, and I forced myself to look away, my knees threatening to buckle with the intensity of his focus solely on me. "Tell me what you'd like to think, and why you're refusing to allow yourself to do so."

I swallowed, hating how he'd just called me out so easily.

"I'd like to think you're good," I answered honestly. "But everyone I know doesn't seem to think the same, so why should I?"

He stood, his towering frame pulling my gaze back to him. I tilted my chin up, the back of my head resting against the building. "Siara, Raiden, Flynt—they don't think I'm good?"

"You know that's not what I mean."

He pocketed the vial, not moving to give me space. "Do others always influence you so easily?"

I scrunched my nose. "No."

He looked down to adjust the sleeves of his leather jacket around his wrists, his fingers brushing my stomach as he did. "Then tell me what you really think of me."

I tried not to breathe as much to keep my stomach tighter in an attempt to keep his touch away from me, but I was kidding myself. I was enjoying this. The little grazes of his fingertips. The way his body dwarfed mine. I didn't want it to stop.

"A lady doesn't share her secrets so easily," I replied, tilting my chin up in defiance.

A smirk pulled at the corner of his mouth. "It's a good thing no secrets are safe around me." His eyes pinned mine in place. "Haven't we been over this, Princess?" He leaned closer, setting a hand on the wall beside my head, and my lips parted on their own accord. I was pressed against the wall at this point, but I didn't want to move, even if given the chance. "It seems to me you want to keep me here—dodging my questions even though you have the answers."

"I don't." I attempted to sound convincing with my words, but failed.

"Then tell me what you're thinking."

My eyelids fluttered as my gaze skipped to his mouth for the flash of a second. Why did I want to know what his lips felt like on mine, and why did I care to find out how he tasted?

"I'm thinking about the paper you shoved in your back pocket," I blurted, needing to say anything but what I was truly thinking. He did *not* need to know where my mind had just gone.

He arched a brow, dropping his hand back to his side. "Is that so?"

I nodded, humming my response. "Mhmm."

He studied me, knowing damn well I was lying. "I guess it goes both ways, then." He looked to the side, eyeing the door I'd come out of before moving his gaze back to me. "A man doesn't share his secrets so easily."

He turned away, moving toward the door to the dining hall. "I'll have Siara replace the pants for you. Get home safe, Auria." Then he disappeared inside, leaving me standing there with my heart racing for an entirely different reason now.

CHAPTER 28

AURIA

The storm had finally let up, raining sunshine down on the town. Lander had gotten over his frustration at being placed in a separate house once he'd heard Bowen had helped me in the caves, and after he saw Siara and Raiden had stood up for me in the dining hall yesterday morning. Paxon was less inclined to change his opinion, as I'd expected after his stunt with Hanklie.

Lander had visited last night to check on me, and despite the late hour he'd stopped by, I'd found it at least comforting to know he cared in the slightest. He'd likely spent his day gambling, the scent of cigar smoke clinging to him giving his whereabouts away. With a brother like Paxon, I didn't blame Lander for using it as a stress reliever.

The choice Paxon had presented me with loomed over my head like a lingering cloud. I got the feeling that with the way he'd held me over the chasm, controlling whether I lived or fell to my death in that moment, if I chose wrong, he'd make sure I paid for it.

His threat hung clear in the air, and since that day at the

chasm, it was all I could think about. My mind was once again a prison with my thoughts, though this time, I had a choice. And while I didn't typically have those, I wasn't feeling very grateful for it now, rather wishing I didn't have a decision to make altogether.

Oh, how the irony was excruciating.

I assumed Bowen was under the impression that I was doing well here in Deadwood, aside from the little spurts of tension, and yet, my head was darker than any cave, deeper than any chasm, overflowing with spiraling thoughts I couldn't keep straight. I wasn't weak only in my body, but also my mind. I couldn't get a grip on it, even when faced with a life or death decision. What strength was found in that?

A knock sounded on the door, and I walked over from where I was seated in my living room. I opened it to find Lander standing with his hands tucked into his coat pockets, much like the night before. His jacket had somehow survived the attack, and though I was certain he wore borrowed clothes underneath, he made sure to wear the colors of his kingdom every day.

"Busy?" he asked with a raised brow.

"What would I possibly be busy with?" I hadn't meant to sound so snappy, but I was stressed. The deadline to be back in Amosite was just around the corner, and with the bridge down, I knew we wouldn't make it.

"Aside from some meals and nearly getting yourself killed in a cave, you've been holed up in this house. Might I interest you in a tour?"

A laugh escaped me. "You're not from Deadwood. How might you give me a tour?"

With a barely-there shrug, he said, "Well, with not much else to do, I've come to find I'm quite the tourist."

I raised a single brow. "And that makes you qualified to show me around?"

He gave a mock bow. "It'd be my honor."

I rolled my eyes, but stepped outside to join him. After a quick look at the clothes I'd chosen this morning to be sure they were appropriate, I closed the door. It was a warm day, but the knee-length dress wasn't suffocating. For a short stroll, I'd be fine.

We walked alongside each other in the direction of the main strip through town. I was thankful Paxon hadn't accompanied him, as my answer to tag along surely would have been much different if he had. With the way Paxon watched me, I wanted to stay far away from him if I could help it. That thought in mind, I figured the easy answer to his ultimatum would be not to choose Paxon's offer, but to continue on with my marriage to Lander. It was the safer option of the two, but something made me believe I'd live to regret it.

I glanced at Lander as we walked. "May I ask you a personal question?"

"Go ahead," he replied.

"What's your power?"

"Power?"

I nodded. "Everyone has them, don't they?" It's what my father had told me growing up, but it was so personal to each person that they kept it a secret. It was why I couldn't talk about my own.

"Humans don't have magic. We mine for it," he said matter-of-factly.

That couldn't be right. Maybe he was just confused by how I had phrased it. "Right, but aside from the magic in the earth. Everyone surely has their own power."

He shook his head. "Fae did, but humans have never."

My steps nearly faltered as we continued walking, his words

blowing apart the fragments of my mind. Was he keeping it a secret, thinking my father wouldn't want me to discuss this either? Or was he being serious?

"Why?" he asked, pulling me from the spiral I was surely headed toward.

I kept my focus on the ground ahead of me. "Just curious."

With my response, he thankfully dropped it. I wanted to question him further, but also didn't want to raise alarm bells. What if he thought I was going insane, coming up with theories and losing my mind being outside of Amosite?

We turned onto the main street to find people walking about every which way. A few children were playing with marbles in the dirt, and on the porch beside them sat an elderly woman patching a hole in a piece of clothing. Guards clad in all leather with protective padding stitched into their outfits stood outside buildings, a few speaking with townspeople in casual conversation. It was unlike what I'd seen in Silicate during my brief visit, where they didn't correspond with the citizens. They simply did their job and kept everyone in order.

The sizzle of meat on a grill sounded from the market as a man stood outside cooking. A woman with graying hair emerged from the open door to the store to hand him a wooden bowl of what seemed to be more marinated protein.

"Fae were people, like us?" I asked Lander, clearly unable to drop what he'd said.

He nodded as we continued on our way. Three horses were tied out front of the next establishment, their riders somewhere inside what looked to be some sort of repair shop. With a quick peek inside the open door, I saw hats, saddles, and other leather items strewn about on shelves and racks, giving the impression they repaired all sorts of things in there.

"In some of the books I've read, they portray them as beasts able to subdue humans. Very few talk of them being just like us. Normal looking, civil," Lander supplied.

"What do the others describe them as?"

He tilted his head in thought, the sun beating down on his lightly freckled cheek. "Monsters. There are drawings of them with horns of all shapes and sizes, pointed ears, fangs. It's hard to believe creatures like that walked our land once."

A woman with dark blue hair tied up in a high ponytail passed us, her narrowed gaze trained on me. She passed without a word, her look anything but comforting.

"Do you believe the stories?" I asked Lander, shaking off the shiver her gaze elicited.

He shrugged. "Hard to trust anything written in those books when anyone can get their hands on them. I guess I'm more of a *believe it when I see it* type of guy. What about you?"

I watched as a plume of dirt rose up in the air as a horse pawed at the ground on the other side of the street. "I never know what to believe anymore."

We stopped outside of a dark red building, the paint chipping off in various places, revealing sun-bleached wood and spots of decay.

"This is my stop," he said, looking up at the sign above the door.

"Barter's Hell?" I read aloud. I guessed the tour was over.

He smiled, though it shone with a hint of shame. "Not much to do in this run-down town."

"I wouldn't tell the residents that," I advised.

"I'll chalk it up to my bad habits, then."

"That was more like a stroll than a tour," I joked, not really caring if he showed me every building or simply kept me company for a time.

He shrugged, a hint of a smile pulling at his mouth. "I never said it'd be an eventful tour."

"Can I come with?" I had nothing else to do but aimlessly walk around, and it might be fun to try my hand at a game or two.

His smile fell as he eyed me. "You don't peg me as the gambling type."

I shrugged. "One can always learn."

He hesitated a moment before opening the rickety door and waving me in. "After you, my lady."

Excitement rang through my veins as I stepped over the threshold. Musty air and the pungent smell of ale hit my nose, the combination only lighting my curiosity like a match. The dark room was littered with tables, men and women alike sitting on barstools and worn chairs. At our appearance, heads swiveled our way. A few raised their noses at me as Lander led us through the maze of the bar, and I did my best to keep my eyes downcast, as if I was worried about my footing. Granted, the floor was quite a mess, so stepping over spilled alcohol or shards of glass was necessary.

"Would you like a drink?" Lander asked as we rounded the far end of the bar.

I felt compelled to decline, but something about being in Deadwood, in this gambling den, turned me into someone else entirely. "Sure."

He ordered two drinks, sliding one in front of me as he paid. Before walking off, I took a sip, my nose instantly scrunching at the pungent taste.

"Deadwood likes their alcohol strong," Lander said, a tilt to his lips at my reaction. Since being here, he'd grown a slight shadow along his jaw, the blond hair growing in quick.

"You've been here that many times already to know that?"

Once we got to the back of the bar, he held a door open, and just in his casualness with finding the entrance, it confirmed what I'd thought. He knew this place like the back of his hand.

"I've a curious mind," he said as I passed.

The next room was dark, the windows—all two of them—covered in black cloth. Smoke hung in little clouds, swirling through the tables in the musky air. Men and women were scattered about, playing games of poker. A few of them had ink that swirled up their necks, some with designs climbing so high that they disappeared under their hair. Large men full of muscle and stern expressions stood around, keeping an eye on the competitions. I didn't want to find out why their presence was necessary.

Some of the men had women perched on their knees with a delicate touch to their chests or shoulders, keeping them company while they puffed on cigars and played their cards. It was hard to imagine Lander as one of them, but I remembered it was the gambling he was addicted to. Not the girls.

Naturally, I would've been put off by the murky scent enveloping the establishment, but I welcomed it with a deep inhale. Though I instantly regretted it, I didn't hate the smell. It was different than I was used to, and for that, I welcomed it.

"Ah, Lander," a man said from one of the tables.

We both turned in his direction, finding a pudgy middle-aged man puffing on a cigar, watching us along with the rest of his table. By the looks of them, it seemed their game had just ended.

"Perkins," Lander replied. "Great day so far?"

"It would be if you'd pay up already," Perkins huffed, his salt-and-pepper mustache moving as he spoke.

"I'm working on it," Lander said rather boldly, as if it was some kind of joke.

Another man spoke up across from Perkins. "Care to make up for it in a game, Bular?"

Lander held his arms out. "It's why I'm here, isn't it?"

An unsettling grin spread across the man's mouth as his

gaze moved to me. "And who's the pretty lady you brought with you today?"

"My fiancée, Auria," Lander answered.

All eyes in the room faced us—no, faced *me*—and Perkins stood from his chair, scooting it back to get his belly past the table. "A game in the back, then."

Lander set a hand on my lower back, guiding me past the tables to follow after Perkins, the man who'd spoken to Lander, and another man with brunet hair. From behind, the latter looked rather fit with a sculpted back and his hair mussed, the top sticking up in odd spots. He shoved his sleeves up to his elbows, revealing a cacophony of black swirls etched into his skin. My movements stiffened at the sight.

He was a thief, just like the rest of them.

As we walked, Lander leaned close to my ear. "That's Crass," Lander murmured, nodding in the direction of the man who'd spoken to him. "And Nemin." He gestured toward the brunet.

"You owe them money?" I asked quietly.

He tossed his head back and forth. "Not exactly."

Before I could ask what he meant by that, we entered a small, more damp room. The air hung thick, and with the flick of a hand from Perkins, the lanterns hanging from the walls and above the table lit, casting a dim amber glow throughout the room.

With a hard swallow and a deep breath to center myself, I followed them toward the table in the middle of the room.

CHAPTER 29

BOWEN

The day after Paxon's outburst before breakfast, I decided I couldn't sit by any longer. With the storm finally ebbing, I had things I needed to attend to.

Things like figuring out why the fuck that bones dragon hit an invisible sort of wall and couldn't pass through it.

Raiden had given me the rundown on what had happened during breakfast to cause Auria to be standing outside covered in food and, very clearly, upset. Meanwhile, Siara had wanted to find Paxon and rip his dick off—her words, not mine—for shoving Auria. His manhood—again, her words, though I wholly agreed—didn't deserve to be intact after his elbow made contact with her.

The moment I had seen Auria standing there with her eyes squeezed shut and her body being held up by the wall, I couldn't have kept going.

No, Auria was the only thing that had mattered in that moment.

"We're going to the caves," I said to Vulcan as I rounded his front leg in the meadow and grabbed one of his scales to heft myself up his body.

Is that the brightest idea, given you and the girl were just nearly killed in there? Vulcan asked, judgment blazing in his tone as it rang through my mind.

"I need to figure out why that dragon couldn't pass through that barrier in the caves." I settled on his back and adjusted my face covering before he took flight with a huff.

His massive wings beat hard against the calming air, and I squinted my eyes against the onslaught of wind as we took off.

Let me guess, I am to be your test subject, Vulcan said.

"If you can fit in the cave, that'd be helpful." Despite his clear reluctance at the idea of it, he'd have no choice. I needed to figure this out.

It took longer than usual to reach the mountain due to the random bursts of wind slamming into Vulcan on our way. Once we made it, Vulcan circled before landing on the rockslide, finding a spot right outside the opening of the cave. His talons scrambled for purchase, digging into the loose boulders.

This is not smart, Vulcan chastised, his grip slipping on one of the rocks. Dragons were strong, but their size wasn't always ideal.

"Scared?" I asked as I descended his muscled leg.

For a being as small as you, yes.

I chuckled. "Always so judgmental."

A burst of steam hit my back as I climbed the boulders, Vulcan close behind in case I lost my footing. I wouldn't, but the sentiment still stood.

Once we reached the mouth of the cave, I peered inside, narrowing my eyes against the endless pit of black to be sure the bones dragon hadn't made it through since we had left.

When no form took shape, I entered, walking a few feet in before turning around to see if Vulcan could fit. He ducked his massive head, bending his neck and curling his body in on itself.

This is not how I wished to spend my day, he huffed, just barely making it through the entrance.

I turned, continuing on my way. "You complain a lot for a dragon."

You demand a lot for a tiny being, he retorted, trying to lift his neck but only resulting in hitting the rocky ceiling.

Bits of loose debris rained down around me from the impact, but I ignored it. "Commenting a lot on my size today. Feeling a little self-conscious?"

No, but I am a tad hungry.

"If we get stuck in here, I give you full permission to eat me."

Really?

He sounded too hopeful.

I shot a glare back at him.

"No."

We walked at a slow pace to accommodate for the awkward position Vulcan was in, and once we reached the spot I remembered seeing the bones dragon last, I held my hand up for him to stop. Claw marks dug into the ground before me, evidence of where the dragon had struggled to get through but had no luck.

Please, do tell what your plan is, Vulcan spoke up, his voice vibrating through my mind.

I stepped to the side, gesturing at the empty space. "Try to get through."

His bored gaze moved from me to the vast nothingness and back again, all the while I stared at him.

You are serious.

"I am."

With a sigh, Vulcan moved. I pressed my back up against

the wall to give him space to fit. As soon as his nose was near the claw marks, he stopped, but not of his own accord. He shook his head against the impact of whatever his muzzle ran into.

He tried again, shoving his forehead into the invisible wall.

Still, no luck.

"Does it hurt at all? Maybe a burn?"

No. Just a wall like any other.

I stepped around his massive foot, holding my arm out and successfully passing through the barrier. "Can you see it or is it nonexistent to you, too?"

Nothing is there. It only prevents me from passing.

It must be that way for every dragon, then. Much like the barrier over the chasm, preventing their entrance to Amosite.

"Have you experienced anything like this before?" I asked, stepping over the claw marks etched into the ground.

Only the same place we all know, Vulcan replied. *The one kingdom we cannot get into.*

It didn't make any sense. How was this here, and why was it preventing dragons from passing through?

I didn't sense any magic, so whatever was powering the invisible wall did a good job at hiding its power source. My only thought was that there had to be something inside Amosite that wanted to keep dragons out. Fae were able to pass through it no problem. It was only the beasts it affected.

Deep in the cave, a crash echoed, pulling both mine and Vulcan's attention to the sound. Seconds later, the bones dragon appeared, racing around the corner with its mouth wide, yellowed teeth bared, and a roar splitting through the air. I quickly stepped back over the line, hoping like hell the wall kept it on the other side. Otherwise, we were screwed. Vulcan could take it down no problem, but with the close proximity and the inability for him to stretch to his full size, it'd be difficult and likely result in the cave collapsing on top of us.

Behind me, Vulcan roared into my mind as his growl filled the tunnel.

"It won't get past." At least, I hoped.

Vulcan's massive mouth was directly beside me, pungent saliva puddling at my boots as the bones dragon advanced. Not even a foot from me, as my heart thumped in my chest, screaming at me to run, it slammed into the wall. A clatter of bones clanking against one another echoed through the cave as the dragon roared in frustration.

It is truly stuck inside, Vulcan observed, schooling his features.

I nodded, watching as it got back on its bony feet. As soon as it did, it opened its massive jaw to release another ear-piercing bellow.

Vulcan's foot disappeared from my periphery, and I turned to find him retreating.

"Where are you going?"

We will not find answers standing in an unstable tunnel. Leave the creature alone.

He was right. The cave could collapse at any moment, much like it had before, and provoking the bones dragon to act out wouldn't help matters. I couldn't help but note the sympathy squeezing through the cracks of Vulcan's typically hard tone either. Seeing the dragon stuck there had to affect him somehow, even if he tried to hide it.

With one last glance at the dragon, I turned around, following Vulcan's massive body out of the cave. The sun was blinding as we exited, the cloud cover finally gone, leaving the sky wide open, and I squinted my eyes until they adjusted.

What is your plan? Vulcan asked.

From where I stood on the edge of the ledge, I stared out at the land, watching as the sun and the reflective rays beat down on the nature surrounding us. I had not a clue where to start with figuring this thing out, other than whatever was powering it was coming from inside Amosite.

"I'm not sure yet."

In the distance, a familiar dark green dragon appeared in the sky, powerful wings coasting along the skyline as it slowed its approach. Perched atop the beast's back was Raiden, and I instantly recognized him on his dragon, Bratus. If he was here, that meant he had something to tell me that couldn't wait until I returned.

Vulcan and I climbed a bit of the way down the rockslide to meet Bratus and Raiden where they landed. Raiden descended the dragon's back, meeting me halfway.

"What is it?" I asked.

"I debated coming at all, but I wasn't sure if you'd be pissed I didn't tell you right away. Dixus, intoxicated as ever, passed me in the street like he usually does on his way home from Barter's Hell. He made it a point to tell me to stop in at the bar."

My eyes narrowed in confusion. "Why?"

"Guess he saw a beautiful woman from another world."

My jaw clenched as what he said registered.

There was only one woman Dixus would be ogling over in his drunken state. The man wasn't even into the female population to begin with.

I silently cursed, not giving Raiden another glance before turning to mount Vulcan.

If Auria was in Barter's Hell by herself, she was in for a rude awakening.

Criminals were all too quick to lose their manners in the presence of pretty things.

CHAPTER 30

AURIA

Each of the men took a seat at the round, dark oak table. Crass and Nemin left two seats open between them, so Lander took the chair beside Crass. I took the last open spot, sitting in between Lander and Nemin, and set my cup on the table.

"Know the rules?" Perkins asked me, sorting through a deck of cards he'd grabbed from the middle.

"I'll teach her as we go," Lander said.

Crass looked over at me, a devilish glint in his eyes. Peeking out of the collar of his shirt was a black twirl, revealing his hidden tattoo. "Let the girl figure it out on her own. She looks like a quick learner."

Perkins began dealing a card to each of us, then did another round before setting the deck down, leaving us each with two cards. As he moved, I eyed a splotch of black on his upper arm, reaching toward his elbow underneath his sleeve.

I glanced at Lander before checking my cards. A pair of spades. "I can do it."

Perkins set two vials of magic on the table, starting the bet.

My brows rose slightly. They were betting with magic. I didn't have any with me, as I had no reason to carry it around, along with coins. If I ever needed to purchase anything during our stay in one of the kingdoms, one of my guards would take care of it for me. But right now, there were no guards. As they were still healing from the attack, none had joined us for days.

Under the table, Lander nudged my leg before shooting me a nervous look. He hadn't thought this far ahead—that much was certain.

"I'm in," Crass said, setting the same amount of vials in the middle.

"Call." The contents of Lander's hand clanked as he placed two vials beside the four now sitting in the middle.

"I'll call," I said hesitantly, getting some kind of understanding of the gist of the term by watching the others. After a lifetime of being kept away from the fun, I was an excellent observer, which I hoped would give me the upper hand through this.

"Have to bet something of equal value, girl," Perkins muttered, eyeing me.

I blinked, trying to think of anything I had on me to give besides what I wore. "My shoes?"

"Your shoes *and* a seat on my lap for the duration of the game will do," Nemin offered up.

I looked at Lander.

"It's fine," Lander said, answering the question in my gaze. He didn't really have a say in what I did, but I also didn't want to mess up our act that we were happily engaged.

Nemin kept his eyes on me, a smirk cresting his mouth. "I don't bite."

By the starved look on his face, I highly doubted that.

I toed off the ankle boots Siara had given me, setting them on the table, then slowly stood from the chair and straightened my dress. The ivory fabric fell just above the knee, exposing more of my legs than I was used to. In Amosite, it never would have been allowed, but in the beating sun of Deadwood, the other black clothes felt unbearable today.

"Keep your hands to yourself, Nemin," Lander warned as I perched atop Nemin's knee.

His hand went to my waist, pulling me back to meet his chest. I was angled in such a way that he couldn't see my cards, but just in case, I laid them flat on the table. I could remember my two spades just fine.

"Raise," Nemin said, placing three vials and a stack of coins on the table.

Perkins set three cards face-up on the table as Nemin murmured close to my ear, "So, Auria, what led you to want to marry Lander?"

"Certainly couldn't be his skills in gambling," Crass snarked.

Perkins let out a low chuckle, the loose skin under his chin wobbling with the act. He added two vials to the table.

"It's more of a mutual thing," I answered, eyeing the jack of clubs, seven of spades, and nine of diamonds. I had to be doing something right as I had three spades in total now.

"Raise," Crass said, following suit with Perkins's bet and a stack of coin on top.

"I'll call," Lander said, tossing in a handful of coins and two vials before taking a swig of his drink.

Crass's gaze landed on me, the amber light reflecting off their boozy sheen. "What'll it be?"

Along with magic, I had no coin on me, but I had to bet something. "My necklace?"

Crass's eyes fell to my collarbones, then lower. "I don't know, Nemin. You think her necklace is worth a wad of coin and some magic?"

My throat worked on a swallow as Nemin glanced from his cards to my necklace, his face far too close to mine. From this angle, he had a clear view of the swell of my breasts, and the thought alone caused a shiver to skate down my spine. "It'll do this round," he finally said.

I reached up to unclasp the chain, then set it in the pile with the rest of the pot. I opted for a long sip of ale in the hopes the alcohol would wash away my nerves.

"I'll raise it." Nemin shoved three vials toward the center along with his coin, his inked arm brushing mine.

Perkins let out a puff of smoke as he set another card in the center, revealing a ten of spades. My fourth spade. That had to be good for something.

"Fold," Perkins muttered around the head of his cigar, a frown pulling the corners of his lips down.

"I'll call it." Crass set two more vials of magic on the table.

Lander chewed on his lip before adding his portion to the pot.

Nemin's thumb pressed into my side, signaling my turn. With nothing to bet, I should've folded, but instead, the word fell from my lips. "Call."

Crass's smirk grew as the rest of the table waited. "With what?"

I mentally checked each item I wore, which wasn't much. I couldn't offer them an abundance of whatever magic they wanted, as it'd give away my abilities, so I only had one other thing to offer. "My dress."

Thankfully, I wore a corset and undergarments underneath, so I wouldn't be entirely exposed if it came down to it.

Nemin raised a brow, his hand gripping the fabric. "Brave girl."

"Braver than you," I snipped, not sure where my boldness came from, other than the alcohol.

A wry smile stretched his lips. "You'd be surprised." He tossed two vials on the table, not taking his eyes off me.

"You're a lucky one, Lander, to have such a temptress," Crass crooned before sipping on his ale.

Lander ignored him, staying silent as his fingers nearly folded the cards in his grip.

The door burst open behind us, and none other than Bowen stormed in, his gaze trained on me, not giving a single ounce of his focus to anyone else in the room. His eyes burned into my skin where he stared at me, and I wondered if it was due to the position I was currently in—perched atop Nemin like some sort of shiny prize.

"What are you doing?" Bowen practically growled.

I grabbed my cards off the table, lifting them a few inches in the air. "Playing a game."

"Not anymore," he said, no room for debate in his tone. Naturally, that would've turned me away, but Bowen's command was one I wanted to heed, and the alcohol was not helping in my persuasion.

I shook my head of its haze, though it did little with the thick cigar smoke hanging in the air. "We're almost done. I think."

Nemin snorted.

"The girl has already bet so much," Perkins said with a false pouty tone, a glint in his eyes as he trailed them down my body. "Let her take her chances."

Bowen let the door fall shut behind him as he leaned up against the wall and crossed his arms. My eyes followed the action, my breath hitching as I noticed the tattoos covering his arms, the same ones I saw the night of Exitium Lunae. From his wrists to beneath his shirt, he was full of black ink. My heart picked up its pace. How had I forgotten he was just as dangerous as the rest of them?

"Care to play?" Nemin asked, not looking up from his cards. His hand gripped my waist uncomfortably, causing me to shift. Bowen's eyes moved to his hold on me.

His jaw clenched, a tick jumping in his cheek as his upper arm muscles bulged when he tightened his stance. His gaze burned into me like a flame—one I welcomed. "I don't gamble."

"Too bad," Nemin tsked. "Some good stakes being thrown about today."

Perkins set another card in the center, then sat back in his chair as he puffed on his cigar, tearing my gaze away from Bowen to inspect the card. Jack of spades. Maybe I wouldn't lose my clothing after all. If the least I had to do was sit on a stranger's lap, I'd call it a win.

"Call." Crass added his bet.

Lander slid another two vials to the center, eliciting a grin from Perkins.

"What about you?" Crass asked, turning those drunken eyes on me.

I wouldn't back out now. My hand had to be good, and I was tired of being weak. I wanted to take chances, and this could be one of them. "I'll call."

Lander swallowed audibly. A sheen of sweat coated his forehead, glistening in the light. Why hadn't he folded if he was worried?

Crass's smirk turned into a full-blown wicked grin. "What else could you possibly give?"

I schooled my features, needing to act confident in my offering. I *would* win. "My corset."

CHAPTER 31

BOWEN

"Auria," I warned through gritted teeth, using all my restraint not to lift her off that piece of shit's lap and cut his leg clean off where she was perched atop it.

"She's only having fun," Perkins dismissed, waving a swollen hand in the air.

Crass, the sick fuck that he was, grinned. "Maybe we'll get a show after all."

My teeth ground together to the point they might break. "Careful, Crass." I wouldn't hesitate to gut him where he sat.

"Raise," Nemin continued, ignoring my warning as he tossed three vials of magic in the center of the table. The group of them got away with too much as it was, and now he was displaying her on his lap like some sort of spectacle, like he fucking owned her.

No one fucking owned her.

Crass set his cards face-up, followed by Lander and Auria doing the same.

Auria's confident smile among the tension in the room did

nothing to ease the need to get her the fuck out of here. "By the looks of it, I think I've won, boys."

Nemin gave the slightest shake of his head, and my fists clenched. "Sorry, pretty one." He laid his cards on the table. "Looks like I've got a full house, which beats out your flush." His lips tilted into a heinous grin as his hand tugged roughly at the fabric of Auria's dress. "Time to strip."

I shoved off the wall, my restraint hanging on by a fucking thread. "No one's fucking stripping."

Perkins, the cocky fuck that he was, took his cigar out from his thin lips. "It's her bet. She loses, she pays up. Those are the rules."

I had rules of my own, and I'd enforce them all the same.

"It's not fucking happening," I gritted out.

Crass stood, his chair scraping against the floorboards as he faced me. "You her keeper?"

"Auria is not taking a single piece of clothing off." The promise of death laced itself in my words.

She was a shiny prize in a room full of criminals—did she really think things wouldn't go south?

"It's the rules of the game," Nemin drawled, repeating what Perkins had already said. It only proved how little brain cells that head of his contained.

"What's her fiancé got to say about it?" Perkins asked, nodding in Lander's direction.

Lander was the perfect picture of a bundle of nerves. He hadn't won, and I was well aware he already owed a debt. He ignored Perkins, but Nemin wasn't going to let it slide as he sat forward in his chair, his chest pressing up against Auria's shoulder. She tried to lean away, but Nemin's grip on her dress only tightened. Pure rage coursed through the haze in the air, emanating off me like a perfume.

"Real quiet now, huh, Bular?" Nemin said.

Auria, the confident woman that she was, said, "Leave him alone." The stern hold she tried to keep on her voice would have made me proud if it wasn't for the risk she was taking speaking out against them. "This is my loss, not his."

Crass stepped a foot in Auria's direction, towering over her in Nemin's lap. "Then pay up."

My teeth ground together, and I swore one cracked. I should have stepped in by now, but Auria tried to hold her own, and I wanted to see her succeed. I wouldn't let them put a damn hand on her, though.

She shoved Nemin's hand off her waist and he reluctantly let go, allowing her to stand. She was a few inches shorter than Crass, but still, she leveled his gaze. "Fine."

Her eyes found mine, the green constellations warring with regret, shame, and uncertainty. She couldn't get a read on me, on what I would do if she took that damn dress off. Her hand came up, a finger sliding under the strap, all while she didn't dare look away from me. She wouldn't do it. She wanted me to stop her, but I was fucking lost in her gaze.

Impatient, Nemin grabbed her dress from behind and yanked, the fabric tearing at her breast. A gasp slipped from her as she attempted to wrench herself from his grasp. I moved without thought, instantly calling to my magic and filling their lungs with the thick smoke that hung in the air. I robbed them of all oxygen, and as the inability to breathe hit Nemin right as he reached for Auria again, his eyes went bloodshot. His mouth opened like a fish out of water as he struggled for air, and a choke escaped him as he staggered forward. On the other side of Auria, Crass did the same.

Perkins's eyes were wide where he sat while Lander held on to the edge of the table like it might keep him alive.

"You boys never listen," I tsked, disappointment and barely contained rage dripping in my tone. The hold on my control was slipping, all because of *her*. "It's a shame, really. But there's only so many chances I give out." And with Auria, they had zero.

Crass gripped the edge of a chair and it fell back, toppling with him to the ground.

Perkins shot up from his seat while Lander finally moved, albeit slowly, going to Auria's side. She clutched her dress to hold it up where it'd torn right above her breast. The top of her corset was exposed, and it only lit the match inside me that much brighter.

"What's happening to them?" Auria asked, panic in her voice as her eyes darted around the room.

"Let them go," Perkins demanded, his chin jiggling as he spoke.

I watched as Crass writhed on the ground, grabbing for his throat as the smoke burned his lungs. "Give the prince his bets back." The last thing Auria needed was her fiancé having a target on his back due to his gambling addiction. Deadwood always made certain that debts were paid, and the citizens didn't care if they had to get their hands dirty to get them.

Nemin's hand wrapped around Auria's wrist from behind, and she yanked away as he gasped for air with wide eyes. The dark, oily wisps snaked in through his nostrils and ears, slithering into his eye sockets as my veins pulsed heavily, my power coursing through me like a welcome embrace.

"Bowen!" Perkins boomed, his face beat red.

"I don't have many rules, Perkins, and yet, you've broken almost all of them," I said. "Not once, not twice, but multiple times now. How can I trust you'll change? That your pathetic hounds will quit engaging in games like these?"

Nemin used the table to hold himself up, leaning his weight into the dark oak.

Lander reached for Auria's hand, and she pulled it back like she'd been burned. The smoke called to me, wanting to infect him, too, but I held it back. I shook my head against the feral rage that threatened to overcome my senses. He was her fiancé. He wouldn't harm her.

"Auria, we need to get out of here," Lander begged. Between losing the game and the chaos ensuing, he was frantic.

"No." Her eyes darted between Crass and Nemin where they struggled for air, suffocating under my wrath. "You go. I'll find you."

He shook his head. "I'm not leaving without you."

Tendrils of smoke whirled around Lander, itching to bite, as Auria said, confidence lacing her words, "He won't hurt me."

My head tilted slightly. She trusted me. Interesting.

"You're so certain?" Lander asked warily.

She nodded, her dress slipping from her grip unknowingly.

Without hesitation, Lander gathered his coin and magic vials off the table, then darted out of the room, careful not to brush me as he slipped past.

"She offered her clothes. We didn't force her to do anything," Perkins defended, and I almost laughed.

Auria carefully stepped around Crass's body on the ground, his face a deep shade of purple now. I regarded Perkins with sheer boredom, the smoke of his forgotten cigar dancing in a frenzied manner all around him.

"She didn't seem very willing to strip, did she?" I asked.

Perkins shook his head, the lantern light glinting off his bald spot. "We won't make her. We won't, right, boys?" He looked to the two men in desperation, but they were in no position to respond.

I didn't give a shit. "Not the first time, Perkins."

"Why punish for it now?" he asked, the tremor in his voice practically calling to the smoke as it begged to take him, too.

"Don't kill them," Auria pleaded, finally speaking up.

My eyes shot to hers as I flexed my fists. She was closer now, but clearly wary to be by my side. Her defense of these pathetic men intrigued me as much as it fueled my rage. She didn't know what they would've made her do had I not shown up.

Suddenly, fear shone bright in her expression, and I fucking hated it. "Please," she whispered.

"I can't do that." Yet no apology rang in my tone.

"You can."

She overestimated my sense of control, as I was finding out all too well I lost it in her presence.

On the floor, Crass had stopped moving, his skin turning a light shade of gray. By the looks of it, Nemin was shortly behind.

Like a switch, those green eyes of hers turned something in me, sending cracks through the stone of my mind. If she wanted them alive, I'd spare them. If she wanted them to rot, I'd wilt their corpses where they laid. She'd made her choice, and in that, I'd honor her.

Tendrils of dark smoke seeped from their bodies, dissipating in the air as Crass gulped down oxygen, his skin turning a deep red. Nemin choked on a cough, clouds of gray rushing from his parted lips.

I paid them no mind. It wouldn't have deflated me in the slightest if they'd died in that moment, but Auria had wanted otherwise.

Stealing one last look at her, I said, "Come with me."

She hesitated, debating if it was wise to accompany me. I wouldn't blame her if she didn't. She knew I was dangerous. But as I opened the door, to my relief, she followed.

~

The late afternoon sun beat into my skin, but it was a welcome reprieve from the musty room I'd found Auria in. She stuck out like a sore thumb in Deadwood, catching the eye of everyone, whether man or woman. Unfortunately, that included Perkins and the men he had hooked under his finger. He was big into gambling, recruiting people to win big and give him a portion. Claimed he was some sort of manager. Truthfully, I didn't give a shit what he did as long as he abided by the rules set in place. I wasn't a strict leader by any means, but a town full of outlaws couldn't get away with everything. They involved a woman without her consent? I'd drop them dead where they stood. Auria was the only reason the three of them still breathed.

Deadwood was a home to some, and a hiding spot to others. For Auria's group, it was a temporary stop. Yet somehow, she'd managed to immerse herself in places she shouldn't be in a matter of a few days, between the caves and now the gambling den. If I had to take a guess on the latter, Lander had had something to do with it. His bad habits were going to get her killed, and I wondered if that was his goal.

"Where are we going?" Auria asked, struggling to catch up as she held her dress to her chest.

I'd wanted to kill Nemin for touching her. For eliciting that scared look on her face. To tear him apart as the smoke infected his lungs, stealing all the oxygen from his body, suffocating him slowly, agonizingly, as it streamed through his veins to blacken his heart. But Auria had spoken up. She hadn't been afraid of me, though it was clear she knew I was the one causing their pain. No, she'd *defended* them after the pig had torn her dress. After they'd wanted her naked in a room full of men. After Nemin had perched her on his knee like a fucking trophy.

Betting or not, a woman always had a way out, and they hadn't given her one.

I didn't judge anyone based on their hobbies, but that look in Auria's eyes had said it all. She hadn't wanted to get that deep into the game. She had wanted the thrill, to do something she hadn't been allowed to do her entire life, but she didn't need to strip in front of sick men in order to find that.

"Bowen," she spoke up, pulling me out of my thoughts.

I slowed my pace, shoving away the rage that fueled every step. She was the only thing stopping me from going back in there and ripping their heads from their bodies and taking pleasure in watching the blood seep from their arteries. "I want to show you something."

She hopped on one foot, attempting to slip on one of her boots. I internally cursed as I stopped to let her put them on. My jaw ached as I surveyed the space around us, making sure no one was copping a look at her exposed corset. To the bystanders' credit, no one dared glance this way. They valued their ability to keep their eyes in their sockets.

She straightened, brushing hair from her face before her hand went back to her dress to hold it in place. The move only put her red-tinged cheeks on display. "Show me what?"

"You'll see."

She huffed. "What a broad answer."

"You don't want to come, Princess, just say so. I'll walk you home right now."

"It's not that. I just—" She shook her head, like she was finally processing what had happened in the gambling den. "You didn't have to do that."

"Do what?" I asked, tilting my head. I wanted her to say the words.

Her lips pursed together. "You know."

"I don't think so." I was messing with her, but fuck, it was the only thing getting my mind off the impulse to turn around and obliterate them.

"You didn't have to hurt them for me. I put myself in that situation," she blurted, like even saying the words left a bad taste in her mouth.

I stepped toward her, causing her to grip the top of her dress tighter. "You would have rather stripped naked for them?"

Her throat worked on a swallow as her eyes fell to the ground. "No. But you could have been nicer."

I couldn't help it. I chuckled, the act sounding a little insane. "You think they were showing you that same respect? Being nice?"

Her gaze hardened as she held back her answer. But she didn't have to. I saw her response clear in her gaze. The look alone fueled my desire to rip their eyes from their heads.

Fuck, I wanted to hurt them a hundred times over again. This feral response to seeing her like that... It was uncontrollable.

I took another step so there was barely any space between us, my silhouette casting a shadow over her. She looked up at the same time I grabbed the thin fabric of her gown.

"Tell me, was he nice when he tore your clothing? Exposed you in a room full of men that would have done anything to see you completely bare, had I not shown up?"

"Bowen," she whispered, the word barely audible with her silent plea to make me stop.

I didn't realize my knuckles had turned pure white from how hard I gripped her dress. I needed to get some of this out.

I let the fabric go and turned, continuing in the direction of the forest.

Her footsteps quickly followed. "Where are you taking me?" she asked again. The slight waver in her voice made me stop in my tracks, my fists clenched. I didn't want her scared.

"To the woods," I answered.

"What's in the woods?"

I looked over my shoulder to find her staring at my back, the town behind her. Her beauty was a shining light in this drab place. "An explanation."

She hesitated, not moving any closer, and I fucking hated the sight of her standing there looking so defeated.

"I will not hurt you, Auria. That much I can assure you."

"Why not?"

My brows furrowed.

"You may have protected me, but how do I know you don't want the pleasure of killing me yourself? Everyone else in this world seems to want to, so what makes you any different?"

Turning on my heel, I closed the distance between us until the hand holding her dress brushed my chest. "If I wanted to hurt you, you'd have bled the moment I saw you in your pretty little castle. If I wanted you dead, you'd be six feet under. Does that answer your question?"

She gave the barest tilt of her chin before stepping around me to continue in the direction we were headed. I easily caught up to her, walking alongside her. Our boots crunched in the dry leaves as we entered the tree line.

"You have magic," Auria said, stepping over a rock.

"Yes."

"Lander lied, then," she surmised. "He said we don't have magic."

I let out a sigh. She knew less than I thought, which only made me want to direct my indignation toward her father. "If what your father has told you is true, then why does he use you for yours? Why not anyone else in Amosite?"

Her steps faltered. "No one else can do what I can. At least, that's what he's told me. When did you figure it out?"

"I put the pieces together after our first dinner when he practically controlled you like one of his aimless guards." The memory of that night alone grated every inch of my being, sending my power thrashing through my body like a caged animal.

"Like his very own puppet," she murmured.

My gaze shot to hers. "You are not a puppet."

She shook her head, adjusting her grip on her dress. "Sometimes, I don't know."

"No, Princess. You're not. You're much, much more than what you may believe."

She was silent a moment, the only sound the leaves crunching under our feet. The last time we had been in the woods together, aside from heading back from the caves, I'd killed three men who had threatened to harm her, and I'd been so close to doing it again today. I *should* have.

Above the trees, massive wings cast a shadow over the land before a rush of air hit us, signaling Vulcan's looming presence. He was listening.

"If you're insinuating humans don't have magic themselves, then how do you explain what you can do?" she asked.

I stuck a hand in the pocket of my pants, palming a vial of fire magic. Taking it out, I twirled it in my fingers, bringing Auria's attention to it.

"Vials don't count," she said.

I rounded a tree that looked to be decaying, stopping at its base. Auria stopped a few feet behind me, and when I called to the magic, lighting a branch on fire, Auria gasped, staggering back.

"What are you doing?" she shrieked.

"Showing you what you want to know." Once a proper fire was started, using the bark as fuel as it climbed over the tree, I pocketed the amber vial, sending a silent appreciation for its use.

The flames licked at the dead leaves, eating its way up the branch toward the trunk as it spread. Once the entire tree was enveloped in fire, I let my magic unleash itself as it'd been longing to do since I'd forced it out of the men's bodies in the den. The familiar feeling of crackling energy built in my veins as they visibly darkened, the tips of my fingers tingling.

"Bowen," Auria said hesitantly.

The smoke sprouting from the tips of the flames swirled as it heeded to me, sensing my power and bowing to my command. In a flash, the smoke turned on its creator and enveloped the fire, snuffing it out as it cut off all its oxygen. The flames suffocated under the barrage of smoke, and all that was left was the swirling fog and charred tree.

The smoke moved wildly as it waited for my direction, and I let it have control as I faced Auria. Her eyes were wide as she took in the state of the tree, then her gaze moved to me. She stepped back, her boot snapping a stick and causing her to flinch. I hadn't held back in my display, and the charm we all wore so easily had dropped, revealing the points of my ears.

Her brows pulled together. "You can control fire?"

I shook my head. "Try again."

A tendril of smoke floated over to her, stroking the side of her cheek. She looked down to find it skirting across her skin, down her neck, over her shoulder, and coasting along her arm.

So soft, my smoke purred, a whisper in my mind meant to antagonize me. It only spoke up when it pleased, more grating on my nerves than Vulcan typically was. All the voices in my head had an opinion, but we rarely ever agreed on anything, making for a chaotic mess if I ever dropped the reins.

"Smoke," she breathed. "A-are you fae?"

Satisfaction curled inside me, along with the need to make her understand what this meant, in order for her not to fear me. Though, by the look of it, intrigue lit her eyes. She wasn't scared. She was enticed.

The smoke ran across her fingers as another thread ghosted

over her collarbone. I watched as it moved on its own accord, exploring her.

If only you could touch her like I can, it taunted. *Comfort her like me.*

My jaw ground together as the tendril slowed, going to her hand that held her dress. I watched with rapt attention as it twirled itself around her fingers, almost like it wanted to help what she was ashamed of. I let it, holding back the jealousy that arose with its ability to go to her right now.

I cleared my throat, cutting my magic off. It instantly evaporated into the air, disappearing completely. "I am."

"Are you all fae?" she asked, and the way she took a small step back didn't sit right with me. I had been reading her all wrong. Perhaps the fear was entwined deep with her curiosity.

Looking up through the branches, the sky was turning an orange hue, the rings setting somewhere on the horizon, along with the sun. "That's a question for another time, I'm afraid."

"Why not now?" Disappointment and frustration laced her tone. A lifetime of questions gone unanswered or responded to with empty lies, and here I was, dismissing her like all the rest. But unless she wanted to be a hungry wolf's dinner, we needed to head back.

"There are dangerous creatures out here," I answered. "Ones that hunt at night." But that didn't mean their threat ceased in the day. They just typically prowled deeper into the forest when the sun was up, taking to the darker parts of the woods.

"Aside from you?" she asked.

I should've expected that retort.

I stepped toward her, mere feet separating us now. "Contrary to what you may think, I'm not the monster."

She pulled her dress higher. "You could've fooled me."

"I've tricked a lot of people, Auria, but you are not one on that list."

"What makes me so different, then? Or are you lying?"

I shook my head, diminishing another foot between us. "I wouldn't lie to you."

"Deceive me, then," she said.

Another step, and my eyes caught on the rise of her chest, my senses focusing in on the pounding of her heart. In an instant, my charm rounded out the points of my ears for her benefit. "It's time to go."

She held her ground as the shadow of Vulcan's wings flashed over us again. He wasn't going to let us fall prey to a bunch of wolves.

I closed the distance, only inches separating us now. "If danger gets you going, Princess, all you have to do is say it, and I'll make some."

Her eyes narrowed slightly. "That's not why I'm standing here."

I leaned into her space, causing her to step back once more. Her back hit the tree behind her, and she dropped her dress, exposing her corset. It took all I had in me not to look at the material. Without thinking, my hand came up to wrap around her throat, pinning her to the tree. I didn't apply any pressure, though. Her breath hitched, and my pants were suddenly all too tight.

"If I had to guess, I'd think you like this, Princess," I murmured.

Her nostrils flared as she tilted her chin higher, almost leaning into my grip.

My devious little thing.

My opposite hand came up to her cheek, my finger trailing over her blushing cheekbone, down to her bee-stung lips. "Do you like my hand around your fragile little throat?"

Her pulse jumped against my palm encircling her throat, blood pumping through me just as fast. To hell with me being dangerous. She was a temptation too sweet for the predator inside me to stay away.

My finger pulled on her lower lip, the flesh bouncing back as I moved my hand to the tree behind her so I could lean in further. Tilting my head, I inhaled her scent, my nose brushing her neck right above my thumb. Daring to get even closer, I let my lips trail over her pulse, reveling in the speed in which her heart beat for me.

"No," she managed to get out, but I could practically taste the lie as it slid off her tongue so effortlessly. A lifetime of them, and she was a pro.

I pulled back just enough to look her in the eye. "Keep telling yourself that. Maybe one of us will believe it one day." I dropped my hold on her, gathering all logical thought in order to take a step back from her. Anyone else, and I wouldn't have cared, but Auria was the daughter of my enemy. I couldn't go there with her. "Go or stay. But don't say I didn't warn you."

I left her standing there, her back still pressed against the tree, and headed back toward town. All the while, I could practically hear Vulcan chuckling in the sky.

She'd be my fucking downfall if I let her get close.

I'd lose everything I'd worked so long to build.

But suddenly, deep in the crevices of my mind, it seemed worth the risk.

CHAPTER 32

AURIA

Sleep had evaded me most of the night. After Bowen left me in the forest, I hadn't stuck around to figure out what creatures he was talking about. After seeing the sandwalkers in the desert, I didn't want to guess what prey lived on the outskirts of Deadwood waiting to strike. As far as I could tell, whatever threats were out there didn't pass the town line, which brought me at least some comfort.

Before heading home, I'd stopped by the guards' house to check on them. They seemed to be doing better after just a few days of rest. Two of them were in worse shape than the other, but in a day or two, they should be on their feet without too much trouble. I was thankful they were doing okay, but I wasn't excited to inevitably be trailed by one of them again. I was enjoying my freedom—perhaps a bit too much.

I'd thankfully avoided Paxon as well as I could, but I was bound to run into him soon. I hadn't wanted to confront the choice he'd given me and what either decision might mean for me. To think he truly wanted the best for me was hard to believe.

After pulling myself out of bed, I'd thrown on a pair of dark leather pants and a form-fitting black short-sleeve shirt. My boots laced up past my ankles, and in the mirror, I'd admired the way the outfit as a whole fit like a glove. I felt less exposed than I ever had in a dress, despite every curve on my body being on display.

I enjoyed the breakfast I'd found waiting in the kitchen of my own house, complete with berries, bison sausage, and a muffin. Then I'd sat on the couch, enjoying the book that was sitting on the armrest. Along with the leather-bound novel had been a half-empty vial of strength magic, its glowing, purple liquid shining in the rays of the sun. I wasn't sure who had been in here while I'd slept, but I took advantage of the forgotten vial, refilling it and reveling in the power that flowed through me like the blood in my veins.

After filling the vial up to the cork, I'd flipped through the contents of the book, taking in every piece of information I could. The pages inside had tiny script and large drawings of various types of dragons. I never would have thought so many breeds existed, and while the knowledge written within the book intrigued me, it was the art I couldn't take my eyes away from. Each was unique, painted with colors to match their true form in order to blend into their natural biome.

My fingers stroked over the painting of a white dragon with ice-blue eyes, nearly identical to the one that'd saved me in the Brimstone Mountains. It felt like weeks had passed since then, but it'd been merely days. The top of the page was titled Snow Dragon, indicating which breed this one was. That had to be what the female dragon was, having shot ice from her mouth to freeze people in place, then obliterate them into tiny chunks with one sweep of her powerful tail.

I'd have never thought this to be possible, but now, it simply amazed me that all of this existed in a world I once thought was simple, boring. Serpentine was far from any of that.

A knock at the door drew my attention away from the pages, and reluctantly, I closed the book, leaving it on the cushion as I headed for the door. As soon as I opened it, Siara appeared with a breath of relief.

"Oh, good. You're dressed. Let's go," she said, stepping to the side and ushering me forward with far too much enthusiasm.

"Where?" Her politeness toward me took me off guard every time, though it was a relief compared to the harshness the majority of people I came across treated me with.

"It's market day!" she exclaimed, throwing her arms out.

I blinked, not understanding the excitement.

She sighed. "When a bunch of tradespeople come through town with rare items from all over the continent, even overseas. I want to shop, and I want you to come."

"That's a lot of wants."

She rolled her eyes. "Flynt's busy, so he wouldn't come with me, and I figured you might want to see what it's all about."

Out of all of her other options in this town, she'd thought to invite me. The sentiment alone sent warmth spreading through my chest.

"I don't have a lot of money on me," I said. One of the guards had given me a few coins in case I needed to buy something while they were healing, but it wasn't enough for any rare items.

She grabbed my hand, pulling me out the door. "That's fine. If you want something, just ask."

I barely had time to close the door behind me as she led me down the porch step and into the street. Ahead, people were everywhere, and my guard instantly went up at the thought of them possibly not being human. Was Siara fae? Was this a trap? But if she was, she hadn't shown any sort of hostility toward me to prove it. Maybe Bowen was right, and they weren't monsters. But if that was true, then why were they thought to be extinct? Why not reveal themselves?

Leaving the small strip of houses, Siara pulled me into the throng of people as we entered the main street. It was an effort not to bump shoulders with some of them, a few casting dirty looks my way when I got too close.

"Siara, are you sure I should be out here?" I asked, trying to keep my voice low. It was no secret who I was related to, and that would always make me a target.

"Stick me with me and you'll be fine," she replied over her shoulder. She must've caught the worried look in my eye because she slowed, walking alongside me. She held a hand up, and between the tips of two fingers, electricity sizzled. The confirmation hit me like a brick.

"You're fae, too," I whispered.

She nodded. "Bowen told me you found out yesterday."

Had he gone straight to her after leaving me in the woods? Was there something going on between the two of them, and I was too naive to see it? But why did I even care? He wasn't mine to be jealous over.

"But you don't need to worry," she went on. "You're safe here."

I almost snorted at the word. It seemed as if I was anything but safe anywhere, let alone in a town full of criminals.

"How do you and Bowen know each other anyway?" I asked, curiosity getting the best of me.

"I was friends with Flynt first, but when Bowen's dad died and he shoved everyone away, I was sort of...persistent. He wanted to wilt away. I mean, the man was doing everything he could to—" She stopped, glancing at me. "I guess I shouldn't get into that part. But long story short, he was a shell of the man he is today, and I helped him get through it. I lost my family when I was young, grew up an orphan, and Flynt always made sure I was fed and had shelter. After Bowen snapped out of it, they just kind of brought me into the group." She gave a little shrug. "Became the family I always wished for, but never got lucky enough to have."

I gnawed on the inside of my cheek, my heart hurting for both her and Bowen, and the pasts they had had to endure. It made me feel guilty for feeling even remotely miserable in my own life when others surely suffered worse.

"But anyway, that's all old news," she said, brushing it off like she hadn't just dropped an emotional bomb. "They're stuck with me now."

"I'm sure stuck is the last word they'd use," I replied.

"You're giving my ability to be clingy far too little credit," she teased, all too aware I was starting to see it bright as day.

"Where do the tradespeople come from?" I asked, curious if this would be as dangerous as everything else seemed to be and taking advantage of the alone time with her to ask questions about anything.

"Not Amosite, if that's what you're thinking," she supplied. "Some come in at the ports from other continents, and others live their lives traveling and selling their creations, never really settling in one place too long."

The sight of the market coming into view as she spoke nearly froze me in my tracks. Booths were set up all along the street, people bustling about. Some had carts full of goods, others overflowing armfuls of supplies. People wore clothes just as me, while others wore more risqué attire. There was no dress code in Deadwood, that much was certain. The freedom to express themselves opened an aching longing inside me. If today was as close as I got to being able to do that, I'd be satisfied.

"Oh, look!" Siara squealed, grabbing my hand and tugging

me in the direction of a booth selling assorted pieces of jewelry. "I think opal would look amazing on you."

I bent over to get a better look at the piece Siara had pointed out. An array of colors littered the white stone, a delicate gold chain attached to the piece. In the sun, the greens turned to purple, to orange and royal blue, shining rainbows with every shift of the light.

"It's beautiful," I said.

The vendor, a middle-aged woman with graying hair and a sun-splotched nose, eyed me, her gaze carousing up and down the length of my body. "Too much for you." She went back to her other customer, lifting another piece up into the sunlight for the patron to admire.

Siara narrowed her eyes on the woman, then set two vials of magic on the table, the blue liquid glinting in the sun. Water magic. "It's for me."

The lady pocketed the vials, waving us off.

Siara picked up the chain, holding it out to me. "Here you go."

"Siara, I can't accept that," I said.

The stone swung in the air as she waited for me to take it, bringing it closer. "Yes, you can."

I shook my head. "I don't have any magic or enough coin to give you."

"Consider it a gift for your travels, then," she said.

The necklace as a whole was exquisite, more eye-catching than any of the gaudy pieces I was forced to wear with my outfits back in Amosite. There, it was to brag of the wealth my father had. Here, I could wear it simply because I liked it. That thought alone convinced me to accept it.

"Fine, but I'm getting you something in return."

She shrugged, then spun her finger in a circle. I turned around and lifted my hair off my neck. She clasped it, adjusting it so it lay directly in between my collarbones. I faced her again, finding a gleaming smile on her face. "Even more beautiful when it's on."

With one last admiring look, she started to head to the next booth, but my attention caught on a burly man pocketing three bracelets and a vial of magic off the table we'd just purchased from.

Without thinking, I spoke up. "Hey! Put those back."

His heated glare landed on me, but I refused to shrink away. From the existing tattoos on his forearms, more lines etched in around his wrists. I wanted to stare at the ink, to watch as the swirls took their shape in his skin, almost like a brand. The work itself was almost like a trance I was sucked into but quickly snapped out of when he stomped directly in front of me.

"What was that?" he gritted out.

I had nothing on him—no strength or height—as he towered a foot and a half over me, but still, I held my chin high. "I said put them back."

His nostrils flared, the piercings on both sides moving with them, and I suddenly wished I would've held my tongue. I didn't know who was fae in this town, and I really didn't want to find out this way. "What are you going to do about it, bitch? Glare at me to death? Stomp on my big toe?"

I opened my mouth to respond, but a hand shot out, landing on his chest. It shoved him back a foot, and a man wearing all black stepped between us. Even from the back of his head, I recognized Bowen. Electricity practically rolled off him, prickling my body with awareness as something inside me swirled in a frenzy with his presence.

"I suggest you leave the lady alone," Bowen warned, his voice eerily calm.

Around his hands and tattooed arms, smoke swirled, and

the tendrils only grew as more joined the cluster from nearby grills and candles.

The man stared Bowen down, his fisted hands flexing before finally backing away. He shook his head once, turning around. I noted he didn't return the jewelry and magic he stole.

"He stole her merchandise," I said. "And a vial."

Bowen turned around. Our chests were too close. In the beaming midday sun, his blue eyes shone brighter than the sky. "That's not for you to take care of."

I crossed my arms defiantly. "Then who will? Or is this town too full of outlaws for you to care about a little piece of jewelry?"

The smoke dissipated as he grabbed my arm, spinning me around so my back was pressed to his chest. He lowered his head, murmuring in my ear, "See those guards posted at every other booth?" He paused, waiting for me to find them. Though they almost blended in with the crowd, now that I was looking for them, I couldn't miss each standing in leather outfits, guns slung on their hips. Daggers filled every sheath on their body, and I didn't want to guess what other weapons or magic they held. "They take care of it so that you, Princess, can enjoy your shopping."

With his body pressed to mine, my back was nearly buzzing. "I'm hardly shopping."

I could practically feel his eyes drop to the opal necklace around my neck, and the memory of his hand against my skin in that very spot heated my core. I couldn't help the rise of my breasts as I tried to inhale. Bowen seemed to suck the oxygen from me with a few simple words.

"Auria! Oh my gods, I thought I lost you," Siara said, hurrying over to us as she shouldered past a stout woman.

Bowen dropped my arm and stepped back. "You did."

I didn't bother looking back at him. "She didn't. I just got sidetracked."

Her eyes darted between me and Bowen, a knowing glint in them as she tried to hide her smile. "Well, it looks like Bowen kept you company instead."

By the look on her face, it led me to believe they didn't have anything between them. If they did, why would she seem almost...elated to see him simply standing with me?

"My lady," a guard, one of *my* guards, said, appearing from the crowd.

His appearance took me aback, as I thought they wouldn't be out and about for another day or two at least. Siara and Bowen regarded him with bored curiosity.

"Are you feeling better?" I asked, seeing as his leg was wrapped from the knee down and he used a stick propped under his arm to hold himself up.

"Quite. I came to grab a few things for the others, but my lady..." His eyes fell to my clothes, then darted back to my face. "I noticed you're not wearing Amosite's colors while you're out, and with orders from your father, you must change. You know the rules, Lady Auria."

My brows pulled together. *That's* why he'd approached me? It was the same bullshit from before. The same thing they'd said to me when I'd checked on them last night. "All of my belongings were destroyed in the raid."

He gave a nervous nod. "Surely Deadwood has something that would work."

"This is mainly all I have." Given the circumstances, he had to understand, right?

"It will not do, my lady. Your father gave us strict orders—"

"The lady can wear whatever she'd like," Bowen interrupted, his voice taking on such an authoritative tone that even *I* felt compelled to heed it.

The guard turned his attention on Bowen. "With all due respect, sir"—he cleared his throat—"King Tenere was very clear—"

Bowen's eyes bored into him. "Are we in Amosite, Soldier?"

The guard's eyes darted to me before looking back at Bowen. "Well, no—"

"Right." Bowen stepped toward him, his entire being the mask of calm control. This side of him was as collected as a king. "She may wear what she'd like while staying in my town."

The guard swallowed, a nervous bead of sweat gleaming off his forehead. To save himself from the scrutiny, he nodded, giving me one last glance before disappearing back into the crowd.

To hell with all of this.

I heaved a breath, then stepped around Siara, heading in the direction of the next booth. Vibrant blown glass vases sat displayed on the white cloth draped over the table, and I wondered how they traveled with such delicate items. Taylin had never mentioned a market such as this visiting Amosite, and I presumed it was yet another thing my father didn't allow his people to take part in.

The thought of Taylin dropped a boulder to the pit of my stomach, and I realized just how badly I missed our daily talks in the gardens. Was she still showing up every day, waiting for my return in case we arrived early? Or had she forgotten about me for weeks, relieved she wouldn't have to make the trek from her home in the city to the castle for a short visit?

Siara admired a few of the vases beside me, Bowen trailing behind us with his hands casually clasped behind his back. He kept a watchful eye on the crowd around us, and I did my best not to glance his way.

"Did you get my gift?" Bowen asked, coming up on my other side as Siara continued onward.

"A book and a half-empty vial is hardly a gift," I snipped, irritated with his presence at the moment. Between stepping in with the man and defending me in front of the guard, I felt embarrassed. The last thing I wanted was for him to feel bad enough for me to leave gifts on top of all of the saving, too. Besides, this was a trip for me and Siara, *not* Bowen.

His chin dipped. "So you did."

I acted more interested in the items displayed before me than the man making my heart race. "Gifts are to be given. You're merely loaning it to me."

"It's yours to have, even after you leave."

I shook my head. "I can't take anything like that back to Amosite. My father would surely—" Surely what? The fact was, I had no clue what he'd do if I brought back souvenirs, let alone an entire book on dragons. Now that I was thinking about it, I didn't believe I'd be able to take the necklace Siara had given me either.

Bowen made a humming sound behind me, but I chose not to pay it any mind. If he wanted to be judgmental, he could keep it to himself.

But then his chin appeared in my peripheral as he leaned over my shoulder, and his voice, smooth as honey, filled my ear. "Trouble at home, Princess?"

I spun on him. "Even if there was, I wouldn't confide in you."

He cocked an amused brow. "Does Father Dearest not know his precious daughter isn't so innocent after all?"

"After this trip, I plan to keep it that way," I gritted out, hoping he got the message *not* to say a word to him, should they speak.

"About the information in that book or the way you like how my hand feels wrapped around your throat?"

My nostrils flared, my cheeks surely reddening. I couldn't let him get under my skin this easily.

"Or maybe"—he leaned closer, and the crowd faded away—"the way your breathing picks up its pace when you see me. Or how your heart rate skyrockets in my presence."

I narrowed my eyes on him before spinning back around to follow after Siara once more, choosing to give him the cold shoulder and not let him succeed in getting under my skin. That's all he was trying to do, and I wouldn't let him.

We moved on to the next booth, finding leather satchels and sheaths for daggers and swords dangling from hooks above the worn table. A man with white hair sat behind the display, etching a design into a strip of leather. He looked young, his skin tan from long hours in the sun.

To the left of me, Siara snorted. "You can get your name etched into a sheath. How cute." Her attention snagged on a small purse hanging from a metal hook, the size just big enough to hold a few vials of magic. She turned it over in her fingers, staring for a few moments longer, then dropped it, moving on to the next booth.

Behind me, Bowen was thankfully caught up in conversation with a guard who'd singled him out in the crowd. While he was distracted, I took some coin out of my pocket and set it on the table. The purse would be perfect for Siara, a gift in return for the necklace she'd bought me.

The man behind the table didn't so much as glance at my coin, so I took the purse off the hook, adjusting the strap over my shoulder.

A hand grabbed my wrist, ripping the leather strap from my hold, and I was spun toward a hard chest. Bowen took the purse, setting it back on the table. "Fucking hell, Auria."

"What?" I asked, exasperated with his tone. What the fuck had I done other than buy a purse?

He ran his hands down my arms, his eyes roaming frantically over every inch of my exposed skin. "Do you burn anywhere?"

"Burn? Why would I *burn*?"

He pivoted my body side to side, then moved my hair off my neck. The act alone sent tingles skittering through me. "When you're marked for stealing, your skin burns where the tattoo forms."

His insinuation struck me. "I didn't steal any magic. It's a *purse*. I put coin down."

He grabbed the bag, opening the flap to reveal a bundle of vials lying neatly inside. "You have to check inside before you try to buy anything. *Nothing* is safe."

My jaw nearly dropped. "Why the hell would there be magic in there?"

"Some beings use these items to move magic."

"*Move* magic?" What the fuck was he talking about?

His lips rolled together. "Not everyone has access to specific types of magic in every region, so they smuggle it." When I didn't reply, because words evaded me altogether, he continued. "You're sure you don't burn anywhere?"

"Yes." I'd know if I did. The sensation was all too familiar to me.

He searched my eyes, likely to see if I was telling the truth. "Best keep that little bit to yourself." He set the purse back on the table.

"Why?" I hadn't technically stolen it, and the absence of the ink was proof of that.

"Do not speak a word of this, Auria." He checked around us to be sure no one had seen. The way my name rolled off his lips etched itself into my brain. His voice wrapped around me like a caress.

I retrieved my coin off the table, pocketing it. "I don't

suppose you're trying to control me now, are you?" I asked, doing my best to keep the irritation in my tone, despite wanting to let it go.

He looked at me again, his eyes narrowing as he leaned closer. "Not in the way you think, Princess."

His gaze moved to something behind me, and I turned when his body stiffened. In the crowd, Paxon stood still among all the bodies moving every which way around him as they shopped and chatted. His eyes were trained on us, watching.

"You keep an eye on him," Bowen muttered, his voice low with warning, like he wanted to say more.

"You don't like him?" I questioned, wondering how much he knew about Paxon.

"I don't trust him."

His reluctance to explain why filled me with annoyance, and I didn't stick around to see what Paxon might do or to hear some bullshit short response from Bowen. Leaving Siara at the booth she'd wandered off to, I joined the crowd of people, not bothering to say a word to Bowen.

"Auria," he called after me, but I ignored him.

I pressed through the throng, warm bodies bumping into me from every angle. I needed air and space, and this market wasn't providing a reprieve for either. I quickened my pace, spotting an empty alley ahead. I shoved my way past the last few rows of people, inhaling the warm air as I stepped into the opening.

As I'd suspected, Bowen followed.

"Auria," he said again.

I ran my hands through my hair, tugging at my scalp. "Why won't anyone just be clear with me?" But the question was left open. I didn't expect an answer. I doubted Bowen had one anyway.

My chest heaved as oxygen filled my starving lungs, and I

pressed my forehead to the wooden wall of whatever business stood on one side of the alley.

This entire world was a mystery to me, and as I'd come to learn, my father kept me in the dark for no good fucking reason. It was all to control me, to keep me naive and willing to follow his every demand. He'd succeeded, and I wanted to hate him for it, but a part of me couldn't. He'd kept me safe, fed me meals, provided me safety and shelter.

"You're okay, Auria," Bowen said, his voice a touch softer than it had been in the market.

I whirled on him, throwing my hands to my sides. "You're an extinct species, Bowen! Hell, this whole fucking town likely is, and I had no clue!"

In a blink, he was in my space, pressing my back to the wall, pinning my hands above my shoulders. "Breathe, Auria."

I tried to shove against his hold, but it was no use. "I don't need to fucking breathe!"

"Your mind is spinning in a hundred different directions right now, so yeah, some deep breaths might help."

I tried again to get him off of me, but his hands remained on mine. I wouldn't look at his eyes, wouldn't let myself get lost in them. He'd deceived me. But he didn't. My father had. If I hadn't been so blind to the world, I'd have known dragons weren't actually in hiding, known fae weren't extinct, that creatures existed past Amosite's chasm. But it all came down to Bowen. Bowen, standing here, pinning me against this godsforsaken wall as a market full of predators bustled mere feet away.

I let out a frustrated groan, shaking my head and squeezing my eyes shut. "I'm spinning because of you, Bowen!" My chest heaved, my mind a whirlwind.

"I'm not your enemy," he said.

I couldn't help it any longer. My eyes met his, and I swallowed the dryness coating my throat. "You're fae." And if I had to guess, they were rumored to be extinct for a reason.

His hands pressed harder against mine, his toned, inked forearms flexing with the movement. "That's right, Auria. I am. Which means I can feel the fear wafting off your skin, hear your heart threatening to beat out of your chest, smell the desire seeping off you every time I walk into the room."

"You're wrong," I spat.

He ignored my protests. "It isn't me you should fear." He dropped my hands, and I realized how much I was relying on him to hold me up when I staggered away from the wall. He was an anchor in the chaos.

"Then who? Because all arrows point to you right now," I said between panting breaths. He'd treated me so nicely thus far, and yet, I couldn't help but have second thoughts that he was the monster lurking in the dark.

He let me have a moment to breathe, to settle the racing of my heart. "Think about everything you knew, and everything you know now. You shouldn't trust anyone. Not in Amosite, not in Deadwood." His eyes held mine, something like pain flashing in them. "Not even your precious fiancé."

He didn't give me the chance to press further as he left me in the alley. It wasn't the first time I had watched him leave, the sight all too familiar after last night, and I wondered if that was how it would always be.

People walking out on me before I could get a real answer.

CHAPTER 33

AURIA

Rather than attempting to explore the rest of the market, I headed home. Bowen had soured my mood, and meandering through a crowd of people would only make it worse. One moment, he was standing up for me, and the next, he was acting as if I were his enemy—just like nearly everyone else had so far, as if the actions from my father were brought onto them by me.

But I wasn't the reason for their hardships. Being kept in the dark for so long, I could only guess what my father had done to tarnish the Tenere name, but with the little details I knew, I had to assume it was his greed that had gotten to him.

If only people knew—

No, they'd never know. To them, they probably assumed I was some spoiled, rotten princess, but the opposite was true. I would never be anything like my father if I could help it. I'd give and give until I had nothing left in me if I could. I drained my energy for my father every day, filling vials like some servant. I was his daughter, and he *used* me.

I hadn't noticed I'd shed a tear until the drop trickled down my cheek. I swiped at it angrily. Neither Bowen nor my father deserved my tears. My rage was mine. I was the reason I was stuck in this situation. Being married off to a stranger—though Lander had become somewhat of a friend through this—and being used as some pawn. It all laid on my shoulders like an anchor on the seafloor. The only one with the power to get me out of this was me, and yet I was too weak to try.

Or was I?

Stepping up onto the porch, I opened the door to the home I was staying in. With the curtains drawn, the living room was dim, but rather than opening them, I walked over to the lantern after shutting the front door. I pressed a finger to the vial, refilling the fire magic inside before lighting the flame.

"Have fun at the market today?" someone asked, causing me to jump.

I spun to find Paxon lounging in a chair in the corner, like he'd been waiting for me. He traced a finger over the cover of the book I'd left out, one leg crossed over the other.

"I did," I said, doing my best to mask my irritation at the sight of him.

"Good." He stood, taking his time as he uncrossed his leg and pushed up from the chair. He left the book on the armrest as he slowly moved toward me. "I saw you there."

When he didn't continue, I said, "Oh?"

"With Bowen." He prowled closer to where I stood in the entry of the room.

"I wasn't exactly *with* him," I clarified. "More like he helped me and stayed near in case something happened again." I hoped that was a good enough cover-up and Paxon hadn't seen us in the alley. Technically, I had been there with Siara, and Bowen had inserted himself into our little shopping trip.

"I'm only going to say this once, Auria. Whatever you are doing with him, it needs to stop."

"Why?" The question was out of my mouth before I could stop it. I should have left it at that. I had no reason to want to be around Bowen any more than I had to, so it should be no problem to listen to Paxon's demand, but something about him trying to tell me what to do, who I could be around, didn't sit right with me. I was tired of people trying to control me.

He stopped within a foot of me. "You're with my brother, aren't you? Or did you forget I gave you a choice not too long ago? A choice of who you could belong to."

His words lit a match in me. "I don't belong to anyone but myself," I gritted out.

Paxon's eyes turned curious, a hint of amusement in them. "You belong to my brother until you make your decision."

"And if I don't?"

In a flash, he grabbed my wrist, squeezing until I swore the bone might break. A little whimper escaped me, despite my effort to hold it in. "Then I will shatter every precious little finger on this hand until you can no longer use your magic. And without those, you are useless. A fragile thing with no purpose."

I tried to keep my breathing controlled as I attempted to yank my wrist away, but it wasn't until he loosened his grip that I was successful. My heart pounded inside my chest, the beat nearly painful as the reality that he'd seen me use my magic on the fire vial set in.

"No more Bowen," he repeated, each word enunciated clearly.

He walked past me, his usual calm demeanor firmly back in place as his threat hung in the air.

"And Auria," he said, turning his head to the side but not looking at me, "the bridge changes nothing. You have until it's repaired and we are able to return to decide."

After the front door closed behind him, my hand tightened into a fist. Frustration ate at me like termites to wood, and I wanted to hit something. To yell, to cry. But all I could do was grind my teeth as I gave Paxon enough time to walk away from the house. Then, once I was sure the coast was clear, I left.

I had a lifetime of staying cooped up to look forward to upon my return to Amosite. I was going to handle my emotions in the one way I knew might erase them for just a few hours—with a couple drinks.

~

THE BARTENDER GAVE me a hefty dose of side-eye as I slid onto a stool in the dimly lit saloon. Patrons that had shopped for hours littered the bar, having spent a bountiful amount of magic on items from the market and were now drinking the rest of their day away. I hoped to be on the same level of buzzing in less than an hour's time.

"Order," the bartender grumbled. He was a big, burly man with bulging muscles and short-cropped brunet hair. It was a wonder he was working behind a bar and not a part of the army.

Having never been in a proper bar before, I wasn't sure what to order. With my hesitation, he seemed to sense my naivety. "I'll get ya an ale."

"Thank you," I said as he moved to grab a thick glass, pouring dark gold liquid into the cup from a spout.

He slid it onto the counter, some of the liquid sloshing out onto the sticky bar top. "Three coins."

I rifled through my pocket, tossing three silver coins onto the counter. He grabbed them, tossing them into a bucket on the floor. That wasn't a very secure payment system.

"What's your name?" I asked as he slung a dirty rag over his bulky shoulder. Black ink stretched up his neck like so many others in this town.

He only glared in response, then moved to fill another drink for a beautiful black-haired woman down the way.

"That's Lux," a man said as he slid onto a stool next to me.

I turned to find Flynt setting his own glass on the bar.

"I take it he's not very talkative," I surmised, grabbing my drink.

"Only with the people he likes," Flynt replied with a half-shrug. "Which isn't many."

Bringing the glass to my lips, I sipped and instantly regretted it. My eyes squeezed shut against the tart taste.

"Nastiest shit, isn't it?" Flynt asked around a smile.

I coughed, setting the cup back down. "How can you even enjoy that?"

Flynt shrugged, taking a large sip of his own. "Not much of a choice. Lux brews it in the back and won't change his recipe. He says it's an 'acquired taste' and we all just need to open our palates."

"It's true," Lux grumbled from the end of the bar as he poured another hefty serving of ale. "You fuckers have no taste."

"I don't think it's terrible," Siara said as she slid onto the stool on my other side.

Flynt scrunched his face. "She's insane."

"Stop giving poor ol' Lux such a hard time. He works hard on his ale," Siara defended. As if on cue, Lux slid a full glass in front of her. She gave him a sweet smile. "Thanks, Luxxy."

Flynt groaned, setting an elbow on the bar and a hand on his forehead, like she was giving him a headache. "Siara, please."

"You're just mad you can't get free drinks by flirting," she said.

A smile pulled at my lips as Flynt said, "Lux, you're looking very handsome today. New tattoo? Bet you stole some real badass magic to get that beauty."

Lux only grunted, walking away.

"You're terrible at flirting, that's the problem," Siara observed, sipping her drink without so much as a wince. "Auria, on the other hand, is amazing at it."

"*What*?" I'd never done such a thing, *especially* not in Deadwood.

Siara swallowed her ale, her glass thumping against the bar as she set it down. "Don't act so oblivious. Bowen's hooked around your pretty little finger." Then she added under her breath, "More than that fiancé of yours."

Flynt's brows rose. This was news to him as much as it was to me.

"I certainly do *not* flirt with Bowen."

She cocked her head, her light blonde hair sliding over her bare shoulder. She was wearing a white sleeveless top and tan pants, the outfit accentuating her curves. "Hm."

I faced her fully in my seat. "What does 'hm' mean?"

Behind me, Flynt said, "Bowen doesn't get attached to women."

I spun on the stool, facing him now. Was he insinuating he went from woman to woman, unabashed?

"Never had a woman worth getting attached to," Siara muttered.

I turned back to her. I was going to get whiplash. "What are you two trying to say?"

Siara shrugged, turning her attention to her ale with a flick of her hand. "You probably don't care. As you said, you don't flirt with him, so it likely doesn't matter to you."

I grabbed my ale, scrunching my nose in an attempt to plug it as I chugged the liquid. I didn't stop until the last drop passed my lips, then slammed it on the bar. This was not my idea of getting my mind off things—not when Siara and Flynt were throwing Bowen's name around like some sort of carefully laid bait. I didn't have enough alcohol in my system to deal with this.

"Maybe we can talk about a man you do like, then," Siara said as Lux grabbed my glass, refilling it.

I tossed three more coin onto the bar, a snort escaping me. "Who might that be?"

Siara stared at me, raising both brows. "Your fiancé, maybe?"

Lux slid the glass back to me, and I cradled it with both hands, watching as the liquid sloshed. "Oh. Right."

Flynt belted out a laugh, slapping a hand on the bar as he leaned closer. "Did you truly just forget about your fiancé?"

"It's a forced marriage." The explanation fell out of my mouth, and I instantly wished I could take it back. The alcohol was making my tongue loose.

Siara perched an elbow on the bar, her knees brushing the cushion on my stool. "Well, we all knew *that*."

"You did?" As far as the other kingdoms were aware, we were marrying to return the peace. Our union was to show that Torbernite and Amosite were coming together in an attempt to restore trade, and it was supposed to be believable. That was the whole point of this trip.

"You're never with him," she said simply.

"That, and you two rarely smile together. Or even frown, for that matter. Two people who like one another usually get under each other's skin," Flynt added.

"I hardly think that's the basis of a healthy relationship." I went in for another gulp of ale, needing the alcohol to work its magic far quicker than it was.

"So, is he good in bed?" Siara asked.

Ale flew out of my mouth in a spray, resulting in a glare from Lux.

"Gods, Siara," Flynt mumbled, shaking his head before sipping his drink. He needed the buzz as much as I did now.

She shrugged. "I'm only curious. He's attractive."

"We're friends," I choked out after my coughing fit.

"Who said friends couldn't have fun?" she asked innocently.

"Please never say that around me or the guys again," Flynt groaned.

"Life's boring if you don't get a quickie in now and then," Siara added, as if that defended her statement.

Flynt's face twisted in disgust. "We're practically your brothers, Siara."

She reached around me to smack him lightly on the back of the head. "I don't mean *you*, idiot. You three aren't the only men in this world. And even if you were, I would never sleep with any of you."

Flynt rubbed at the back of his head. "Thank the gods. I love you like family, Siara, but—"

"Flynt, hate to cut you off, but this isn't about you. I hear about you enough." Siara turned her gaze back on me. "About the fiancé."

I spun the glass on the counter, the liquid sloshing up the sides. "There's not much to tell."

"You truly haven't jumped his bones?" Siara asked, disbelief in her tone.

"No." And I didn't plan to. We didn't even want to get married to one another, let alone have sex. "We're just marrying to"—my face scrunched—"restore peace." I rested an elbow on the bartop, my chin falling into my palm. "But I don't know if that's *really* the reason." The admission slipped past my tongue before I could stop it. Damn Lux's ale.

Over me, Siara and Flynt shared a look, but I couldn't decipher what it meant.

Siara let out a dramatically loud sigh, breaking their stare. "Everyone is so damned boring in this town."

I snorted, ignoring how they didn't acknowledge what I'd said. Lander and I were a mess these two probably didn't want to get too involved in. "You're in a town full of criminals and outlaws, and you think that's boring?" My eyes widened on my drink for emphasis, my brows raising as I looked at her. "Try living in Amosite."

Something akin to pity flashed across her face as her features softened, and I shook my head. "Oh, no. Don't look at me like that."

"Like what?" she asked, her voice even softer now.

"I don't need your pity," I said before downing the rest of my ale. My mind was finally starting to feel the effects of the alcohol, and I was glad for it. "Go back to asking about my sex life or something."

"It's not pity," she defended, not even a shimmer of intrigue lighting her gaze with my suggestion.

I slid the glass forward, hoping Lux would fill it soon. I couldn't tell if the taste was growing on me or my body simply wanted the buzz so bad that it didn't mind the pungent flavor anymore. "What do you know of my father anyway? Does everyone know what he does?" Like keep me locked in a castle. Or literally any other terrible thing he had done.

"Besides the fact that he's the reason for a lot of people's suffering?" Siara questioned.

Flynt instantly shot her a look that screamed, *Shut up*.

I froze, my eyes stuck on a particularly sticky spot on the counter top. "What?"

Siara glanced at Flynt. "If he's not going to tell her, then I might as well."

"That's not your place, Siara," Flynt warned.

"What aren't you two telling me?"

Flynt shook his head subtly. "Siara, don't."

She stared at him, an entire argument playing out between the two of them in that look alone.

Unbeknownst to the war raging in front of him, Lux filled our glasses once more before moving back to the other patrons. With the silence stretching between Siara and Flynt, I stood from the barstool and tipped my head back to guzzle the ale down. After slamming the glass on the bar, I tossed three coins on the counter, then looked to them both. "I'm heading home, but next time you two want to hang out, make sure you're willing to talk about the things you bring up."

All of my anger truly wasn't directed at them, but I wanted to enjoy my buzz, not wallow in it, so leaving was the best option.

But that didn't mean I was going back to the house I was staying in.

No, the options were limitless in Deadwood, and the thought alone excited me all the more.

CHAPTER 34

AURIA

Despite the late afternoon sun reflecting off the rings in the sky, there was a cool breeze battling with the heat. I welcomed it as the wind rustled the leaves high above. The woods called to me. Each time my mind wandered, I wanted to go here. Perhaps it was the deprivation from a lifetime in Amosite with no forest to traipse through, but the various oaks and pines settled me, bathing my body in their endless shade.

Being enclosed in walls most of my life, the open expanse of the desert or meadows made me feel too vulnerable, exposed. Whereas the trees, huddled mere feet apart, gave me a wide, yet comfortable space, compared to the stone I knew so well.

I reveled in the last few days of freedom I had with no guard trailing me everywhere I went. Though helpful in some instances, they made being wholly myself difficult at times. Their injuries were bittersweet, along with the conversation I'd walked out on in the saloon.

Siara had insinuated that my father was the reason for people's suffering, and while I wasn't blind to his treatment of the citizens in Silicate now that I'd witnessed it firsthand—though my experience was brief—I got the feeling she was hinting at a much bigger picture, and yet again, information was withheld from me.

Was it me?

Did I seem that naive to give the impression that I couldn't handle the world for what it was—cruelties and all?

"Trouble in town not enough for you?" a deep voice spoke up, pulling me from the alcohol-induced spiral I was headed toward.

I set a hand on the trunk of a tree, glancing over my shoulder to find Bowen standing a few trees back. "I was simply enjoying the silence of the forest." I faced forward again, stepping over a root as I continued walking. "And you are currently interrupting it."

By the crunch of leaves, I could tell he was following me. "Ah, Princess, with that head of yours, I doubt it's ever truly silent."

I rolled my eyes, despite him being unable to see it. "Do tell. What do you suppose I'd be thinking about to make my mind so loud?"

He hummed as he grew closer to my back, and still, I continued walking. "I could guess a few things."

"Go on."

Without pause, he listed, "The ring that will one day feel too heavy on your finger. Why this land is so vastly different from your own. How you finally don't have a guard trailing you like a lost puppy. But on top of all that"—he exhaled a breath, close enough now that it raised the hairs on the back of my neck—"what most stands out in that pretty head of yours is the way you feel when you're around me."

My cheeks heated, and I was glad he stood behind me so he couldn't see what he really did to me. I scoffed in an attempt to act as if his words hadn't affected me. "I feel nothing around you."

I could practically sense his smirk. "The princess is a liar."

I whirled, finding him all too close as he nearly rammed into my chest. "I am *not* a princess, and I feel *nothing*, especially around you."

His voice lowered. "Besides the fear?"

My eyes narrowed. "Why are you out here?"

"I could ask you the same thing."

I let out a frustrated groan, turning back around to take another step.

"Tell me something honest," he went on.

I tried to focus on the tiny bits of green grass reaching up through the pine needles and leaves covering the ground, searching for sunlight as they brushed along the sides of my boots. His question made me want to laugh. Out of everyone here, I was the most honest of all of them, and yet, he wanted veracity from me?

"Honest." The word tasted bitter on my tongue. "That's so funny, considering no one tells me shit, including you."

"I've never lied to you."

My eyes turned to slits at his statement, but I couldn't deny that I believed him. I might be foolish, naïve, but nothing he'd ever said to me before felt like a lie. Not like the spun truths my father presented me with.

With a sigh, I admitted, "I'm not upset that the bridge collapsed."

When he didn't respond, I turned around, finding him still standing where I'd left him. His brow was cocked, his gaze curious. "Really?"

I picked at a piece of bark on the tree to my right, studying the rough, brown piece as if it was the most fascinating thing on this planet. "I mean, of course I'm upset about it. I was meant to be back in Amosite before..." I shook my head. My father would be irate. "It's just nice to be somewhere other than the castle for a change."

"I know. You don't get out much."

I moved my attention to him. He remembered me saying that so long ago?

"I'm the daughter of a king," I explained. "I can't exactly just stroll around wherever I'd like."

"Why not?"

My brows pulled together, his question taking me back. Was the reason not clear already? "What if I was injured? Or worse?"

He held a hand out, gesturing to the forest surrounding us. "You're walking around right now, aren't you? No guard, no order. Just you, on your own free will. Slightly buzzed, too, if I'm guessing correctly."

He was idiotic. "Well, as you can see from the market incident, my free will is not always the best. It sometimes leads me to being deceived." Yet the last part was not in reference to the market. It was a jab at him. I shook my head and continued, "I shouldn't have said anything about the man stealing."

"So, what? You'd rather lie down and let him?" he asked, as if he wasn't the one to step in when I had almost been pulverized. Well, at least that's what I assumed would have happened if Bowen hadn't shown up.

"I'm the king's—"

He stepped forward, interrupting me. "I don't give a fuck about your king."

The anger in his tone shocked me, leaving me standing there with no response. In seconds, he was in front of me. "You want to know something, Auria? Just ask."

My mouth dropped open. Was he *serious*? "You're acting like you'd just simply answer my questions now."

He held his hands out. "Ask away."

"How do I know you won't twist some wicked answer for your own benefit?"

"You truly think I'm so cruel," he surmised.

"Fine!" I huffed air out of my nose. "What clouds your mind, then?"

He looked rather bored as he said, "Aside from knowing the nauseating feeling that overcomes you when you don't use your powers?"

I nearly froze in place. "How do you know about that?"

"We both have powers, don't we? Using them can become somewhat of an addiction, and your father has you riding that high so thoroughly that your body loathes being cut off from it."

My head shook of its own accord. "My magic comes from me. I control it."

He chuckled, the sound full of breath and pity. "You've never been taught how to control it—those urges that hit you when you haven't fed it, I know all too well. Magic is alive, Auria, and sometimes it bites."

Suddenly, the forgotten book and half-empty vial made sense. He knew my magic—my own self—better than I did. I felt like a fool. So my next question came calculated.

"Why did Siara say my father is the reason for a lot of people's suffering?"

For a moment, he looked almost taken aback, like that was the last thing he expected me to ask. I wanted to say, *Don't worry, I have a list*, but settled on taking it one question at a time.

"He's the reason we have to stay in hiding," he started.

I blinked, then shook my head as I tried to comprehend his answer. "Fae?"

Bowen nodded, crossing his arms. A topic he was defensive of, then.

"How? That's not possible. My father doesn't have that much power. Or any, for that matter." My eyes trailed to the ground in thought.

"Anything is possible, Princess. You just have to open your eyes to it."

"He's just one man."

"One man, with enough power to wipe out an entire civilization."

My father was feared by fae because of *his* magic? "But fae are more powerful than humans." I looked up at him. "Aren't they?"

He leaned a bit closer, his eyes brighter than the sky itself. "Humans don't have powers, Auria. So yes, that is correct."

The entire world slammed into me at once, and I flung a hand out to the tree to steady myself. "What did you just say?"

"Lander was telling you the truth when he told you humans don't have powers."

"But I—"

"*You* are a unique case."

Why? Why me? "Am I fae?"

"I'm not sure," he admitted.

My voice rose as I said, "You're not *sure*?"

"You may be half, the lineage possibly going back centuries in your bloodline, but without knowledge of what your mother was, I couldn't guess entirely."

I swayed on my feet, the truth of his words making the alcohol sour in my stomach. I'd never suspected my mother was anything but human in the few years she'd been alive. "How can you be so certain?"

He grabbed my waist, steadying me. Whether it was the buzz or the truth making my head spin, I wanted him to keep his hold on me. Keep me grounded to this earth, in this moment, rather than letting me spiral out of control. "I can sense something is different about you," he said softly.

"That's why you hate me."

His eyes flashed like pain physically hit him with my assumption. "I don't hate you, Auria."

"Then that's why *they* hate me. Why every kingdom I've visited on this wretched journey has loathed me, made their hatred of me clear."

His gaze darkened, his fingers straining not to grip my waist tighter. His arm flexed with the effort. "They will not harm you. I would never let that happen."

My eyes, welling with tears I refused to let fall, found his, holding his stare. "You don't understand. They already have. All of this, and I'm supposed to what? Go back to that suffocating castle and live out my days, as if my father is the saint he claims to be?"

"You don't have to go back."

I shoved his hand off me, reeling as I spun around and plunged my hands through my hair. "Don't say that like it's an option."

"You have choices, Auria."

I laughed, the sound anything but comforting as I turned on him. "Choices aren't afforded to pawns like me, Bowen."

"This isn't his game to win."

"So, what? Your plan is to what? Kill my father?" I hated the pain that laced itself with those words. How terrible would it be if my captor was gone? The man who was supposed to love me unconditionally, who instead held me locked in his idea of a suitable life. If he died, I'd be left with my stepmother, and she—

He stepped into my space again, cutting off my thoughts before they went places they couldn't come back from. "If that's what you want, say the words. Say you want him dead, and I'll drive the knife through his heart and set you free. You can fly, Auria. You just haven't left the nest."

"I'm out of his damn cage right now and look at me!"

He did. His eyes devoured me, taking in my body, every dip and divot, like a feast. "Freedom looks astonishing on you."

And then it hit me.

I wasn't the only prisoner here. He was hiding, too. He was fae. His prison looked a lot different than mine, but we were both held stagnant with no place to go. He couldn't truly be himself, let his fae side out to play, unless he was sure no human was watching. And me? I couldn't be me, period. There was no escaping this endless hell for me. But maybe for him, there could be.

And maybe...it wasn't me who couldn't handle the world.

Maybe the world couldn't handle me.

"I have one more question," I said, needing to move the topic off of me.

"Is that so?" he replied, sarcasm lacing his voice, like he knew damn well I had a hundred more.

"For now." I dipped my chin before meeting his gaze. "Why were you in Torbernite the night of Exitium Lunae if you weren't celebrating? You clearly have no ties with them."

He inhaled, his shoulders rising with the act. "I was looking for something, and I figured infiltrating their castle on a night when everyone was distracted celebrating a mass slaughter was the best time."

My brows rose at least six inches in the air. "I'm sorry, what? A mass slaughter? Lander told me it was a holiday to honor equality."

He let out a chuckle, the sound holding no amusement. "Yeah. That's what they tell themselves. Is it equality to hold a tradition where you party until the sun rises if you're celebrating the day they tried to wipe out the entire fae population? Not to mention, they thought they were successful. Every year, we get to watch humans drink and dance and enjoy themselves over the murders of our innocent population."

My mouth opened and closed like a fish out of water. "That can't— But he said—"

"He's manipulating you." His voice sounded strained as the veins in his hands blackened, the web of dark strings climbing up his neck.

"Lander is educating me," I defended. "Something no one else has offered to me. How am I supposed to know who to believe?"

He stepped closer, bending forward so our noses were nearly touching. "Maybe the man who's saved your life countless times now, and given you the option to get out of the situation that's *killing* you."

My breath stuck in my lungs. He was right. Bowen had shown no ill will toward me. He'd helped me, taken my people in, saved me from certain death, whereas Lander had been all too comfortable with the circumstances at hand, not thinking twice about bringing me back to my father.

I had to trust Bowen. He'd given me no reason not to.

With that thought in mind, I wanted to make the most out of my time left with him.

"I have one request before I leave."

He waited, that raw hunger still shining bright in his eyes.

"Take me to see the bison."

CHAPTER 35

AURIA

After a night of restless sleep, I met Bowen in the meadow clearing behind Deadwood. It had been too late in the day for him to take me as soon as I'd asked, so he'd promised this morning that he would follow through on my request to see the bison. To my surprise, he was waiting where he'd told me to meet him with his back against a tree, one leg kicked up with a foot resting on the bark as he bit into an apple.

"Sleep well?" Bowen asked, pushing off the tree as soon as I entered the grassy expanse surrounded on all sides by thick groups of trees.

"As well as I could," I replied, suddenly thirsty for an entire bucket of water. The ale had dehydrated me, and I greatly regretted overindulging.

He crossed the field, holding the apple out to me. "Long night from the anticipation of seeing me again, or the alcohol?"

I ignored his offering as well as his snarky question. "Are we walking to the bison?" They had seemed far off in the distance on our way into Deadwood, so I doubted it'd be a short trip on foot.

He dropped his hand. "You know, there are far more interesting things to see in Deadwood than a herd of bison."

I quirked a brow. "Oh, yeah? What did you have in mind?"

He shrugged, eyes scanning the trees behind me. He was about to open his mouth when my memory struck me. "Actually, now that you mention it, I do recall seeing some sort of building in the forest."

His gaze shot to mine, and it seemed he was trying to cover his surprise at my acknowledgment of it. "When did you see that?"

A smile tugged at my lips for taking him off guard, but I stifled it. "The night I went to the cave."

A gust of wind blew through the trees, rustling my hair, but neither of us took our gazes off each other.

"Best to stay away from there," he finally said.

"The building or the cave?"

"Both."

With the vulnerable look in his eyes, I assumed that, whatever the structure was, it meant something to him, so I decided to let it go. "I suppose we'll have to settle on the bison, then."

He tossed the apple in the air, his casual demeanor slipping back into place seamlessly, and caught the half eaten fruit again. "Might want something in your stomach for this, Princess."

"How do you know I haven't eaten breakfast already?"

He admired the fruit like it was the most interesting thing he'd seen all week. "I think you rushed here first thing, forgetting to even have a sip of water."

My eyes narrowed on him. He had no right guessing correctly. I plucked the apple from his fingers. "Fine. I'll eat as we walk."

I took a step but immediately stopped in my tracks as a massive, midnight black dragon landed directly in front of us.

The earth shook as it set massive, taloned feet on the ground, the ends digging up soil. My grip on the apple slipped, and it tumbled to the ground as I hurriedly stepped back, though it was a feeble attempt as the dragon could easily eat me whole if it wanted, no matter how far I was. It folded in its wings, the grass and leaves rustling in the breeze it created with the movement.

Bowen simply stared up at the beast like it was just another day for him. "That's how we're getting to the bison."

My eyes widened, darting between Bowen and the dragon. As it shifted, the tips of its black scales sparkled a shimmering gold. "We're *riding* it?"

"*Him*," the dragon corrected, his voice like a landslide in an empty cave as it filled the space around us.

I gawked at the beast.

"This is Vulcan," Bowen introduced, like he was some kind of close friend rather than a fucking dragon.

"He has a *name*?"

Bowen fought to keep a smile at bay, clearly finding amusement in my reaction to the dragon, who stood taller than the trees, huffing in front of us.

I spun on Bowen. "How am I even supposed to get on that thing?" The pitch in my tone was high, doing little to hide my nerves.

The ground beneath me shook, causing me to stumble as I faced the dragon again. He'd come closer.

Vulcan's nostrils flared, his pitch black eyes narrowing on me. "*Does the burned one have no manners*?"

My jaw nearly fell to the lush grass. The *burned one*?

Bowen stepped forward, his shoulder slightly blocking me from Vulcan—as if that would do anything against the beast—with all traces of his smile now gone. "Vulcan, this is Auria." He accentuated my name, putting emphasis on it.

The dragon's tail swished through the grass, the movement anything but settling.

"That is what you will call her from now on," Bowen warned. Was he really ordering a *dragon* around?

"As for your question," Bowen said, turning to me, "I'll help you up."

"I'll need at least a twenty-foot ladder to get on him." There was no way I could manage this just by a helping hand. Bowen was tall, but not *that* tall. The dragon dwarfed us. To him, we were the ants littering the ground.

Vulcan seemed almost reluctant as he bent, lowering his wing to the grass. The gold flakes shimmered as he stretched the limb, but the beauty was nothing compared to the deadly look of his talons, dirty and sharp, along with his dripping fangs hiding behind a scaled mouth that surely held a few dozen more, primed and ready to swallow me whole.

I shook my head. "I take it back, I don't want to see the bison. I would much rather hang out with Siara, or even Lux, or really do *anything* but this."

Bowen stepped in front of me, doing his best to block my view of Vulcan but failing miserably. "He won't hurt you."

A disbelieving laugh escaped me. "He's a thousand times your size."

Bowen cocked a brow.

"I mean that he's not going to listen to you!"

Behind him, Vulcan practically rolled his eyes—if dragons could even do that.

"He has no reason to eat you, if that's what you're worried about," Bowen said.

"Until he does," I hissed out.

Bowen looked over his shoulder at the dragon, impatiently waiting with his wing still lowered to the grass. "Did you hunt this morning?"

"*Only innocent people*," Vulcan replied, bored.

My mouth fell open again.

Bowen faced me, grabbing both my hands and giving a reassuring squeeze. "He's only kidding." Then, louder, "Right, Vulcan?"

"*I suppose*," the beast purred. His voice, deep and full of gravel, grated over my body, sending chills prickling across my arms.

"If you truly don't want to ride on him, I can saddle up some horses and we can be on our way. He's the quickest means of getting there, but horseback is fine if that's what you'd prefer." It almost shocked me how willing he was to accommodate me if I didn't wish to ride a fortress of a beast.

I stared at Vulcan's shimmering wing, finding it almost hypnotizing. If Bowen said it was alright, I had no reason not to trust him with this, too. Right? Surely, he'd done this before, and so far, he'd proved that keeping me alive and unharmed was important to him. After all he'd done for me thus far, he wouldn't put me on the back of a dragon who would drop me from the air like a flea on his back and be done with me.

Hopefully.

"No," I said, shoving all the confidence I could muster into the word. "We can do this."

"We?" Bowen repeated. "Princess, I've ridden him hundreds of times. It's you who needs convincing."

Refusing to lose the confidence I'd just meagerly gained, I stomped past Bowen, my boots flattening the grass as I approached Vulcan's wing.

"Auria—" Bowen called out, but I didn't stop.

I reached up, grabbing hold of the bony part at the tip of his wing. With a swivel of his head, he shot me an irritated glare, a rumble sounding in his throat as the bottoms of his very sharp, very horrifying teeth bared at me.

"Auria, it was a joke," Bowen said after I hefted myself up, digging the toe of my boot into Vulcan's scales with a white-knuckled grip on his wing.

"What?" Was he kidding me? Now I looked like an idiot. Riding a dragon—

Bowen placed strong hands on my waist, lifting me off the wing and bringing me back to the ground. The warmth of his skin seeped through my loose, leather corset where it sat over my white blouse. Every nerve in my body focused in on his touch, but then, somewhat reluctantly and to my slight disappointment, he dropped his arms to his sides. "You climb up his leg, not his wing."

I let out a frustrated huff of air, tossing my head back. "Gods, save me."

"*Not even a god can save you from this, burned one,*" Vulcan muttered, lifting his wing in a high arc before stretching out his front leg before me and Bowen. The size alone made me have to swallow the nerves that crawled up my throat. He was massive—almost the same size as the snow dragon in the Brimstone Mountains.

"Vulcan," Bowen reprimanded, glaring up at the beast.

Vulcan chuffed, a puff of warm vapor rising from his nostrils. "*You call her by a different name as well.*"

Bowen's jaw clenched. "Not to degrade her."

I snorted. "That's not how I've taken it."

His eyes held mine. "Maybe in the beginning, Auria, but not now."

Like a trance, he pulled me in with words I so badly wanted to hear. Something was changing between us, and maybe it wasn't anything big, but the subtle shift that had occurred between when we first met and now wasn't lost on me. I only hated that whatever this was was temporary.

"*Her name does not suit her,*" Vulcan defended shamelessly, breaking our short stupor.

"Your attitude does not suit you," I spit back, trying to find a place to grip onto his scales. Behind me, Bowen set his hands back on my waist, and I froze. They fit so perfectly—like they belonged in that tiny divot between my ribs and my hips.

"Careful, Princess. He can bite." Bowen lifted me higher, helping me get my footing. Though Vulcan's leg was outstretched, it still gave us a steep incline.

Vulcan stared out at the tops of the trees, waiting for us to get our act together. Well, I supposed just me. Bowen was apparently a pro. "*Yes, and I'm feeling a bit snappy.*" For emphasis, he made the closest resemblance a dragon could to a smile, bearing his yellow teeth dripping with saliva.

Bowen shook his head behind me as I breached the top of Vulcan's shoulder, climbing onto his back. With his size, it wasn't as difficult as I thought it would be to stand and get my footing. Still, though, Bowen kept a hand at my waist, his touch light, to keep me from losing balance. I didn't want to know how far of a drop it would be, even on the ground.

"Sit here," Bowen instructed, gesturing to the center of Vulcan's shoulders.

"We just...sit? There's nothing to hold on to?" I asked.

Bowen must've seen the slight fear in my eyes because he stepped behind me, his chest brushing my back.

"You can hold on to me if you'd prefer," he murmured in my ear, brushing his hands down my arms to grab my hands. He helped lower me to straddle the peak in Vulcan's spine. Once I was seated, his hand slid down my outer thigh toward my knee, then back up to my hip. "You hold on here"—he trailed his hand back down to my calf where it was slightly angled toward him—"not here. He doesn't like when you dig your heels in."

In response, Vulcan blew a burst of steam through his nose. From this angle, I could barely see over the arch of his neck to the back of his head. But even from here, he was just as menacing.

"Ready?" Bowen asked, situating himself behind me in a similar position. His knees brushed the backs of my legs, his body flush with mine.

I gave a stern nod, despite the flutter of my heart. From fear or Bowen's presence, I wasn't sure. "Ready."

His hands fell to my waist like an anchor, and my stomach dropped as Vulcan flared his wings, beating them against the wind. My eyes wanted to squeeze shut, every instinct in my body screaming to lie flat and hold on for dear life, but I held my position. Almost reassuringly, Bowen's thumb brushed the skin peeking out from under my shirt. I wasn't sure if the sensation was more thrilling than the ride itself, but I didn't have time to think about it as Vulcan banked left, throwing my body to the side. Despite gravity trying to pull us down, Bowen kept me in place until Vulcan straightened out. The sound of his wings was like a steady heartbeat, and once we were off the ground, the flight became almost peaceful.

"You're doing so good," Bowen praised, and his words shot straight to my core, heating me from the inside.

To distract myself from our position in the sky and Bowen's hands on me, I focused on the gold shimmers hidden in Vulcan's black scales, the sun dancing over them almost like the blazing ball of fire was meant to do just that. The glimmering splotches stole the rays, soaking them in and spitting them out with ten times the vibrance, the beauty almost blinding me.

"They manipulate the light when he needs them to," Bowen explained, his mouth close to my ear in order for me to hear him over the howl of the wind. "Comes in handy sometimes."

"Manipulation?" I clarified.

I felt him shake his head, his chin coasting over my shoulder. "No. Working together with an unlikely ally."

I assumed the sun could make a dragon a target for predators—if they even had any—so the trick of the light would definitely seem helpful to Vulcan in some circumstances.

Daring a glance over the side of Vulcan's wide body, I looked down upon the tops of the trees, their size seeming almost insignificant from this high up. On one side, the mountains stood in the distance, looming over the land like they, too, knew their beauty and held it proudly. In the opposite direction, the terrain held the desert, bordering the other side of Deadwood. Ahead, the forest ended, opening to a large expanse of green grass. The fields stretched forever, butting up to what seemed to be a river in the distance.

Little brown specks popped up among the sea of green as we flew closer, revealing themselves to be a herd of bison. I sucked in a breath, the confirmation that they were truly alive and indeed not extinct almost threatening to take the air from my lungs. I remembered eating bison as a delicacy growing up, the memory as vivid as when my father told us they had been killed off, never to be seen or hunted again.

Minutes later, Vulcan landed in the field, far enough away from the herd that I had to squint my eyes to make them out. Vulcan dropped his shoulder so Bowen could help me down his scaled leg. All the while, my heart raced with anticipation. For the most part, it wasn't seeing them that amazed me, but more so the confirmation that my father had lied. It made me wonder how many other things he had twisted for his own benefit—and why.

Vulcan made himself comfortable, finding a spot to lie in the shade, as Bowen walked through the tickling grass beside me. The breeze blew the blades as clouds cast shadows over the ground all around us.

"Your father made the announcement of their extinction almost two decades ago," Bowen said.

I glanced at him. "How did you know that?"

With his gaze focused on the herd ahead, he said, "It was when he cut off all trade with Deadwood."

My brows furrowed. "Why would he do that?" The town was full of criminals, but if they provided a staple, surely my father would've negotiated a deal good enough for the both of them.

"How well do you think you truly know your father?"

"Enough to know he's greedy," I replied.

Bowen dipped his chin, the grass rustling around his boots. "That's a start." He hesitated, thinking on his next words. "He doesn't think he needs to rely on any other kingdoms to remain flourishing." He glanced sidelong at me. "And I assume that's because of you."

"I hardly think I have much to do with it." I couldn't produce food or other goods with my power, only duplicate magic that was already in front of me.

Bowen stopped, a finger ghosting my wrist to cause me to face him. "Don't underestimate your value, Auria. Before I saw you, truly saw you, I did the same. Which was foolish of me, might I add. But you are much more magnificent than you've been led to believe." He stepped forward, a lock of hair blowing over his brow. "That man and those walls are not your end, Princess."

I swallowed, slightly taken aback by his affirmation of my magic. Still, it felt odd to hear someone speak about it so... openly. But not only that, his confession. His demeanor toward me had changed since my group arrived in Deadwood, and he noticed it, too.

"Your father thinks that with you, he can create all that he needs," he continued.

"But wealth is not the only thing keeping Amosite alive," I explained. "They need to eat, to drink, have shelter and clothes."

He cocked his head slightly, studying me. "When you went into Silicate, did you get that impression? That the people were taken care of?"

The conditions of the citizens had been clear, and Bowen's point was proven. I shook my head in response.

"Your father's greed is killing your kingdom. Other kingdoms, innocent people—they're all suffering at his hands. He doesn't like Deadwood? He cuts us off. My people have suffered just as much."

My head tilted at his phrasing. "Your people?"

He sighed, looking up to the sky like it might give him the restraint he needed.

"Bowen. What are you saying?"

His forehead creased as his eyes met mine again. Already, I could tell he was choosing what to tell me, picking each word carefully. Normally, I'd feel upset over that. But if this topic was sensitive to him, a subject he didn't take lightly, I wouldn't take it to heart. Not all things were meant to be known.

"Deadwood is a ruined kingdom."

CHAPTER 36

BOWEN

"What?" Auria asked, her voice laced in disbelief. The look in her eyes pained me. Another detail of this world once unknown to her, being thrown at her with the rest of the secrets she'd been unraveling. That look alone made me want to keep her in Deadwood. Fuck the bridge and her father.

There was so much she didn't know, and I wanted to be the one to tell her all of it. But piling too many stones on an unstable pile would surely topple the structure.

"Deadwood was one of the many kingdoms fae called home before the moon ruptured. After the humans barricaded themselves in Amosite, leaving the dragons to take out the population of fae, multiple civilizations were wiped out in the destruction. My people came out lucky, even though our population is a fraction of what it once was, but the others were burned to the ground. Their buildings and people succumbed to the chaos wreaked among villages."

Her brows pulled together as she tried to piece it all together, and I saw the moment it hit her—the moment her perception of me would change, likely forever. "You're a king?" Her voice was barely more than a whisper.

I loosed a breath. "Yes."

"But—" She shook her head. "Why don't they regard you as such?"

"I don't want them to," I admitted. I'd never wanted the title, but it had been thrust upon me at a young age when my father was murdered. "I'm one of my people, not some greater male sitting high above them. We are all equals, and the titles should remain as such. As was how it should've stayed between humans and fae."

"Stayed?" she repeated.

My lips rolled together. There was so much to say, and so little time until she left. "Fae were always more powerful than humans, sure. But they never used their abilities in that sense —only to aid. Yet, the moment humans got the upper hand, they took over, trying to eliminate the fae species altogether."

In the slight sheen of her eyes, I could tell her mind was spinning. "But how did they manage to—"

"Auria," I interrupted, taking her hands in mine. It wasn't solely my decision whether she could know about our plan, and in telling her more, it would surely end up in questions I couldn't answer without potentially upsetting my friends. I should talk to them first, but even if they disagreed, I wasn't sure I was willing to keep anything from Auria. "Can we talk about this back in town?"

Her eyes, so full of betrayal—not from me, but for what she'd been taught to believe—searched for my honesty. I wouldn't keep anything more from her unless it was to ensure her safety, but discussing it in a field with any listening ears wasn't wise. And by the glare Vulcan was aiming my way, he was hearing every word.

"Okay."

"So why did you want to come out here, exactly?" I asked, reluctantly dropping her hands.

"To see the bison. I told you that."

I stepped over a hump of dirt as we continued walking. "Yes. But why?"

"Well, obviously I've never seen them in person before," she explained, "and I figured, if I'm to go back to Amosite once the bridge is repaired, I might as well see all that I can while I have the chance."

"You don't think you'll be able to leave Amosite again," I said, coming to the conclusion myself.

She looked ahead, her gaze so full of hope. I commended her for gaining that emotion during her stay here, despite knowing that once she went back—once she left Deadwood—she'd likely never be able to leave those castle walls again. Some days, even I lost sight of hope. But without it, what good were the days ahead?

"I got my wish, so I'm content," was all she replied, though I heard what she wasn't saying. She would never truly feel as serene as she did right now if she was back inside that castle, so she was soaking up every moment of this while she still had the chance.

"And what was your wish?"

She was quiet a moment, likely debating whether to tell me or not. I wouldn't blame her if she didn't.

"Meadows and forests. People and conflict. The world, really. One can feel quite small inside stone walls, but out here, I feel...invisible, but in the best way possible."

"Like nothing can touch you," I guessed.

She glanced at me. "Yes," she admitted, her voice quieter than before. "Which is funny, I know, to feel untouchable outside of the prison rather than within, but..." She trailed off, and I silently wished she'd continue. I wanted to know what happened to her inside that demented palace.

"No harm will come to you here," I said, filling in the silence so she didn't feel obligated to.

Walking the rest of the way without another word shared between us, I stopped us a good distance away from the bison. Though seemingly peaceful, they were aggressive when they felt threatened.

We sat in the grass beside each other, her leg only a few inches from mine.

She watched as the bison grazed, bringing her knees to her chest and wrapping her arms around them. I'd seen the herd hundreds of times, sometimes helping the male who watched over them and ensured they were healthy. My eyes didn't stray toward them. Instead, they remained glued to Auria like honey in the combs of a hive. She was so different from what I'd expected, and I, like so many others, was guilty of assuming she was anything like her father. She had a heart bigger than any I'd ever seen in this world, longing for a taste of the life the rest of us got to live. But that feeling, sitting deep in my gut, wasn't pity. It was longing. Longing to be the one to show her everything she had never gotten to see, to be the one to experience things with her for the first time. To watch those green eyes light up at the thought of doing something new.

"What are you looking at?" Auria asked, turning toward me and pulling me out of my trance. As of recently, she often had that effect on me—sucking me in so deeply, I never worried if I'd come out. It was a hole I jumped into willingly.

"You."

Her breath coasted off my cheeks like a whisper—her face so close I could count the light spattering of freckles on the apples of her cheeks that had bloomed during her time here. If she stayed, would more appear? Would her beautiful eyes somehow turn more vibrant? Would her hair lighten a shade or two with the sun beating down on her for the rest of her days?

Even if Deadwood changed her, took the darkness off her shoulders and out of her mind and brightened her entire being, she'd be just as devastating as she was right now. Just as breathtaking as the night I saw her at the masquerade ball.

I'd been attracted to her since the beginning—there was no hiding that—but *gods*. Auria was every star that speckled the night sky, every ray of sunlight shining upon fresh blooms in the meadows. She was a temptress ensnaring me with her sweet scent.

Somehow, we both leaned closer to each other, like neither of us was aware of it but accepting of it all the same. Her sweetness enveloped me, tugging me closer. Her eyes fell to my lips, so many emotions warring in them, but the one that stood out the most had my body lighting like a flame—desire.

I wanted to give in, to close the distance and find out what she tasted like. At the thought of her ass pressed against my groin on Vulcan's back, my smoke stirred inside of me, excitement and anticipation funneling like a tornado through my veins. It, too, wanted me to claim her. To press my lips to hers, and—

We couldn't. Not here. Not now.

It was just the predator inside of me, aching to consume the woman who had taken over my every waking thought.

So I spit out what first came to mind as I pulled away—what had been interrupting my thoughts all too often recently. "Does he touch you?"

Her eyes widened slightly as she dropped her arms from around her legs and straightened where she sat. A flash of disappointment and confusion crossed her face before she asked, "Who?"

Who else? I wanted to ask, but shoved the jealousy away best I could. "Lander."

Her gaze turned back to the herd. "No." She let out a sigh. I'd definitely upset her to some extent. *Fuck*. "We're friends, if you couldn't tell."

I hadn't seen them together all that much to get a read, but the knowledge settled my mind the slightest bit.

"It's more so his brother who's pushing all of this," she went on.

That piqued my interest, shoving away some of my remorse. The hairs on the back of my neck raised. "Paxon?"

I stared at the side of her face as she nodded. She looked like she had so many things she wanted to say, but— "I'm not sure that my hand in marriage is all that's going to come of this."

My eyes fell to the grass in thought. "Does Lander know of your ability?"

She shook her head. "Only you and my father know, as far as I'm aware." But one glance at her told me she wasn't telling me something.

I didn't mention that Siara had tried to come to the conclusion of what Auria could do. Siara could read anyone. Though her ability was to wield lightning, I would've believed her if she had told me she could figure out anyone's intentions based on looks alone. It was impossible to hide anything from her.

"Are you open with him?" I asked.

Her brows pulled together as she studied me. "Are you jealous?"

I almost choked. "Only curious."

She hummed a disbelieving sound, a smile pulling at her lips.

I quickly stood, holding a hand out to her. "We should head back," I said, needing to change the topic at hand.

To my surprise, she grabbed it, allowing me to pull her to a stand. "Thank you."

I gave a small nod, dropping her hand. "Anything you want to see, Auria, just ask."

She offered a closed-lip smile before we turned to head back to Vulcan. Something had changed between us in this field—something I didn't want to allow myself to think too deeply about, for fear my heart wouldn't handle her inevitable departure well. Out of self-preservation, I shoved those thoughts aside, choosing to instead focus on the mutual understanding we had landed on. I wouldn't harm her, and she wouldn't share my secrets.

Perhaps what this was was trust.

It was a start.

ON OUR FLIGHT BACK, a light sprinkle of rain had started. By the time we landed, it was a full on downpour. The sky had turned an ugly gray, masking the silver rings and the late afternoon sun. We'd been in the field longer than I'd thought.

I helped Auria down from Vulcan's back, her balance already better than it had been when she first mounted him. The rain made his scales slick, making it difficult to find stable footing on the way down, but Auria didn't seem to mind. If anything, she seemed to be enjoying the rain.

With a pat on Vulcan's leg, he took off, flying toward the mountains. A majority of the dragons from the rocky biome congregated there to rest or catch up on anything happening around Serpentine. Though dragons usually stuck to the terrain they were born into, they crossed into other habitats if needed. It wasn't impossible for them to thrive in other conditions—just inconvenient at times. They flourished where they were from, but dragons were stubborn. They'd do anything just to prove they could.

I swiped a wet lock of hair off my forehead as our boots trudged through the mud in the forest. It was pointless to shout over the pelting rain, so we hurried through the downpour, walking between two buildings to come out on the muddy street.

Immediately, I found Raiden standing by the saloon door. He left the guard he was talking to, aiming right for me. Auria stopped by my side as soon as she saw him approaching.

"Bowen," Raiden said in his usual cool tone. Only someone who knew him like I did would catch the stiffness hidden beneath his calm exterior.

The look in his eyes confirmed something was wrong. "What is it?"

"A word?" He didn't have to say it for me to know he didn't want to speak about whatever it was in front of Auria.

I glanced at her. Her wet hair was stuck to her dripping cheeks, and her shirt clung to her form, leaving little to the imagination. Rather than let my mind wander, I mentally gauged the distance to the house she was staying in. It wasn't far, but I still didn't feel right leaving her.

As if she had read my thoughts, she said, "I'll be fine. No one's out anyway. It's a short walk."

Still, I hesitated, and Raiden took notice, that speculative look appearing. He was all too observant.

"It's not very far—" I started, but she cut me off, stepping closer so she wouldn't have to raise her voice over the rain.

"No one will harm me. Isn't that what you said?" she asked, rain streaming down the bridge of her nose.

She had me there. "Okay. I'll have Siara come check on you

to make sure you made it home." She held my gaze, looking so damn beautiful despite the storm raging around us. I mentally shook myself. "I'll see you around, then?" As of now, all our run-ins had been coincidental, aside from the times I had watched her from afar. People were on edge with Auria's presence in town, so I excused my concern for her as maintaining peace. Keeping her alive meant keeping her father off my back —nothing else. At least, that's what I had told myself.

She looked as if she wanted to say something else, her mouth parting, but she settled on, "Have a good night, Bowen."

She gave Raiden one last look before she walked away. My eyes didn't stray from her drenched form, the way her hips swayed under the soaking fabric of her clothes. How her hair dripped down her back, the long strands even darker with the rain. Maybe it wasn't to keep her father off my back if something happened to her that I had kept an eye on her in Deadwood and the night of Exitium Lunae. Perhaps it had been for my own selfish reasons—my predatorial side declaring that if anything were to happen to her, it'd be at my hand, no one else's. Weeks ago, I might've felt my bloodthirsty instincts come out to play with that thought, but now, it was a different part of me not wanting to see another's hand laid on her. I had gone from being okay with her fending for herself to being overly protective.

After she rounded the corner to head toward the rows of houses, Raiden and I headed off toward my home on the back side of Deadwood. It was nothing grander than the residences the citizens lived in. When my father had been killed, I wasn't interested in sitting on the throne in that castle hidden in the woods. I wanted to be among my people, and to lose the title altogether. I made smart choices, so I hadn't felt compelled to pass the enthronement to anyone else. My only request was that I wouldn't be regarded as their king, but as an equal. Well, as much of an equal as I could be when the decisions fell on my shoulders. But that was why I had Flynt, Raiden, and Siara. The three of them helped me rule Deadwood. Raiden handled the army, Flynt was in charge of bringing me information regarding other kingdoms, and Siara helped keep us all in check, as well as keeping an eye on the town for any internal threats, though she had appointed that role to herself, wanting to be more useful.

As much as Deadwood was a home to many, it was also a hiding spot for criminals. Stealing magic, in our eyes, wasn't punishable by death, but to other kingdoms, it was. If you were spotted with ink anywhere on your body, you were killed on sight. Deadwood gave refuge to those who had made bad decisions in the past, so long as they stayed in line with our rules. No murder, no rape, and you respected your peers. If someone was getting to the point that they were stealing, either for survival or boredom, they needed help, not the afterlife. Though, at times, the rougher groups could get rowdy, Raiden and our guards kept the peace. But still, my track record remained. I wouldn't hesitate to cut someone's throat and tear a limb from their body, and the people knew it.

Raiden held the door open for me as I shucked my muddy boots off, leaving them on the porch. As I stepped inside, the blazing fire instantly warmed my rain-soaked clothes.

"Gods, there you are," Siara said, standing from the couch like they had all been waiting on me for hours.

"I leave for an afternoon and you all can't handle my absence," I grumbled, stepping into the kitchen to grab another apple. Auria had clearly needed my first one more than I had, even though my offering had been futile, given the apple was now likely caked in mud and debris where she'd let it fall to the ground. I could forgive her for that, though, given the circumstances at the time.

Raiden stood with his back against the wall, crossing his arms. "Well, that simple afternoon stroll was the same amount of time it took for the patrons at the bar to start a riot and cause a fuck ton of mayhem."

Swallowing my bite, I said blandly, "A riot, huh."

Flynt stepped up to the counter, both hands resting on the edge. "Fights broke out, chairs were destroyed—"

I raised an eyebrow, taking another bite.

"Why are you so calm about this?" Siara asked, her voice taking on that high octave it always did when she was growing annoyed of me—which happened quite often.

I set the apple on the counter, dusting my hands off. "Let me guess. This is because of Amosite and Torbernite's group."

"Did you coordinate this or something?" Flynt asked, incredulous.

I crossed my arms. He wanted to point fingers, and I was *not* the right guy to blame. "Now why would I do that?"

Raiden shrugged from his spot on the far side of the room. "Bored, maybe."

My eyes narrowed on him. "If I was bored, Commander, I'd simply challenge you and beat you at your own game." Raiden was skilled, but we were almost equal in the fighting department—both with swords and fists. It was always a fun time trying to rile him up.

"Then let's go," he challenged.

"You're all boys! Children, even," Siara shouted. Her blonde hair was tied back, though strands had fallen loose from the rain, still wet from being outside. They'd shown up here not long ago, then.

"They need to go," Flynt interrupted, his voice soft, like he didn't want to say the words as he steered the conversation back on course.

My teeth nearly ground to dust at the thought of sending Auria back to Amosite anytime soon.

I brushed past them, moving to the living room. "Not until the bridge is repaired."

"There has to be another way in," Siara said, following closely on my heels.

I spun on her, stopping her short. "I said no."

Flynt pulled her back by the shoulders, stepping in between the two of us. I would never hurt Siara, she was practically my sister. But Flynt was protective. A downfall for us all, actually.

"This delay is only going to cause more problems," Flynt warned.

Again, my eyes narrowed. "Are you insinuating something, Flynt?"

His gaze was hard as he held my own. "You can't protect everyone. Not when we have our own agenda. A plan, might I add, we are this fucking close to finishing." He held his fingers a breath apart for emphasis.

I stepped toward him. He was barely an inch shorter than me, and I never used the dominance tactic with my group, but he was suggesting I practically throw Auria to the wolves, and for what? My own benefit? It wouldn't be to anyone's benefit for her to go back, *especially* not hers. What happened to them liking her?

"I will not be sending them away until that bridge is complete. Is that clear?" But even then, would I be able to? I knew what awaited her—the fate Auria was set to have. Even her marriage to Lander would still be controlled by her father. If she never left Deadwood, it couldn't happen. But that wasn't my decision to make.

"What do you think will happen when people find out you're protecting them?" Siara asked from behind Flynt.

"I'm not protecting them," I stated, which was only half a lie. I somehow had come to the point of protecting *her*.

Siara's brows shot up. "You seriously think we're that naïve? Maybe the boys are, but not me. You don't think I saw you step in for Auria at the market?"

"You weren't going to," I defended. "You walked away, losing sight of her so easily. Does she mean that little to you?" I paused, giving her a moment to let that set in. "You and Raiden stood up for her in the dining hall against Paxon, the son of Torbernite's leaders. I threatened one of our own. There's a difference."

Her eyes flashed, hurt shining in them. My dig was too close to home, and I instantly regretted it. "Make your own decisions, Bowen, but remember where your loyalties lie. You can't save everyone."

I could.

"I thought you were her friend," I said instead.

"I am, but I know it will end. She can't stay forever," Siara replied. "None of us *want* her to go back, but there's no other option. Her father will tear this place apart, and we'll be right in his path."

But she *could* stay forever.

I shook my head, dragging a hand down my face. There were no options here. Auria would have to leave at some point. Deadwood would never accept her because of the target her father put on her head. It would take a lot of convincing, otherwise. And they were right. We had a plan to keep moving forward with.

"How long until the bridge is repaired?" I asked, forcing myself to accept the inevitable, all while trying to come up with a way out of it.

"A week, maybe," Flynt answered.

I pressed my lips together in a firm line. "Then they'll be gone in a week."

"Bowen..." Siara started, presumably seeing the hurt in my gaze. It wasn't over me wanting to keep Auria here. It was what I knew she'd go back to.

"Drop it, Siara," I muttered.

Raiden shoved off the wall, taking a few slow steps into the living room as he finally spoke up. "Maybe there's a way—"

But he was cut off as the front door opened, and a small form stumbled in, falling to the ground.

CHAPTER 37

AURIA

I had to force myself not to look back at Bowen as I walked away. Even among the pounding rain, I would've known if he had left before I disappeared, but instead, he watched me go, and the thought was somewhat comforting. I nearly wanted to reach up and touch my lips, the memory of how close we were in that field making them tingle. We'd almost kissed, and yet, he'd pulled away, asking about Lander. I guessed I should've been thankful for that, though. Kissing him would've only made things complicated.

As my boots trudged through the muddy street, his words replayed in my mind. *That man and those walls are not your end.* But did he know I had nowhere else to go? Anyone else to be? I was Auria Tenere, a prisoner in my own home for the benefit of others, but never for myself. I didn't get choices or freedom or a chance at another life. I lived the one I got, and I learned to be content with it. Better an occasional burn from my step mother than to die at the hands of an enemy. At least, that's what I used to think. I wasn't so sure anymore.

But if Bowen thought hope was a trait I held proudly, he

was wrong. Hope was what tore me down to depths I could hardly fathom when disappointment presented itself. Better to not set your sights high at all in order to save yourself from the landslide of dejection.

The dark, cloudy sky and onslaught of rain made it difficult to see as I attempted to shield my eyes from the massive drops. The downpour pounded into my shoulders, the storm refusing to let up. What I thought was the sound of rain coming down harder, quicker, turned out to be footsteps, but before I could turn to see who was approaching, something hard hit me in the side of my head, sending me straight to the ground. Mud splashed up around me, coating my clothes as my hands dug into the slimy sludge.

I tried to blink away the rain as I slipped in the mud, attempting to push myself up. The effort was useless as the toe of a boot landed in my ribs, stealing the oxygen from my lungs. I collapsed on my stomach, my body flat in the squelching mud as I tried to suck in air. The pain was excruciating with each breath, and I feared a rib had cracked. Before I could satisfy the emptiness of my lungs, a hand gripped my shoulder and flipped me onto my back. Another rough hand wrapped around my neck, cutting off my ability to breathe entirely. It squeezed, and through the storm, I saw two men standing above me.

My slippery hand wrapped around his wrist, trying to pry it off, but he only held tighter. I blinked through the downpour, and the moment they came into focus, the blood in my veins froze. The men from the gambling den.

Nemin and Crass.

"How does it feel to suffocate, bitch? Doesn't feel so good when it's you, does it?" Crass seethed, looming over me like death itself. Vengeance shone so bright in his eyes, the look alone felt like blades in my chest. Or maybe it was the loss of oxygen sending my body into shock.

With the thought, I snapped back into motion, digging my nails into his wrist in a poor attempt to make him let go. As if a few scratches would stave off this amount of hatred.

"Grab her hands," Crass called over his shoulder as my lungs burned.

Nemin took my hands in a punishing grip, slamming them into the mud to hold them beside my head. With my fight restrained, Crass added a second hand to my neck, squeezing tighter.

But it couldn't be this easy for them. I wouldn't allow such a fate. I refused to die in some muddy puddle, lying in the middle of a street. If they wanted to kill me, I'd make sure they had to fight for it.

I kicked out, my foot finding purchase between Crass's legs. It wasn't as hard as I would've liked it to be, but it was enough to make him let go. I sucked in air like a starved animal, my lungs on fire with their hunger.

Nemin immediately moved to pin my thigh with his knee, digging my hands deeper into the mud. Every point of contact pulsed with pain, the man nowhere near gentle. I was covered head to toe, and my head was spinning from the loss of oxygen and initial hit. But that wouldn't stop me. It couldn't.

Crass grunted, likely getting his bearings, and I wasted no time as I turned my head to the side, biting down on Nemin's wrist. He yelled out, releasing me, only to use his good hand to slap me. My head whipped to the side, mud coating my hair and cheek as a metallic flavor filled my mouth. I realized it was blood. From me or Nemin, I wasn't sure.

While Nemin was distracted, rubbing at his bite wound like a hurt dog, I folded at the waist, enough to bring my foot up and kick him in the face. Nemin fell back with a gruesome groan as Crass pounced at me again. Before he could land, I spun away, rolling a few times before glancing over my shoulder. Crass landed on his hands and knees, a snarl aimed my way as he scrambled after me. I twisted away once again as he reached for my ankle, and he let out a frustrated grunt, slinging foul names my way over the thunder cracking in the distance.

On my back now, I leaned on my elbows and waited until he was close enough to lift my leg and put all my force into kicking him square in the nose. A sickening crunch filled the air, somehow louder than the rain, and blood instantly poured from his nostrils. His hands came up to cup his nose, but I didn't wait to see if he'd strike again. I hurried to my feet, taking off in the direction of town and ignoring the pain in my ribs with each heaved breath. If Bowen was still in the street, he'd help me.

My boots slipped through the mud, each flail putting more pressure on my torso as I fought to keep traction on the slick ground. Nearly every inch of me was coated, my hair knotted and heavy, but none of the mess mattered. Not when Crass and Nemin were possibly on my heels. I couldn't waste time looking back as my body sang with adrenaline. If they got to me a second time, they wouldn't let me get away alive.

I rounded the corner back into the main part of town, but the street was empty. Not a single guard stood out in the storm. A part of me was thankful there wasn't a soul milling about. They could see my state of weakness and strike as well. I couldn't trust anyone here, so what made me think Bowen would help me? He'd stood up for me in the past, but now? He could just as easily leave me for dead.

I had no idea where he lived, and even if I found houses in the direction they might have gone, would he even be there?

At the spot I'd left Bowen and Raiden, fresh boot prints led off toward the edge of town. They had to be theirs. With the rain, any older tracks would've been washed away by now. It was my only lead, and without any other options, I followed them. Each second that passed, the prints became harder to make out, but I trudged on, my boots sticking in the mud with each step. I had to blink profusely to keep my vision focused through the drops of rain glueing themselves to my lashes. That, and the exhaustion creeping into me with every step from the fight and loss of oxygen.

Finally, I came upon a row of houses, and at the end of the path of footprints, I found a pair of boots sitting caked in mud on a porch. Upon closer inspection, I figured they had to be Bowen's. And if they weren't... Well, I'd take my chances.

It wasn't Lander or Paxon or any of my guards on my mind when it came to needing help in this moment. It was Bowen. I chose not to look further into that, blaming it on the pure need for survival.

I stepped onto the porch, but the sticky mud caked on the sole of my boot had me grabbing for the wooden post holding up the makeshift roof in order to not fall flat on my face. To get to the door, I had to let go, but the moment I did, my boots slid like ice was underneath me. My arms flung out, trying to grab hold of anything, but instead of the wall or another post, I hit the door. It opened so easily, spitting me out onto a warm, wooden floor.

Then footsteps sounded, and I curled in on myself, bracing for the worst.

CHAPTER 38

BOWEN

The mud-coated woman folded her body into a ball as I hurried over. Raiden had his hand on his dagger, not sure yet if she was a threat or not. Flynt and Siara stood back, giving us space and keeping their guard up in case the person was a distraction for something bigger.

"Please. Please, don't hurt me," the girl cried, wrapping her arms tighter around her legs. "I-I'm looking for someone."

That voice. So smooth and buttery, yet so full of fear and desperation.

Instantly, my veins awoke with a fury I'd never felt before. Smoke trailed through me, hunting, stalking, searching for a target.

Where, my smoke whispered. *We will kill them. Slowly suffocate whoever touched her.*

"Auria." I knelt beside her, setting a hand on her dirtied arm. She was covered in thick mud to the point she was almost unrecognizable.

She flinched at my touch, her shoulder hiking higher, as if

to protect her face. I glanced over my shoulder at Siara. "Start the shower. Hot water."

Siara nodded her response, hurrying up the stairs.

I looked over what I could see of Auria's body to find any blood mixed with the sludgy brown substance, and to my relief, there was none. Still, my teeth ground together, my jaw popping. I had to keep myself under control.

We will end them, it promised, the statement laced with lethal intent.

"Auria," I said again, forcing that voice into the depths of my mind, far from where I could hear it. I needed to focus.

As if her ears finally opened, she released her hold on her legs, tilting her head to look up at me. "Bowen." Relief hung to my name on her lips like a prayer. "I-I'm sorry. I didn't know where else to go—"

I shook my head. The tremble in her voice was killing me and lighting me up all at the same time. The need to take care of her and obliterate whoever put her in this state was so strong, my magic pulsed, ricocheting inside me. "You did the right thing. I'm right here." But it fucking pained me that she even had to come. That she was in a position where she needed somebody. But if she had to choose, I was glad she chose me.

I brushed her tangled hair from her face, my eyes narrowing in on her bloody lip. Whoever did this to her would live to regret it. I'd tear them limb from limb, decimating them from this planet entirely. But not before I made them suffer. "Who did this to you?" My voice was rough, like the tip of a knife along splintered wood.

She tried to push herself up on one hand, muddy water dripping from every inch of her. Her hand slipped as a gasp tore from her lips, and I quickly wrapped an arm under her. Despite the need to find whoever did this and make them suffer, she needed me more. I wouldn't leave her side while she was like this. She was quickly becoming, if not already, more important than a lot of things.

"I'm going to pick you up, okay?"

She nodded, and the look on her face, the relief she felt seeing it was me and not someone else touching her in this moment—it fucking killed me.

I slid my hands under her shaking form, lifting her into my arms. A whimper escaped her, and I feared her injuries were far worse than what met the eye. Standing, I looked to Raiden and Flynt. "You two go home. We'll talk more later."

They both nodded as Siara came down the stairs. "Water's on."

"Thank you," I said to her. "I got it from here."

Sympathy and worry mixed in Siara's features, and I knew she regretted saying Auria needed to leave. She herself had grown attached to her. Siara wasn't great at making friends, having a hard time trusting people, and seeing Auria in this state pulled at her, too. None of us knew what we were doing, and it was impossible to make judgment calls for the better of anyone but ourselves. Even tonight, I'd thought Auria would be okay getting home, but something as simple as that had almost killed her. In turn, we blamed ourselves for it. Even Raiden. The concerned look on his face was proof of that. Above that, he was furious with himself. His job was to protect—and here he'd been.

After the three of them left, I headed up the stairs, arms wrapped delicately around Auria like she might break in half if I moved too quickly or gripped too hard. The side of her head lay against my shoulder, a small noise escaping her lips as a shudder moved through her body. In an attempt to soothe her, my thumb brushed her thigh as I walked us down the short hall to my bedroom. Steam billowed out from the bathroom door as I entered.

The bathroom was big enough to fit the tub in the corner, a toilet and sink, and an open shower. To prevent mold, I'd laid brown stone tile on the ground. Two small woolen rugs sat in front of both washing areas.

"Clothes on or off?" I asked. She needed this mud off of her so I could examine her injuries, but I didn't want to be impolite.

"Off," she muttered into my still-damp shirt.

"Are you okay to stand?"

She nodded.

Gently, I lowered her to the floor, keeping a hand on her waist to steady her as she swayed.

"I can step out—"

She quickly shook her head, fisting my shirt where she kept her hand on my shoulder for balance. Despite the mud, the smear of blood by her lip, and rain mixing the two substances together, her green eyes shone brighter than the meadows in the spring. "Please don't leave me."

I'd stay forever if she asked.

"I won't." Dropping to my knees in front of her, I hesitantly reached forward, looking up to find her watching me. "May I?"

She nodded, her hand still propped on my shoulder for support.

With deft fingers, I worked at the sodden laces of her boots. Once one foot was undone, I gently grabbed her ankle, indicating for her to lift it. She did, and I slid the boot off, tossing it aside. After her foot was back on the ground, I got to work on the other.

"You didn't answer my question," I stated, lifting her other foot to slide the second boot off. "Who did this to you, Auria?"

"They were wearing hoods," she answered, a tad too quickly.

Standing, I leveled her gaze. "Why are you protecting them?"

"I'm not."

"You are. You know exactly who they are." My fingers worked on the front laces of her corset, undoing them before shoving it to the ground behind her. Her gaze on mine while I did so awoke a craving so deep, I nearly couldn't hold it back, but now wasn't the time.

I moved to her blouse, my hand wrapping around the hem, now completely brown and soaked through, and gently lifted it. I watched to make sure no doubt crept into her eyes. "And by the looks of it, you fought them off."

Despite her current condition, her chin tilted up slightly. "I did."

Pride seeped in. "Good girl." In one swift motion, I lifted the shirt off of her, tossing it to the ground beside her boots. She wore nothing underneath, and it took all I had in me not to look, clenching my jaw to fight off the allure of her. "Pants next." An inch closer, and my fingers were working on the tie of her leathers. Her breath, so warm and inviting, heated my neck as I kept my eyes on hers. This was torturous when it shouldn't be.

Hooking my fingers in the waistband, I slid them down, letting them fall to the ground once they were past her knees. A brush of my hand found her underwear still perfectly placed. "These, too?"

She nodded, her throat working. We both knew she was capable of taking them off herself.

My cruel, tantalizing Auria.

Her lips parted as my thumbs hooked in the band. I was gentle with the sheer fabric, tugging them down until they slid the rest of the way off, landing atop her pants.

Her gaze fell to something behind me, her eyes vacant. "They asked how it felt to suffocate," she said quietly, her voice almost lost in the spray of the shower. It was all I needed to know exactly who had done this. My smoke flickered inside me, urging me to go find our target.

"Well, you'll never have the answer," I told her. They wouldn't live to see the morning.

"I did," she admitted. "For a moment, I knew what it felt like."

My hands, thankfully not touching her in this moment, instantly tightened into fists, my fingers nearly breaking as I imagined crushing them to pieces.

"Shower's ready for you," I gritted out.

I stepped to the side, giving her space to pass, but the moment her hand left my shoulder, she stumbled forward a bit. I gripped her elbow, steadying her. Had they broken a bone? Injured her worse than I thought? She wouldn't be able to stand on her own in the shower.

But then my eyes fell to the contact her body had with mine, where her breasts brushed my leather jacket. Fuck, she was beautiful, so godsdamned jaw-dropping, even in this condition.

As she exhaled, I could see her stomach and the bruise blooming on her side.

"You're hurt," I ground out, my hand moving on its own accord to brush over the blue and purple galaxy already painting her side.

She let out a small, breathy laugh, but winced as she regretted it. "I didn't think it was a secret that I was."

But this was worse. Her ribs could be broken. Shattered.

I'd fucking destroy them for touching her.

"Maybe a bath would be better," I muttered.

She shook her head, her cold hand coming up to wrap around my wrist. "You can help me."

My eyes shot to hers.

Gods, what was she doing?

"I'd have to get in," I explained.

"Okay." She said it so easily, like that was exactly what she wanted.

Pulling myself out of my stupor, I helped her step into the shower and went to follow after her when she paused, eying my shirt under my jacket. "You don't need to be shy."

Even in her battered state, she was making me lose my mind.

"Auria..." The warning was evident in my tone. She was dancing along a line thinner than parchment, knowing damn well it'd never hold up.

Rather than responding, she stepped under the spray of water, mud instantly washing into the drain as the drops warmed her skin and trailed between her breasts. She was a goddess, and I'd do her bidding. Whatever it was—Auria had ensnared me.

I wasted no time shucking my damp clothes to the ground, leaving all of me bare, and stepped into the shower with her. The hot water sprayed off of her, misting me where I stood in front of her. I grabbed the bar of soap from the small shelf on the wall while she ran her face under the water. Foolishly, I was almost jealous of the droplets as they cascaded down the curve of her jaw, streaming down her neck to disappear beneath her breasts. Unable to help myself, I began to run the bar of soap along her collarbone, watching the rise and fall of her chest with each breath.

With the mud washing away, fresh bruises exposed themselves, littering the delicate skin of her neck. My vision nearly went red as the natural instinct to end those who had done this surged through me.

Her eyes, lit like the forest trees in the midday sun, found mine. That look alone thawed me, stealing my attention once more. I trailed the bar lower, over one breast, then the other.

Once they were both coated and glistening, I moved down to her stomach, my gaze following the trace of the suds as they bubbled over her skin. My other hand found her waist on its own accord, my fingers tracing over the deepening bruise on her side. The absence of dirt and grime revealed what broke me inside—her pain.

While I practically worshiped her body with the bar of soap, she watched me. If she was looking for anything other than pure awe, she wouldn't find it. She was the embodiment of beauty.

Bringing the soap back up, I ran it along her cheeks, ridding her skin of the mud that once coated it. Her face, so close to mine, reddened slightly, but I excused it for the hot water. I cupped her head at the base with my free hand, and once her eyelids fluttered closed, I tilted her head back to wash the suds away.

This entire moment was far too much, even for me, but I couldn't step away. I'd wither away to a prune if it meant I got to stay in this shower with her, blocking out the world and any outside forces telling me I shouldn't go further with her. And yet...

I stepped behind her, gently wrapping my hand around her hair to lift it off her neck, revealing her back. As soon as my eyes traveled down, everything within me froze. Her skin was littered in scars, old and new. It felt as if my breath had been stolen away and locked somewhere I'd never find it again. Auria had that effect on me all too often, but this time, it was with torture.

"You have scars," I gritted out.

The slightest fall of her shoulders, the tilt of her head, and I knew shame and embarrassment had filled her.

"Bet you didn't think a princess like me would have those," she murmured quietly. She threw the nickname at me like quiet venom, and I wanted to rip my own tongue out for ever using it in such a way.

"Not that you would, but that you shouldn't. Who gave you these?"

While I waited for her to respond, I ran the soap through her hair, doing my best to gently untangle the strands. Minutes passed, and I couldn't remain quiet any longer. "Auria."

"Not my father," she answered, though it didn't tell me *who*.

The smoke from the sconce in the corner swirled with the mist fogging the room, sensing my magic building to its breaking point.

"He leaves a different sort of pain," she admitted, her voice too frail and vulnerable for my liking. If I didn't leave and get this out now, the room would be nothing but ruins. I needed a release, and fast.

I set the bar of soap back on the shelf. The familiar gray streaks were crawling up my veins all too quickly. Against my better judgment, I left her standing under the spray as I stepped out of the shower and grabbed a towel from the rod. With too much force, I wrapped it around my waist, nearly tearing the fabric.

But rather than a polite goodbye or sticking around to make sure she was alright, I managed to grit out, "I want names."

And left.

~

THE GROUND SHOOK as Vulcan landed, his talons digging into the soaked earth.

"You knew," I spit at him.

"*You have hurt her on top of it,*" Vulcan replied, knowing exactly what I was getting at. He could feel her emotions from inside the house and most likely came to the conclusion I'd left her due to them. But it wasn't because of the scars. It was because I wanted to rip the world apart, and I couldn't feel that way. Not when it came to her.

It was unfortunate dragons could sense the emotions of those who were vulnerable, whether fae or human, for it gave us the underhand when they decided to use it to their advantage.

I stepped forward, not giving a shit about our size difference. We could both kill each other where we stood, and yet, I felt no fear in front of him. "I'm doing what's best for her."

A flash of white flew past us before giant wings folded in on the snow dragon's massive body, her landing almost causing me to lose my balance. "*Staying away from every being on this planet is what is best for the girl.*"

Glacies had something coming to her if she thought taking Auria away would benefit her. "You try to take her, and I'll—"

But my voice was cut off as she snapped vicious teeth at me, the razor sharp fangs dripping with bloodied saliva, indicating she'd likely been hunting before coming here. Before she could come any further, Vulcan let out an ear-splitting roar, and Glacies swiped her tail at him, knocking it into his neck. The two of them never got along, but when it came to Auria, Glacies was protective for reasons I didn't know. She had been the one who saved Auria when the bandits had attacked.

With blazing red eyes aimed at Glacies, who growled deep in her throat, Vulcan said, "*She will not take the burned one.*"

"Call her that one more time," I warned.

"*Do not be so sure,*" Glacies gritted out, ignoring my threat toward Vulcan.

Vulcan stepped forward, his footfall as loud as the thunder that pelted the sky. "*She is too valuable.*"

The rain had slowed, but the night was dark, the rings dimmer through the lingering clouds.

"*For all the wrong reasons,*" Glacies hissed, her eyes glowing a bright blue as her ice threatened to release itself all over Vulcan.

As if called to the presence of power, smoke curled around my arms, nipping at my skin like a rabid dog wanting to attack. I was surprised it had stayed silent as I spoke. "Stop speaking of her like I won't end either of you where you stand."

Glacies swung her head my way, her large nostrils flaring as ice crystals formed in the air. She had a temper, and it was showing. "*You defend her, yet you could just as easily use her like she is nothing.*"

"I would never use her." I, more than anyone, did not want to see Auria have to make a choice between her life and our mission.

"*He is not thinking with his brain,*" Vulcan sneered, shooting me a judgmental look.

"I won't do it." Bringing Auria into this would mean risking her life, and by the scars on her back, there was already someone in that castle who didn't care whether she lived or died. I wouldn't be the reason for another crater in her skin. "We can find it on our own."

"*Years, and you are still coming up blank,*" Vulcan's voice boomed through the meadow. "*How long until the corrupt king finds out? Until he not only attempts to decimate faekind again, but us in the process.*"

"I won't let that happen."

Vulcan's face was in mine in an instant, heat radiating off his breath as it turned to steam. "*You are a single fae. You do not* let *anything happen. It* happens."

Glacies watched both of us with an intense stare. If she assumed there had been a shift in my loyalties, she didn't speak of it.

"I do what I can for my kind, as well as yours. I don't see you snooping around castles you have no business being in." They had no hope if it wasn't for me. After the dragons had wiped out the fae—so the humans believed—they were left to their own devices, so long as they didn't come near the human kingdoms. If they did, they were shot down, killed on sight. The humans saw them as simply an unlikely ally, but they didn't ever stop to think that dragons might have ulterior motives of their own.

Vulcan huffed, the burst of air warming my arms. "*I could torch them where they stand.*"

"Yet you don't. Why is that?" I knew exactly why, but I wanted to hear his over-confident self say it. Dragons hated admitting their weaknesses, and I wouldn't advise anyone to encourage them to do so, but Vulcan would never harm me. He'd just threaten roasting me like a kabob until the day he died—which would likely be never.

Glacies chortled to the side, her breath coming out in little puffs of white. "*You are a cruel one, even for a fae.*"

Refusing to answer, Vulcan turned around, his massive tail almost taking me out in the process. Dark magic worked just as harshly on them as it did on fae, and he wouldn't risk dragonkind—despite his ego screaming at him to let his aggression out to play. He was a lot, but he wouldn't risk his species.

Our conversation was cut short as the sound of light footsteps crunching over soaked leaves came from behind me. All three of us turned just in time to find Auria emerging from the brush.

CHAPTER 39

AURIA

After Bowen had left me in the shower to finish cleaning the mud off myself, I'd rinsed and dressed in the clothes he'd laid out on the bed, only to find he had left the house altogether. Though it wasn't wise, I'd gone to find him, but I hadn't expected to find Vulcan and a white dragon standing with him in the forest clearing, too.

A closer look confirmed it was the white dragon that had saved me during the bandit attack. Somehow, my body knew it was her.

Bowen stepped toward me. "Auria—"

I held up a hand. "No. Before you tell me to go back, that it's not safe out here, tell me why you left."

If there were a brow on his head, Vulcan would've raised it. "*Trouble in paradise?*"

I sent a glare at the monstrous beast. "You stay out of it." Bowen opened his mouth to reply, but I wasn't done. "You think some scars are a good enough reason to run away? That my pain is your suffering? Well, guess what, Bowen. It's not. It's *mine*, and for you to judge me because you think you have the right to take that on for me is ridiculous. You're a king, my father's equal in sense of rank, and you think—" But I hadn't realized we'd drifted closer until he grabbed my wrist, halting the finger that prodded at his chest.

"I am *not* his equal. And if you think I'm judging you, you're sorely mistaken. I *admire* you. What you've been through your entire life, and yet, you remain loyal to a family that only sees you fit for upping their egos and monetary gain?" He shook his head. "I could never judge you for the evidence of the hell you've been put through."

My breathing was hard as I wrenched my wrist from his grasp. Rather than feel relieved by his words like I'd expected I might, they only enraged me, twisting a knot deep in my stomach. "It's your ego that's the problem, not theirs."

Something like surprise passed over his features. "You're defending them."

"They're all I know! They keep me safe, fed, and I'm fine!"

Our chests bumped into each other as smoke practically billowed from his ears. Gray lines crawled up his neck. "What's happened while you've been out of Amosite? Huh, Auria? Look around." He threw his arms out for emphasis. "You're still alive. You're fed, safe—"

I pointed to my lip. "Do you call this safe?" My hand moved to my side, cupping my aching ribs. "This?"

Regret filled his eyes, and I hated myself for it. It wasn't his fault, and yet he took the blame. Carried it on his shoulders like the weight was only his to bear. "That was my mistake for leaving you."

"You can't be by my side all the time out here. So yes, I will defend my home, because that is the only place I can expect what's coming." I hated the taste of the words as they passed my lips. But what did he want me to say? That he could take away the hurt, carry the burden of my past, and for what? For me to cloud his mind and distract him? He clearly had other things to do than look after me.

He shook his head, and I could tell he was disappointed. I think I was, too.

"If the dramatics are done," the white dragon drawled from the side.

My anger toward Bowen's disappearance at the house quickly dissipated as the sight of the snow dragon set in. Though still unnerving where she stood, she was less petrifying than that day in the mountains.

"This is Glacies," Bowen said, his tone calmer now as he took a step back, almost like it was an admission that I had won. But if this was winning, I didn't want it. What was wrong with me? Why had I blown up on him after all he'd done since I stumbled into his home?

Instantly, I missed the warmth that emanated from his body. The smoke had gone back into hiding, the lines gone from his skin. I ached for their presence to return, too.

"We've met," I murmured, staring up at her. White eyelids blinked over icy blue irises as we studied one another. "You're a lot less menacing now, though."

Vulcan chuckled, steam flowing from his nostrils. *"The girl is good at compliments."*

Glacies shot him a glare.

"Thank you," I stuttered out. "For saving me."

Glacies tapped a talon on the ground, the sharp edge digging into the mud. *"Those dregs deserved nothing but death. A few others, too."*

Before I could respond, her tundra eyes shot in the direction I'd come from as she took a protective step forward.

Leaves rustled behind me, and I spun to find Lander stumbling into the meadow. "Lander?"

"Auria." He gulped down air. "I heard about the attack. Are

you alright?" He approached rather quickly, and Glacies's growl reverberated through me.

At my side, Bowen shot her a warning glare.

My brows knitted together in confusion. "You heard about it? How?"

Lander stopped a foot in front of me, his eyes landing on my split lip before they trailed to the bruises around my neck. He glanced nervously at Bowen and the dragons, doing a double take on the latter before speaking. "They're talking all about it in the saloon. Guess someone saw the scuffle. You got 'em good."

"You *saw* them? They're there, right now?"

He nodded, and a wisp of smoke ran up the inside of my wrist, hidden from sight as it caressed my skin. "Got a good punch in when Crass started talking, too. Came looking for you and saw you walking out here."

"You've been hiding in the bushes?" I asked, my voice rising in pitch. He'd seen my argument with Bowen, then. Saw me thank a *dragon*. Fuck, he was seeing the dragons right now. I wasn't sure if that'd be a problem, but it couldn't be good, right?

His forehead creased, as if he couldn't figure out why that'd bother me. "I wanted to make sure you were okay—"

That tendril of smoke weaved through my fingers as my frustration rose, almost like it was trying to comfort me. My head was still foggy from the hit, and I was beyond exhausted, making my temper shorter than ever before. Gods, what was wrong with me? "Clearly, I'm fine. You didn't have to follow me out here—"

Vulcan's nostrils flared as his eyes narrowed on the tree line. "*The air reeks of human stench.*"

Bowen nodded his head in the direction of Lander, as if to say, *And here's your reason.*

Lander tugged a hand through his disheveled hair, his

knuckles red. "Dragons, Auria? They'll kill you just as easily as Crass or Nemin could have." He shook his head. "Easier, even." He craned his neck back, looking up at Glacies with fear in his expression. Fear he failed to cover up. He focused on me again. "What are you doing out here?"

His assumption that the dragons would hurt me only fueled my rage, causing me to step forward, but Bowen cut me off, getting in between the two of us. "Best to not make assumptions you can't hold yourself up against, Prince," he said, ignoring Lander's question.

The two of them shared a look, a threat warring in their gazes.

"It's been a long day for Auria," Bowen continued, cooling his expression. He reached behind himself to set a gentle hand on my waist. "We'll be going inside now. I suggest you turn in for the night yourself." Though it was aimed at Lander, Glacies and Vulcan took off, beating wings blowing cool night air across my heated neck as they disappeared into the sky.

Lander looked around Bowen's shoulder at me. "You're sleeping at his house?"

Gods, this was all wrong. I wanted to scream. My stomach churned, causing me to flatten a hand against my abdomen. Something didn't feel right.

"I'm walking her to where she's staying," Bowen clarified.

My head swam as Lander said something in response, but I couldn't make it out over the fog. I stood there, blinking into space. Had they hit my head that hard? Did I have internal bleeding? Surely, there wasn't any lasting damage. This felt different than in the street, like a tingling in my mind.

"Auria." Bowen's voice filled my head, and I shook it, clearing the haze to find him standing directly in front of me.

I searched the clearing. "Where's Lander?"

Bowen's brows pulled together. "He left." A step closer, and he set both hands on my upper arms. "Are you feeling okay?"

He'd blame himself if I told him something felt off. Despite what he might think, this wasn't his fault. "I'm fine. Just tired."

He hesitated, not fooled by my words, but didn't push. Already, my stomach was feeling better, but I didn't understand the wave of dizziness or why it seemed to pass so quickly.

"Let's get you home," he said. Any trace of his gray tendrils was gone.

We headed through the dense brush, branches catching on our clothes as we walked. A few steps ahead, Bowen did his best to hold the spindly twigs away so they wouldn't fling back and hit me.

"Why did they leave?" I asked.

He knew I meant Glacies and Vulcan. "They don't like petty drama."

"Is that what Lander and I are to everyone?" The thought that others might view us that way wouldn't surprise me. What Lander and I were forced to do together seemed so...minuscule compared to the world around us.

Holding a particularly thorny branch to the side so I could step into the clearing that led to Deadwood, he said, "To some. It's no secret your marriage was arranged for a reason." Marriage slid off his tongue like one might spit out bad tasting food.

"To bring the kingdoms back together," I offered.

"And that would benefit Torbernite?" he asked as we walked side by side between two houses, entering the town.

"What do you mean?"

"They were doing just fine with their arrangements with Sulphur and Feldspar. It's Amosite they all have problems with."

I tilted my head in thought. "Are you saying this was only for my father's benefit?"

Bowen shrugged. "Perhaps the Bulars had their own reasons."

With not a clue what those might be, I said instead, "So you're *friends* with Glacies."

A glance at Bowen showed the corners of his mouth twitching into a smile he fought to keep at bay. "I wouldn't say I'm particularly friends with the dragon. Or any dragon, in fact."

"What would you call it, then?"

We walked down the main street. A few burly, drunk men were hanging around the front of the saloon as we passed.

"An alliance, I suppose. We help them, they help us," Bowen explained.

"We, as in..."

"Fae," he filled in. "We have a sort of bond with dragons, and Vulcan happens to be my bonded pair. He loathes being connected to anyone, but we complement each other." With the two of them being just as intimidating as the other, I believed it.

"How does this connection work, exactly?" It'd be hard to believe they had some sort of written agreement.

"Like with a partner, your feelings grow attached. But rather than gradually, it's instantly. Dragons have a sense that fae don't—being able to mentally tell when their bonded fae is injured. But if the dragon gets hurt, their fae companion almost feels it like a phantom pain. It's such an inner connection that living without your dragon... It'd be agony. The mourning never stops. Your heart breaks, day after day." He was silent a moment as the knowledge settled in my mind, his eyes on the squelching muddied street. "Many fae choose death over the pain."

The thought of how it would feel to be so deeply connected

to a being and then to lose them only made me sympathize with the fae more. Would Bowen choose death if Vulcan were to die? He seemed too strong. Too unbreakable. The thought of something like that causing his end forced a foreign unease to run through me. I didn't want to think of that happening to him.

"Why were they in the clearing in the first place? Did you call to them or something?" We rounded the end of the street, walking through the lined up houses.

He shook his head. "They wanted to discuss something. And I was a little...pent-up."

"What was it?"

He looked at me with resigned eyes. "Auria..."

My lips pressed into a thin line. "I just want to help." A purpose while being stuck in this town would be nice, but I gathered I wouldn't find it with Bowen. Not that I should have expected to in the first place.

He faced forward again, shoulders stiff. "We don't need your help."

I reared back, almost as if he'd slapped me with his words. Thankfully, my house was straight ahead. I didn't hesitate before quickening my pace, closing in on the porch.

"Auria, wait."

As I reached the step, I spun, and he halted feet away. "No, I get it. Nobody really needs me anyway."

"That's not what I mean, and you know that," he defended.

As if he didn't just say the words himself. I propped my hands on my waist and narrowed my eyes. The movement reminded me of the pain in my ribs. I'd need to find a healing vial soon. "I clearly don't know you like I thought I did. So no, Bowen, I don't know that. No one will open up to me about anything, and maybe that's how it always ought to be."

"I tried—"

I let out a snort in disbelief. "By telling me about dragons? That's not you."

"It *is* me. It's part of who I am. There's a lot you don't know," he started.

"That's the problem," I muttered.

"But it's too much for me to tell you all at once. And it's not solely my decision whether I can tell you all of it or not. The bridge will be back up in a few days, if that—"

"You're going to tell me what's too much?" I dropped my hands. I'd thought we were getting anywhere with our moment in the field. With the shower. With him helping me. I had been a fool to go to him. "Being hidden away from everything my entire life is *too much*, Bowen. Being told I can't handle the truth or that I shouldn't be told something is *too much*. Not being honest with me is *too much*. I can't take it anymore—the deceitful people in my life deciding what I can and can't know."

"Yet you defend your father every chance you get," he bit out.

I could *scream*. He didn't understand any of it. A wolf could be fed by its abuser every day, and it had no choice but to love the hand that fed it, even if it was the same hand that hurt it. When you were given such few options, you worked with what you got. I couldn't bite the hand that kept me safe. But in thinking that, was I admitting that my father's treatment of me was unfair? That my home truly was cruel, and I'd simply lived to become accustomed to it? Maybe Bowen's distaste toward my defending of my father was justified, then. But an outside eye would never understand the comfort hell could provide.

Doing my best to reel in the unruly emotions that refused to stop showing themselves tonight, I said, "I appreciate your help earlier, but like you said, it's been a long day. Goodnight, Bowen."

If he saw the hurt in my eyes, he didn't speak of it. I stepped inside the house, softly shutting the door behind me. Truthfully, my past wasn't Bowen's burden. If anything, he was the only one who had given me some sort of reprieve to the silence I'd been given my whole life. My pain was not his fault, nor was the way I grew up. Maybe he was right in that I couldn't handle all this information at once. After all, I'd only ended up upset with him each time I got a taste of this world.

And maybe, the self-deprecating thoughts spiraling through my mind weren't anyone else's fault but my own, too.

CHAPTER 40

BOWEN

The moment Auria shut the door, I was heading in the direction of the saloon. I didn't want to think of the look of betrayal in her eyes before she disappeared inside. We needed to work on this communication between the two of us—

I shook my head. She was leaving. There was nothing to work on.

My boots pounded in the mud, globs of it spraying upwards as I walked. If Crass and Nemin thought they could get away with attacking Auria, they had less brain cells than I'd given them credit for. I'd had problems with them playing dirty in the past, but nothing like this.

They hurt her, and that wouldn't go unpunished.

Finally, my magic whispered in my mind. *I've been waiting.*

"You and me both," I muttered, mere feet from the saloon.

My smoke was way ahead of me, shoving open the door to the saloon so hard the wood split as it slammed against the wall. Instantly, the tendrils were hunting for them. It was a game we both enjoyed, the predator inside me coming out to play.

The patrons were in pure chaos when I entered, fists aimed at one another, a dagger or two drawn, a gun pointed at some man who probably deserved it, if the blood on his knuckles was any proof of that. A chair was thrown at the wall, breaking into pieces while a table was overturned.

But as my magic's presence became known by the way it weaved between all of them, searching like a hound its prey, they ceased in their fighting, all heads in the room turning to me.

Raiden would be jealous of how quickly I had been able to stop what had to have begun as a riot and seemingly quickly turned into one side disagreeing with the other. I had no doubt that once Raiden had left here, they had gone back to business. By the looks of the place, I likely wasn't far off with my assumption.

It was because of Auria.

But so was this.

Ribbons of smoke darted for the back corner, finding my two targets chuckling over a game of poker. The idiots were so wrapped up in their game, they hadn't even realized my presence like the rest of the place. Those laughs quickly turned to choking as I approached, the smoke taking punishment into its own hands. But I wanted to have my fun, too.

As the other men scattered from the table, chairs knocking over in their haste, I called for the smoke to retreat back to me. It spiraled out of their mouths and nostrils reluctantly, darting around me in clouds of frenzy.

"Bowen," Nemin stuttered out as Crass's eyes watered from his coughs. Both their cheeks were beet red. From fear or overindulging in alcohol, I didn't care. "What are you doing here?"

"My town, isn't it?" I righted one of the chairs, taking a seat to face them. "Or did you forget that when you went after one of my people?"

Crass, the poor, brainless bastard, snorted. "Your people?"

My smoke didn't like that. It darted for its target, pooling in Crass's eyes, swimming around like it enjoyed the pain it inflicted.

I knew I did.

I crossed a leg over my knee, unsheathing a dagger from my boot. "She's currently under Deadwood's protection. And, you see, two of Deadwood's notoriously problematic residents going after her just doesn't look good."

"W-we didn't know," Nemin, the pathetic man that he was, whimpered, his words pouring over one another. "We only wanted a little payback, to scare her a bit."

Gray fog surrounded his legs, crawling up his waist to his neck. I was half tempted to let it have the reins.

I picked at my fingernail with the tip of my blade. I knew he was lying. They had attacked with the intent to kill her. Auria didn't wear bruises as bright as hers without death having been a breath away. "Why is that?"

Crass rubbed relentlessly at his eyes, but no amount of scratching would soothe the burn.

Nemin's gaze darted between Crass and the smoke curling up his body. "She never paid up."

I sat forward, elbows on my knees, dagger dangling from my hand. "Rumor has it, you two haven't been truthful about your debts either."

Nemin's eyes widened as the smoke wrapped around his neck, the veins nearly bursting through his skin. "W-we have. We're always h-honest."

I hummed, sending the smoke from Crass's eyes through the sockets and into his lungs. Immediately, he began gagging as I stood from the chair, tossing the dagger into the air to catch it by the handle.

Shoving Nemin's shoulder back, I forced his hand flat on the table. "Lying to your king isn't a good look." Even saying the word burned the back of my throat. Rearing my arm back, I brought the dagger down. The blade cut clean through his wrist, and his hand disconnected completely from his body.

Behind me, the rest of the saloon cleared out, wanting nothing to do with the punishment I dealt. They might be outlaws—fae who committed crimes for the good and bad—but I was the most feared in this town. That fact would always remain.

Nemin's screams filled the emptying building as Crass's choking ceased, his body lying lifeless on the ground.

I knelt, getting right in Nemin's sweat-soaked face. "Don't ever fucking touch what's mine again."

I wiped the blood dripping from my dagger on his shoulder, then left him to his own misery. He'd suffer, but he wouldn't die. I'd have gladly killed him, but I wanted him to serve as a message to the others.

If anyone wanted to lay a hand on Auria in my town, they'd answer to me.

Smoke trailed me as I walked toward Lux, who still stood behind the bar. He ran a rag over a glass, business as usual, as if I hadn't just killed a man and tortured another in his establishment.

It wasn't the first time.

I was too antsy to sit, so I leaned against the edge instead, my elbows propped on the sticky surface. "Sorry about the riots."

Lux set the glass down next to the other clean ones, giving me a hard look. "Not gonna apologize for chasing my moneymakers out?"

"You know I never do."

He grunted. "I know. So don't feed me some bullshit apology about a couple pissed off fae."

I sighed, hanging my head.

"Besides," Lux went on, tossing the rag in the sink, "the girl is growing on me."

My gaze moved back to his, a smile pulling at the corners of my mouth. Lux never admitted shit like that. "What was that?"

He shot me a glare, grabbing a handle of whiskey and pouring a shot before sliding the small glass toward me. "You keep standing up for her, and people are going to get suspicious."

I knocked the amber liquid back in one swig before setting it back on the bar. "I'm lenient, Lux. They know that. But not when it comes to this."

My eyes focused on the clear glass as my mind went back to Auria's muddy form. The scars on her back. The bruises on her neck. Her ribs.

Lux must've sensed the anger growing because he said, "We'll handle the riots. You just keep her safe, alright?"

Again, my attention moved to him. I'd never heard the man speak like this.

I dipped my chin in response.

He waved a hand my way, eyes darting to my arms and back. "Now get the fuck out of here before you smoke the place out."

I hadn't even realized the familiar gray crawling up the path of my veins.

Tapping the edge of the bar once, I shoved off and left the saloon, the color in my arms refusing to dissipate as it reveled in the chaos I'd just created.

Despite my conversation with Lux and having enacted some sort of revenge, though, I didn't feel an inkling of reprieve knowing Auria had been hurt tonight, and I feared that feeling would never leave me from this point forward.

THE COOL NIGHT air did nothing to calm the rage that remained filtering through me like magic trapped in a vial. Tendrils of smoke traced gray veins from my elbows to the tips of my fingers, and even after I'd wilted the leaves of a nearby oak tree, it refused to be contained. My power fed off my fae side, and both were currently pits of uncontrollable feral energy.

Piss and blood is almost a step up from human stench, Vulcan grumbled into my mind as he stuck taloned feet into the mushy soil behind me, folding his wings in on himself as he landed. *Still unbecoming, though.*

I shoved the sleeves of my jacket up farther, the leather tight on my biceps. "I took care of the problem." My voice was hoarse. Tired.

Whose problem may that have been? Vulcan asked as I turned to face him.

I shook my head. I wasn't doing this with him again. He didn't want me anywhere near Auria unless it was to use her, and yet, that didn't sway me. Little of what Vulcan had to say did. He was an opinionated dragon whose input I didn't need.

Scaled eyelids blinked over dark, gold-flamed irises, and the judgment in his gaze was all too apparent. *Are you so willing to go against your people for harming a girl who means nothing to you?*

I scoffed, ribbons of smoke curling toward him. He didn't bother glancing at the approaching threat as a low growl reverberated through his chest. "Order is to be kept in this town."

You have guards for that, he reminded me.

"I like to get my hands dirty sometimes." I refused to be a

leader who made others do all my bidding. I wasn't afraid of a fight. If anything, I rejoiced in them.

Vulcan did his best attempt at an eye roll. *Ever the king.*

"I am *not* a king," I gritted out. Twice in the span of a few hours, the word tainted my tongue. I wouldn't replace my father, and I wouldn't be like the other leaders on this continent.

Flynt and his stone dragon, Silax, along with Siara and her water dragon, Azurina, landed on either side of the clearing.

Lovely.

They both slid off their dragons' backs. Azurina watched Vulcan with a curious eye. She was a dangerous dragon when provoked, but otherwise shy. Her quietness was polar opposite to Siara's volume.

"Bridge is looking good so far," Siara announced, running her fingers through her thick, blonde strands to untangle them from flight.

"Still thinking the same completion date?" I asked.

Flynt nodded. His hair was windblown and his cheeks were splotched in red. "Doubt it will be longer than a week now."

They were making good progress. It was bittersweet. "Good."

"Are you thinking of checking out Torbernite again?" Flynt asked, taking his leather gloves off and shoving them in his jacket pocket.

"Maybe next week," I clipped.

Flynt raised a suspicious brow before eyeing the charred tree nearby, likely getting the gist of just how stir-crazy my magic was making me.

"*He would have been successful the first time had he not been distracted by the girl,*" Vulcan muttered, speaking aloud so the others could hear his judgment.

Silax, the lazy dragon that he was, lay in a ball, releasing a huff in response. The dragons weren't happy with how long our plan was taking, but a civilization couldn't bestow major changes overnight.

"What happened with what girl?" Siara asked, always the curious one.

"Nothing happened with any girl," I bit out, shooting Vulcan a warning glare to keep his putrid mouth shut. "I have this covered. I just need to go back, do some more digging, and we can move on."

Steam misted the grass below as Vulcan chortled.

"Need I remind you not to insult our own, Vulcan," my voice boomed, yet the dragon didn't stand down. He stepped forward, bringing his head to my level. "Or perhaps you're jealous."

From my peripheral, Silax moved to a stand, sensing the rising tension.

"*She is distracting you. Or do you not see that? I thought you were smarter, King.*" Vulcan's voice was dangerously low, the gold flecks in his scales flaring brighter as he spoke.

I refused to let him provoke me with the title, but his indirect insult of Auria was reason enough for my smoke to wrap around his legs like a coil ready to spring. "This is not her fault."

"*Tell me, then, if she had not shown up, would you be infiltrating their supply right now?*"

Siara, the brave one that she was, stepped between us. "Alright, boys. No need to whip them out and measure. We'll get this sorted out. In the meantime, let's all stop blaming Auria for shit that doesn't involve her."

Her words were a slight shock as just earlier, she had done the same. I'd been right, then. She was just as attached.

Mentally, I shoved the word away. I couldn't allow myself to grow attached to Auria. She was to leave, and I'd likely never see her again. It was better this way.

"Siara's right," I said as Vulcan dropped the act, giving me space. He'd never dare put a gnarly talon on me, and I'd likely never do the same to him. That never stopped the threats from flying, though. "None of this is her fault. She'll be gone in a few days, and we can get back to the plan."

After the incident earlier, I was thankful Glacies wasn't here for this. She was overly protective of Auria, and I didn't need that interfering with any of this.

"Flynt, were you and Silax able to find a weak spot over the chasm?" I asked, turning to them. I'd sent them to see if their attempt ended the same way the bones dragon's had when it had hit the invisible wall in the cave.

He shook his head as Silax stepped up behind him. His light brown scales were muted under the silver rings casting a glow upon the meadow. "We tried to fly over multiple different areas of the chasm, even tried over the ocean, but there's something blocking dragons from entering at all angles. Clearly, fae can get in, so it's only for them."

"We tried, too," Siara added. "No luck."

Off to the side, Azurina nodded, green hooded eyes sparkling in the night.

"We need to figure out why, and soon." There'd be no way to follow through with all of this if the dragons couldn't fly into Amosite, and after my experience in the caves, we couldn't get them in through there either.

Something had to be powering an invisible wall of sorts. We just had to figure out what that was and destroy it.

"The plan is still on," I said, more so to assure Vulcan. "We'll make this happen, and we'll get what we've been fighting for. My father didn't die for nothing, and neither will we. Is that clear?"

Dragons and fae alike gave nods of approval.

Now we just had to figure out how to do this without truly making the fae population extinct, and possibly bringing the dragons down with us.

CHAPTER 41

AURIA

Despite the exhaustion, I'd barely slept last night due to my mind spinning, repeating the conversation with Bowen over and over. I'd been so angry at myself for the attack, as if it was somehow my fault. Granted, my part in the poker game had presumably started all of this, successfully putting a target on my back, but I was tired of not living. Though the little bit I had gotten the chance to do ended up in bruises staining my neck, a broken rib or two, and a steamy shower with a man I couldn't seem to stop arguing with. It was almost like a twisted version of foreplay, yet Bowen and I would never get past the bickering.

He'd said they didn't need me. While it shouldn't have been a shock, the statement had echoed through the dense forest of my mind until the early hours of the morning, every leaf dangling from unstable branches screaming his words at me.

Well, I didn't need *him*.

After using the healing vial I'd found set beside the book to mend my ribs, I'd pulled on a long, deep blue dress with a revealing neckline that dipped into a low V between my breasts. The slit in the thigh went nearly to my hip bone, and with each step, it revealed more. The outfit showed far more skin than I'd ever felt comfortable with before, but with only days remaining until the bridge was crossable again, I wanted to do as much as I could, and that included wearing risqué dresses. Second on my agenda for the day was to act as if the attack hadn't affected me at all. If anything was going to show them not to fuck with me, it'd be me exuding confidence out in the open, not hiding away, scared for my life.

I clasped the opal necklace around my neck, the pads of my fingers brushing over the tender bruises painting my skin. I'd only healed my ribs, keeping the bruises there to heal on their own. I wanted people to see what had happened, and that despite it all, I was still standing.

I'd been so close to death last night, and in that moment, when the air squeezed from my lungs and burned a hole in my soul, I'd found it truly wasn't a fate I wanted to meet anytime soon.

I left my hair down, thrown over my shoulders to cascade down my back in silky waves. For once, the strands had obeyed, and they were less frizzy than ever.

A glance in the mirror sent satisfaction coursing through me at the intrepidness that seemed to radiate off of me by appearance alone. I headed for the door, but as soon as I opened it, I stopped short.

Bowen stood with his back against the post of my small porch, tossing a dagger up in the air, only to catch it by the handle. His heel was propped up against the wood, his stance casual but stiff, like at any moment, that blade might land true.

"Princess," he greeted, not looking my way.

"What are you doing here?" I questioned, closing the door behind me as I stepped into the midmorning sun. There was no breeze, yet the air held a chill, causing goosebumps to freckle my chest.

"Enjoying the lovely day," he replied, now admiring the glint off the blade from the blinding rings in the sky.

I stepped past him, looking out at the street. "Well, I'm going out."

The sound of dirt shuffling filled my ears as he presumably straightened behind me. "I'll come with you."

I turned my head to the side, my eyes cast on the ground. "I never said where I was going."

"There's nowhere in this town I haven't been, a spot in this land I haven't seen. Wherever it is, wherever you go, I will be there. And if you choose not to tell me, I will find you."

I turned then, facing him, and as his devouring gaze took me in from head to toe, his hand froze on the hilt of his dagger. "I'm going to the saloon."

He gave no indication that he had heard me, his eyes heating as they turned to twin flames, visually devouring the display set before him. The dress clung to every curve, accentuating my hips, waist, breasts. And every inch the fabric covered —and the spots it did not—he admired like a starved animal set in front of a feast after a long hibernation.

His eyes, so vibrant under the blue sky, met mine. The look alone made me want to torture him day in and day out, just to see that hunger—that need—blaze in his gaze. But not only him, it was me who was vexed by a life I'd never live with a man I could never have. Based on the tortured look on his face, I'd say he wanted me, too. He just didn't want to admit it.

So I'd find a way to make him beg.

I faced the street again. "Coming?"

One glance back showed him snapping out of his all-consuming stupor, his throat working on a swallow as he sheathed the dagger in one fluid motion. My eyes followed the blade, the way his hand held the deadly weapon like a delicate wildflower. Would he one day handle me with such precise, lethal confidence?

He came to my side, and we walked alongside each other without another word, heading through the rows of houses until we entered the main street.

"Long night?" I asked to break the silence. Chatter filtered onto the road from the shops, people bustling about as they went about their business, but it wasn't enough to break the pressing quiet that hung between me and Bowen like a bow on a string ready to snap.

"It was nothing special," he answered. "And you?"

He didn't ask if I was alright. He knew that I was, based on the thorough visual examination of my body he had done.

A woman didn't dress in such a way the day after being attacked to simply cower like an injured animal.

"Good as a night could be, given how the day before went." I wouldn't lie. Despite the outfit, I was distraught over what had happened, but I had to keep my chin up, lest they get the upper hand and take advantage of a fragile state of mind.

He sent me a sympathetic glance, and I wanted to fall into it and wrap myself up in his care. Out of the entire evening, my mind kept wandering back to him in the shower. Standing in front of me with water dripping down his bare chest, the light dusting of hair across his skin dampened, his eyes that had taken me in with nothing but concern. He hadn't hesitated to take care of me, to bring me upstairs and make sure I was okay. To wash the filth, grime, and shame from my skin. He'd just... done it. I had once thought he hated me, but then he had scooped me up, and I had never wanted to be put down again.

If that was hate, consider me loathed.

"You don't need to worry." Something in him had changed last night. I could feel it in the tone of his voice, in the way my skin hummed near his, our arms nearly brushing as we walked.

What a simple reassurance when my life could have been ripped from me in seconds.

"I'm not." The words were light, a slight tremble to them, and he sensed I wasn't speaking my mind. But rather than pointing it out, he let me believe my own words for the sake that maybe, if he didn't refute them, I'd find them to be true.

We approached the saloon, and without hesitation, he held the door open for me, stepping aside to let me pass him. After yesterday, him being okay with my being here somewhat shocked me. But that's what stood Bowen apart from the rest of the people in my life. He didn't tell me where to go. Rather, he followed, giving me the freedom to make my own decisions.

Until he shoved me away.

A constant push and pull with him, leaving me seasick on stable ground.

With that thought in mind, I didn't bother thanking him as I stepped over the threshold. I was still mad at him for saying he didn't need my help, and I wanted him to know that.

The musty air immediately stung my nose as cigar smoke whirled in the rays of the sun streaming in from the dirt-caked windows. Dust mixed with the clusters, creating a cacophony of fluttering debris. Stronger than before, the smell of that putrid ale combined with the pungent scent of whisky hit me as Bowen let the door fall shut. I hadn't realized I'd stopped walking, my mind racing with the thought that Nemin and Crass could be in here, that I'd have to look them in the face after what they'd done to me.

A gentle hand rested in the dip of my waist, giving a light squeeze as a thumb brushed over the fabric of my dress. "You're safe," Bowen murmured, his chest brushing my back.

But it wasn't his words or the knowledge that no one would

touch me with his presence that soothed my speeding heart—it was him. His body near mine, his breath on my skin, his eyes only on me. I never wanted him to remove his hand from that spot. I wanted him to touch me like he had in the shower, with such careful precision, like he could play me as a musician might pluck the strings of a harp. Delicate and with meaning, only to elicit the most beautiful harmony. His caress made my skin sing, my senses tingle, and I wanted to feel it for the rest of my days. To hear the tune we silently sang in the presence of each other.

But all too soon, his hand was gone, leaving a cold breeze in its place.

I pasted on a smile. "I think I want to play a game." I went to step forward in the direction of the pool tables, but his grasp was back, holding me in place.

Perfect.

He moved around me, his face now directly in front of mine. "You have to bet magic, and you have none to offer."

With the tilt of my neck, my eyes locked on his. "I'll just play with yours."

A challenge, and I wanted him to bite.

A look of amusement lit his face, the slight arch of a brow, a small curve of his mouth. "Is that so?"

I moved closer. His breath skated down my cleavage with the dip of his chin. "Yes."

"You don't barter with magic that isn't yours, Princess."

My eyes fell to his neck, skirting down the peeking tips of his tattoo to the black shirt that stretched across his chest. If I reached out, I'd feel his heart. Was it beating as erratically as mine—wanting more as badly as I did?

"Consider it borrowing, then," I replied, meeting his gaze again.

He released my waist once more, and I hated how badly I

wanted it back again. Was he a drug, and I was addicted? "I don't let just anyone borrow my magic."

My finger moved on its own accord, connecting with his hard chest, trailing up, up... "It's a good thing I'm not just anyone, then, isn't it?"

His chin dipped further, and I knew people were watching, but *fuck*, I didn't care. His tongue swept out to wet his lips, and the act alone nearly sent me to my knees. But before I could get further caught up in the mysteries of his mouth, his hand grabbed mine, flipping it palm up. His other arm moved, and then something cool landed in my grasp, glass clinking together. "Two vials. One game. No more."

My fingers wrapped around the vials. "Bossy today, are we?"

His voice lowered, and I wanted to bottle the words that came with it. "You don't know what bossy looks like, Auria, but I'd be happy to show you."

I almost considered taking him up on his offer. *Almost*. But instead, I stepped back, satisfied enough with the vials in my hand and the knowledge that I'd gotten under his skin. "I'll pass."

Walking around him and the knowing smirk on his lips, I found an empty pool table with a muscled man leaning against it, massive arms crossed. It was a shock his skin didn't burst from the size of the muscles themselves.

Setting the two vials on the table, I gave the man a saccharine grin. "Care to play?"

Unfolding the boulders disguised as arms, he grabbed his cue where it was leaned up against the table and took one giant step toward me. For a moment, I thought he might crush me where I stood, but instead of pulverizing me, his hand shot out to the right and he dropped two vials next to my own. I took that as his silent agreement that he was in.

To my surprise, Bowen didn't try to step in. Rather, he

leaned back against the nearest wall, cast in shadow as he faced the pool table. His feet were shoulder-width apart, his arms crossed over his broad chest. He didn't move once as he watched my every shot while I played against the quiet giant of a man.

~

FIFTEEN MINUTES LATER, I wasn't surprised I was losing. Truly, I'd only wanted to have fun. Well, that, and to have Bowen's eyes on me the whole time. He thought he didn't need me? I'd make him crave me instead.

A few people had stopped by to strike up a conversation with Bowen, but all the while they spoke, his simmering eyes never left mine. If I had to be honest, a big reason I was losing as badly as I was was due to my focus barely being on the game in the first place. My entire body was lit like a match under his ravenous stare. Bowen was dangerously distracting, and I feared my tactic to rile him up was having the opposite effect I'd wanted it to.

My opponent, who I'd learned went by the name Brick—it fit, really—had played a fair game, and I was a bit deflated our round was almost over. I wouldn't ask Bowen for more magic, though. Not that I felt bad taking any, but because I didn't trust myself to get that close to him right now. Our bodies, warm and soaking, in that shower, had awoken something in me. We'd both been laid bare, emotionally and physically, and I'd seen a part of him I wondered if anyone else ever had. My entire being was hyper focused on that version of him, but I had to remind myself that the Bowen I had seen last night wasn't who he truly was. Not all the time, at least.

"Busy night last night, I hear," a man said, offering Bowen a drink. The last conversation had been mumbled words, but this one I heard loud and clear from where I stood pondering over the game.

He shook his head at the mug of ale, declining it. "Just another day," Bowen replied, and a glance his way found his eyes still glued to my every move.

With it being my turn, I surveyed the table, finding the best shot on the far end. Perching up on the tips of my toes, I knew Bowen could see down the front of my dress as I bent at the waist, and yet, I didn't move to take my shot. I studied the angle of the ball to the hole like it was the most important decision of my life.

"Nemin went to the infirmary frantic as hell. Couldn't tell if the guy had more tears or piss drenching him," the man said before taking a long swig of ale.

I took the shot, the crack of the balls filling the saloon, but it missed the hole. I didn't give a shit, though. Not after what that man had just said to Bowen.

I straightened, slapping the cue on the table. Bowen's jaw ground together as he waited for my next move.

Whatever Nemin was doing at the infirmary, it wasn't because of my attempts to fight him off.

"Keep the vials, Brick," I muttered, abandoning the table and beelining for the door.

I made it outside right as Bowen's hand wrapped around my wrist. "Auria."

I spun, shaking him off me. "Why was he in the infirmary, Bowen?"

His eyes flashed, something lethal passing through them, but not toward me. "Why do you think?"

"What did you do?" But rather than irate or full of rage, my voice was soft, just above a whisper. He hadn't just helped clean my muddied skin, made sure I wasn't majorly injured, he'd...

"I cut his hand off and suffocated Crass. He's dead. Nemin got lucky."

Nausea rolled through me, but I held it back with a hand to my stomach. "Why?"

His forehead knotted. "Why did I make them pay for what they did to you?"

Dropping my hand to my side, I shook my head. "You said you didn't need me, so why protect me? Why not let them try to kill me again? It'd only take the problem off your hands."

He wrapped a callused hand around my wrist, his grip firm but feather soft all at the same time, and pulled me around the side of the building. He didn't let go of me as he spun around, or when he pressed my back against the wood siding, or as he pressed the bulge in his pants to my lower stomach, leaning into me. "Feel that, Auria?"

I refused to respond. The pressure alone sent sparks careening through me.

"Tell me that feels like you're a problem to me. That I don't need you. That I don't crave you every moment since the day I met you. Every night since you arrived in Deadwood, I've laid in bed, thinking of you, imagining ways I could make you stay for my own selfish reasons." He heaved a breath, and I forced myself to do the same. His words made me dizzy in the best way possible, an even sweeter buzz than alcohol could even dream of eliciting swirling through my mind. "Is that what you want me to tell you to make you believe you are needed?"

I could only blink at him, words lost from my tongue as all it wanted to do was taste his, to know what it felt like to part those lips and lose myself in the current of him.

Finally, I managed a nod.

"Then I'll say it every day you remain in Deadwood, if that's what you desire. All you have to do is say the words, and I'll remind you every damn day how needed you are on this planet." He braced his hands on the wall, caging me in with tattooed arms as he lowered his head. "You are needed."

I was quickly coming to realize that Bowen had enveloped every thought in my mind in just a matter of days.

But it wasn't days. No, it'd been over a month now since the night of the ball. While he'd royally pissed me off the night my father had announced my engagement, his irritable comments had stuck like honey, his voice replaying in my head. And then he'd shown up the night of Exitium Lunae and killed three men without even blinking. He'd done that for me, and yet, I'd questioned him. Wondered if he wished the worst for me.

And in this moment, those thoughts were only damning me. With my eyes on his lips, and his on mine, there was only one thing that mattered in this alley. If I leaned a few inches forward, angled my head a bit to the right...

But Bowen was a criminal. Someone my father hated. He was a leader, but not a king, and worst of all, I barely knew anything about the world.

But I knew more about him than anyone else. Didn't that count for something?

No. I was being a fool.

I pulled back, my head nearly hitting the wall. "I'd like to go home."

He blinked, likely studying the way the words had spilled from my mouth, how they were rushed, unsure, and clearly a lie. What I really wanted to say was, *Kiss me and make me forget this is temporary*, but instead, I was a coward too afraid to take that leap.

His throat bobbed with a swallow, and he stepped back, dropping his hands from the wall. Instantly, my body mourned. The place he'd pressed his cock to my body, only thin fabric separating us, went cold. I should take back what I said, tell him how I truly felt—

"I'll walk you home," he said, his deflation clear.

And it was set in stone.

Maybe this was best. I'd be leaving soon anyway.

His hands flexed before I shoved off the wall. He didn't want to have restraint when it came to me, and I was right there with him. I wanted to live in a world where I could ravage any man I wanted, to be free to kiss whoever I thought fit just because I could.

But instead, I lived where not only a castle was my prison, but my mind as well.

Walls didn't just hold me back from my desires. It was the thoughts—the consequences—that would surely follow.

We walked back to the house in silence so thick, I thought I might get lost in the fog. And when he left me at the door without a word, I wished my mouth had never opened, and my lies had never been spoken.

CHAPTER 42

AURIA

As soon as I stepped past the threshold, I knew I wasn't alone.

I silently closed the door behind me, walking farther into the house. I paused in the opening to the living room, my heart nearly stopping.

Paxon sat calmly in one of the chairs much like before, but as soon as he stood, the tight line of his mouth told me he was anything but serene.

Gods, not right now. I wasn't in the mood. Though, was I ever when it came to him? "What are you doing here?"

"Where were you?" he asked.

I scoffed, heading for the kitchen.

There had to be some sort of alcohol in here. Rifling through every cabinet, I finally found a decanter shoved in the far corner on a bottom shelf. Rich, amber liquid sloshed in the glass as I grabbed it.

"I won't ask twice," Paxon warned, but I didn't give a shit.

I uncapped the bottle and took a swig, but as soon as the liquor hit my tongue, the glass was flying out of my hand and onto the wood floor. I barely had time to swallow before Paxon had me shoved against the counter, a firm grip on my upper arm. "You reek of alcohol and smoke."

"Bowen's outside," I said hurriedly, the liquor burning my throat as I nearly choked on it.

A menacing smile spread across his face. "That man can't protect you."

"He would against someone like you."

He leaned closer, and I arched back, the edge of the counter digging into my lower back. "Someone like me, huh?"

My words were strained, my eyes slits. "Someone who touches me without permission."

For emphasis, he yanked on my arm, bringing my chest to his. I suddenly regretted wearing the revealing dress. "Remember my little warning? I don't think you've listened." His other hand raised, and he jerked as if to slap me. I flinched, squeezing my eyes shut to brace against the oncoming sting. The pathetic act alone made him chuckle as he released his grip on my arm, not laying a hand to my cheek. "Be careful, Auria. I wouldn't put so much faith in a man that may not be all that he seems."

As he stepped away, my body stayed guarded, stiff with the fear that he was letting me believe it was over, but it was anything but. Like a lion toying with its prey.

"Bowen isn't a liar like half this continent is," I defended.

He straightened the sleeves of his jacket, adjusting one of the buttons, as if I'd rustled them purposefully. "Oh? I overheard them talking about a little plan they have for Amosite."

My brows pinched together. If he was baiting me, I couldn't tell. "What do you mean?"

He shrugged like it was just a simple conversation between two friends. "They want to destroy the entire kingdom."

Blood froze in my veins. "No, they don't." They couldn't.

Bowen wasn't like that. He wouldn't destroy an entire kingdom. Not with innocent civilians in the crossfire. I knew him well enough to be sure of that.

Satisfied with the state of his sleeve, Paxon looked at me. The glint in his eyes was anything but settling. "If you want proof, I'm sure you can find some in his house."

With that, he headed for the door, leaving me standing there with alcohol flooding the floor and the fragile state of my mind threatening to shatter like the glass among the mess.

He couldn't be telling the truth. But if he was...

Could I really trust anyone?

"I came to see if you made a decision," Paxon said, stopping before he twisted the handle.

I didn't move my eyes from the mess. "You told me I have until the bridge is repaired."

He was quiet a few moments too long, unease creeping through my limbs with each passing second. "A wise person never waits until the last minute."

My jaw clenched. "I'll take every moment I get." Because I had no fucking idea what to choose. Not with everything seeming to crumble down around me.

~

I WAS DETERMINED to figure out if what Paxon had claimed about Bowen was true, so as soon as I woke the next morning, I dressed in a white blouse with a leather corset that stopped right below my breasts and pulled on a pair of brown pants, the waistband just reaching the bottom of the corset. I passed on breakfast, not bothering to grab a snack on my way.

There would be no more secrets. No more staying in the dark. If there were things to be found out, I'd find them. A life of imaginary walls with doors only others could open when they chose was not a life I wanted to live anymore. I'd open them all, and I'd learn all I wanted to learn, have knowledge on any topic I wanted. As soon as I returned to Amosite, I'd demand my father allow it. I'd already discovered so many things on this trip, so what more could the rest hurt?

I swung open the front door but skidded to a halt as I took in Lander standing before me, his hair neatly combed back to show off his freshly shaven face.

A smile crested his lips. "Good morning."

"Uh, hi," I greeted, glancing behind him. "Did you need something?"

"Just wanted to spend some time with my fiancée." Still, the word sounded odd rolling off his tongue, and he knew it just as well by the look on his face.

"I'm quite busy at the moment, actually." I glanced over his shoulder again as a mother and her daughter walked past, the child skipping along in the dirt.

His brows furrowed. "You don't look very busy to me."

"I was actually just on my way out—"

"We haven't seen each other much since we've arrived in Deadwood, and that's my fault." His eyes truly did look sympathetic, and I suddenly felt bad trying to skip out on him. "I've been caught up, wallowing in my emotions over our engagement—which is actually something I'd like to talk to you about. But I figured we could explore while we chat? A friend at the saloon told me all about the mines, and I thought we could check them out."

Exploring sounded a lot more enticing than sneaking around Bowen's house trying to find information that might not even exist. For all I knew, Paxon was trying to pit me against Bowen. I shouldn't fall for the bait so easily.

"That sounds great, actually." I stepped over the threshold to close the door behind me.

"I've brought you a horse." He gestured to the gray mare standing tall and alert by the post, all tacked up and ready to ride. "She's quite sweet."

I walked over to her, lifting a hand to rub her muzzle. "She's beautiful."

He stood by the stirrup, gesturing to the saddle. "May I?"

I nodded, coming around the side of the horse and setting a hand on the horn. He helped me into the saddle with a hand on my waist, then handed me the reins. Once situated, he mounted his own horse, a beautiful red color, and we headed toward the edge of town, my horse following his easily.

Lander glanced at me, doing a double take as he noticed my stiff posture. "Have you ridden before?"

The movement of the animal below me felt odd, but nothing compared to the ride on Vulcan. That was something I'd never forget the feeling of—his powerful body splitting through the wind, his wings beating with strength that utterly amazed me.

"No," I answered. "Though I've always wanted to."

A smile lit up his face as we emerged from between two houses, entering the forest. "Another new thing to tack under your belt."

"Do you know where the mines are?" I asked. I'd never seen the ones in Amosite, so of course, seeing them here piqued my interest, but without a proper guide, I was curious how Lander knew where to go.

"The guy said to keep going north, and eventually we'd find the hole in the mountain."

"So the mines are different from the caves?"

He shifted in the saddle. The sun was causing our legs to heat against the leather. "Typically, yes. Some kingdoms will branch off existing cave systems to mine for magic, but others create new tunnels entirely."

"Do they ever close them?" My father had told me ours were closed, given I produced magic for him, but it seemed other kingdoms were under the impression we still had workers in them.

He reached down to shove away a long branch that tried to get caught on his stirrup. "Not typically, no. Though Amosite claims to have closed their dark magic mines, no one has confirmed if that's true."

"Why wouldn't it be true?" As far as the continent was aware, fae were extinct, so humans didn't need any more dark magic to null the fae's abilities.

He shrugged. "Not a lot of people trust your father, as you know, but even more so since he won't let anyone near that area to even check it out."

I added it to the growing list of things I wanted to know. I was sure my father would be simply ecstatic to know I was curious about so many off-limits topics.

Speaking of off-limits topics...

"About the dragons..." I started.

"What dragons?" Lander asked, sending a wink my way.

Relief rolled off my shoulders like a wave. With everything else going on, I wanted to make sure Lander wasn't going to rat all of us out for being near them. He'd been angry at first, but his demeanor toward me being near them was a complete turnaround now. Had he just drank too much that day?

"Why did you truly bring me out here?" I asked, moving on as I did my best to maneuver my horse around a large rock in the path. The trees became fuller the deeper we headed into the woods, and I was thankful for the break from the beating sun.

"I wasn't lying when I said we haven't seen each other much since we ended up here. Truthfully, I haven't seen the guards often either. They've barely left the house they're staying in, but as far as I've been told, they're healed enough to be walking around for a few days now."

"Maybe they're mad at us for being the reason behind them losing so many of their friends?" I wondered aloud, shooing a bug out of my face.

"Maybe," he agreed. "Or they're scared."

"Scared of what?" Deadwood was indeed different from Amosite and Torbernite, but not enough to keep them locked away in an old house out of fear.

Lander was quiet a moment, chewing on his lip. "Bowen."

I pressed my lips together, choosing to ignore his answer.

"You seem to like them a lot more than you do me and my brother," Lander continued.

I glanced at him. "Why is it always a package deal with you two?"

"We're family," he stated, like that much wasn't obvious.

"But you're so much...better than him."

His horse stepped over a thick branch, mine following suit. "Not everyone would agree with that."

"I highly doubt that."

We headed up a slight incline, the trees growing denser, the air a bit cooler.

"It's true," he said. "I reckon that's why they offered me to marry you rather than Paxon. He's too smart, while I sit there and do their bidding as I'm asked, so long as they let me do what I want in my free time. It's a flaw, really."

I studied him, wondering if he truly felt it was a flaw that he followed his parents' demands with the promise he'd get the freedom to do as he pleased. "Well, if it makes you feel any better, I'm elated they chose you to marry me instead of him." I didn't think I'd survive if I was to marry Paxon. From what little I knew of him, I loathed him. He was too controlling, like many of the people in my life were.

"Is that so?" He tried to hide his smile.

I had a hard time hiding my own. "Don't get your hopes up."

He leaned forward in the saddle, helping his horse up the small hill, so I did the same. "Speaking of the marriage. Do you think we should call it off entirely?"

"Do you truly think they'd let us call off the marriage they forced us into?" I hardly believed they would.

"You never know. I mean, in the end, it's our choice, right?"

I nearly wanted to laugh. "I don't get much of a choice in anything, Lander. I'm just told what to do and expected to do it with no complaint."

"I'll talk to them, then." He sounded so sure, like he could persuade them to jump off a cliff if he wanted.

"Have at it." Humor laced my tone. If he was successful in convincing them to call off the wedding, that'd mean I wouldn't have to make a choice between the marriage or allowing Paxon to get me out of it. I'd be free from all of it. Maybe not my life, but the arrangement I had been forced into. And that was a start.

"Do you think that guard truly abandoned his post that night?" I asked, referring back to the beginning of the trip.

With a glance his way, I noticed his creased forehead, a pondering expression taking over his face. "It's possible."

I heard what he didn't say. "But?"

"But...not likely. If he did, your father would have him hunted down and executed. All the guards are aware of the consequences."

I gnawed on my bottom lip, getting my next question out before I could talk myself out of it. "What that guard said about our arrangement... Do you think this is all for something else?"

He looked at me as the small breeze rustled the leaves around his horse's hooves. "What else would it be for?"

I shrugged. "I don't know. Some petty, royal drama, maybe?"

He snorted. "If it's because of drama between our parents, let them settle it however they see fit. Getting involved in that can be messy."

"That must be why you're so reluctant to act a prince, then," I teased.

Lander shot a smile at me from his horse, but as he opened his mouth to reply, he was cut off by a low growl. Then, a beast nearly equal in size to my horse pounced from behind him, and I screamed.

CHAPTER 43

AURIA

A horned wolf with teeth larger than any dagger clamped down on Lander's horse's neck as he made a sad attempt to dodge the attack. Blood spurted in all directions as the horse let out a strangled whinny, and at the sight, my horse spooked. She reared, front legs flailing in the air with wide, frantic eyes as another wolf with horns larger than the first cleared the thick brush. My heart threatened to pound out of my chest, but quickly ceased beating at all as I slipped from the saddle, free-falling to the ground.

The air punched from my lungs as I landed on my back, my ass taking the brunt of the impact. I had no time to register the pain that bloomed through my body as a third wolf appeared, while the second darted after the gray horse as she attempted to run. Her coat was splotched with masses of red as she took off into the trees, and the wolf easily lost interest in the chase, instead turning on me.

While the first wolf laid into the other horse, Lander aborted, having no choice before the stallion pinned him as he fell.

"Lander!" I shouted right as one of the wolves bounded toward him.

He spun just in time, unsheathing his dagger in the same movement, but one look at the tiny blade and I knew it wouldn't be enough to fend off the beasts. The wolves were massive, almost taller than us, with paws that dug into the earth.

Drool fell in thick globs, puddling in the soil as the wolf lunged, teeth bared in his direction. I didn't have time to watch Lander defend himself as the other set eyes on me, yellow teeth a contrast to its black fur. The animal had eyes as gold as the sun. The sight would have been beautiful had the predator not been trying to eat me.

I slowly pushed myself to a stand, ignoring the way my hip twinged as I held my weight. I needed a better advantage. I had no weapon. No defense. I searched the ground hurriedly, looking for anything I could use to fend it off. Finally, my eyes landed on a rock at least five times the size of my hand. Almost like the wolf knew what I was planning, it snapped its massive jaw, spit flying in my direction. With no other options, I dived at the same time it did, my hands landing hard on the rock as my lungs were once again deprived of air. My knees dug into the earth as I scrambled to get leverage on the stone. With no time to dig it from the dirt, I flipped onto my back. One of the wolf's paws immediately pinned my arm to the ground.

With my other hand on the rock, I grappled with the rough surface, finally getting it free. I used all my force to heft it up, striking the wolf right as it chomped inches from my face. Then Lander yelled, the sound full of pain and frustration. A snarl tore through the air at the same time, but I couldn't look. Death was knocking, and I had no time.

The wolf standing above me shook its head from the hit, its large, slightly curled horns swinging back and forth with the movement, narrowly avoiding stabbing me in the process. It quickly recuperated, returning to baring its teeth in my face. I tried to pull my arm out from under its massive paw, but I couldn't get it free. If I couldn't get out from under it, I'd be dead in seconds.

The beast was too heavy, using all its weight to keep me pinned down. Its nostrils flared as its tongue darted out to lap across long fangs. Right as I thought I might have made an ounce of progress, my arm popped, and I bit down on a scream. My shoulder roared, flames enveloping every sense in my body.

But it wasn't fire. I wasn't burnt.

It was just my shoulder dislocating. Breathe.

But pain always clouded my senses. Brought my mind back to the hurt I knew too well. I couldn't go to that dark place now. I needed to survive.

Lander yelled out again as claws dug into my skin, likely ripping the thin layer. A feeling like water cascaded over my arm, but it wasn't water. It was blood. *My* blood.

The wolf made a noise like I would've never thought imaginable, and I realized it was done playing with its food. Its enormous mouth opened, and I looked straight into the jaws of death itself. I opened my mouth to scream, but as its teeth clamped down on the spot between my shoulder and neck, no noise came out. My ears rang, my entire body on fire. Maybe it was a flame, and the wolf was the harbinger of all pain. Every bad sensation ever felt was brought to the surface by the beast, my skin buzzing with the desire to go numb.

There'd be no dulling this.

Light, brighter than any ring in the sky, any star in the universe, shot out as Lander cursed loudly somewhere in the distance. His voice was an echo in my mind as I shut my eyes against the blaze. Perhaps the whole world was burning, and we had all met our fate.

A river flowed over me, scorching, then cold, and the backs of my eyelids went black as a yelp pierced my ears. Suddenly, I was weightless, no force holding me down. My soul wanted to float, my body aching to move, but all I could do was lie in the moistening soil.

"Auria," a voice, so panicked and hoarse, said from above me. Or was it below? My mind was too tired to tell.

It repeated my name, and hands clasped my shoulders, then another touched my cheek. The skin wasn't rough, not like the texture I'd come to enjoy on my body. Instead, it was soft. Soft among the never-ending flood of pain. Pain. Pain.

"Auria, open your eyes," he commanded, but I wasn't sure I could listen.

Fingers tapped my cheek—or was it a palm?

My eyelids fluttered in an attempt to check, but as soon as I saw more than just black, I regretted it. Lander was covered in blood, his blond hair stained. Was it his? Did he kill the two wolves? What about the one that had been on me?

Lander's hand left my cheek, and then he was searching my body, movements frantic as he lifted my torn shirt. When had it torn?

"You're going to be okay," he assured, but it sounded more like he was trying to convince himself. Maybe he was. Maybe it was that bad.

Despite the sun high in the sky, my toes were cold, a chilling sensation flowing up my legs as water dripped onto my neck.

Where was the water coming from?

My blink was slow as my head tried to loll to the side. My entire body suddenly felt heavy, and I was tired.

"Auria," Lander said, his voice so rushed while my mind was so slow. "Hey." His hand was back on my cheek, moving my head back to face him after it had fallen to the side. "I'm going to get help, okay?"

A shadow passed behind Lander, and I wondered if it was getting dark. We couldn't be in the woods past sunset. Bowen wouldn't want that.

"Bowen's not here, Auria. I am," Lander said. Had I spoken out loud?

I forced my eyes to stay open, but it was becoming more of a battle, and suddenly, I didn't mind if I lost. A nap might do me well anyway.

Lander shoved off his jacket in one swift motion, placing it beside my head. I hissed in a breath as the fabric stung across my skin, lighting every nerve ablaze. I wanted it off. Off. *Off*. I reached up to shove it away, but my arm wouldn't move, so I tried the other. He held my hand back.

"You have to leave it, Auria. It'll help stop the bleeding."

I was bleeding?

He swiped at the beads of sweat coating his forehead, and one look at his hand told me his statement was true. His fingers dripped red, blood smearing his skin as a drop landed on the high point of his cheek.

"Fuck," he muttered, breaths quick while mine slowed.

I tried to talk, but my tongue was caught in my throat. I coughed, the sound wet and clogged. Water splashed my face, oozing from my mouth, but Lander's widening eyes told me it wasn't what I thought.

The liquid was blood.

There was no rain, no river.

I was dying.

"I'm going to get you out of this alive," he promised, but his voice wasn't very convincing as it wavered.

My vision went hazy at the edges as I coughed again, trying to swallow whatever constricted my throat. Maybe I'd choke, or my lungs would fill with blood, or I'd bleed out, my body going cold. Whatever chose to take me, it could have me. My body was frozen, my mind a spinning cloud, and my eyelids were too heavy.

Just one more dose of pain, and it'd be over forever.

"Auria, keep your eyes open." Pressure increased on my shoulder, and I wanted to scream, but I couldn't conjure a single noise to come out.

"Auria," Lander repeated, but then his voice faded into the rest, and the storm in my mind finally calmed, letting gray clouds envelop my being.

CHAPTER 44

BOWEN

"People are always causing some kind of problem," Raiden muttered from where he stood next to me outside the store. He'd been keeping an eye out after a passerby had stolen some of Dee's canned goods. Not all the people who used Deadwood to refuel after a long trip were conniving, but every now and then, we got a thief whose hands were a little too grabby.

A chorus of shouts and hollers rang out right as a horse coated in blood galloped into the town, emerging from between two buildings and stampeding through a group of people waiting in line outside the butcher's. Raiden and I shoved off the wall as the horse stormed past with no intention of stopping. A strap of white cloth was stuck to the saddle, and my senses instantly lit up in alarm, my smoke curling within me, searching for a threat.

No one was out in the forest today that I was aware of, but that was one of our horses. Worst case scenarios flashed through my mind as Raiden looked in the direction the horse had come, likely waiting to see if anything else appeared. But while he was looking at ground level, my eyes were trained on the sky as Vulcan circled once, then landed in the middle of the street, leg outstretched to me.

It is the girl, Vulcan said hurriedly. He never panicked, and the concern in his voice ringing through my mind had me moving.

"Stay here," I called back to Raiden, not bothering to see if he had heard me. The amount of blood on that horse... If it was Auria's...

I couldn't think of that. She was alright. There was no other option. I mounted Vulcan faster than ever, and before I was even situated on his back, his wings were pounding the air, darting us into the sky.

"What happened?" I shouted over the roar of the wind.

Wolves, was all he said.

My veins turned to ice. If she'd been bitten, the venom would kill her quicker than blood loss.

I wanted to urge him faster, but he was already going at a speed I'd never seen before. The way even he was frantic did nothing to settle me. He knew it was bad.

Trees rushed by in a blur before Vulcan was mere inches from the branches, finding a spot to land. As soon as his feet hit the ground, I was off and sprinting toward the small, bloodied form on the ground. A horse, torn open at its neck and belly, lay deceased, and three giant horned wolves littered the ground around the scene, their chests not moving as they lay dead. Blood was everywhere, but through all the chaos surrounding the area, I could only focus on Auria.

My knees slammed into the ground as I lowered myself beside her. Lander was there, holding a blood-soaked jacket to her neck.

"Auria," I said hurriedly, but with no response, I leaned down closer, setting both hands on her blood-streaked cheeks.

Her skin was so cold, but with the faint rise of her chest, I had hope. "Auria, open your eyes."

Lander let out a strangled sound. "She passed out."

I wanted to kill him for letting her lie here, bleeding out and dying. Why hadn't he gone for help? Done anything but sit here and watch her fucking die?

But I couldn't focus on him. Auria needed me. I could handle him later.

I leaned down farther, sliding an arm under her shoulders, the other under the bend of her knees, and murmured in her ear, "I'm sorry, Princess. I'm here. Stay alive for me, okay? I'm going to get you help, but you have to stay alive."

I stood, careful not to jostle her too much. The jacket fell to the ground with a thump, the fabric heavy from her blood. One look at her neck and the black that etched its way through her delicate skin like ribbons told me we didn't have much time. Her arm slipped, dangling at an awkward angle, and I realized all too quickly that it'd come out of its socket, the joint loose. I gently righted the limb, holding it close to her body. Knowing the pain she must have felt sent rage skating over my skin, my power flicking at my bones, aching to take vengeance. But revenge didn't matter—not right now. Keeping Auria alive did.

I rushed over to Vulcan, who'd lowered himself as far as he could to help me get up. Once I was on his back, Auria's limp body cradled in my arms, he took off in the air, leaving Lander behind. I'd have Siara or Flynt go back to get him, but right now, Auria was all that mattered.

As Vulcan's wings beat relentlessly in the air, a whimper escaped Auria's lips. I brushed the caked hair away from her forehead, shushing her. "I've got you. I won't let you die. Not today. Not any day."

Her skin was so pale, and now more than ever I wanted to see her bright eyes, hear her yell at me, or call me names, or tell me she hated me. I wanted to feel her warm skin, see her glimmering smile, and watch the way her nose scrunched the slightest bit when she was fighting her emotions. I wanted to toy with her, tease her, be the one who stole all her attention.

But that wouldn't happen if she died, and I realized with all too much clarity that if she left, it'd be the same feeling I felt right now. I'd never get any piece of Auria again, and that wasn't a fate I was willing to accept.

Vulcan banked to the right, landing behind my house and lowering himself once more. I quickly, but extremely carefully, dismounted, sliding down his leg to the ground. Raiden and Doctor Quinn emerged from the house, and one look at Auria's frail form in my arms had Raiden's jaw going taut.

Doctor Quinn acted immediately, holding the door open wide for us to enter. "What happened?"

"Wolf bite," I told her. "And a dislocated shoulder. I don't know what else."

I wanted so badly to take Auria's pain away. I'd do anything to make sure she was okay. That she felt none of what was to come.

Her wound gushed blood down my front as I took the stairs two at a time, a stream of it following me up the steps. I brought her directly to my room, Quinn rushing behind me to her medical bag sitting on the small table by the wall. She rifled through it until she held up a large needle, dark, murky green liquid sloshing inside the syringe.

I laid Auria on the bed, not bothering to pull back the sheets. I could clean and deal with those later.

Quinn stood on the other side of the bed, checking the dosage. "Anti-venom," she explained. "I don't know how long it's been in her, so this may not work—"

"Just do it," I urged, my tone hard and laced with panic.

Tears threatened to fall, but I wouldn't let them. I had to be strong.

She was going to be okay. There was no other choice. Auria Tenere would not die on me today.

Quinn moved Auria's blood-soaked hair away from the wound, and the moment she did, Auria started to thrash.

"It's burning her veins," Quinn said, as if the explanation would soothe me one bit.

I set a palm on Auria's cheek, and instantly, she calmed, yet her breathing remained rapid. "I'm right here, Auria." Gods, all I wanted was to see her eyes. To know she wasn't on the verge of death. "I'm not leaving your side." *I'd never leave you.*

Doctor Quinn slid the needle into the skin by Auria's wound, injecting every last drop of the serum. As soon as the needle was gone, Auria yelled out, and the sound tore through every last defense I had, obliterating them entirely. Tears sprung to my eyes, but I tried to keep them at bay.

I couldn't be weak now. Not for her.

I framed her face with my hands, resting my forehead against hers as she thrashed again. "It's going to be over soon, Auria. Just a little longer. I promise." My voice broke on the last word. I wasn't even sure if she could hear me as she let out another scream, the veins in her neck bulging.

My smoke was dormant, eerily still and just as worried as I was over the potential outcome of this situation.

"What's happening?" I gritted out, wishing like hell I could erase the sound of Auria's pain from my brain forever.

"The serum is trying to null the venom, but it's deep in her bloodstream." The way Quinn's sentence dropped off held no comfort.

Tears rolled down the sides of Auria's face, and I tenderly wiped them away, despite the scream that ripped out of her, the sound ending on a whimper as her back bowed.

I tried to calm the frustration rolling through me, but it was no use. Auria's life was out of my hands, and I fucking hated the helpless feeling that overtook me.

"You're going to be okay, Princess. You have to be. I won't let it be any other way."

As if spilled from a bucket, black liquid sloshed out of her wound, coating the bed in a sticky slime. Once the substance stopped spurting, Quinn attempted to clean up the mess, and I helped replace the pillow under Auria's head.

"That was the venom," Quinn explained. "I can heal the wound and put her arm back in place now."

She walked over to her bag, grabbing a healing vial, and returned to Auria's side, uncorking the glass. Before she could tilt the vial to Auria's lips and apply it to her injuries, the green liquid moved on its own accord, flowing out of the open glass in a floating stream.

We watched as ribbons cascaded through the air to caress the bleeding wound at Auria's neck, stitching the skin back together like a doctor might with needle and thread. As it wrapped around her shoulder, her arm moved on its own, setting the joint back in place, and the red, sensitive skin went back to its pale color. The green substance hovered over her body for a moment, almost like it was checking for other injuries, before dissipating into her skin.

Quinn watched with wide, curious eyes. "I've never seen such a thing before. Magic has never behaved so...willingly."

But despite the phenomenon that had just happened before us, I couldn't take my eyes from Auria's face. I couldn't tell Quinn why the magic might have treated her so tenderly, willingly healing her without command, without sharing Auria's secret. The magic cared for her like she always did for it, and this was its repayment.

"Thank you," I croaked, my throat raw and swollen from unshed emotion.

"She may be out for a while," Quinn said, walking back to her bag across the room. "Days, even. But she'll be okay." She stowed the syringe away, along with the now-empty vial. "She needs lots of rest, even when she does wake. Make sure she takes it easy."

I wrapped my hand around Auria's limp fingers. My knees had gone numb against the hardwood floor. My lips met the back of her hand as I gripped it, my elbows propped on the edge of the bed. She was so frail and weak in my giant bed, her breaths shallow and slow.

I wouldn't leave her side until she woke. Until those big, glassy green eyes met mine.

"You saved her life, Bowen."

I looked over to find Doctor Quinn watching me, curiosity etched into her gaze.

I shook my head, my thumb moving over Auria's pale skin on its own accord. "You did, and I'm eternally grateful for it."

She moved her bag from one hand to the other, coming up behind me to set a gentle palm on my shoulder. "She wouldn't have made it if it wasn't for you. Get some rest. She'll be here when you wake."

Quinn left, closing the door behind her, but I think she already knew I wouldn't be able to close my eyes until Auria awoke. Until then, I'd stay by her side. For when she did wake, I'd be there for her till the end of my days or if she told me to go. Even then, she'd have to force me.

Almost losing her had proved I wasn't okay with her leaving. Hell, if she wasn't asleep right now, I'd beg where I sat on my knees, pleading that the only space safe enough for her was by my side.

Auria had broken through the walls surrounding my heart

as if they were merely thin as eggshells, and now that she was in there, I wouldn't be letting her go.

No war could keep me from her, no feud big enough to make me stay away.

And if for some reason, she didn't feel the same, I'd find a way to let her go.

I only feared it might break me in the process.

CHAPTER 45

AURIA

No breeze caressed my bare skin through the open back of the chair as I awaited the all too familiar burn. Heidi commanded the fire magic, but it flickered in her mental hold on it, resisting. The magic knew, though, that it could not fight against its holder.

Magic was to be used, not allowed an opinion.

"This is for your own good," my stepmother said, circling behind me. "You never learn, child."

But I was no longer a child.

Years and years of unnecessary punishment, only doled out to cure her boredom in this grand castle. I, on the other hand, was sent to work, exhaust myself, and sleep to pass the time, while Heidi chastised to her heart's content.

"There is nothing to learn from this," I muttered, not caring for my brash tone. What worse could she do that she had not already done?

A fist wrapped around my hair, and my head was yanked back, but the fire that erupted on my scalp was nothing compared to the one her flame would elicit.

"You speak out of turn one more time," she seethed, her perfect composure shattered by rage. I wasn't scared of her, though. I never would be.

My stepmother was a monster, but I knew there were bigger battles to fear.

"That is not an admirable quality," she continued. "It must be purged from you."

She let go of my hair, and the fire roared to life in her palm. Heat licked at me, indicating it was bigger than she usually let it get. Typically, she was careful, precise in the size to be particular with the wounds, but today, she was reckless.

I'd invited myself to one of their meetings with an advisor from another kingdom. After a few glasses of wine, my tongue had grown slippery, making bold comments in front of the man. She'd had to hold her composure throughout the entire hour, but once it was done, she had managed to haul me up here, where a guard ripped the back of my dress open.

Many beautiful dresses were ruined by her.

The ball of fire hit my skin, right below my shoulder blade. As she held it there, the scent of burned flesh filling my nose, it felt as if my entire body was alight, not only the patch.

Usually, I'd count to ten, and it'd be done. But today, my silent numbers passed fifteen, then twenty, and I was screaming in agony.

"Please," I begged, which I never did. Not with her. "Please, stop."

Tears rolled down my cheeks as thirty seconds, then thirty-five, passed. It was never-ending. A miracle my skin hadn't melted clean off the bone.

Then, it was gone, and I was panting, sweat, drool, and tears cascading down the front of my body. But I didn't feel the droplets. Not past the excruciating pain.

And that was how I sat.

For minutes.

Hours.

Tied to the chair, my arms and legs bound, as my skin sizzled.

"SHE'S STILL RESTING," a deep, lush voice said, breaking into the foggy night of my mind.

"Did she say how long?" a woman asked, and I strained to put a face to their voices.

My eyelids would not obey, staying clamped shut and heavy. My shoulder felt as if a phantom flame crawled along the skin, and I quickly wondered if I was in Amosite. Had my father come to bring me back home?

"She guessed it could be days," the same man said, and it hit me.

Bowen.

I wanted to scream for him, to reach for him, touch him, hold him.

Bowen.

A hand gripped mine.

"Has he seen her?" the woman, who I now realized was Siara, asked.

"No." His voice was so stiff, so full of gravel. Was he upset?

A light footstep on the wood floor. "He's her fiancé, Bowen."

"He's the reason she's injured." His tone dripped with malice, and I wanted to reach out to him, but nothing more than the twitch of a finger would respond. "She can make the decision on her own when she wakes."

"And if her father shows before she does?" Siara asked, her voice so soft, like feathers drifting through the air.

The hand on mine tightened.

"I will not let her out of my sight until I know she's okay."

But then the fog became a storm, and I drifted on the wind.

MY THROAT WAS SANDPAPER as my eyes peeled open, feeling like the thickest glue had been stuck to the lids. As my lashes fluttered, adjusting to the dim light, I tested moving my fingers, thankful when they did as I asked.

My head rolled to the side, the soft pillow cushioning my cheek as my eyes landed on Bowen. He was slumped in a chair in the corner, his neck kinked at a weird angle and his hair in disarray. The position looked uncomfortable, but there he sat, watching over me. Had he moved at all?

I managed to move my arms in an attempt to push myself up to a sitting position, but as soon as I did, an ache rolled through my shoulder, down my arm to the tips of my fingers. I let out a small whimper as my elbows gave out, a burst of air flowing through my nose.

Bowen's eyes snapped open, immediately landing on me. "Auria." Relief was evident in the way he said my name. He shoved out of the chair and instantly moved to stand by my side, setting a gentle hand on my shoulder. "It's going to ache for a few days."

"What happened?" My voice almost didn't sound like my own. My memory was foggy after the bite, but I remembered the wolves vividly. Their snarls still echoed through my mind.

"Your arm was dislocated, but we set it back in place. And we were able to extract the venom from the wolf bite—"

My eyes darted to his, causing my head to spin. "Venom?"

His brows pulled together, and he lowered himself so we were eye level, setting his knees on the rug. "Wolves have a substance in their saliva that can kill someone in minutes, but thankfully, Quinn was able to get it out just in time."

The realization that I truly could have died hit me. In moments, my life could have ended. Would anyone have mourned me? Or would my father have simply heard the news and been irate that his daughter was no longer there to provide for him?

"Hey," Bowen said, interrupting my spiral. His hand found mine, his thumb stroking over the back of it. I watched the movement. "You're okay."

"How long have I been out?" I asked.

"Two days."

I stared at his thumb moving over my skin, trying to process how I'd been down that long.

"How much do you remember?"

I swallowed, my mouth dry. He grabbed a glass of water from the nightstand, allowing me to sip before I answered. "The wolves, the bite, then a burst of light, and it was all over..." My forehead creased, my mind straining to remember anything more. "After that, nothing."

His brows pulled together. "A light?"

My mind replayed the flash over and over again. "I was being attacked, and then I was blinded by it, and it all just... stopped. After that, the wolves stopped attacking, but it could just be the holes in my memory. Maybe they kept going, and I imagined it."

"Did you see where it came from?"

I shook my head. "I was kind of..."

His lips flattened into a thin line. He knew what had occurred after that. "Vulcan saw what happened and came to get me. He took me to where you were, where Lander was just sitting there like a fucking fool rather than trying to get you help."

Lander.

My eyes widened slightly. "Is he alive?"

Bowen nodded, though his eyes were lethal. "Vulcan brought us here, but Flynt went back for him. He's okay. A bit scratched up, but nothing Quinn couldn't handle." He shifted closer. "How are you feeling?"

It was a loaded question. I felt foreign in my body, like a chunk of my life had been stolen away by the gap of lost memory. It wasn't anything major, but still, lying in this bed for two days while the unknown happened around me...

"No one was allowed in the room aside from Siara, Flynt, and Raiden to bring supplies," he explained, reading my thoughts, as I was sure my face showed my quiet panic. "I never left your side, Auria." His tone fell, his throat tightening. "I'd never let anything happen to you under my watch."

I couldn't blame Lander for bringing us into the woods. He hadn't known what could happen, yet I knew Bowen was furious with him.

"I feel okay," I finally answered. Summing up how I felt both mentally and physically seemed too much of a chore at the moment, so the response would have to suffice. "Sore, but alive."

He gave a closed-lip smile, holding so much back in that look alone. Had he feared I would slip away in my sleep? Watched the rise and fall of my chest for two days to make sure I was breathing? It was hard to believe Bowen cared that much, but if what he said was true, I had no choice but to take his word.

"Are you hungry? I can have Flynt bring some food if you are."

I shook my head, a slight headache blooming behind my eyes. "No, I'm okay. Thank you. I think I'm just tired." Two days of rest had left me feeling exhausted, surprisingly.

"Get some sleep," he said, pushing to a stand.

Before his hand could leave mine, I gripped it. "Stay."

He peered down at me, a war brewing in his eyes as his brows furrowed. "I'm not leaving you alone in this room."

"No." I pulled the sheet back, indicating what I meant. "Stay with me."

The crease between his brows deepened. "Auria..."

"Please. Just for today."

Despite how I would have thought things between us would transpire, Bowen made me feel safe, and right now, I wanted to be wrapped in that feeling. Him being in this bed with me didn't have to mean anything. It was just for the day.

Or at least, that's what I told myself.

Succumbing to his inner battle, he let go of my hand, shoving the sheets back farther. He helped me scoot over the slightest bit, making room for himself. I rolled onto my side, expecting him to keep his hands to himself, but instead, he wrapped an arm around me, his chest pressed to my back.

"For as long as you'd like," he whispered against my hair, pulling me closer and wrapping me in his warmth.

We fell asleep like that. Two lost souls in a universe full of pain, finding solace in each other.

CHAPTER 46

BOWEN

I slipped out of bed, careful not to wake Auria as she slept. It was dusk now, and she'd need food when she awoke. I hadn't planned to fall asleep holding her, but after nearly losing her, I wanted nothing but to feel her body in my grasp. To hear her breathing unlabored, to see her cheeks the slightest shade of pink as the healing magic brought life back into her.

She'd been so pale when I'd carried her inside, and I swore, on the back of Vulcan, that her breathing had stopped for seconds, minutes. By some miracle, she had survived. When I'd woken at the sound of her whimper, saw her eyes were open, my heart had lit like a torch in the darkest of night, burning brighter than any flame could ever dream of doing. I didn't want to remember how my chest had felt like a hollow chasm at the thought of her not making it, how rage had flowed through me on the current of smoke tendrils, my veins blackened and my power angry, thrashing, demanding I do something—*anything*. That if she hadn't woken up, I'd have to live with the fact that I'd avoided my growing feelings and she'd have never known how I truly felt.

I vowed to change that.

Stealing one last look at her petite form under the blankets, I quietly opened the door, slipping out into the hall. I inhaled a long, full breath after clicking it shut. Auria robbed all the oxygen from my lungs, leaving me breathless in her presence, but in her near death, I wasn't able to breathe for all different reasons. As I had waited for her to wake, I hadn't given a single thought to what her father might have done if his daughter had died in my territory. I'd only thought of myself losing her. Of her never experiencing everything she wanted to. I hadn't thought of my people, and for that, I felt ashamed. Selfish. Now more than ever, with our plan making headway, they needed me focused.

But Auria was a distraction I welcomed with open arms, and I didn't want to be free of her. Not like I had originally thought I would want to be.

I planned to head down to the kitchen to make her something to eat, but Lander crested the top of the stairs before I moved away from the door, and my entire body instantly went on guard. He was the reason she was hurt. The reason I almost lost her. Smoke licked at my skin, clouds of gray forming around my hands.

"You need to leave," I ground out before he could make it down the hall.

I'll end him where he stands, my smoke whispered, its pledge to make Lander suffer clear.

I held it back. I was only feet from where she slept, a thin wall separating us. I didn't want to wake her if things turned ugly, but I wouldn't hesitate to rip his head from his body.

"I have a right to see her."

My fists flexed as my power urged me to strike. It was just as protective of Auria as I was. "Not in my kingdom, you don't."

"We're engaged," he defended, as if the title made all the difference in the world.

I took a step toward him so as to prevent my voice from drifting into the room. "You were one second away from not having a fiancée at all. If I had found her even one minute later, she would have *died*. She'd be dead because you were too much of a coward to take the proper precautions."

"This is *not* my fault."

Smoke thrashed in my veins, demanding to wrap ribbons around his throat. I held it back. Barely. "You brought her out there knowing damn well you couldn't protect her. You didn't keep her safe, so yes, it is your fault, Prince." I spit the name like an insult, and he recoiled.

His eyes narrowed, and I wished he'd strike so I had an excuse to rip him apart, piece by piece, letting my smoke have its way with him while I did it.

Give him a reason, my magic purred. *Let me loose.*

I inched closer, fury radiating off me in waves. "And don't pretend the two of you are set to be married. I know everything that goes on in this town, including every word that's uttered. You're in this for yourself, Bular, and I won't let Auria get caught in the middle of whatever it is your family has planned."

His molars ground together right before a creak sounded behind me. Lander's eyes shot over my shoulder. I looked back to find Auria standing in the hall, a hand on the doorframe. Instantly, I moved to her, offering my hand. She was weak, still healing, and we'd woken her.

"Let's get you back to bed," I murmured, gently wrapping a hand around her elbow, the other steadying her waist.

"You can leave us be," Lander commanded behind me.

I ignored him, knowing if I reacted, I'd likely rip his throat out. The primal side of me wouldn't leave these two alone with her in this state. So instead, I led Auria back into the room.

"I want to talk to him," she croaked, her voice slightly raspy from sleep. She leaned into my touch, and I welcomed the feel of her.

Power surged beneath my skin in warning, but I ignored it. "Okay."

I guided her to the bed, helping her ease down on the edge of it. Lander moved into the room, watching her with a hesitant eye. I gave her space, leaning against the wall at the head of the bed with my arms crossed. I wouldn't be leaving him alone with her. He hadn't directly injured her, but he was the reason she was out in those woods in the first place. He might as well have done the damage himself.

I glared at Lander. "Whatever you have to say, get it out and leave."

"Call off your guard dog," Lander said to Auria, eliciting a snort from me.

"How do I know you're not a threat to her?"

Lander turned on me, nostrils flared.

"Stop." Auria shoved off the bed, wobbling on her feet. "Please. Just stop."

I wanted to go to her, wrap her up in my arms and never let go, but I stayed put against the wall.

She kept her stare on Lander, steadying herself on her own. "What do you want?"

He looked down at her, noticing she wore my shirt. His jaw pulsed. "Tell him to leave."

"Whatever you have to say, you can do it in front of him."

The corner of my mouth threatened to lift in a smirk as Lander sucked on his teeth, unpleased with my presence and the fact she'd just chosen me over him in this moment.

Finally, he dropped his fight. "Auria, I'm sorry. I didn't mean for you to get hurt. I didn't know the wolves hunted during the day. I thought they only came out at night and that we'd be safe."

Her lashes fluttered, and I could tell she wasn't ready for this. The attack was all too fresh.

Lander moved forward and took her hand in his. My body tensed with the urge to slice every finger that touched her off his body. He lowered himself to one knee, and I nearly rolled my eyes at the dramatics. Though, it did send a bit of satisfaction coursing through me at the sight of him practically begging for forgiveness. I just hoped she wouldn't give in.

She dipped her chin, looking down at him. Her hair was slightly mussed from slumber, my shirt hanging loosely around her upper thighs. Siara had helped me change her clothes while she had been passed out. The ones she wore before had been caked in blood, and I'd wanted nothing but to get her out of them as soon as she was healed enough for us to move her.

"Please know that it wasn't my intention to leave you vulnerable out there."

"It's always a risk," Auria whispered, pain laced in her words.

"I know. And I was an idiot for thinking it was safe to bring you to the mines."

I arched a brow. The mines? Why would he have been taking her there?

"It's safe if you take the proper precautions." If Auria wanted to see them, I didn't want her to fear the thought of ever visiting them. I'd take her, if she'd let me. "Your spur of the moment decision to take her out there with no backup, no proper weaponry, could have gotten you both killed. The forest is passable if you're smart."

"Are you calling me dumb?" Lander asked, dropping her hand as he stood to face me.

I shrugged. It was too easy to get under his skin. "If the shoe fits, *Prince*."

"Leave." Auria's tone left no room for argument.

Lander shot her a questioning glance as I kept my eyes locked on him. One wrong move, and I'd sink a dagger in his throat and watch as the blood drained from the wound. "You heard her."

He rolled his lips together, likely contemplating staying. "We'll talk about this later."

He turned on his heel, leaving me and Auria alone in the room. I watched as she stared at the door, wondering what she was thinking. Did she hate him? Forgive him? Want to end his life as badly as I did?

"Can I get you anything?" I shoved off the wall and dropped my arms to my sides.

She shook her head, sitting back on the bed almost as if in a trance. From feet away, my gaze caught on the tear that escaped her eye, rolling down her cheek to drip off her chin. In an attempt to hide it, she turned her head away from me. But out of everyone, I was the last person she needed to hide her emotions from.

I crossed to her, easing down to my knees, and gently grasped her chin between my thumb and pointer finger. I used my other hand to wipe another droplet away. "Don't waste a single tear over him." I held her eyes with my own, darting between the two, before coasting my gaze down to her shoulder, sliding down the pale skin of her arm as my hands fell to the bed on either side of her. Not long ago, she had been broken—dying in my arms. And she very well could have, had Vulcan not come to grab me in time.

What if he had been minutes later?

Seconds?

What if she had died before I arrived?

What if she never knew it was because her coward of a fiancé hadn't a clue what to do to stop the bleeding or that he could attempt to remove the venom?

I was kidding myself, though. He wasn't smart out in the world—only in his castle hidden away in Torbernite, where his parents and brother told him what to do and when. He wouldn't have sacrificed his life for her, and that was the difference between him and me.

I'd give anything to keep Auria breathing, even if for just one more breath.

"Bowen—"

I snapped my focus back to her, finding her lips sealed shut, like she'd thought better of whatever she was about to say.

"What?"

She shook her head the slightest. "Nothing."

As her cheek moved with the obvious sign that she was chewing on it from the inside, I could tell she was keeping something from me. But if she didn't want to tell me, I'd let that be her secret to decide to share.

I had other concerns.

"Why was there glass littering your kitchen floor?"

Her forehead creased. "You were at the house?"

"Siara was. To grab some things for you. But she saw the mess and came straight back."

She blinked, her hands intertwining together in her lap. "Right."

I waited silently for her to go on. Maybe a glass had slipped through her wet fingers—

"Paxon was there, waiting for me."

Instantly, smoke flickered in my veins, prowling through my body with the urge to hunt. "When."

She slackened slightly, leaning closer as she felt me go on

alert. One glance at my arms and we'd see the graying veins as my magic feasted on the need to keep her safe.

"After you left me the other day."

"Why didn't you go back out and get me?" My voice was full of lethal calm, grating as I fought the impulse to go out there and find him myself.

She unclasped her hands, setting them on top of mine on either side of her. Slowly, I turned mine over so our palms touched.

"He wouldn't have let me if I tried," she said, defeat clear in her tone. I fucking hated it.

"I would have killed him if he so much as laid a hand on you."

With the way she averted my gaze, I knew he'd done something.

"Where did he touch you?"

"Bowen—"

"Where, Auria?"

Her eyes turned pleading, and fuck, that look alone would've sent me to my knees if I wasn't already there.

"It's in the past, Bowen. I'll clean the glass before I leave—"

"I'm not worried about the fucking glass, Auria. I'm worried about *you*."

The words left my tongue on their own accord, begging to be voiced.

A slight crease was etched between her brows as she processed my words, my mind doing the same. Admitting I was attracted to her—fine, that was nothing. But this admission felt like...more.

"I'm okay," she whispered.

I stood, my hands opening and closing without her warm, delicate skin against mine. "You could have died."

She got to her feet, no longer unsteady as she did. "I didn't."

"But you could have!" My voice boomed through the room, and I hated how it rose. Hated the things she brought out in me.

"I'm not made of glass!" she shot back.

I froze with only her in my vision. Is that what she thought? That she'd shatter under the wrong circumstances? She'd already overcome more than many could say in their lifetime, and she'd only gotten to live hers for a few weeks.

If Auria Tenere was anything, it was steel.

My hands fisted at my sides as I shoved my magic back down, erasing it from my veins. "You won't break that easy, Princess."

Her stiff shoulders eased the slightest, the smallest hint of a smile tugging at the corners of her mouth, and I thought maybe she believed me. Or maybe, she was starting to believe in herself.

"No, I won't."

And I knew now that she did.

CHAPTER 47

BOWEN

The night air did nothing to ease the stiffness of my muscles as I walked to the meadow clearing behind Deadwood. Auria was inside the house asleep while Flynt kept watch at the door like I instructed, but even without the command, he would've done it willingly. He was worried about her, too.

I needed to burn something, to swallow the flame and let my power surge like it demanded. Auria had almost fucking died, and I couldn't get the image of her, bloodied and torn open, out of my mind. Couldn't get her pained screams to stop echoing through my ears whenever silence filled them.

And her scars...

Pain was no stranger to her, and I wanted nothing more than to tear everything down that could harm her. That *had* harmed her. To obliterate her father, whoever put those scars on her, Lander, and most of all, Paxon. I didn't know what his motive was, but I had to believe that Auria was strong enough not to let him get to her.

Anytime he was near, my power would hum, snaking its

way through my veins and itching underneath my skin to find his lungs and choke him where he stood. He was human, and yet, my fae side went on full alert when he was near, telling me something else was at play, and he was in control of it.

If I had half a mind, I'd dig his grave tonight.

As soon as I reached the other side of the clearing, I palmed the fire vial in my pocket, and the tree in front of me burst into flames. The wild streams of orange and yellow flickered as it licked its way up the bark to the drying leaves. My magic thrummed as it pulsed through me, etching my arms and every other part of my body with blackened ribbons as it called to the smoke elicited by the fire. The two joined midair, dancing together as if in harmony, then attacked the flames as if in battle, snuffing it out in seconds.

"*I see your control has slipped,*" Vulcan said from behind me, judgment clear in his tone. I hadn't heard him land, hadn't felt the ground shake while I was too distracted with thoughts of Auria.

With my back to him, smoke curled around me before darting his way. Heat blasted my skin through my leathers, and I turned in time to see his gold fire fizzling out between us.

"*Do not threaten me, King,*" he growled.

I shrugged, shoving my hands in my pockets. "It just wanted to play."

A burst of wind shoved my hair back as Glacies landed between Vulcan and me. Immediately, her yellowed teeth were in my face, spit flying every which way as she bellowed a low, violent growl.

She kept her lips curled as she demanded, "*Where is the burned one.*"

I stood my ground. "Not sure who you're referring to."

Her throat vibrated as another growl emanated from her. I was tired of the fucking nickname. Auria was not only known for her pain or her past—she was more than just a sum of all the bad things that had happened to her.

"*The girl is hurt, and you are standing out here like a child unable to control himself,*" Glacies spit. In the moonlight, her white scales reflected an almost silvery blue, the sight nearly blinding to the eye.

My eyes narrowed on her. "I'm the reason she's alive."

Behind Glacies, Vulcan muttered, "*As if I didn't help.*"

"*Have you forgotten I can smell every ounce of her pain, King?*" Glacies asked, her tone malignant.

I was growing tired of them calling me that when they were angry. If anyone needed to get their emotions in check, it was them. All these fucking nicknames were pissing me the fuck off.

"I've done all I can to make her comfortable." But if she was still hurting, why hadn't she said so? I could've done more. I wouldn't have left to release the built-up energy inside me—

"*It is not enough. You weak, helpless fae never care for anyone but your own. It is vacuous that we even have to keep our peace with you. Much rather obliterate your kind like we were meant—*"

I took a step toward her, careless of her dripping fangs. "And then what, Glacies? Have no help against the humans? Get every dragon killed because you're too stubborn to be nice for once?"

"*I am nice when I so please!*" she roared. "*I saved the girl, too. There is no reward for doing so.*"

"Only avoiding war," I reminded her. There was no doubt in my mind that King Tenere would ruin Serpentine if harm came to his daughter. Oh, if he could see her now.

"*There is more she is not saying,*" Vulcan spoke up.

Glacies swung her head in his direction, her neck cocked at an odd angle. "*Speak, and I will rip your throat from your body.*"

I raised a brow. She didn't want him telling me, and that only intrigued me more.

"What is it?"

Glacies's warning growl filled the air, and Vulcan narrowed bored eyes on her. They were nearly equal in size, but Vulcan had the upper hand here.

"*She is protective of the girl,*" Vulcan said, and Glacies's deadly tail swung my way as she turned. I narrowly missed it, jumping back a foot as she darted for Vulcan with an open mouth.

Vulcan's roar filled the air as he pinned his wings to his sides and clashed with her in the middle of the meadow. I wasn't bothered by their fighting—not as his words settled in my mind.

Glacies was protective of Auria. I knew that. So why was she so mad about him speaking the words aloud?

Unless...

"You bonded with her."

But dragons didn't bond with humans. They hated everything they stood for, how weak they were. The only reason they put up with fae was because we had strength, power.

But Auria didn't need vials to use magic. Could that be how she'd protected herself from the wolves? Was that what she was about to tell me inside?

Which meant...Auria might not be human after all. I'd gone back and forth on whether she might be full-blooded fae from a royal bloodline that had died off after the moon exploded, but if she was, that meant they weren't extinct either. And that her father had been with a fae. The creature he despised.

A cacophony of growls and snapping teeth filled the meadow as Glacies took her anger out on Vulcan for speaking her truth into existence.

"When?" I questioned, raising my voice.

"It is not of your concern," Glacies hissed before attempting to sink her fangs into Vulcan's leg. He dodged it, batting his wing to keep his balance.

"When?" I asked again, louder. For the time being, everything about Auria was my concern.

Fuck, not just now. Forever. I didn't think I could ever rid myself of thoughts of her.

Glacies backed up a few steps from Vulcan, turning her anger on me. She must've seen the concern in my eyes, for hers softened almost instantly, her lips falling to cover her razor sharp teeth.

Her head hung as glistening white eyelids blinked over frozen eyes. *"The moment I saw her in the mountains."*

"And you're just now telling me?" Anger laced my words, despite my attempt to keep it contained.

She lifted her neck, tucking her wings in. *"It is not meant to be."*

"But it is. Because it happened." There was no undoing a bond. They were connected for life. "Does Auria know?"

Those piercing blue eyes shot to me. *"No. And she will not."*

"That's not something you can decide for her. What if you get injured? She would feel it and not have a clue what's happening."

Glacies's eyes narrowed, like that was some kind of insult. *"I do not get injured."*

I scoffed, shoving a hand through my hair as Vulcan came up beside her. His gaze was filled with worry, and I had no fucking clue what to do.

"I want to see her," Glacies demanded.

"No."

Panic pooled in her eyes. *"You cannot keep me from what is mine."*

"You just said it yourself—you don't even want her!" The thought had my stomach turning.

Vulcan stepped forward, blocking Glacies from me. His voice quieted, aiming his words directly at me. "*Let Auria make this choice for herself.*"

I shook my head in disgust. "Glacies wasn't going to give her that option. She has no idea why she even likes the short-tempered beast."

A low growl filled the air behind Vulcan, indicating she'd heard.

Good. I wanted her to know I was aware of that little fact about her. If that temper ever turned itself on Auria, I'd rip her wings from her back myself.

"*As the universe allows, let it be how it will be.*"

I stared up at Vulcan, hating the wisdom he randomly decided to spew. I much preferred his backhanded comments and dramatic eye rolls.

"Fine." Vulcan moved out of the way, allowing Glacies and I to face each other. "You get ten minutes with her, and if you so much as think about taking her and flying off—"

"*Her safety means more to me than taking her from here,*" Glacies admitted, her tone softer than I'd ever heard it before.

With a nod, we headed in the direction of Deadwood.

I LEFT Glacies and Vulcan behind the house as I went inside to see if Auria was awake. Glacies had made it a point to say that she was, but I got the feeling the dragon would find a way to wake her even if she wasn't.

Heading in through the front door, I took the steps two at a time. Flynt was right where I'd left him, his back leaned up against the doorframe and arms crossed over his large chest. His eyes caught mine as I walked down the hall.

"Has she come out at all?" I asked, even though I hadn't been gone long.

Flynt shook his head, adjusting his stance to give me room. "Not a peep from the room." As I reached for the door, he added, "There were no knife wounds on the wolves, Bowen."

I paused, meeting his gaze. "None of them?"

He shook his head, confirming my suspicions. Whatever light Auria had seen was the thing to take them all out. I didn't dwell on the fact that it only made me hate Lander more, knowing he hadn't even stabbed one of them.

We'd figure this out later.

Carefully, I twisted the handle and slowly opened the door to peek in.

She was sitting upright on the bed, her back against the stacked pillows with her gaze on the door. "I'm not some caged tiger waiting to strike."

I opened it the rest of the way to step in. "I didn't want to wake you." Her eyes drifted to the comforter pulled up to her waist as she picked at a stray strand. She looked...hopeless. "What's wrong?"

Her chest rose under the large shirt she wore as she moved to rub at her finger. "What are we to do when the bridge is back up?"

I moved without thinking, crossing the room to sit on the side of the bed. I pulled her fidgeting hands into my own. "We will figure it out when the time comes."

The truth was, I didn't have an answer. I couldn't keep her here—not without inciting a war between Deadwood and Amosite.

She shook her head. "I am forever his, Bowen." Glossy eyes

found mine, and my hands squeezed hers. "Never yours, nor mine."

She studied me for my reaction, but I had none. It couldn't be this way. I wouldn't let it.

"This wasn't supposed to happen," she whispered.

"I know," I murmured, my thumb coasting over her skin. I wanted to tell her she could stand up to him, fight him on this, somehow find a way to gain her freedom, but we both knew that would never happen. Not so long as he lived.

How would that affect Glacies's bond with her? To never see her other half? She had no way of even getting into Amosite if she simply wanted to visit.

"Are you up for some company?" I asked.

She blinked, and all the pain seemed to wash away in that act alone. "*I* have company?"

I pressed my lips together. "Of a sort."

She arched a brow in response.

I stood, helping her off the bed. Her bare legs were no longer uncertain, so I reluctantly dropped her hands. My palms itched with the craving to have her skin back on mine, causing my fists to flex as we walked. She wore only my black shirt, the hem brushing her upper thigh.

Auria took her time descending the stairs, holding on to the railing as she went. I stayed right behind her in case she needed me for balance, but she made it to the bottom successfully on her own. Once we were outside, we rounded the corner of the house to head toward the back. Auria didn't stop walking when she saw Glacies. Rather, she continued to approach her, craning her neck back to look up at the towering dragon.

I stayed a few feet back as Glacies lowered her head in one fluid motion, sending a small gust of wind to blow a couple strands of hair off Auria's face. The dragon's giant, white nostrils flared as she took in Auria's scent, likely checking her for lingering injuries. Auria didn't move as Glacies inhaled deeply, and when the spot right above Glacies's eyes furrowed slightly, Auria reached out a hand.

On instinct, I took a step forward, worried she was overstepping, but a low growl emanated from Vulcan's throat, silently telling me to leave them be. I obeyed, but kept a sharp eye on the two of them. One wrong move, and I'd be getting Auria the fuck away from her. Just because they were bonded didn't mean Glacies was giving her a welcome invitation to treat her as a pet, but regardless, Auria had no knowledge of it to know any better.

Auria's palm rested gently between those glacier eyes, and instantly, Glacies's eyelids fluttered shut against her reassuring touch.

"I'm okay," Auria whispered.

Glacies brought her nose closer to Auria's side, the fabric of her clothing catching slightly on the edges of her scales.

As if Auria could sense Glacies was finished in her inspection, she removed her hand, and Glacies raised her head. The dragon didn't take a step back as she regarded me with disdain.

"*You are lucky you get to live another day,*" Glacies said, her voice thick with what had to be emotion. I was sure she could still smell the lingering pain in Auria's body, sense what she had gone through on that dreaded flight back from the forest.

I dipped my chin, giving her the benefit of the doubt, knowing she wasn't in the best state of mind to have a bickering competition at the moment. Glacies was a stubborn dragon. I hadn't crossed paths with her often, but when I did, she was always up for a battle, whether verbal or physical, despite weather or circumstances.

Glacies took a few steps back from Auria, her frozen eyes hinting at concern as she studied her. "*I said it before, and I will tell you again. Be careful who you trust, burned one.*"

"I would prefer if you call me Auria."

Her response shocked me to my core, and then I was moving without thought as I stepped beside her, positioning her just behind my shoulder in case Glacies decided to strike. And with the shift in her features, I didn't doubt she was thinking about it.

But she and Auria were bonded... She would never—

"*As you wish, Auria,*" Glacies replied before flaring her wings and darting off into the starry sky.

I shot a look at Vulcan, who read the message loud and clear as he took flight, heading after Glacies. He'd make sure she was okay, though I was certain the dragon would want to be alone. Dragons didn't handle heavy emotions very well, especially ones they didn't have the answers to. They wanted solutions, and most of the time, feelings got in the way of that.

Slowly, I turned to find Auria staring up at the sky, the stars reflecting in her pupils like pops of sparks from a fire.

"I think I'd like to sleep right here," she murmured, not taking her gaze from the galaxies looming above us. She seemed to be in some sort of haze, transfixed by the world and what it could offer. What it could take. "For one night."

If savoring the midnight sky was what she wished, I'd make it happen. To give her the world and more in just a few short days would be my greatest honor.

"For one night," I repeated.

After finding Flynt, he made that happen, bringing down blankets, pillows, and water. I worked on setting up the makeshift sleeping arrangement while Auria kept her gaze on the sky, and it took all I had in me not to admire her the way she was the stars. A universe of beauty, and I could only see her.

Once the blankets were laid out neatly and the pillows were in place, Auria lay beside me, one blanket between her and the grass, and another draped over her body up past her breasts.

"We can't see as many stars in Amosite because of the city," she said quietly.

I forced my gaze to stay trained on the sky, for if I turned her way, I feared I might do something reckless. So instead, I spoke. "When we first met, you told me the stars were bright."

"Yes," Auria replied.

I swallowed, inching my hand just the slightest bit closer to hers where it rested directly beside me. My skin hummed with the nearness of her. Under these stars, with Auria beside me, I feared my brain was malfunctioning as my tongue listened to my heart and let slip an admission I should've kept tightly locked away. "They'll never shine as bright as you, Auria. Not in my eyes."

And for that one night, we fell asleep in silence under the stars, dreaming of a world much different than the one we were given, and wishing of a universe in which this might work.

Knowing that it wouldn't.

CHAPTER 48

AURIA

It'd been a day since I reassured Glacies in the clearing, and every hour that ticked by since, I thought of her. Why had she been so concerned as to seek me out to be sure I was okay? She didn't belong in Deadwood with her natural biome being in the Brimstone Mountains, yet she was here. It was no secret that she lingered either. She'd passed over the house with her massive wings and blinding body reflecting the sun about five times.

I hadn't bothered to ask Bowen if he knew what was up with her, instead enjoying his company while I could. After hours of eating, hydrating, and napping on and off, he'd asked if I was up for a stroll through the forest, reassuring me multiple times that I'd be safe and no other attacks would occur. I hesitantly agreed. That was three hours ago, and we were still riding.

He'd only brought one horse to the house, insisting I ride with him so I didn't tire myself out too much. I hadn't objected. Being close to him was quickly becoming my favorite place to be.

Bowen dropped the rein from one of his hands, setting it

over mine where it sat on the horn of the saddle. "Are you doing okay?"

I nodded. This was not the first time he had asked. His constant checking in on how I was feeling made my heart flutter. "I'm okay. Would you care to tell me where we're going now?"

He stayed quiet, returning his hand to the rein.

I heaved a heavy sigh. "Bowen—" I started, but quickly snapped my mouth shut as we crested the top of the hill. The sight before us stole the breath from my lungs.

Rather than make some smart-ass comment, he gently tugged on the reins, stopping the horse as he watched my reaction, my eyes taking in everything in front of us. Or was he admiring my awe? I wasn't sure. Not when I'd never seen a sight such as this or even dreamed of one remotely similar.

At the base of a towering mountain sat a spring surrounded by crystals of all colors and sizes jutting up from the rock and soil. Every shade imaginable glittered in the setting sun as it cast shadows over the land. Clusters of crystalline spikes darted out of the ground like knives, beautiful yet glaringly deadly.

"This is Iris Vere," Bowen explained, finally taking his eyes off me to look over the beauty before us. "The Rainbow Spring."

True to its name, the water glowed a rich pink, swirls of other colors mixing with the fuschia. As if protected by the mountain that loomed above it, there wasn't a ripple to be seen, the top of the spring like stained glass.

With my mind caught in the trance of its beauty, I hadn't realized the horse had begun walking again, only stopping once he hit the edge of the spring. There was a small bank where no crystals sprang up from the ground, just wide enough for us to dismount.

"It's beautiful," I said, the words barely a whisper as I stared down at the strawberry-colored water.

"There are so many places I want to show you," he admitted quietly.

I didn't voice what we were both thinking. That time wasn't on our side.

"Would you like to get in?"

My head spun in his direction at the question, the saddle creaking as I shifted. "Can we?"

"Some springs aren't safe to swim in because of the veins of magic that run near the water, but this one is fine."

"There are others?"

He glanced over his shoulder, like he might see one he could point out. "There are quite a few scattered in and around the Sunward Mountains."

My eyes widened slightly. "*In*?"

His gaze caught on mine as he turned back to the spring. "We've happened upon a couple in the caves, but we don't go near them for obvious reasons. Between earthquakes and the risky magic buried deep in the earth, it'd be too dangerous."

"Well, thank you for bringing me to one of the safe ones, I suppose."

"You're welcome," he replied, his voice teasing.

"What makes the water this color?" I asked, though I think I knew the answer.

"Minerals. The spring is far enough away from any major pockets that it won't hurt us, but the crystals hold raw magic that sometimes leaks into the water, mixing with the minerals and changing the water different shades. It's why we call it the Rainbow Spring."

I nodded my response, speechless by the idea that this naturally existed, sitting here undisturbed.

He jumped down from the horse, then set both hands on

my waist before I could attempt to swing my leg over and lifted me down himself. He removed his hold on me, and my stomach dipped at the craving to have them back.

With our focus now on the calm body of water in front of us, I said, "So how do we do this, exactly?"

"We undress, then get in," he explained, as if that didn't include us getting naked or dipping into a pool of magic.

He must've sensed my hesitation because he said, "Come on, Princess. Not like we haven't seen every inch of each other already." His fingers gripped the hem of his shirt and tugged it up over his head.

Instantly, my cheeks heated. When he noticed the color of my skin matching that of the pink water, a smirk pulled at the side of his mouth.

"I don't bite," he added.

"How do you know I don't?" I asked.

He tossed his shirt in the plush grass behind us, and his bare chest brushed my shoulder, sending tingles down my arm. "Because if you did, you would have already."

"Maybe I'm waiting to strike."

He leaned a little closer, his breath smelling of mint and something faintly fruity. "Then take aim, Princess. I've been waiting for you."

A breath of a second later, he shucked his pants off completely, underwear and all, and dove into the spring. I jumped back as water sprayed up at me. Rather than the cold I expected, the droplets were warm as they coasted down my skin to the soil beneath me.

The horse, completely unbothered by us, stepped back up into the grassy meadow and began grazing.

Bowen emerged from the water, wiping his dark hair out of his face. The sight of him wet and knowingly naked below the surface heated my core. He was so painstakingly beautiful in this moment, everything I remembered from our moment in the shower, and fuck, I wanted to wrap myself up in him and never leave.

He sent a smile up at me, and I tried to hide my own, shaking my head with the effort. I tried to shove the utter need for him away with no success. Getting in this spring with him was dangerous, if any other time we were alone together was proof of that. So why was sinking into the warm water with him so enticing? Like an addiction I wanted to form, but had never had a taste of before.

With his eyes glued to mine, he swam backwards until his back hit the wall of crystals behind him. Blues and golds glistened over his tanned skin like a painting, and I wanted to capture the sight forever to keep a sliver of the life I could've had with him inked into my memory.

He didn't encourage me further as I stood there, staring at him as if I could find some sort of confidence in his gaze. It wasn't that I was nervous to bare no clothes in front of him, but more so the idea of us being alone in the water, with nothing to do but explore each other. That night in the shower had been for a reason, and right now, this was purely for pleasure.

And I was stupid to be robbing myself of it.

I yanked my blouse off, and my breasts were on full display as I bent to pull down my pants. Once those and my shoes were off, I straightened, watching as Bowen drank me in from across the spring. He looked parched, like not even all the water in this spring could sate him of his sudden dehydration.

Slowly, I dipped my toes in. The water was just as warm as it was when it had splashed me, if not more so. Finding the smooth stone bottom, I submerged both my feet, walking toward him. After a few steps, the water was up past my breasts, the waves gently rippling against my skin as I waded forward.

I stopped mere inches from Bowen, staring up at him as he

towered over me, despite the spring being somewhat deep. My eyes fell to the tattoos covering every inch of bare skin on his chest and stomach, weaving around the tops of his shoulders and down his arms.

"Are they from stealing?" I asked, bringing a finger up to trail over the one cresting his right peck.

"They are," he replied, his voice lower, huskier than usual. "Does that scare you?"

I shook my head, finding his eyes again. "I believe people can do bad things for the right reasons."

"And you assume my reasons are justified when you don't know what they are?"

My palm flattened to his chest as I drifted closer. "I think you'd do anything to keep your people alive."

A sort of predatory glint took form in his gaze, and I looked down, focusing on where my hand made contact with his skin. My core heated, every nerve in my body lighting up like a match as my palm tingled against him. His finger hooked under my chin, lifting my head so that I had no choice but to face him.

Everywhere we connected sparked like a life source flowed through our touch alone. Something darkened in my peripheral, and at first, I thought it might've been the sun finally disappearing for the day, but upon closer inspection, it wasn't that at all.

The water was turning a deep purple.

I went to draw my hand away from Bowen, but he grabbed my wrist, holding it in place.

"Why is it doing that?" I asked, confusion and slight panic lacing my words.

"It feels you," Bowen answered, but provided no further clarification.

Violet ripples collided with our bodies as my brows furrowed. "*Feels* me?"

"It's not just the minerals working alone to cause that color, but the magic, too. It can sense your emotions. How you're reacting to being in this spring with me."

The furrow of my brows deepened. None of what he was saying was making this any clearer.

"I saw you in the tunnel," he admitted. "With the fire magic. How it reacted to you, and you to it. How it didn't ink you that day in the market."

I shook my head in disbelief. "It's just magic—"

"You don't have to hide from me, Auria." With his finger still hooked under my chin, he moved to place his palm against my cheek. "I see you. All the things you try to keep secret, I notice. All the hurt you try to keep bottled inside, I feel."

"I'm engaged," I blurted, scared of what his words were doing to me. How they were making me feel. I didn't want to hurt him when I left, and these feelings he was admitting... They would only lead to heartbreak.

But it wasn't as if my engagement mattered anymore anyway. Lander and I had both agreed to call it off as soon as the bridge was rebuilt and we made it home, which would be any day now.

"Who do you think you're fooling? Because it's not me."

"I don't take you as a fool," I defended. He was anything but.

"Then what do you take me as?" As if an answer to that question might be so simple.

And it truly wasn't. I didn't have an answer because I was quickly coming to find that I took Bowen as *everything*. The reason I was able to step out of my comfort zone and feel safe. The reason I was alive. The reason I'd been second-guessing returning to the place I had grown up—the place that'd only served as my prison. He had shown me what freedom could look like. How the sun felt on my skin if I let myself bathe in it.

That my magic wasn't something to be ashamed of, but rather proud of.

How my heart seemed to skip a beat every time I saw him.

"Give in, Auria," Bowen murmured, his voice a caress on the part of me that wanted to do exactly that. "Stop holding yourself back from the things you want most in this life and *give in*."

And maybe it was the water, or the chill catching on the dusk air as the sun fell behind the horizon, giving us the privacy we desired, or the words he spoke so blissfully that drew my lips to his.

Or maybe it was simply what I wanted, and I was able to do it.

"Fuck this," I muttered, right before our mouths molded together in an explosion of hunger and need.

My hand slid up his chest to wrap around the back of his neck at the same time his fingers tangled in my hair, pulling me flush against him. Our lips fit together like they were meant to be, and I wasn't sure if it was me or the spring, but the water seemed to warm around our bodies.

A wisp of air floated up the center of my back, and I realized it was his smoke that caressed me as his tongue slipped past my lips. I welcomed him, my own dancing with his in a rhythm only the two of us could make together. As if that sparked a match, the kiss became ravenous, our mouths became rougher, starved of the other like this wasn't enough. We were each other's oxygen, our only source of life flowing between our ravaging kiss.

Our breaths melded together, and he inhaled deeply as he consumed me, pressing his forehead to mine. "I can smell what I do to you." His hands tightened in my hair, like it was almost painful for him to admit that. "All I want is to taste your sweetness on my tongue."

A small whimper escaped me at the thought of him doing

just that, and he swallowed the sound with another kiss. He pressed his lower body to mine, his hard length a tease where it rested against my stomach. Suddenly, my senses became overloaded with a wave of honey and sugar.

"Make that sound again," Bowen pleaded, murmuring the words into my mouth before he pulled his lips from mine to pepper kisses down my jaw, to my neck.

He wrapped an arm around my waist as my back bowed, my head tilted up toward the sky as I exposed my neck further for him. He kept me upright when my legs wanted to give out from the surreal need for him, and a wave of dizziness came and went. Never mind the vulnerability in this spring—I didn't think anything could stop me from wanting more of him. Of *this*.

Bowen's other hand tugged at my scalp as he drew his mouth farther south, sucking my breast into his mouth with the smallest graze of his teeth. A gasp sprang from me at the shock, and his tongue lapped over the bud to soothe it. He elicited a thrill from me I wanted to chase, and I got the feeling Bowen would deliver willingly, should I want more.

When he gave a little bite, another moan was pulled from me, causing his fingers to dig into my back. His mouth popped off my breast, and he looked at me with lust-heavy eyes. "It will be my personal goal in life to elicit those sounds from you." His mouth was back at my neck. "Again." Another kiss to my collarbone. "And again." To my jaw. "And again."

When his mouth finally crashed into mine, another whimper climbed its way up my throat. We were a cacophony of clashing teeth, panting breaths, and heated skin. The arm wrapped around my waist slid away, only for his hand to grab my breast in a pleasuring grip. My nails scratched at his neck, but neither of us seemed to care. Not as his magic slithered around my body in ribbons of black, snaking over every inch of my skin. I was a bundle of goosebumps, every nerve alive and homed in on the two of us.

My palms slid to his chest, and I shoved him backwards so his shoulder blades hit the crystal wall behind him, his hold on me now gone. A look of shock passed over him before my mouth was on his neck, licking and sucking. Rough hands gripped my hips punishingly as my breasts pressed against him.

Bowen moved his hold to my ass, then hooked his hands under my legs to hoist me up. My legs wrapped around him seamlessly, my lips not once leaving his tattooed skin.

I never wanted this to end. Never wanted to think of Amosite again or what a world without Bowen looked like. I'd been robbed of so many things in this life, and I couldn't let it happen again. Couldn't be deprived of the feelings Bowen wrung from me.

In between moving my mouth from his neck to his lips, I caught sight of the water turning indigo.

"Don't think," Bowen commanded against my lips. "Feel me, Auria. It's just me and you in this moment." One hand left my thigh to weave back into my hair. "Get out of that beautiful head of yours."

Heeding his words, I tightened my grip around his waist, melting deeper into our kiss. Warm smoke coiled around my nipple, tickling the sensitive skin. Our mouths broke apart as my lips parted on a sudden inhale.

"I want to feel you," I begged, my voice breathless. "More than this."

"Auria—"

"I know what I want," I cut him off. "Please." *Don't rob me of this, too.*

I would never.

My eyes shot open at the sound of his voice echoing

through my head, but before I could question it, he was gliding his hands down my front, between my breasts and over my belly, causing it to jump at his touch. Then, his hand was between our bodies, poised at my entrance.

Answering the questioning look in his eyes, I nodded. A single finger slid inside me, and my mouth fell open, my breath hitching.

A sensation like no other coursed through my body at the feeling of him, and slowly, he retreated the digit before gliding it back in. On the next pass, he added another finger, and a noise like none I'd heard before fell from me.

His mouth was back on mine in an instant as he pumped his fingers in and out of me at a pace that was torturous. Needing something—anything—to hold on to, my hand came up to his neck. His back leaned further into the crystals behind him, and I was sure they were biting into his skin, but neither of us cared. Not when everything about this moment was earth-shattering.

My forehead pressed against his as my fingers dug into the side of his neck, gripping gently. As if hearing my silent plea, he added a third finger and picked up speed. My thighs felt like slush as I tried to keep myself tangled around him. When my hold almost slipped, his smoke lashed out to support me. The tendril around my breast curled tighter, another gliding down my stomach to flick across my clit.

Another moan ripped through the dusk air, and it only stoked Bowen further. He pressed a kiss to my cheek, keeping his pace steady and fast.

"Just like that." *Please. Please don't stop.*

I wouldn't dream of it, Princess.

His words in my mind fueled me, and when the ribbon stroked over my clit in a soothing circle, my stomach tightened and my legs went stiff. My scream echoed off the crystals as my head fell to Bowen's shoulder.

He pressed a kiss to the crook of my neck. "That's my good girl. Come on my fingers, Princess. Take what you need from me."

The only thing keeping me up was his power and the hand still wrapped around my thigh as my body shook. My orgasm rippled through me like nothing I ever could have imagined, and once the waves tapered off, I peeled my eyes open to find that the water was back to a deep violet, swirling around our connected bodies.

Bowen slowly withdrew his fingers from me, moving to rest his hand on my thigh. But I didn't want soft, and I most certainly didn't want this to end. Not now. Not when I just got my first taste of him.

Lifting my head from his shoulder, I didn't give him a chance to speak before my mouth was back on his. With my strength coming back, I tightened my legs around him.

Auria.

"No," I mumbled into our kiss. I didn't want him to tell me to stop. That we shouldn't go further. *I want more.*

And we will. But—

He heard that?

"No," I repeated, but it was nearly drowned out by the sound of flapping wings. Following the noise, a rush of cool air slammed against my back.

Bowen pulled me closer to him, likely to shield my naked body from whatever dragon had decided to interrupt us. It almost broke me as our lips parted and Bowen focused his attention behind me.

"What is it?" Bowen asked.

"King Tenere is on his way, and he brought company."

CHAPTER 49

BOWEN

If Vulcan was concerned, that meant things were far past bad. So bad that he'd barely had the patience to let us get dressed while he gave us a moment of privacy. He couldn't care less about seeing us with no clothing, but for Auria's sake, he was polite for once.

We'd left the horse in the meadow, knowing he'd find his way back on his own. Horses were smart, always returning to where they knew food was. I had no concerns he'd find his way.

On our flight back to Deadwood, Auria seemed reluctant to lean into me, keeping an inch of space between her back and my chest at all times, despite my arms wrapped tightly around her waist.

"Something wrong, Princess?" I murmured in her ear, the wind sweeping her hair back and over my shoulder. My chest felt warm where it made contact with her, much like it had in the spring. The sensation had come out of nowhere, almost too hot to endure at first, but then it had evened out, staying constant beneath my skin. I ignored the fact that I shouldn't have been able to scent her arousal in that spring. Fae couldn't smell others' pleasure, not unless they were—

I'd deal with that another time.

"No."

Her stubbornness lifted one corner of my mouth as my thumb ran along her ribs, right under the swell of her breast. "The erratic beating of your heart says otherwise."

She kept quiet as Vulcan pumped his wings harder over the trees below.

"Do I need to convince you to tell me?" My lips coasted over the crook in her neck as I spoke, making it impossible to miss the goosebumps that freckled her skin in their wake.

"You didn't want to go further," she said quickly, her words rushing over one another, like she didn't want to voice them to begin with.

My mouth froze on her neck, my thumb following in its pause. "I did."

Subtly, she shook her head, but not in answer. In disbelief. "Was it too much? Was I bad or—"

"Auria." I brought my other hand up to grab her chin, making her turn sideways so she could see me. "You are perfect. Please believe me when I say it had nothing to do with you, and rather a particular interruption from a certain pain in the ass." The last bit of my sentence was louder with the intent for Vulcan to hear.

A low growl rumbled beneath us in response.

Auria's eyes searched mine, like she wanted to believe me, but her mind was planting seeds of doubt and willing them to grow stronger than the effect of my words.

"Stop getting lost in your head. If I could, I'd take you on the forest floor right now, tasting every inch of your body." My thumb stroked her jawline. "Hearing every little moan pass your lips." Her mouth parted. "And feeling you come apart beneath me." I searched her eyes, tempted to say, *Fuck it* and demand Vulcan land so I could make good on my promise. "I would like nothing more than to do all of that right this instant. Forget the world and get lost between your legs. But we have other matters to attend to."

I hated the way I sounded like a king at the end rather than a man with feelings. As if ruling came first.

I wouldn't let my leadership role come between us, but if King Tenere was on his way, we needed to be in Deadwood when he arrived, lest he decimate the town trying to find his daughter.

"We will have our time," I promised her, trying to convince her as much as myself that our moment in the spring would not be the last opportunity we got to explore each other and what this could be.

She gave the barest nod, a sliver of doubt leaving her eyes before she faced forward again. The silence, save for the wind rushing past us, barely lasted as she asked in a quieter tone, "How did you do it?"

Do this? I questioned privately.

From the side of her face, I saw her lashes flutter, like my voice wrapped around every sense in her mind, twirling through her core like a meaningful embrace.

"Yes," she confirmed, releasing a breath. "That."

The truth was...I shouldn't be able to. It'd surprised me as much as it had her, and in her moment of pure bliss, she'd been able to respond. It seemed she didn't know how without such emotions driving her.

Our kiss was just that good, Princess.

She shot me a glare over her shoulder. "Don't play with me, Bowen."

It means dragons aren't the only ones with this ability.

I didn't mention how my smoke could communicate with me if it so pleased.

"Can you talk to anyone else like that?" she asked.

Right now didn't seem like the best time to explain what this meant. With her father on his way and what had transpired in the spring, I didn't want to confuse Auria with more questions weighing down on her shoulders. She wasn't fragile, not in my eyes anymore, but one could only take so much in a day. Even I knew that.

Like what? Like how when you released around my fingers, gripping them beyond comprehension, I wanted them to break inside of you so they would never have to leave your body?

I didn't miss the heat that crawled up her neck into her cheeks at my words. It had the desired effect, both igniting her and making her questions cease.

I'd tell her everything once I knew we were safe and without threat of her father burning Deadwood to the ground.

It was time.

No, Princess. It's just you and me in this bubble, and I intend to use it—my lips ghosted over her shoulder—*to my advantage.*

Within minutes, we were landing in the town square of Deadwood. Dust kicked up around us in a cloud as we descended Vulcan's leg. As soon as Auria was steady on her feet, he took off, his shadow coasting over the crowd of irate people.

"He'll try to kill us!" a man shouted as a few individuals closed in on us.

"The girl! The girl is the reason for his visit!"

"Send her to the desert, he can grab her there!"

"If we're lucky, the sandwalkers will get to her first!"

Slight panic flooded Auria's features, and smoke licked at my veins, begging to be unleashed.

Let me out, my magic purred. *I will end them all where they stand.*

I shoved its voice to the black depths of my mind as Raiden shoved his way through the crowd, coming to stand on Auria's other side. "They're not happy."

"I couldn't have guessed," I muttered.

"Once word got out, they went feral," Raiden informed me, eyes scanning the crowd for any advancing threat.

"They forget they're fae."

"You forget he has dark magic."

At the mention of dark magic, my smoke banged against the steel wall I had forced it behind, demanding to be released.

"I can leave," Auria spoke up, and both our gazes shot down to her. She was staring out at the roaring crowd, now kept a decent distance away by Flynt and Siara waving them backwards after they had showed up shortly behind Raiden.

"Auria—"

"They're right." A sheen coated her eyes as she looked up at me. "I'm the reason he's coming. If I leave, he won't storm Deadwood."

"We don't even know what his intentions are." Aside from taking Auria back to that prison. Away from here. From me.

"We know enough. My father is not a peaceful man. It's no secret, and they're all aware of that."

Raiden's attention turned back to the roaring crowd, giving us a moment to speak.

My fists clenched at my sides, fingers threatening to break. "You're not leaving, and that's final. He can march into Deadwood all he wants. Burn the damn town down if he so wishes." That earned a worried glance from Raiden. "We didn't survive all these years just to cower in his presence. Neither did you."

Auria stared up at me, a thousand words shining in those green depths.

"You two need to get out of here," Raiden said, interrupting our silent promise to each other. We wouldn't let anything happen to either of us or this town. "The crowd will calm down eventually, but I don't think it's wise to keep Auria in their sights at the moment."

I gave him a nod of understanding. She wasn't the problem, but the townspeople didn't know that, and they surely hadn't been convinced during her stay, which meant they most likely wouldn't be swayed in the next few minutes.

A flash of lightning split the air right above our heads, but not one of natural occurrence. My smoke shot out, wrapping around the electrified thread before it got the bright idea to do any damage. Hazy ribbons snuffed the bolt out, the air instantly smelling burnt. A guard aimed for the attacker, though if they'd wanted it to strike, it would have landed true. They were sending a warning shot, demanding answers.

My fingers laced through Auria's, pulling her close to my side as a wall of smoke fanned out on either side of us, causing the outraged citizens to part as I tugged her through the crowd, back toward the forest behind town. They wouldn't follow—not if they wanted to keep their lives.

"Will they kill me?" Auria asked, causing my steps to falter.

I glanced down at her, doing a double take before stopping. My hands gripped her shoulders, turning her to face me. "No. I wouldn't let them, even if they wanted to."

"They're angry, Bowen. You can't be so sure of that." Her eyes held a sheen, one I wanted gone.

"My p— The citizens of Deadwood don't want violence. That, I'm sure of."

She tilted her head in question. The only light illuminating the two of us was from the rings glowing silver in the sky. "A town full of criminals doesn't want violence?"

"We have always strived for peace. That's been our goal

since the beginning. It's—" My words cut off at the sudden change in her face, like realization was hitting her.

"What?" she asked.

I shook my head, dropping the subject. "Nothing."

"You think I'm too fragile to tell me," she surmised, deflation coating her voice.

My brows pulled together. "What? No. That's not it, Auria."

"Then what?"

"If I don't protect you, then it's your father—his kingdom—who's after me." If anything happened to her here, he'd have my head on a spear for the harm that came to her, even if it wasn't my doing.

Her body went stiff before she stepped out of my hold. "Then why let us—*me*—stay here until the bridge is rebuilt if you're so scared of the consequences when something happens to me?"

The way she said it made it sound as if she was so sure harm would always come to her. "Nothing will happen to you."

But *fuck*, she'd already been attacked here. Injured by both people and animal.

She shook her head, knowing this, too. "You don't know that. My father would have killed you had any of those times ended in my death. He'd flatten Deadwood to nothing but dirt and dust." Her head fell like it was just now hitting her that the dangers of being here might be too much to bear.

"I do know that, Auria, because I'm the one making sure no one puts their hands on you. Not again."

Again, her head swung back and forth. She was in denial. "I was a fool to kiss you," she whispered. The way her words hit felt like she meant it more for herself than me.

I opened my mouth to reply, but my words were cut off as a twig snapped somewhere deeper in the woods. Without hesitation, I grabbed Auria's arm, pulling her to the nearest tree to pin her between my body and the trunk.

Don't say that, I spoke quietly to her.

Her forehead creased, eyes boring up at me as her chest heaved in frightened breaths.

I will never regret what we did, Auria. Not even if you begged me to.

"Please, do tell why you have my brother's fiancée pinned to a tree." Paxon's voice grated every nerve in my body like a knife against wood.

Smoke coiled in my veins, desperate to strike, but I kept the tendrils concealed.

My jaw ached as my teeth ground together. Reluctantly, I stepped back, leaving only a foot between my body and Auria's.

Take the reins, Auria, or I'll kill him.

Yes, my smoke chanted, its voice echoing through my mind. *Let us kill him.*

I shoved it away best I could, along with the urge to decimate Paxon where he stood.

She blinked, processing my words drifting through her mind, then pinned a glare on Paxon, who was watching from mere feet to the side of us. "This is none of your business."

I kept my back to Paxon, for I feared if I saw his face, my smoke would unravel. It wanted to take control, and I wanted to let it.

"Oh, there's a *this* now." Paxon tsked. "It very much does concern Lander if you're showing public displays of affection with another man."

A deep, condescending laugh rumbled through me as I shook my head.

"He's just looking out for me," Auria defended, sensing the rising tension and shoving off the tree. "We agreed to call the marriage off," she added.

I could almost feel Paxon's brow raise at my back. "So you've made a decision, then."

That froze me to the spot, magic pausing its surge through my veins to stand at attention. My gaze found Auria's. Her eyes quickly grew panicked.

"What decision?" I asked, a growl behind my words.

"Interesting," Paxon practically purred behind me, but I paid him no mind. My smoke, on the other hand, returned to its frantic state, coiling and spinning inside me with the urge to suck the oxygen from his lungs. I felt my control over it slipping like a thin thread.

"Nothing that concerns you," Auria said quickly, alarm in her tone. Her words landed like a hit to my stomach.

Shoes crunched over leaves behind me, indicating Paxon was retreating—to where, I wasn't sure, but as long as he wasn't here, I didn't give a shit.

"Is that how you want to be now?" *After everything.* I'd been as open with her as I could.

Hurt flashed in her eyes, but I could see the war she waged within herself. Her mind was likely a storm, clouds swirling with the push and pull of her desire to tell me and her usual impulse to keep things bottled up inside.

I'd give her the ability to decide, but time was quickly running out.

"Do what you must," I said, taking another step away. I told myself she didn't mean it. She was confused, too much happening at once. She'd come around.

"Bowen—"

Unlike everyone else in your life, I won't force it out of you.

Something akin to gratefulness shone in her gaze now, but it did little to mask the storm brewing behind her eyes.

"Go back to the house. I have matters to attend to." More

hurt shone in her gaze. I fucking *hated* it. "I will come to you once I'm done," I assured her.

Though her reluctance to open up to me stung, I understood it.

Things didn't change overnight.

Before I could second-guess my decision, I turned around, heading away from Auria and into the chaos.

CHAPTER 50

AURIA

I should've known I was going to be followed. Paxon wasn't done simply because he had walked away in the woods. He only wanted me alone.

With that knowledge, I should've barricaded the front door as soon as I came inside, but not even seconds after walking in, the door was flying open.

Paxon shut it behind him, not moving from his spot near the entrance as he stared me down. I stood in the kitchen, bottle of bourbon in hand, just about to take a sip. Between Bowen feeling betrayed by me for not telling him what Paxon had meant, my father coming to Deadwood to retrieve me, and the kiss in the spring, my mind was a tornado. Alcohol might only make that worse, but it might also numb the thoughts I couldn't get a grasp on. The only coherent one that rang clear was the one I didn't know what to do with.

Leaving here was not what I wanted.

"Drinking is a bad habit," Paxon chastised.

"So is trying to control the people around you, but alas." I threw my head back, the rich liquid stinging my throat as it went down. The glass hit the wood counter with a dull thud as I set it down.

Paxon's gaze roamed the room, as if he hadn't seen it multiple times before. "Those who sit and wait rarely get what they desire."

"And what is it you desire?" I asked, only to make him get to the fucking point.

Those sharp, devious eyes planted their sights on me. "Power."

I scoffed. "You'll hardly get that with me. A war is more likely."

He ignored my statement. "You and Lander have come to an agreement to end the engagement."

Satisfaction shone in his gaze now, whether at the fact that Lander and I didn't have the ability to end it or that my only option was to go with him if the wedding truly wasn't going to happen. I hadn't forgotten his ultimatum.

Marry Lander or go with him.

"I haven't made up my mind yet," I lied.

"I gave you until the bridge was repaired, and with King Tenere currently on his way, it seems that time is up."

"Not yet." The bridge might be repaired, but I was still in Deadwood.

I should have told Bowen what Paxon had meant. I should have told him a long time ago, if I was being honest with myself. Bowen had given me no reason not to trust him, and yet, I was always on high alert around him. Maybe not in the way I was when in danger, though. Perhaps I had been reading myself wrong, and it was desire that coursed through me like a river. Whatever it was, I could lean on Bowen. That much was certain.

Paxon's head cocked to the side, like he could sense my thoughts. "You want to stay in this wasteland."

My lips pressed together as I refused to voice my answer. It was an unreachable dream, and yet...

Paxon threw his head back in a laugh, the sound echoing through the too-quiet house, despite the chaos that ensued just outside the walls on the main street. "I should've known," Paxon continued. "Auria, the daughter of a king, wants to live with lawless lowlifes."

If only he knew just how powerful Deadwood really was, he wouldn't be making these accusations.

Still, I did not speak.

"Are you more upset about having to choose between Lander and my offer or that you'll be leaving your precious, worthless Bowen?"

"He is *not* worthless," I defended, falling right into his trap.

A devilish smile pulled at his mouth. "You're right," Paxon admitted. "Not with the plans he has in place."

With that, he turned, pulling open the door to leave me in the silence. His words bounced around my head, but I wouldn't believe them. Not after seeing who Bowen truly was. Paxon was trying to plant a seed, and I wouldn't let it bury itself in my mind.

Not being able to take another second of the quiet, I headed for the door, leaving the bottle of bourbon uncorked on the counter. I closed the door behind me and beelined for Bowen's house. He was the only one who could settle any doubts creeping up on me.

I wouldn't let Paxon win in his effort to turn me against Bowen.

I crossed the porch and tapped my knuckles against the wood door, waiting. I knocked again, but heard no footsteps from within. I should've gone back to my house and waited for him, but I didn't want to be there or chance seeing Paxon again.

I tried the handle, and to my surprise, it was unlocked. Stepping across the threshold, I closed the door behind me, surveying the room.

"Bowen?"

Silence met me, so I took to the stairs, heading for his room. The door was wide open, and the familiar sight made me stop in my tracks in the doorway. The space was so empty without him in it. Memories of my healing from the wolf bite flashed through my mind. Bowen lying in that bed with me while I healed, holding me through my nightmares as my mind brought me back to my dark past while in my vulnerable state.

Bowen seemed to have changed that day, seeing me in a new light. One so bright that his eyes had opened to a whole new possibility between us. One I hadn't considered myself, but welcomed willingly. Through all the bickering and slight disdain for each other, Bowen had grown on me.

I crossed the room, trailing a finger up the smooth sheet covering his bed. My hand reached his pillow and paused, tracing where his head might lie when he rests. When his mind finally let its guard down for a short period of time to wonder up dreams he wished were reachable, or possibly nightmares that anchored him during the day, keeping his defensive mood on strike at all times. Perhaps he'd thought of me at times while his bed comforted his tired body, imagining me beside him, like I'd let my mind wander to a time or two before.

But not in this life could that happen.

A perfect circle of moisture dropped to the fabric, and I swiped a hand under my eye to find it was a tear. Wiping my cheeks dry, my fingers trailed to the necklace resting over my collarbone, fiddling with the charm, like it might bring me some sense of hope that there was a good outcome after all of this.

But my hope didn't sit in Amosite or with my father. It sat with Bowen and the hospitality he showed me and my people, even though he didn't have to. He'd protected me time and time again, and after tonight, I would never see him again.

I didn't want to think of the possibility of it, but I knew it was the truth. Today might have been our last day together, and I'd kept something from him, hurting him in the process. That wasn't how I wanted to leave.

I didn't want to leave at all.

Bringing my hands around the back of my neck, I pushed my hair out of the way, draping it over one shoulder to unclasp the necklace. Resecuring the clasp, I laid the jewelry on his pillow, then took a step back.

My eyes wandered the room, taking in everything I was too shy to look at before. The trinkets on the bookshelves lining one of the walls, and all the spines begging to be opened. I crossed to what had to be hundreds of books, admiring the gold foiling adorning so many of them.

I trailed the tip of my finger through the dust on the rich brown shelf, walking until I got to the end, when my focus snagged on a piece of paper sticking out between two pieces of text. Letting curiosity get the best of me, I slid the parchment out. It had been folded multiple times.

Carefully opening it, my eyes scanned the paper, finding it to be a map of a building and its outer perimeter. Multiple x's covered specific areas of the map, and upon closer inspection, recognition hit me in the gut.

It was a drawing of a castle.

Amosite's castle.

My home.

My brows furrowed as I searched the parchment, looking

for any indication of what the x's might mean or why Bowen might have a perfectly drawn map of the place I had grown up.

Was Paxon telling the truth? That Bowen wanted to destroy Amosite?

Was this a log of rooms they had cleared for some reason? Combed through? Were they planning an ambush of some kind?

Why would Bowen need to keep track of something like this? For *what*?

Realizing I would find no answers staring at a paper with a potential plan to decimate my home, I quickly folded it to its original state and shoved it back where I'd found it. Crossing to the bed, I grabbed my necklace from the pillow and beelined for the door.

Whatever the map was, it couldn't be good. To mark x's over specific rooms in the castle? There was *no* good reason for that.

Bowen might be able to explain, but—

Excuses.

I'd let myself believe his words, let him kiss me. Let him see parts of me I'd never let anyone else see, only to find this?

A dull ache started to form with the thoughts spiraling through me. If nothing was truly as it seemed, was I even capable of making decisions? Could I trust anyone at this point?

My mind swirled with heavy emotions, causing the pang to quickly turn into a pounding headache as I descended the stairs and stormed outside. As soon as I was on the porch and the humid air hit me, a sharp pain split through my head. With the necklace grasped in my palm, I held my forehead, setting my other hand on the wooden beam to support myself.

My stomach soured as the pain became almost unbearable. A gasp passed my lips as something sharp and cold hit me in the side of my neck. Immediately, my vision went blurry, and the beam tilted sideways. Or was that me?

It had to have been the latter as my shoulder slammed into the splintering wood porch, sending a shockwave of pain through me. Polished boots appeared in my vision, and I tried to look up to see who they were attached to, but my eyes were too heavy, and my mind was going dark.

Strong hands gripped me as the fog took over, and everything went black.

CHAPTER 51

BOWEN

"Are you going to tell Auria?" Flynt asked as we walked through the throng of citizens. Fae of all different backgrounds pulsed around me, their powers practically beaming out of them with the concern they held for their lives.

They had such doubt in their ruler that they believed I might let them die under King Tenere's wrath? I'd just have to make it clear to them that I'd do anything to keep that from happening.

I shoved through the brothel's front doors. "No."

"Glacies won't be able to get to her—"

In the middle of the open room, I spun on him. "Do you think I don't know that?" I'd given him a quick rundown of what Glacies had told me and Vulcan regarding her bond with Auria. I didn't want him taken off guard if Glacies put up a fight when King Tenere arrived to take his daughter back.

Patrons, men and women alike, quieted their tones as they sent nervous glances our way.

"It could sway Auria to stay," Flynt said, lowering his voice to not draw more attention.

"If she doesn't already wish to be here, I don't need to try to change her mind." If not for me, I highly doubted she would stay for a dragon she hardly knew. The creatures were new to her. I couldn't tell her, and have her leave and wonder for eternity what the bond meant.

Glacies and Auria could survive apart from each other, but after a while, they'd feel as if a hole had been dug through the center of their chests, wishing to be filled. Auria would likely believe it was her mourning the life she had experienced for such a short time, while Glacies would know the truth. She'd ache, call out for her, want nothing other than her other half, but she'd never cross the chasm. It was impossible, even if she wanted to.

But if Glacies got hurt... No matter how far Auria was, she'd feel it.

It wouldn't make any sense to her, but I had no fucking clue what to do, and it seemed Glacies didn't either.

"You're just going to keep it from her, then?" I heard the accusation in his tone loud and clear.

Turning, I set a hand on the worn metal railing and climbed the spiral staircase. Flynt's boots echoed a beat behind mine. "It's not for me to tell. The bond is between Glacies and Auria. If Glacies is keeping it from her, then she has her reasons. I won't put myself on her bad side for the sake of persuading Auria to stay."

As I approached the top, the flames in the sconces on the walls flickered shadows along Triss, one of the brothel's original courtesans, who stood on the edge of the wooden porch, overlooking the town. She wore a flamboyant red dress that had a slit all the way up to her waist on one side, exposing her sheer thigh-high stockings. Her brunette hair sat in a bun atop her head, and as she turned to me, she puffed the lingering smoke from her cigarette between her lips. The smoke curled around me, avoiding contact with my skin as my magic sensed its presence.

"I need your perch. Should only take a moment," I said to her as Flynt stopped right at my back.

"I suppose I won't be upset you're not here to request my presence," Triss moped.

I glanced behind her to the people below. "Never am. You could take Flynt here off my hands, though."

Triss's eyes found him over my shoulder, a devious smile cresting her painted lips. "He might be a fun ride."

"Triss, honey, I mean no offense by this, but I don't do…" A hand ghosted my back as he presumably tried to pull the right words from the air.

"Men with feelings can have their fun, too," Triss purred, puffing on her cigarette. "It's not a crime."

"Not much is in this town," I reminded her, sliding past her to set my hands on the cold railing. On the horizon, gray clouds cluttered the near-black sky. A storm was coming. One I hoped we were prepared for.

Triss waved a hand to the crowd. "Take your time. The perch is yours." She left Flynt and me to the ruckus below, making sure to close the double doors behind her.

"Bowen—"

"I can't think about that right now, Flynt." I kept my voice calm as I turned to him. We both ignored the eyes of the crowd turning their attention on us. "Glacies will tell her when she's ready."

"And if Auria decides to go before she can tell her?"

"Then that is the consequence Glacies has to live with." And Auria would feel the ramifications of it as well. Was it really something I wanted to hold back from her? I brushed the thought away. It wasn't my secret to tell.

Understanding shone in his eyes that I wouldn't make the decision for the dragon.

We both faced the street below. It was littered with irate people demanding answers.

"Probably a wise decision," Flynt said. "If the citizens of Deadwood have you stressed, imagine facing the wrath of a snow dragon."

"I wouldn't be stressed at that point." I adjusted my grip on the metal railing, thinking through what I'd say to them. "I'd be dead."

Flynt's lips rolled together before he raised a hand, and the crowd went silent.

I let a breath of a moment pass before speaking. "As you are all aware by now, King Tenere is on his way here as we speak."

Hushed murmurs flowed through the crowd as eyes remained glued to me. One look confirmed that none of the people from Auria's group was among them. They were likely hiding away in their temporary housing, fearing they'd be at risk of harm from the frantic townspeople.

"I don't know what his intentions are, past coming to retrieve his people, so I won't pretend that I do. We gave them sanctuary until the bridge was repaired, and as of a few hours ago, the crossing has been restored."

"When will he arrive?" one of the men asked.

"Late tonight," I answered, which earned more whispers rolling amongst the people. "He has guards with him, likely for his safety."

"What if they find out we're fae?" a woman with a baby on her hip asked.

The sight of the two of them caused a wave of uncertainty to hit me. Not only was Deadwood a refuge to criminals, fae, and anyone that needed a place to rest, it was also a home to many families. Families that had felt safe enough to settle down here. The determination to do everything in my power to keep them safe had me saying, "They won't. Not unless we make it known, which is exactly why everyone must give their utter respect and act cordially. All this is is one leader visiting a town to bring his people home. It is not an act of war. No one will be harmed."

The group remained quiet after my words ceased echoing through the street. Slowly, a murmur began, and I was thankful for it as I turned to Flynt. "Siara—"

He dipped his chin. "It's done. She's made sure the dragons know to stay away tonight."

My chest eased the slightest, knowing they would be out of the crossfire should anything happen. Humans didn't have an alliance with the dragons, other than believing they took care of the fae population. The last thing we needed was King Tenere aware they were aligned with us should he discover what we were.

"We should go down," I said, glancing back at the town.

"Bowen."

Flynt's voice had me turning to him.

"Are you okay?" he asked.

The question had me swallowing my doubts. I wasn't sure if I was, but the people of Deadwood were counting on me. "I have to be."

"It's okay not to have all the answers," Flynt said, a crease forming between his brows. He might get on my nerves from time to time, but Flynt had a heart. On the days I worried I'd lost my own, he reminded me it was still beating stronger than wings on the wind.

"Not today it isn't."

After making our way down the spiral staircase and letting Triss know she and her coworkers should stay inside the building the rest of the night, we waited. Lander showed up shortly after we exited the brothel and stood cast in shadow by one of the buildings, not uttering a word to anyone. I scanned the area for Paxon but didn't find him.

After three hours of waiting, I ordered the citizens to return to their homes, unless they were in the brothel or the saloon. The entire time, all I'd wanted was to go to Auria, to make sure she was sleeping well and not sitting in bed terrified of what might happen tonight. I would have hours ago, but the last thing I needed was the town to create another riot and King Tenere to show up early. I also wasn't sure if I'd be able to keep myself from hiding Auria away where no one could find her. So instead, I stayed standing, my feet planted like twin anchors in the dirt.

On the fourth hour, I debated sending the guards still standing tall in the street to refuel with food and water, but I thought better of it when my magic sprang to life with the scent of smoke in the air.

They are near, my smoke whispered, satisfaction coursing through the tendrils in my veins with the hope of attacking them. I let it anticipate the worst, knowing this could go haywire fast.

It was a miracle the sandwalkers hadn't torn the group's limbs from their bodies the moment they stepped foot in the desert. The only things keeping the shadowed creatures at bay were the lines of torches on either side of King Tenere's horse-drawn carriage. As the group got closer, I became certain he was comfortably inside while the others were exposed to the monsters that lurked in the dark.

Before entering the town, the guards at the head of the group stopped. They stood with straight backs, squared shoulders, and their torches held high. The driver pulled the reins on the wagon, and once the horses slowed, I spotted a second carriage behind the first, more elegant one. Only two horses pulled the smaller coach, compared to the four on King Tenere's.

Raiden stood to my right as Flynt flanked me on my left. Siara was behind all of Deadwood's guards that waited behind us, ready to alert the town in the event that chaos ensued. I hoped it wouldn't come to that, but King Tenere was unpredictable. I'd almost expected him to send only his guards to retrieve his daughter, but maybe the man was smart after all and was finally coming to learn that his men weren't the best trained. Obedient, sure, but prepared for battle? Hardly.

Out of the near hundred men that flanked the two carriages, one moved, opening the door to the first. Meanwhile, movement to my right caught my attention, and I turned to find Paxon finally joining us. I hadn't a moment to wonder where he'd been as King Tenere stepped out. Even in the flickering flames, the bags under his eyes were all too noticeable. The slightest bit of satisfaction coursed through me at the thought of him losing sleep over the daughter he treated like he couldn't care less if she lived to see another day.

How terrible it was to lose a gem you had never once valued.

Smoke twirled around my fingers, itching to creep into the people of Amosite and suffocate them where they stood. I reined it in, keeping it hidden beneath my skin. If I didn't have a town behind me I needed to protect, I'd let my magic have its way with every single one of King Tenere's guards, stealing the oxygen from every lung, infecting their blood and stopping the beating of their hearts.

As soon as King Tenere's polished boot touched the ground, Paxon and Lander were moving, leaving our group to join theirs. I was nothing other than fucking relieved to see their retreating backs. They could have them, but I'd be damned if they touched Auria.

Three guards emerged from the shadows of an alley, two limping and the other clutching a dangling arm, his wrist swollen and blue. We'd offered them aid, but all three had refused. Either because they loathed Deadwood or feared their king wouldn't approve of them seeking further help from the enemy.

King Tenere watched as Lander sidled past him, but rather than sticking with his brother, Paxon paused to mutter something in the king's ear, facing away from me so I couldn't try to read his lips. With the dip of the king's chin, Paxon continued on, joining his brother near the three guards behind the second carriage.

"Bowen." King Tenere regarded me as he stepped away from his guard, facing me and my group with a bored stare.

"King Tenere," I replied blandly. "I'd say it's nice to see you again, but I think we'd both rather skip the false pleasantries, with all the creatures waiting to demolish your group just beyond the line of light."

He didn't fall for my threat, but many of his men did, turning to nervously glance around them. Every couple seconds, when the breeze caught a flame, it'd illuminate the sandwalkers waiting on the outskirts of their lights. A few of the men shifted on their feet, likely thinking they might die tonight.

They were right to be scared.

One wrong move, and their torches would snuff out. A mistake they didn't know they had made, given my smoke was more than eager to be released upon them. All that stood between their life and the afterworld was those little tendrils of smoke pouring from the tips of their flames. A shame they decided on the old-fashioned way of light rather than magic. But I assumed that was due to resources running thin with Auria being gone so long. I had no doubt she'd be worked nearly to death upon her return, and it made me all the more inclined to stay quiet about her whereabouts.

"Where is she?" King Tenere asked, doing his best to sound civil but utterly failing.

I cocked my head in question. "Who?"

"My daughter," he gritted out, his tone taking a bit of an edge.

My eyes narrowed in thought. "Sorry, you'll have to be more specific."

His teeth ground together. "Auria."

With her name, my brows raised. "Ah, I remember her."

"I am not a fool, Bowen. I know she's here. I received word that she and my guards took refuge in this pit of a place. Where is she?"

"Asleep, along with the rest of this town. You should really think about coming in uninvited at a more reasonable time if you desire an audience."

His hands flexed at his sides. "It is time for her to return home."

"Is that what Auria wants?" I asked, folding my hands together behind my back. Despite the casual stance, my magic thrummed in my veins to the beat of my heart, thrashing inside me wildly, like it sensed danger and needed to get out.

Something wasn't right.

"She is needed back in Amosite, so that is where she will go," King Tenere declared.

"Is that so?"

He inhaled a deep breath, then raised a hand, signaling a guard. The man moved, walking past the horses to the second carriage. We watched as he opened the door and reached inside. A muffled protest came from within, and then a woman was being yanked from the coach. She stumbled on her feet, despite looking fine otherwise, and with a closer look, I recognized her instantly.

He had brought Auria's best friend, Taylin, along for the ride. Auria had briefly told me about her, and it was no secret the two meant a lot to each other. This was about to get ugly rather quickly.

Taylin slumped into the guard as her worn shoes tripped on each other in the sand. Flynt must have realized that she was drugged—heavily—at the same time as me because his stance stiffened, his hand moving slowly to the dagger at his side.

"I didn't want to involve her little friend," King Tenere began as the guard brought Taylin a few feet from the king. "But she has left me no choice."

He was desperate. Barely a few words exchanged, and he was resorting to manipulation.

"Sure. Torturing Auria's best friend will definitely make her want to go back to Amosite with you," I said before I could catch myself.

King Tenere's brows peaked at that. "She does not wish to go, then?"

I shrugged, trying to keep up the fucking casual act and feeling anything but. "Not my decision. It's Auria's."

"She doesn't get a choice. I am her father," he boomed back as a guard rifled through a long, cylindrical bag to his left. Taylin swayed on her feet slightly as she continuously blinked, likely trying to get ahold of herself.

"Everyone has a choice," I replied.

The busy guard pulled a short, thin stick from the bag, and I quickly realized it was a small arrow. The tip glowed a bright orange, casting a hue across the man's face.

He proceeded to hand it to another guard with a bow. Beside me, Raiden's hand went to his dagger, ready to take aim and put the blade right between the man's eyes if he nocked it back in our direction.

"Not everyone," King Tenere said.

The guard with the bow pulled back on the string, the tip of the arrow pointed at the sand.

Then, as his aim shifted, Flynt moved to step forward, but I set a hand out, his chest slamming into my palm. "Don't," I muttered, despite my instincts screaming at me to do *something*.

Flynt began to protest, but the words died on his tongue as the guard aimed at Taylin and released the arrow. It flew through the air, crossing the short distance in the blink of an eye, and landed in the center of her thigh.

Her scream filled the night air, echoing over every inch of the valley. Flynt's dagger was out not a moment later, taking the hit Raiden had meant to claim himself as the tip of the blade landed in the back of the guard's neck. He fell, his face buried in the sand as blood pooled on the ground around him.

The guard with a hand on Taylin's arm kept her standing as tears rolled down her cheeks, groans of pain ripping from her trembling form. The arrow stuck straight out from her flesh, and her entire body leaned to one side, her exhaustion craving the reprieve of the ground.

"Let her go," I called out. If he didn't, I feared a war would be started over Flynt's desire to protect every soul.

"I want my daughter, Bowen," King Tenere replied, that confident lilt back in his tone as he gained the upper hand.

My lips pressed together as everything inside me begged not to, but I had no choice. I couldn't let this town be ransacked and Taylin be tortured. But I also couldn't let Auria go back.

Gods help me.

"Siara," I called out, keeping my gaze trained in front of me. "Fetch the king's daughter, would you?"

But she knew in the way I had phrased it that she would only warn Auria, not bring her to us. Siara would hide her before King Tenere could send his guards into the town. Staying inside her home wouldn't be protection enough. Would I be either, though?

Auria, I called to her silently as my eyes stayed glued to Taylin where she struggled.

When no response came, I assumed she was either too far or deep asleep.

Flynt looked about ready to destroy the very earth King Tenere and his guard stood upon, and I had half a mind to let him. Paxon and Lander both stood to the side, not making a move. As if I didn't have reason enough to regret letting them stay in Deadwood temporarily. Lander at least had the sense to look worried, like he wanted to do something but knew it'd be no use.

I was feeling the same right about now.

Tense silence carried across the empty space between Amosite's people and Deadwood as we awaited Siara's return, the only noises penetrating our ears that of Taylin's suffering, making it all the more gut-wrenching to stand by and watch.

An eternity later, Siara appeared at my side, holding out a hand. I grabbed the object she held out to me and did a double take at the delicate piece of jewelry that dangled between my fingers.

She'd given me Auria's necklace.

"She wasn't there, Bowen. I found this outside your house," Siara said quietly.

My eyes moved to her, searching for the truth behind her words. We'd planned this out—she'd get Auria to a safe, hidden place, and return with no sight of her. But the way she'd said it...

So minuscule a move, she shook her head, and I knew for

sure she was being honest. Auria had gone somewhere, and we had no idea where.

Auria, I called to her again. *I need to know you're safe.*

Still, no response, but then I remembered she hadn't done it again after the spring. She didn't know how.

I silently cursed as my fist wrapped around the jewel and chain.

"I don't see my daughter," King Tenere said, the warning clear in his tone.

"She's not here." And this time, I was certain of it.

With a twist of his hand in the air, King Tenere sent his guards flooding into our town. We held our ground, letting them pass in the hopes they wouldn't touch the people. They were just looking for Auria. She wasn't here.

This was useless.

"You're wasting your time," I said to King Tenere. "Taylin will bleed out, and it will all be for nothing."

He didn't spare Taylin a glance as she let out a whimper at my words.

"She is not my concern," he replied.

"She should be."

King Tenere loosed a sigh, like it was such an inconvenience to hear me speak. "Why is that?"

My jaw clenched. "Because she is one of your people."

Rage seemed to seep into his bones as he stepped forward, his anger shaking the loose flesh of his neck. "My daughter is one of my people, and yet, you will not give her back."

"As if she is a pawn to be handed off?"

"She—" He sputtered, but I cut him off.

"Tell me, King Tenere, why don't you ever use her name?"

He blinked, taken off guard by the question. "I do."

I tried my best to ignore the shouts of men, women, and children in the distance as Amosite's guards broke into their homes, searching for Auria as they ripped doors off their hinges, shattered windows and tore apart furniture. Still, Deadwood wouldn't fight back, not unless I gave the signal. They would be safe. We could replace materials. It was their lives I needed intact. "Never when speaking respectfully of her."

His nostrils flared.

"Auria is not here," I repeated. He needed to leave so I could stop wasting my fucking time and find her. "Call your guards off."

"I'd be a fool to trust an imposter leader." He intended for the words to hit where he wanted, but they didn't land. Unfortunately for him, I never missed.

"Better an imposter than corrupt."

Before he could lose himself to the anger building inside him, a guard approached him, coming from the town. He muttered something to the king, then stepped to the side.

"Drop her," King Tenere ordered without so much as a glance Taylin's way.

The other guard let go of Taylin's arm, the only thing keeping her up, and she collapsed to the ground on a sob, landing hard on her side. Her hand instantly went to her leg, hovering near the wound as she squeezed her eyes shut. Her clothing was soaked through with blood. She was losing too much of it. Flynt kept his eyes trained on her the entire time, watching her every move, his muscles straining as he held himself back.

"Let this be a message to my daughter," the king said as more of his guards began returning to surround the carriages once more. In the distance, the sky began to lighten, indicating dawn was near. "If she is hiding, I will find her. And the longer she takes to come home, the more innocent people will suffer."

King Tenere retreated to the comfort of his carriage, and

once he was tucked inside, the large group of guards began moving, heading back in the direction they had come.

As soon as the last man was barely ten feet away, Flynt moved, not wasting a second. His sheath bounced against his hip before he crashed to his knees in the sand beside Taylin's shaking, sobbing form. Two of Deadwood's guards joined him, attempting to assist him in calming Taylin down so they could get her to the infirmary. I wanted to help her, but I couldn't, knowing that Auria wasn't here. I had to go to her. Above all else, I had to find her.

"Siara," I called.

She spun from where she stood discussing something with a distraught woman.

I held the necklace out in my palm. "Take me to where you found this."

CHAPTER 52

BOWEN

I left Flynt and the rest of them to take care of Taylin as I followed Siara through the crowd of men and women armed and confused. King Tenere had almost been...too nice, given the fact his daughter was missing and she was the one who supplied his kingdom with magic. He should've been irate, ready to burn Deadwood to the ground in order to find her. His departure after a simple wound to Taylin's thigh and wrecking some houses was unsettling, but I couldn't worry about what his plans might be as we hurried toward the back of the town.

Rather than taking me to the house Auria was staying in—where I thought she'd been hiding this entire time—Siara led me toward my own residence. To where she'd found Auria's necklace.

"Here," Siara said, pointing to the corner of the porch. "It was dangling off the edge."

I scanned every inch of the wood, finding nothing but more questions with no answers.

"Do you think she left it on purpose?"

She shook her head. "Don't you think she would've left it in a better spot if she had?"

She was right, and it only worsened the souring of my stomach.

The ground shook as a massive, white form took shape in my peripheral. The gust of wind from Glacies's landing sent specks of dirt twirling through the air. I turned to her, finding her teeth bared as saliva dripped from her fangs.

"*You let the girl go,*" she growled, low and menacing. I should've cowered, but her words sparked a question.

"I didn't *let* her do anything. She was supposed to stay put," I gritted out, straightening from where I'd been bent over the porch. "You saw her leave?"

A cloud of frosted air shot from her nostrils as they flared. Siara's eyes narrowed in Glacies's direction, likely guessing if she was going to end me where I stood.

"*If I had seen her, I would have stopped her.*"

Curiosity clutched me. "You finally wanted to tell her? Moments before she was to return home?"

A clawed foot stomped forward as she moved closer to me. Behind her, Vulcan landed, his back curved in a defensive manner as he watched her every move.

"*I wanted to save her life,*" Glacies snapped.

"From her father?" Did she think he'd kill her?

Teeth snapped in my direction, and Vulcan closed in on her from behind. He'd stop her if she tried anything... I hoped.

"*Fae are not as smart as we once believed,*" she chortled under her breath. "*No.*" Another puff of frozen air shot out, the cold raising goosebumps along my arms. "*Someone else wants her dead.*"

My brows furrowed as I cleared my thoughts, wondering if I'd heard her correctly. "I'm sorry. Say that again?"

"Someone does not want her back in Amosite. Not alive, at least. They want her dead."

Siara froze, then asked before I had the chance, "How are you so sure of this?"

"I hunted groups of people heading in this direction days ago. I have only put the pieces together now, after overhearing their discussion of taking out a favored target." Something akin to disappointment coated the last of her words.

"You *killed* them?" Siara asked, her voice higher in pitch.

"I was hungry," Glacies stated.

My gaze dropped to the necklace dangling from my hand, more and more questions arising with each passing second. Was her father so willing to leave because he had taken Auria? Did someone have something to do with her disappearance, and she hadn't run away like I suspected? The necklace was proof of that.

Possible scenarios flew through my mind like a whirlwind. *Where the fuck was she?*

Raiden approached, the rising sun reflecting off his worn leathers.

"How's Taylin?" I asked, needing something else to think about to ground myself. I wouldn't get anywhere if I let the spiraling thoughts win.

"King Tenere had given her a sedative for the trip, but the shock of the wound seemed to pull her out of it. Flynt carried her to the infirmary, but she's lost a lot of blood. Quinn's looking at her now, trying to figure out how to get the arrow out the smoothest way possible," Raiden answered, reciting the information like he was trying to keep his emotions at bay. He, too, had no idea what was at play here.

I shook my head at the questioning look in his eye. I was unable to form the words to say that I had no clue where she was.

"We'll find her," Raiden assured me.

My fingers wrapped tighter around the delicate chain. "I know."

"Why do you think he left so easily?" Siara asked, her eyes somewhere distant, like she was trying to pick apart every possible scenario.

I watched as the opal stone glistened in the rising sun, the rays shooting out in all directions. I had a suspicion, but...

"What are you thinking?" Raiden asked, studying me.

"I think he's using Deadwood as bait to get her back. Wherever she is, he thinks she'll show up back here if she's avoiding going back home. He didn't burn our town to the ground because he needs it standing to take her back." I looked at my two friends, their curious gazes trained on me. "But we're going to find her first."

We had to.

"Where do we start?" Siara asked. She looked exhausted. Another glance at Raiden told me he was, too. I was sure Flynt could use some rest as well, but I doubted he would if I told him to.

Smoke snaked through me, calm and deadly all the same, mirroring how I felt with her disappearance. The sensation was like a cold blade slicing through my beating heart.

The rising sun did nothing to warm my cold skin as Glacies rose to her full height, watching my every move to determine what I might do to fix this.

But I already knew what I'd do.

From the beginning, it wouldn't have been a question.

"With tearing apart every inch of this world until we find her."

CHAPTER 53

FLYNT

Blood. So much blood. More blood than anyone should have lost over an arrow wound, human or fae. My shirt, my hands, even my arm where Taylin's leg had laid limp in the crook of my elbow as I carried her clear across town, were stained red.

But despite the ocean of crimson coating the table and my skin, all I saw was blonde waves and blue pools of pain.

Her screams...

I gripped the edge of the table, forcing myself to stay out of the black hole I was on the verge of getting sucked into.

"Jestin," Doctor Quinn called out, a soaked hand putting pressure on the wound as she surveyed the arrow sticking straight out of Taylin's thigh.

She was panting, every breath pained and full of her plea to make it stop. I wanted nothing more than to take all of it from her. To bottle up her hurt and pour it into me. She didn't deserve this—

She is not your sister, my magic hummed, worried I was losing myself. I feared I was already there.

I didn't even know the girl, and I was teetering on the edge.

"I need a healing vial and more towels before I can pull this out." Doctor Quinn listed off other supplies, items I couldn't focus on as Taylin's head shook back and forth.

"No, no, no. Please, no. Please," Taylin pleaded, tears rolling down the sides of her face. The sedative had worn off on our rush to the infirmary, bringing her back to a confusing and treacherous present.

Quinn set a bloody hand on Taylin's shoulder, attempting to keep her still. "We have to get it out."

"Is there nothing you can give her?" I asked, tugging a hand through my hair and pulling on the strands from where I stood a couple feet from the table, giving them space to work.

"I need her awake to make sure her vitals don't drop," Quinn said as Jestin rushed over with a pile of supplies.

Taylin's panicked eyes darted back and forth. "Please. Just—just—"

"Hey." I knelt beside the head of the table and set a hand on Taylin's upper arm, pulling her attention my way. "I know it hurts. Okay?" I bit down on my lip as her eyes filled with more tears, willing myself to stay calm. "It's going to hurt a hell of a lot more, but then it won't anymore. Once the arrow is out, Quinn can heal you, and it will all be over."

"You promise?" Taylin asked, her voice a hoarse whisper.

I nodded, my thumb running along her cold skin. "I promise. Just keep your eyes on me, okay?" I moved my other hand to hers. "Squeeze my hand if you need to."

"I don't want to hurt you." A tear slipped from her eye, running along the bridge of her nose.

I gave her hand a gentle squeeze. "You can't hurt me. Nothing can." I offered a weak smile.

I didn't look as Quinn and Jestin, her assistant, worked on

securing the wound around the arrow, and in turn, Taylin didn't either.

"That's not true," she whispered, her lips glistening with the saliva spewed from them with her screams.

"It can be if I believe it hard enough." But even my past came around in times like these to prove that I wasn't impenetrable. "Do you believe in a lot of things, Taylin?"

She winced as Quinn shifted her leg slightly, a trickle of sweat sliding down her forehead. "Yes."

Quinn started giving Jestin orders on what he was to do once the arrow was out, but I didn't want Taylin to hear. Didn't want her falling into another panic.

"Tell me about them."

"Butterflies are a sign something good is coming," she murmured. "And bedtime stories aren't just stories."

My thumb continued its strokes along her skin. "What are they?"

"Twisted tales of the truth." She swallowed hard, clearly parched. "My dad used to tell me that."

The corner of my mouth twitched with a smile. "Smart man."

She tried to smile back, but it fell flat. "The smartest."

Before I could ask what else she believed in, her brows pinched, her eyes squeezing shut.

"Squeeze my hand, Taylin."

She tried, but her grip was weak, and then she let out a scream, her neck arching as her head pressed against the table, her back bowing.

I looked to find Quinn hadn't even touched the arrow yet, which meant something was wrong. My memory flashed back to the sight of the arrow as the guard nocked it back, right before I killed the fucker where he stood. Amongst the flames of the night, the head of the arrow had been glowing. Orange. Bright orange.

"Quinn..." I started.

More drops of sweat fell from Taylin's hairline. Her hand was cold in mine. This wasn't right. She shouldn't be having these reactions over a wound like this.

But before I could say more, Quinn's hand wrapped around the shaft and pulled. I tried to block out the squelching sounds as the point emerged from Taylin's thigh. The arrow was thrown to the side as Jestin popped the cork on the vial, instantly drizzling it over the wound. Taylin's panting filled my ears, and I turned to find her eyes rolling back into her head.

A pained roar sounded from somewhere in the distance outside the infirmary.

"Quinn!" I shouted, moving to stand above Taylin.

Her hand went limp in mine as her eyes drifted shut, her breathing instantly turning shallow.

"What's happening to her?" I demanded.

Done emptying the vial, Jestin bent to pick up the arrow, lifting it to eye level. "Doctor Quinn..."

Quinn turned at the same time I did, and we both stopped at the sight.

The tip of the arrow was still glowing orange, the magic vibrant and alive as ever.

But it wasn't magic...

It was—

"Poison."

CHAPTER 54

AURIA

Dim light seeped through the cracks of my eyelids as they fluttered. Fog seemed to cloud whatever room I was in, but after blinking to clear the haze, I found it was my sight, not the air. Blurred lines attempted to come into focus, but my mind spun as I struggled to gain control over myself.

Everything felt...cold. Wet. Hard.

Bars formed in my line of sight, twisting and folding in on themselves as my vision whirled. My head was heavy, unable to lift itself. My arm was folded at an odd angle, but after many attempts, I found not even that limb would move.

My neck ached, but the sensation was quickly trumped by the splitting pain that rolled through my mind. The only light came from an open doorway in the stone, but past the blinding sight, I could see nothing more.

Then, my ears, muffled as they were, perked at the sound of a drum.

No, not a drum. Footsteps.

"She's awake," someone announced to whoever had entered.

A few more steps, and the sound ceased.

"Finally. It's been days." The voice was feminine, somehow familiar.

But who?

More steps came from the same direction, and another person, male this time, said, "The correct dosage was hard to predict, and I wanted to be safe. Now that she's awake, we can start the tests."

Water dripped somewhere in the distance, and everything inside me focused in on the high-pitched sound of the drops. I tried to hold on to that one noise as my mind spun again, but then, the pain in my head became too much.

I groaned, wishing I could roll onto my back. Move. Get off this ground.

But I couldn't—no matter how much I begged my limbs to work.

My blurred eyes roamed the room, trying to make out something. Anything. With the light behind whoever stood near me, I couldn't make out who they were. My sluggish gaze trailed to the side, finding a heap of white rubble piled on the damp cobblestone.

No, not rubble.

A dragon.

Glacies?

Panic seized me as I couldn't wrap my mind around the possibility of her being here, spurring my tongue to work.

"He'll come for me," I managed to get out on a hoarse whisper. He would get us out of here. Wherever here was.

A chuckle, then the man crouched before me, only his dangling hands in my line of vision, blocking Glacies's still form from my sight. "Your precious Bowen won't save you this time."

I coughed, sending a wave of pain through my head. "He will."

Fingers brushed my cheek, moving my hair from my face. The act was chillingly repulsive, but it caused the man to move closer, bringing his face into my sight. And when it did, my heart stopped.

"Don't you know he hates you?"

I tried to shake my head, but the effort only made my mind spin more. "That's not true," I croaked. But even saying the words, I was unsure. I didn't know what to believe anymore.

"Oh, you poor thing." Lander tsked. "He could never care for the daughter of the man who killed his father."

ACKNOWLEDGMENTS

I have to give the biggest thank you to you, the reader. Without you, I couldn't do this, and for that, I'm forever grateful.

To my husband, for being my loudest cheerleader as I wrote Deadwood and went through all my highs and lows. I never thought I'd be able to write a fantasy, and you gave me the courage to keep going. You're such a big part of this series. I owe everything to you and our love.

To my son, thank you for not dropping naps in the middle of writing this. I love you to the moon and back, my love.

Bobbi, Bobbi, Bobbi. We all know I owe so many things to you. For being my brainstorm buddy and listening to my endless voice memos about plot, to being the best editor a girl could ask for. You're truly such a big part of my process, and I love you.

My wonderful PA, Shaylee. Thank you for taking on such a big load while I worked on this book. For always being there to help me at a moment's notice. To hold my hand through my anxiety and overthinking. To helping me market the heck out of this baby. I love you!

Kimberly at Twisted Tales PR, thank you endlessly for taking me on and doing so much for me. You gave me the spark I needed to remember how fun marketing can be, and I can't wait to see where our journey together takes us.

Brittany Price!!! You are the most amazing, wonderful,

talented human on this planet. I am so beyond thankful for you and the work you've done for me. The cover, the chapter header art, the part one and two dragons, just all of it. I'm so obsessed with your work, so I fear you're never getting rid of me. Thank you for being so supportive of me with this project. I can't tell you enough how much I appreciate you.

Thank you to Violet for making the most beautiful map I've ever seen. You saw my sketch at its worst and made it into something beautiful. Your talent never ceases to amaze me, and I'm so thankful for the work you've done for me.

To Emily, my lovely proofreader, for fitting me in last minute when I realized I can't balance everything on my plate anymore.

Thank you to my grandma for putting this love for dragons inside of me at such a young age. For having all those books on your shelves and making my imagination run wild. I got my love for reading from you, and this book wouldn't be what it is without you in my life. I just know you're flying with all the race horses and dragons.

Thank you to all my beta readers for spending the time to comb through the very early versions of this book. It was a little rough in the beginning, but you all gave me the confidence to tweak and change as I needed, and it wouldn't be what it is today without all of you. I'm eternally grateful for each and every one of you.

To the thousands of people who signed up for an ARC, thank you for taking an interest in my silly little Wild West romantasy with dragons. You're the reason my nerves are a little more at ease for this release and switching genres.

To the ARC readers on my team, thank you for always being my cheerleaders. For screaming about my books from the rooftops. I owe you all so much, and am so fricken grateful that I have you all on my team.

I'm probably missing some people, but just know that if we talk at all, I'm so thankful for you and your support. I love that I get to do this author thing, and befriend some of the most amazing people.

MORE BY KARLEY BRENNA

Bell Buckle Series

Spur of the Moment

Beat around the Bush

Scrape the Barrel

Bite the Bullet

Whiskey Ridge Series

Swallow Your Fear